Rafael Sabatini, creator of some of the world's best-loved heroes, was born in Italy in 1875 and educated in both Portugal and Switzerland. He eventually settled in England in 1892, by which time he was fluent in a total of five languages. He chose to write in English, claiming that 'all the best stories are written in English'.

His writing career was launched in the 1890s with a collection of short stories, and it was not until 1902 that his first novel was published. His fame, however, came with *Scaramouche*, the much-loved story of the French Revolution, which became an international bestseller. *Captain Blood* followed soon after, which resulted in a renewed enthusiasm for his earlier work.

For many years a prolific writer, he was forced to abandon writing in the 1940s through illness and he eventually died in 1950.

Sabatini is best-remembered for his heroic characters and high-spirited novels, many of which have been adapted into classic films, including *Scaramouche, Captain Blood* and *The Sea Hawk* starring Errol Flynn.

TITLES BY THE SAME AUTHOR
ALL PUBLISHED BY HOUSE OF STRATUS

FICTION:
ANTHONY WILDING
THE BANNER OF THE BULL
BARDELYS THE MAGNIFICENT
BELLARION
THE BLACK SWAN
CAPTAIN BLOOD
CHIVALRY
THE CHRONICLES OF CAPTAIN BLOOD
COLUMBUS
FORTUNE'S FOOL
THE FORTUNES OF CAPTAIN BLOOD
THE GAMESTER
THE GATES OF DOOM
THE HOUNDS OF GOD
THE JUSTICE OF THE DUKE
THE LION'S SKIN
THE LOST KING
LOVE-AT-ARMS
THE MARQUIS OF CARABAS
THE MINION
THE NUPTIALS OF CORBAL
THE ROMANTIC PRINCE
SCARAMOUCHE
SCARAMOUCHE THE KING-MAKER
THE SEA HAWK
THE SHAME OF MOTLEY
THE SNARE
ST MARTIN'S SUMMER
THE STALKING-HORSE
THE STROLLING SAINT
THE SWORD OF ISLAM
THE TAVERN KNIGHT
THE TRAMPLING OF THE LILIES
TURBULENT TALES
VENETIAN MASQUE

NON-FICTION:
HEROIC LIVES
THE HISTORICAL NIGHTS'
ENTERTAINMENT
KING IN PRUSSIA
THE LIFE OF CESARE BORGIA
TORQUEMADA AND THE SPANISH
INQUISITION

The Carolinian

Rafael Sabatini

HOUSE OF
STRATUS

This edition published in 2002 by House of Stratus, an imprint of Stratus Books Ltd., 21 Beeching Park, Kelly Bray, Cornwall, PL17 8QS, UK.
www.houseofstratus.com

Typeset, printed and bound by House of Stratus.

A catalogue record for this book is available from the British Library and the Library of Congress.

ISBN 07551-152-9-5

Contents

PART ONE

Contents (contd)

PART TWO

PART ONE

Chapter 1

Two Letters

With compressed lips and an upright line of pain between his brows, Mr Harry Latimer sat down to write a letter. He had taken – as he was presently to express it – his first wound in the cause of Liberty, which cause he had lately embraced. This wound, deep, grievous and apparently irreparable, had been dealt him by the communication in the sheets which hung now from his limp fingers.

It had reached him here at Savannah, where he was engaged at the time, not only on behalf of the Carolinian Sons of Liberty – of which seditious body he was an active secret member – but on behalf of the entire colonial party, in stirring the Georgians out of their apathy and into co-operation with their Northern brethren to resist the harsh measures of King George's government.

This letter, addressed to him at his Charles Town residence, had been forwarded thence by his factor, who was among the few whom in those days he kept informed of his rather furtive movements. It was written by the daughter of his sometime guardian, Sir Andrew Carey, the lady whom it had been Mr Latimer's most fervent hope presently to marry. Of that hope the letter made a definite end, and from its folds Mr Latimer had withdrawn the pledge of his betrothal, a ring which once had belonged to his mother.

Myrtle Carey, those lines informed him, had become aware of the treasonable activities which were responsible for her lover's long absences from Charles Town. She was shocked and grieved beyond expression by any words at her command to discover this sudden and terrible change in his opinions. More deeply still was she shocked to learn that it was not only in heart and mind that he was guilty of disloyalty, but that he had already gone so far as to engage in acts of open rebellion. And at full length, with many plaints and upbraidings, she displayed her knowledge of one of these acts. She had learnt that the raid upon the royal armoury at Charles Town in April last had been undertaken at his instigation and under his personal direction, and this at a time when, in common with all save his fellow traitors, she believed him to be in Boston engaged in the transaction of personal affairs. She deplored – and this cut him perhaps more keenly than all the rest – the deceit which he had employed; but it no longer had power to surprise her, since deceit and dissimulation were to be looked for as natural in one so lost to all sense of duty to his king.

The letter concluded with the pained assertion that whatever might have been her feelings for him in the past, and whatever tenderness for him might still linger in her heart, she could never bring herself to marry a man guilty of the abominable disloyalty and rebellion by which Harry Latimer had disgraced himself for ever. She would pray God that he might yet be restored to sane and honourable views, and that thus he might avoid the terrible fate which the royal government could not fail sooner or later to visit upon him should he continue in his present perverse and wicked course.

Three times Mr Latimer had read that letter, and long had he pondered it between readings. And if each time his pain increased, his surprise lessened. After all, it was no more than he should have expected, just as he had expected and been prepared for furious recriminations from his sometime guardian when knowledge of his defection should reach Sir Andrew. For than Sir Andrew Carey there was no more intolerant or bigoted tory in all America. Loyalty with him amounted to a religion; and just as religious feeling becomes intensified in the devout under persecution or opposition, so had the loyalty of Sir Andrew Carey burnt with a fiercer, whiter flame than ever from the moment that he perceived the signs of smouldering rebellion about him.

To Harry Latimer, when his generous, impulsive young heart had first been touched four months ago in Massachusetts by the oppression under which he found the province labouring, this uncompromising monarcholatry of Sir Andrew's had been the one consideration to give him pause before ranging himself under the banner of freedom. He had been reared from boyhood by the baronet, and he owed him a deep debt of love and other things. That his secession from toryism would deeply wound Sir Andrew, that sooner or later it must lead to a breach between himself and the man who had been almost as a father to him, was the reflection ever present in his mind to embitter the zest with which he embraced the task thrust upon him by conscience and his sense of right.

What he does not appear to have realized, until that letter came to make it clear, was that to Myrtle, reared in an atmosphere of passionate, unquestioning devotion to the King, loyalty had become as much a religion, a sacrosanctity, as it was to the father who preached it.

At the first reading the letter had made him bitterly angry. He resented her presumption in criticizing in such terms a conduct in him that was obviously a matter of passionate conviction. Upon reflection, however, he took a more tolerant view. Compromise in such a matter was as impossible to her as it was to him. He would do much to win her. There was, he thought, no sacrifice from which he would have shrunk; for no sacrifice could have been so great as that which he was now called upon to make in relinquishing her. But the duty he had taken up, and the cause he had vowed to serve, were not things that could be set in the balance against purely personal considerations. The man who would yield up his conscience to win her would by the very act render himself unworthy of her. Lovelace had given the world a phrase that should stand for all time to serve such cases as his own: "I could not love thee, dear, so much, loved I not honour more."

There was no choice.

He took up the quill, and wrote quickly; too quickly, perhaps, for a little of the abiding bitterness crept despite him into his words:

"You are intolerant, and therefore it follows that your actions are cruel and unjust. For cruelty and injustice are the only fruits ever yielded by intolerance. You will never again be able to do anything more cruel and unjust than you have now done, for never again will you find a heart as fond as mine and therefore as susceptible to pain at your hands. This pain I accept as the first wound taken in the service of the cause which I have embraced. Accept it I must, since I cannot be false to my conscience, my duty and my sense of right, even to be true to you."

Thus he double-bolted the door which she herself had slammed. A door which was to stand as an impenetrable barrier between two loving, aching, obstinate, conscience-ridden hearts.

He folded, tied and sealed the letter, then rang for Johnson, his valet, the tall, active young negro who shared his wanderings, and bade him see it dispatched.

Awhile thereafter he sat there, lost in thought, that line of pain deeply furrowed between his brows. Then he stirred and sighed and took up from the writing-table another letter that had reached him that same morning, a letter whose seals were still unbroken. The superscription was in the familiar hand of his friend Tom Izard, whose sister was married to Lord William Campbell, the royal Governor of the Province of South Carolina. The letter would contain news of society doings in Charles Town. But Charles Town society at the moment was without interest for Harry Latimer. He dropped the letter, still unopened, pushed back his chair and wearily rose. He paced away to the window and stood there looking upon the sunshine with vacant eyes.

He was at the time in his twenty-fifth year and still preserved in his tall, well-knit figure something of a stripling grace. He was dressed with quiet, patrician elegance, and he wore his own hair, which was thick, lustrous and auburn in colour. His face was of that clear, healthy pallor so often found with just such hair. It was an engaging face, lean and very square in the chin, with a thin, rather tip-tilted nose and a firm yet humorous mouth. His eyes were full without prominence, of a brilliant blue that in certain lights was almost green. Habitually they were invested with a slightly quizzical regard; but this had now given place to the dull vacancy that accompanies acute mental suffering.

Standing there he pondered his case yet again, until at last there was a quickening of his glance. He stretched himself, with a suggestion of relief in the action. The thing is evil indeed out of which no good may come, which is utterly without compensation. And the compensation here was that at least there was end to secrecy. The thing was out. Sir Andrew knew; and however hardly Sir Andrew might have taken it, at least the menace of discovery was at an end. This, Mr Latimer reflected, was something gained. There was an end to his tormenting consciousness of practising by secrecy a passive deceit upon Sir Andrew.

And from the consideration of that secrecy his mind leapt suddenly to ask how came the thing discovered. That they should know vaguely and generally of his defection was not perhaps so startling. But how came they informed in such detail of the exact part he had played in that raid upon the arsenal last April? His very presence in Charles Town had been known to none except the members of the General Committee of the Provincial Congress. Then he reflected that those members were very numerous, and that a secret is rarely kept when shared by many. Someone here had been grievously indiscreet. So indiscreet, indeed, that if the royal governor knew that Harry Latimer was the author of the raid – a raid which fell nothing short of robbery and sedition, and amounted almost to an act of war – there was a rope round his neck and round the neck of every one of his twenty associates in that rebellious enterprise.

Here was something to engage his thoughts.

If his activities were known in Sir Andrew's household, it followed almost certainly that they would be known also in the Governor's. He was sufficiently acquainted with Sir Andrew to be sure that, in spite of everything that lay between Sir Andrew and himself, the baronet would be the first to bear the information to Lord William.

And then he realized that this was no mere indiscretion. In-discretion might have betrayed some general circumstance, but it could never have betrayed all these details of which Myrtle was possessed; above all it could never have betrayed so vital and dangerous a secret. He was assailed by the conviction that active, deliberate treachery was at work, and he perceived that he must communicate at once with his friends in Charles Town, to put them on their guard. He would write to Moultrie, his friend and one of the staunchest patriots in South Carolina.

Upon that thought he returned to the writing-table, and sat down. There Tom Izard's letter once more confronted him. Possibly Tom's gossip might yield some clue. He broke the seals, unfolded and spread the sheets, to find in them far more than he had expected.

"My dear Harry," wrote the garrulous man of fashion,

"Wherever you may be, and whatever the activities that are now engaging you, I advise you to suspend them, and to return and pay attention to your own concerns, which are urgently requiring your presence. Though on your return you should call me out for daring even to hint at the possibility of disloyalty in Myrtle, I cannot leave you in ignorance of what is happening at Fairgrove.

"You know, I think, that soon after the fight at Lexington last April, Captain Mandeville was sent down here by General Gage from Boston against the need to stiffen the lieutenant-governor into a proper performance of his duty by the king. Captain Mandeville has remained here ever since, and in these past to months has acquired such a grasp of provincial affairs in South Carolina, that he continues as the guide and mentor of my brother-in-law, Lord William, who arrived from England a fortnight since. Mandeville, who has now been appointed equerry to his lordship, is become the power behind the throne, the real ruler of South Carolina, in so far, of course, as South Carolina is still ruled by the royal government.

"In all this there may be nothing that is new to you. But it will be new, I am sure, that a kinship, real or pretended, exists between this fellow and your old guardian, Sir Andrew Carey. That stiff-necked old tory has taken this pillar of royal authority to his broad bosom. The gallant captain is constantly at Fairgrove, whenever his duties do not keep him in Charles Town. Let me add on the score of Mandeville, who is undeniably a man of parts and finds great favour with the ladies, the following information obtained from a sure source. He is a notorious fortune-hunter, reduced in circumstances, and it is well-known in England that he accepted service in the colonies with the avowed intention of making a rich marriage. His assets are not only a fine figure and the most agreeable manners, but the fact that he is next heir to his uncle, the Earl of Chalfont, from whom I understand that he is at present estranged. I do not myself imagine that a man of his aims and talents would be so very diligent at Fairgrove unless in Carey's household he saw a reasonable prospect of finding what he seeks. You will be very angry with me, I know. But I should not be your friend did I not risk your anger, and I would sooner risk that now than your reproaches later for not having given you timely warning."

There followed a post-scriptum: "If your engagements are such that it is impossible for you to return and attend to your own concerns, shall I pick a quarrel with the captain, and have him out? I would have done so out of love for you before this, but that my brother-in-law would never forgive me and Sally would be furious. Poor Lord William would be helpless without his equerry, and he finds things devilish difficult as it is. Besides, I understand that, as commonly happens with such rascals, this Mandeville is a dead shot and plaguy nimble with a small-sword."

At another time the post-scriptum might have drawn a smile from Latimer. Now his face remained grave and his lips tight.

A definite conclusion leapt at him from those pages. It was not a question of Sir Andrew's having informed the Governor of Harry Latimer's seditious practices. What had happened was the reverse of that. The information had been conveyed to Sir Andrew by this fellow Mandeville of whom he had heard once or twice before of late. If Mandeville's intentions were at all as Tom Izard represented them, it would clearly be in the captain's interest to effect an estrangement between Latimer and the Careys. And this was what had taken place.

But how had Mandeville obtained the information? One only answer was possible. By means of a spy placed in the very bosom of the councils of the colonial party.

Upon that Mr Latimer took an instant decision. He would not write. He would go in person. He would set out at once for Charles Town, to discover this enemy agent who was placing in jeopardy the cause of freedom and the lives of those who served it.

His work in Georgia was of very secondary importance by comparison with that.

Chapter 2

Cheney

William Moultrie, of Northampton on the Cooper River – who had just been appointed Colonel of the Second Provincial Regiment of South Carolina, under a certificate issued by a Provincial Congress which was not yet sufficiently sure of itself to grant commissions – was aroused from slumber in the early hours of a June morning by a half-dressed negro servant, who proferred him a folded slip of paper.

The Colonel reared a great night-capped head from his pillow, and displayed a broad, rugged face the bone structures of which were massive and well-defined. From under beetling brows two small eyes, normally of a kindly expression, peered out, to screw themselves up again when smitten by the light of the candle which the negro carried. "Wha...wha...what's o'clock?" quoth the Colonel confusedly.

"Close on five o'clock, massa."

"Fi...five o'clock!" Moultrie awakened on that, and sat up. "What the devil, Tom...?"

Tom brought the slip of paper more definitely to his master's notice. Puzzled, the Colonel took it, unfolded it, dusted his eyes with his knuckles, and read. Then he flung back the bed clothes, thrust out a hairy leg, his foot groping for the floor, and commanded

Tom to give him a bedgown, draw the curtains, and bring up this visitor.

And so a few minutes later Harry Latimer was ushered into the presence of the Colonel, who stood in the pale light of early day, in bedgown, slippers and nightcap to receive him.

"Odsbud, Harry! What's this? What's brought you back?"

They shook hands firmly, like old friends, whilst the gimlet eyes of Moultrie observed the young man's dusty boots and travel-stained riding clothes as well as the haggard lines in his face.

"When you've heard, you may say I've come back to be hanged. But it's a slight risk at present, and had to be taken."

"What's that?" The Colonel's voice was very sharp.

Latimer delivered the burden of his news. "The Governor is informed of the part I played in the raid last April."

"Oons!" said Moultrie, startled. "How d'ye know?"

"Read these letters. They'll make it plain They reached me three days ago at Savannah."

The Colonel took the papers Latimer proffered, and crossed to the window to peruse them. He was a stockily built man of middle height, twenty years older than his visitor, whom he had known from infancy. For Moultrie had been one of the closest friends of Latimer's father and his brother-in-arms in Grant's campaign against the Cherokees, in which the elder Latimer had prematurely lost his life. And there you have the reason why Harry sought him now in the first instance, rather than Charles Pinckney, the President of Provincial Congress, which the royal Government did not recognise, or Henry Laurens, the President of the Committee of Safety, which the royal Government recognised still less. The offices held by these two should have designated one or the other of them as the first recipient of this weighty confidence. But to either, Latimer had taken it upon himself to prefer the man who was in such close personal relations with himself.

Whilst still reading, Moultrie swore once or twice. When he had done, he came slowly back, his brow rumpled in thought. Silently he handed back the papers to the waiting Latimer, who had meanwhile taken a chair near the table in mid-apartment. Then, still in silence, the Colonel took up one from a bundle of pipes on that same table, and slowly filled it with leaf from a pewter box.

"Faith," he grumbled at last, "you don't lack evidence for your assumption. Nobody outside of the Committee so much as suspected that you were here in April. God knows the place is crawling with spies. There was a fellow named Kirkland, serving in the militia, whom we suspect of acting as Lord William's agent with the back-country tories. We durstn't touch him until he was so imprudent as to desert, and come down to Charles Town with another rogue named Cheney. But before ever we could lay hands on him, Lord William had put him safely aboard a man o' war out there in the roads. Cheney was less lucky. We've got him. Though, gadslife, I don't know what we're to do with him, for unfortunately he isn't a deserter. But that he's a spy only a fool could doubt."

"Yes, yes," Latimer was impatient. "But that kind of spy is of small account compared with this one." And he tapped the papers vehemently.

Moultrie looked at him, pausing in the act of applying to his pipe the flame of the candle which the servant had left burning. Latimer answered the inquiry of the glance.

"This man is inside our councils. He is one of us. And unless we find him and deal with him, God alone knows what havoc he may work. As it is there are some twenty of us whose lives are in jeopardy. For you cannot suppose that if he has betrayed me to the Governor he hasn't at the same time betrayed the others who were with me, whether they actually bore a hand or merely shared the responsibility."

Moultrie lighted his pipe, and pulled at it thoughtfully. He did not permit himself to share the excitement that was setting his visitor aquiver. He came and placed a hand affectionately on Harry's shoulder.

"I'm not vastly exercised by any threat to your life, lad – at least not at present. Neither the Governor, nor his pilot, Captain Mandeville, want another Lexington here in South Carolina. And that's what would happen if they tried any hangings. But as far as the rest goes, you're right. We've to find this fellow. He's among the ninety members of the General Committee. Faith, the job'll be singularly like looking for a needle in a bottle of hay." He paused, shaking his head; then asked a question: "I suppose ye've not thought of how to go about discovering him?"

"I've thought of nothing else all the way from Savannah here. But I haven't found the answer."

"We shall have to seek help," said Moultrie, "and after all it's your duty to Pinckney and Laurens, and one or two others to let them know of this."

"The fewer we tell, the better."

"Of course. Of course. A half-dozen at most, and those men that are well above suspicion."

Later on in the course of that day, six gentlemen of prominence in the Colonial party repaired to Colonel Moultrie's house on Broad Street in response to his urgent summons. In addition to Laurens and Pinckney, there was Christopher Gadsden, long and lean and tough in the blue uniform of the newly-established First Provincial Regiment, to the command of which he had just been appointed. A veteran firebrand, President of the South Carolina Sons of Liberty, he was among the very few who at this early date were prepared to go the length of demanding American Independence. With him came the elegant, accomplished William Henry Drayton, of Drayton Hall, who, like Latimer, was a recent convert to the party of Liberty, and who brought to it all the enthusiasm and intolerance commonly found in converts. His position as President of the Secret Committee entitled him to be present. The others making up this extemporaneous committee were the two delegates to Continental Congress, the Irish lawyer John Rutledge, a man of thirty-five who had been prominent in the Stamp-Act Congress ten years ago, and famous ever since, and his younger brother Edward.

Assembled about the table in Moultrie's library these six, with Moultrie himself presiding, listened attentively to the reasons

14

advanced by Mr Latimer in support of his assertion that they were being betrayed by someone within their ranks.

"Some twenty of us," he concluded, "lie already at the mercy of the royal Government. Lord William is in possession of evidence upon which to hang us if the occasion serves him. That, in itself, is grave enough. But there may be worse to follow unless we take our measures to discover and remove, by whatever means you may consider fit, this traitor from our midst."

There followed upon that a deal of talk that was little to the point. They discussed this thing; they pressed Latimer for details which he would have preferred to have withheld as to the exact channel through which this information had reached him, and they were very vehement and angry in their vituperation of the unknown traitor, very full of threats of what should be done to him when found. Several talked at once, and in the general alarm and excitement the meeting degenerated for a while into a babel.

Drayton took the opportunity wrathfully to renew a demand, which had already once been rejected by the General Committee, that the Governor should be taken into custody. Moultrie answered him that the measure was not practical, and Gadsden, supporting Drayton, furiously demanded to know why the devil it should not be. Then at last John Rutledge, who hitherto had sat as silent and inscrutable as a granite sphinx, coldly interposed.

"Practical or not, this is not the place to debate it, nor is it the matter under consideration." Almost contemptuously he added: "Shall we keep to the point?"

It was his manner rather than his words that momentarily quieted their vapourings. His cold detachment and his obvious command of himself gave him command of others. And there was, too, something arresting and prepossessing in his appearance. He was in his way a handsome man, with good features that were softly rounded, and wide-set, slow-moving, observant eyes. There was the least suggestion of portliness about his figure, or, rather than actual portliness, the promise of it to come with advancing years. His dress was of a scrupulous and quiet elegance, and if the grey wig he wore was clubbed to an almost excessive extent yet it was redeemed from all suspicion of foppishness by the formal severity of its set.

There was a moment's utter silence after he had spoken. Then Drayton, feeling that the rebuke had been particularly aimed at himself, gave Rutledge sneer for sneer.

"By all means, let us keep to the point. After long consideration you may reach the conclusion that it's easier to discover the treason than the traitor. And that will be profitable. As profitable as was the arrest of Cheney by a committee too timid to commit anything."

That sent them off again, on another by-path.

"Yes, by God!" burst from the leathery lungs of Gadsden, who had been preaching sedition to the working-people of Charles Town for the last ten years, ever since the Stamp-Act troubles. "There's the whole truth of the matter. That's why we make no progress. The committee's just a useless and impotent debating society, and it'll go on debating until the redcoats are at our throats. We daren't even hang a rascal like Cheney. Oons! If the wretch had known us better he might have spared himself his terrors."

"His terrors?" The question came sharply from Latimer, so sharply that it stilled the general murmurs as they began to arise again. At the mention of Cheney's name, he remembered what Moultrie had said about the fellow. An idea, vague as yet, was stirring in his mind. "Do you say that this man Cheney is afraid of what may happen to him?"

Gadsden loosed a splutter of contemptuous laughter. "Afraid? Scared to death, very near. Because he doesn't realize that the only thing we can do is talk, he already smells the tar, and feels the feathers tickling him."

Rutledge addressed himself scrupulously to the chair. "May I venture to inquire, sir, how this is relevant?"

Leaning forward now, a certain excitement in his face, Latimer impatiently brushed him aside.

"By your leave, Mr Rutledge. It may be more relevant than you think." He addressed himself to Moultrie. "Tell me this, pray. What does the Committee propose to do with Cheney?"

16

Moultrie referred the question to the genial elderly Laurens who was President of the Committee concerned.

Laurens shrugged helplessly. "We have decided to let him go. There is no charge upon which we can prosecute him."

Gadsden snorted his fierce contempt. "No charge! And the man a notorious spy!"

"A moment, Colonel." Latimer restrained him, and turned again to Laurens. "Does Cheney know – does he suspect your intentions?"

"Not yet."

Latimer sank back in his chair again, brooding. "And he's afraid, you say?"

"Terrified," Laurens assured him. "I believe he would betray anybody or anything to save his dirty skin."

That brought Latimer suddenly to his feet in some excitement. "It is what I desired to know. Sir, if your Committee will give me this man – let me have my way with him – it is possible that through him I may be able to discover what we require."

They looked at him in wonder and some doubt. That doubt Laurens presently expressed. "But if he doesn't know? And why should you suppose that he does?"

"Sir, I said *through* him, not from him. Let me have my way in this. Give me twenty-four hours. Give me until tomorrow evening at latest, and it is possible that I may have a fuller tale to tell you."

There was a long pause of indecision. Then very coldly, almost contemptuously in its lack of expression, came a question from Rutledge:

"And if you fail?"

Latimer looked at him, and the lines of his mouth grew humorous.

"Then you may try your hand, sir."

And Gadsden uttered a laugh that must have annoyed any man but Rutledge.

Of course that was not yet the end of the matter. Latimer was pressed with questions touching his intentions. But he fenced them

17

off. He demanded their trust and confidence. And in the end they gave it, Laurens taking it upon himself in view of the urgency of the case to act for the Committee over which he presided.

The immediate sequel was that some two or three hours later Mr Harry Latimer was ushered into the cell in the town gaol, where Cheney languished. But it was a Mr Latimer very unlike his usual modish, elegant self. He went dressed in shabby brown coatee and breeches, with coarse woollen stockings and rough shoes, and his abundant hair hung loose about his neck.

"I am sent by the Committee of Safety," he announced to the miserable wretch who cowered on a stool in a corner and glared at him with frightened eyes. On that he paused. Then, seeing that Cheney made no shift to speak, he continued: "You can hardly be such a fool as not to know what is coming to you. You know what you've done, and you know what usually happens to your kind when they're caught."

He saw the rascally, pear-shaped face before him turn a sickly grey. The man moistened his lips, then cried out in a quavering voice:

"They can prove naught against me. Naught!"

"Where there is certain knowledge proof doesn't matter."

"It matters. It does matter!" Cheney rose. He snarled like a frightened animal. "They durstn't hurt me without cause; good cause; legal cause. And they knows it. What have they against me? What's the charge? I've been twice before the Committee. But there never were no charge: no charge they durst bring in a court."

"I know," said Latimer quietly. "And that's why I've been sent: to tell you that tomorrow morning the Committee will set you at liberty."

The coarse mouth, about which a thick stubble of beard had sprouted during the spy's detention, fell open in amazement. Breathing heavily, he leaned on the coarse deal table for support, staring at his visitor. Hoarsely at last came his voice.

"They...they'll set me at liberty!" And then his currish demeanour changed. Now that he saw deliverance assured a certain truculence invested him. He laughed, slobbering like a drunkard. "I knowed it!

18

I knowed they durstn't hurt me. If they did they'd be hurt theirselves. They'd have to answer to the Governor for 't. Ye can't hurt a man without bringing a charge and proving it."

"That," Mr Latimer agreed suavely, "is what the Committee realizes, and that is why it is letting you go. But don't assume too much. Don't be so rash as to suppose that you're to get off scot free."

"Wha – what!" Out went the truculence. Back came the terror.

"I'll tell you. When you are released tomorrow morning, you'll find me waiting for you outside the gaol, and with me there'll be at least a hundred lads of the town, all of them Sons of Liberty, who'll have had word of the Committee's intention and don't mean to let you go back to your dirty spying. What the Committee dare not do, they'll never boggle over. For the Governor can't prosecute a mob. You guess what'll happen?"

The grey face with its shifty eyes and open mouth was fixed in speechless terror.

"Tar and feathers," said Mr Latimer, to remove the last doubt in that palsied mind.

"God!" shrieked the creature. His knees were loosened and he sank down again upon his stool. "God!"

"On the other hand," Mr Latimer resumed quite placidly, "it may happen that there will be no mob; that I shall be alone to see you safely out of Charles Town. But that will depend upon yourself; upon your willingness to undo as far as you are able some of the mischief you have done."

"What d'ye mean? In God's name, what d'ye mean? Don't torture a poor devil."

"You don't know who I am," said Mr Latimer. "I'll tell you. My name is Dick Williams, and I was sergeant to Kirkland – "

"That you never was," Cheney cried out.

Mr Latimer smiled upon him with quiet significance. "It is necessary that you should believe it, if you are to avoid the tar and feathers. I beg you then to persuade yourself that my name is Dick Williams, and that I was sergeant to Kirkland. And you and I are going together to pay the Governor a visit tomorrow morning. There, you will do as I shall tell you. If you don't, you'll find my lads waiting for you when you leave his lordship's." He entered into further details, to which the other listened like a creature fascinated. "It is now for you to say what you will do," said Mr Latimer amiably in conclusion. "I do not wish to coerce you, or even to over-persuade you. I have offered you the alternatives. I leave you a free choice."

Chapter 3

The Governor of South Carolina

Mr Selwyn Innes, who was Lord William Campbell's secretary during his lordship's tenure of the office of Governor of the Province of South Carolina, conducted with a lady in Oxfordshire a correspondence which on his part was as full and detailed as it was indiscreet. The letters, which have fortunately survived, give so intimate a relation of the day-to-day development of certain transactions under his immediate notice that they would be worthy to rank as *mémoires pour servir* were it not that history must confine itself more or less to the broad outlines of movements and events, and can be concerned only with the main actors in its human drama.

In one of these garrulous letters there occurs the phrase:

"We are sitting on a volcano which at any moment may belch fire and brimstone, and my lord taking no thought for anything but the mode of dressing his hair, the set of his coat, ogling the ladies at the St Cecilia concerts and attending every race-meeting that is held."

From that and abundant other similar indications throughout the secretary's letters, we gather that his opinion of the amiable, rather ingenuous, entirely unfortunate young nobleman whom he had the honour to serve was not very exalted. A secretary, after all, is a sort of valet, an intellectual valet; and to their valets, we know, few men can succeed in being heroes. But with the broader outlook which distance lends us we know now that Mr Innes did his lordship less than justice. After all, no man may bear a burden beyond his strength, and the burden imposed upon the young Colonial governor in that time of crisis by a headstrong, blundering government at home was one that he could not even lift. Therefore, like a wise man – in spite of Mr Innes – he contemplated it with rueful humour, and temporized as best he could whilst awaiting events that should either lessen that burden or increase his own capacity.

There is also the fact that whilst, like a dutiful servant of the crown, he was quite ready where possible to afford an obedience that should be unquestioning, it was beyond nature that this obedience should be enthusiastic. He had examined for himself the lamentable question that was agitating the empire; and the fact that he was married to a Colonial lady may have served to counteract the bias of his official position, leading him to adopt in secret the view of the majority – not merely in the Colonies, but also at home – that disaster must attend the policy of the ministry, driven by a wilful, despotic monarch who understood the cultivation of turnips better than the husbandry of an empire. He cannot have avoided the reflection that the government he served was determined to reap the crop that Grenville had sown with the Stamp Act, determined to pursue the obstinate policy which – the phrase is Pitt's, I think – must trail the ermine of the British King in the blood of British subjects. Lord William perceived – indeed, it required no very acute perception – how oppression was provoking resistance, and how resistance was accepted as provocation for further oppression. Therefore, he remained as far as possible supine, thankful perhaps in his secret heart that he was without the means to execute the harsh orders reaching him from home, and obstinately hoping that conciliatory measures might yet be adopted to restore harmony between the parent country and the children overseas whom she had irritated into insubordination.

Towards this he may have thought that he could best contribute by bearing himself with careless affability, as an appreciative guest of the colony he was sent to govern. He showed himself freely with his Colonial wife at race meetings, balls and other diversions, as Mr Innes records, and he affected an amiable blindness to anything that bore the semblance of sedition.

In the end, as we can trace, Mr Innes came to perceive something of this, and I suspect that he began to make the discovery on a certain Tuesday morning in June of that fateful year 1775, when Captain Mandeville, his excellency's equerry, waited upon Lord William at the early hour of eight.

Captain Mandeville, who was himself lodged in the Governor's residence in Meeting Street, came unannounced into the pleasant spacious room above-stairs that was Lord William's study. The equerry found his excellency, in a quilted bedgown of mulberry satin, reclining on a long chair, whilst his aproned valet, Dumergue, was performing with comb and tongs and pomade his morning duties upon the luxuriant chestnut hair that adorned the young governor's handsome head. In mid-apartment, at a writing-table that was a superb specimen of the French art of cabinet-making, with nobly arching legs and choicely-carved ormolu incrustations, Mr Innes was at work.

Lord William looked up languidly to greet his equerry. His lordship had been dancing at his father-in-law's – old Ralph Izard – until a late hour last night, so that the air of fatigue he wore was natural enough.

"Ah, Mandeville! Good morning. Ye're devilish early astir."

"Not without occasion." The captain's manner was grim, almost curt. It was obviously as an afterthought that he bowed and added a shade less curtly: "Good morning."

Lord William observed him with quickened interest. He knew no man who commanded himself more completely than Robert Mandeville, who more fully conformed with that first canon of good-breeding which demanded that a gentleman should at all times, in all places and circumstances, control his person and subdue his feelings. Yet here was Mandeville, this paragon of deportment, not only excited, but actually permitting himself to betray the fact. And it was not only his voice that betrayed it. There was a touch of heightened colour in the captain's clear-cut, clear-skinned, rather arrogant countenance, whilst in his clubbed blond hair there was more than a vestige of last night's powder to advertise the fact that the captain, usually so irreproachable in these matters, had made a hurried toilet.

"Why – what is it?" quoth his lordship.

Captain Mandeville looked at Innes, disregarding the secretary's nod of greeting; then at the valet, busy with his lordship's hair.

"It will keep until Dumergue has finished." His tone was now more normal. He sauntered across to the broad window standing open to a balcony wide and deep and pillared like a loggia. It overlooked the luxuriant garden and the broad creek at the end of it, whose waters sparkling in the morning sunshine showed here and there through the great magnolias that spread a canopy above them.

His lordship's glance followed the officer's tall graceful figure in its coat of vivid scarlet with golden shoulder-knots and the sword thrust through the pocket, in compliance rather with the latest decree of fashion than with military regulations. His curiosity was aroused and with it the uneasiness that invariably pervaded him where colonial matters were concerned.

"Innes," he said, "let Captain Mandeville read Lord Hillsbrough's letter while he waits." And he added the information that it had just arrived by the war sloop Cherokee and had been brought ashore an hour ago by her captain.

Dumergue interrupted him at that point by thrusting a mirror into his lordship's hand, whilst holding up a second one behind his lordship's head.

"Voyez, milor'," he invited. "Les boucles un peu plus serrés qu'à l'ordinaire…"

He waited, eyebrows raised, head on one side, his glance intensely anxious.

In the hand-glass his lordship calmly surveyed the back of his head, as reflected from the second mirror. He nodded.

"Yes. I like that better. Very good, Dumergue."

Audibly Dumergue resumed his suspended breathing. He set down his mirror and became busy with a broad ribbon of black silk.

Lord William lowered his own glass to meet the eyes of Captain Mandeville observing him across the document which the equerry had now read.

"Well, Mandeville? What do you think of it?"

"I think it is very opportune."

"Opportune ! Good God, Innes! He thinks it's opportune!"

Mr Innes, a sleek young gentleman, smiled and ventured even a slight shrug. "That was to be looked for in Captain Mandeville." His voice was gentle, almost timid. "He is a consistent advocate of...of... strong measures."

His lordship sniffed.

"Strong measures are for the strong, and to do as Lord Hillsborough commands us – "

He broke off. Captain Mandeville was holding up the hand that held the letter.

"When your excellency's toilet is finished."

"Oh, very well," his lordship agreed. "Make haste, Dumergue."

Scandalized by the command, Dumergue began a protest.

"Oh, milor' ! Une chevelure pareille...une coiffure si belle..."

"Make haste!" His lordship was unusually peremptory.

Dumergue sighed, and cut short his ministrations. With a final touch he perfected the set of the ribbon in which the queue was confined; then he gathered towel, scissors, comb, curling-tongs and pomade into a capacious basin, made his bow, and retired with wounded dignity.

"Now, Mandeville."

His lordship sat up, swinging his legs round. They were shapely legs in pearl-grey silk. He considered them complacently. They were among the few things whose contemplation afforded his lordship unalloyed satisfaction.

But Captain Mandeville required his lordship to pay attention to very different matters.

"Lord Hillsborough is quite definite in his instructions."

"It's so devilish easy for a politician to be definite in London," grumbled his lordship.

Captain Mandeville paid no heed to the comment. He lowered his eyes to the sheet he held, and read: "The Government is resolved to make an end, a speedy end, of the ungrateful and unfeeling insubordination of the American colonies, which is occasioning so much pain to his majesty's ministers."

"Oh, damn their pain!" said their South-Carolina representative.

The equerry read on: "The excessive leniency hitherto observed must now be definitely abandoned, and coercion must at once be employed to subdue these mutinous spirits.

"Therefore I desire your excellency to act without delay, seizing all arms and munitions belonging to the province, raising provincial troops if possible and making ready to receive the British regulars that will be embarked with the least possible delay."

His lordship laughed. "Not without humour, Mandeville – of the unconscious kind, that so often has a tragic flavour. I am to raise provincial troops. Gadsmylife! As if the provincial troops were not raising themselves, whilst I look on, acquiescing in the damned comedy; pretending not to know the purpose for which they are being raised; regarding them as the ordinary militia which they scarcely trouble to pretend to be. They swarm in the streets until the place looks like a garrison town. They parade, and march and drill under my very nose. Indeed, I marvel that I am not asked to sign their officers' commissions. If I were I suppose I should have to do it. And Lord Hillsborough, snugly at home in England, writes ordering me to raise provincial troops! My God!"

He rose at the end of his bitterly humorous tirade, a tall, handsome, almost boyish figure. "And you, Mandeville, think this letter opportune!"

"It is opportune with the business that brings me," said the equerry. "You are forgetting the back country. Charles Town itself may be a hotbed of rebellion. But up there, beyond the Broad River, they are loyal and tory. And they'll fight."

"But who wants to fight?" Lord William was almost impatient. "I am sent out from home with orders to play a conciliatory part – which is the only part I have the means to play, the only part that I believe it is sane to play. Other orders follow. I am to coerce; I am to arm. I am to prepare to receive British troops. The latter I can do. But the rest – "

"That, too, if you have the will," said Mandeville.

"How can I have the will? Who could have the will whilst there is the faintest chance of conciliation. And why should there not be?"

"Because these people have determined otherwise. Lexington showed us that clearly enough. Up there in Massachusetts – "

"Yes, yes. But this isn't Massachusetts. The enactments which have weighed heavily on the Northern provinces haven't touched the people in South Carolina."

"They have touched their sympathies," Captain Mandeville reminded him. "And there are enough dangerous spirits here to keep those sympathies at fever-point."

"And more who are urged by self-interest to remain quiet. It's not for us to stir them up."

"Yet their Provincial Congress and its very active committees exist, the Society of the Carolinian Sons of Liberty exists. And between them, these illegal bodies rule the province. They rule you."

"Rule me?" Lord William stiffened. "I don't recognise their existence," he declared.

"That is not to abolish them. They exist in spite of you. They come to you with their seditious demands wrapped in constitutional language, and force their measures down your throat, making a mock of your authority."

"But they are as unwilling to come to blows as I am; and since they have the force, and I have not, it says much for their fundamental loyalty that they are as anxious for conciliation as I am. I believe that in my heart – nay, I know it. Haven't I close relatives among those you would call rebels?"

"What does your lordship call them?"

Lord William looked at him, and flushed. He was annoyed, and yet he curbed the expression of it. He recognized that Mandeville, who had already spent two months in Charles Town, was infinitely better acquainted with Carolinian affairs than himself, who had arrived there only a fortnight ago. And he was completely dependent upon Mandeville in his struggle with the constitutional Commons House of Assembly unconstitutionally transforming itself into Provincial Congress and operating through equally unlawful subordinate committees. Therefore he suffered in the equerry certain liberties which in another would never have been tolerated.

"What else, indeed, can you call them?" Mandeville insisted after a moment, on another tone. Then his manner became more brisk. "But I've something else for your excellency this morning. Cheney is here."

The Governor looked up in sharp surprise. "Cheney?"

"He has been set at liberty."

The young face lighted suddenly. "There! You see! That's a proof of their disposition."

"But no explanation is offered of his arrest. Much less regret, as he will tell you if you'll see him."

"Of course I'll see him."

"He has a friend with him, another back-country settler, an intelligent-looking fellow who was sergeant to Kirkland."

"Bring them in. Both of them."

Mandeville handed Lord Hillsborough's letter back to Innes and left the room. The Governor paced across to the window and stood there looking out, pensive, his chin in his hand!

The news of Cheney's release brought relief to Lord William who had seen his authority in peril of being openly defied. It was perhaps as a result of this that his reception of the man was more than ordinarily cordial when presently Captain Mandeville ushered him in, together with his companion, Dick Williams.

"He was sergeant to Kirkland," Mandeville repeated as he presented the latter.

"And before that?" his lordship inquired, simply out of the interest inspired in him by this young man, so personable and attractive despite his shabbiness.

"A tobacco planter in a small way," said Williams. "I have some land, held by the King's bounty, between the Saluda and the Broad. Haven't I, Cheney?"

"Ay, that's a fact," said Cheney, who wore a hang-dog look.

His lordship thought that he understood the fellow's loyalty.

"And therefore you are properly grateful, sir? That is very well. I would all were as dutiful in the back country settlements. But what of you, Cheney? What grounds did the Committee give for your arrest?"

"Just that I came down with Kirkland, as did Dick here. Lucky for him though, he weren't seen in Kirkland's company."

"But they couldn't hurt you for being with Kirkland."

"They might ha' done, if I hadn't denied it. I swore their spy was mistook when he said I came as a lifeguard to Kirkland. I said Kirkland and me had met on the Indian trail beyond the town; that we did happen to come in together, but that I knew naught of him being a deserter from the provincial army. I held to that tale, though they tried plaguy hard to shake me out of it. And when they found they couldn't, why they just let me go. But I ain't safe in Charles Town, my lord."

"Why not, since they've let you go...?"

"Ay, ay, but they may find out something about me yet, and if they take me up again..." He broke off, distress on his dull face.

"What then?"

Williams answered for him. "They may tar-and-feather him," he said casually.

His lordship made a sharp gesture of abhorrence.

"Why? Because he's a king's man! That's a bugbear. Why don't they tar-and-feather me?"

There was a half-smile on the lean face of the false Dick Williams.

"Your lordship is a great man, protected by your station. We are small fry, whom no one would miss. We play this game with our lives on the board and if we're put to death," he shrugged and laughed, "no more notice will be taken of it."

"Nay, there you are wrong. I should see them punished."

"That would vindicate your authority, but hardly profit us."

"They daren't do it. They daren't!" Lord William was emphatic.

"They'll do it to Kirkland, if they get him. And they want him, eh, Cheney?"

"Ay, it's a fact," said Cheney. "The Committee made no secret of it. They'll put Kirkland to death if they lay hands on him, and any other spy."

"So they hold that against him, do they – that he's a spy?"

"Ay, and if they'd had grounds enough to hold it against me I shouldn't be standing here now. If your lordship don't protect me, I'll go in fear of my life."

Lord William turned to his silent, observant equerry. "What's to be done, Mandeville?"

"Send them both to join Kirkland," said Mandeville shortly.

"Ay, ay; but where's Kirkland going?" quoth Williams boldly.

"There's nothing yet decided," Lord William answered him. "Meanwhile he's safe aboard the *Tamar*."

From Kirkland's pretended sergeant came a frank, pleasant laugh that held a note of recklessness.

"Your lordship may send Cheney there if he's a mind to go. But I don't strike my colours yet. I've come to serve the king, and myself, too, at the same time. There's a fellow named Harry Fitzroy Latimer with whom I've an old account to settle."

At the mention of that name Captain Mandeville very obviously awoke to keener interest in Dick Williams. His eyes – dark eyes that seemed invested with a singular penetration from being set in so fair a face – levelled a very searching glance upon him.

"Latimer!" he cried sharply, and added after a breathless pause:

"What is there between you and Latimer?"

Williams hesitated, as if the sharp tone had intimidated him. "Does your honour know him?"

"I asked you a question," said the captain stiffly.

Williams smiled, with a touch of deprecation. "My answer might offend you, captain. Maybe he's a friend of yours."

"A friend of mine!" It was the captain's turn to laugh, and his laugh was not pleasant. "D'ye think I have friends among the rebels?"

"Oh, but this one." Williams turned to his lordship. "Mr Latimer is one of the richest planters in the province, in all the thirteen colonies maybe, and he has a mort of friends among the tories. Why, there's Sir Andrew Carey of Fairgrove Barony as red-hot a tory as any man in America, and Latimer to marry his daughter."

Mandeville looked at him contemptuously. The fellow was not so well-informed after all.

"That may have been the case. It is so no longer. Sir Andrew is my friend, my kinsman; and I have it from himself that this scoundrel Latimer shall never darken his doorway again. I'll add that I do not know him, that I have never seen him, though his deeds are well enough known to me as they are to Lord William."

"Ay," grumbled his excellency. "The fellow's a nasty thorn in our flesh. If the province were rid of him and that firebrand Gadsden, there'd be more hope of a settlement."

"So speak your mind freely about him," the equerry invited. "What is there between you?"

"Just a matter of some fifty acres the grasping scoundrel has filched from my bounty lands, by artful shifting of boundaries."

William's voice quivered with scorn. "There's a noble gentleman for you! A man as rich as Dives, and not above thieving land from a Lazarus like myself. But that's the spirit of these rebels. They're all alike. Where there's no loyalty to the king, there's no fear of God, nor virtue of any kind."

"But there's a law to which you can appeal," Lord William reminded him, shocked by this revelation of turpitude.

"A law!" Dick Williams laughed outright. "The law's dispensed by such men as Mr Latimer in South Carolina. The province is ruled by these wealthy planters. And they'll never legislate against one another."

"We shall alter all that, Williams, when these troubles are settled."

"That's my hope, my lord. That's my faith." Enthusiasm kindled in the blue eyes, a flush crept into that lean, pale face. "And that's why I'm ready to spend my life in the king's service. So that in the end we may have justice of such nabobs as this Mr Latimer. He keeps the state of a prince out of his plunderings. A kite-hearted scoundrel."

"You'll have justice, don't doubt it," said Captain Mandeville slowly. "The fellow is weaving a rope for his neck. Egad! He's woven it already."

"Ye don't say, captain!" Williams was suddenly very eager.

"Oh, but I do," Mandeville answered him, and snapped his lips together on that subject."

Williams showed a desire to pursue it. At least he hesitated now, twirling his shabby hat in hands that were none too clean. Then Lord William diverted the channel of their talk, or, rather, brought it back from that digression.

"What have you in mind to do, Williams? Where do you propose to go?"

"I? Why, back whence I came. Back beyond the Broad. So if your lordship has any messages or letters for Fletchall or the Cunninghams or the Browns, or any other of the loyal folk up yonder, I'm the man to carry them."

"Letters?" said Lord William, and he smiled. "Yet if it were known you came with Kirkland... No, no. Besides, I have no letters for them."

"If you had you'd find me as safe as the others that have carried for your lordship."

"For me?" His lordship looked surprised. "Nay, I have sent no letters. Who says I have?"

"It's what I'm supposing, your lordship. For how else should you correspond?"

"Certainly not by letters," said his lordship, with the air of a man who knows his business.

"By word of mouth, then. There I'm your man. You'll have some message for them?"

"Why, nothing but to bid them keep the men in good order."

"But you do not yet sanction them to take up arms?"

"Not yet. Not without they have ammunition in plenty, and think they're strong enough."

The comely young face of Williams lengthened. "They're not strong enough, nor have they ammunition in plenty. That I know. Besides, Drayton has been up there preaching sedition to them, and that has thinned their ranks."

"Stale news," put in Captain Mandeville.

"Ay, I suppose it is," Williams agreed, and sighed. "If they could depend upon His Majesty's Government for arms."

"Bid them be patient," Lord William answered him, "and should it become necessary – which God send it may not! – the arms shall presently be forthcoming."

Again the face lighted eagerly. "How, your lordship?" he asked breathlessly.

The young Governor sauntered over to the writing-table. "I could not have told you yesterday. But today I have a letter here from the Secretary of State." He held it up a moment, and Williams observed that his face was gloomy, his eyes sad. "His Majesty is resolved to enforce submission from one end of the continent to the other. Tell them that in the back country."

"It will rejoice their hearts, as it rejoices mine, my lord. Does your lordship mean that soldiers will be sent from England?"

"That is what I mean – here to Charles Town." There was no exultation in his voice. "Unless the rebels bend their stubborn necks this place will shortly be a seat of war."

"Now that's good hearing, on my life!" The young man glowed with satisfaction, until Captain Mandeville and even the silent secretary, Innes, smiled to see so much enthusiasm. Lord William alone remained grave.

"There's only one piece of news would gladden me more than that," Williams added after a moment. "And that would be really to know, to be sure, that Latimer was as safe to be hanged as your honour seemed to promise. If you've those journeys of his in mind, to Boston and elsewhere, I doubt if there's much in that you can act on. He's not done as much as Drayton's been doing, and others that you know of. And if you can't proceed against those, what can you do against Latimer?"

"We've something more than that against him," said Lord William.

"If it's anything about which ye're still lacking evidence, it would be a joy for me to get it for your lordship."

"Nay," said his lordship affably. "I think the evidence is complete. Ye're a good fellow, Williams. I'll show you something that'll make you certain of the recovery of your land, with perhaps a few of Mr Latimer's acres added to them by way of interest; something that'll encourage you to continue to serve your king as stoutly as you have been serving him." He turned to his secretary. "Innes, give me that April list."

Mandeville moved across to his lordship's side. "Is it…quite prudent?" he asked.

Lord William frowned. It seemed to him that Captain Mandeville was permitting himself a liberty greater than usual.

"Prudent? And where is the imprudence? What do I betray that may not be published in Charles Town?"

Mandeville pursed his lips. "Provided that the source of the information is not divulged. That is too precious to be risked in any way."

"Your talent, Mandeville, is for pointing out the obvious."

"That is because the obvious sometimes eludes your lordship," Mandeville answered him with that quiet smiling insolence that he was rather prone to use.

"Be damned to you for your good opinion of me! Let it quiet your timid heart that the obvious does not escape me now." He took the document that Innes proffered and unfolded it. He held it out so that Williams could read it. "What name do you find there at the very top?"

Dick Williams was studying the document as if with effort.

"I... I do not read easily," he said.

Mandeville's dark eyes flashed upon him with a sudden look of suspicion. "Yet your speech, sir," he said, "is hardly of one who does not read."

"Oh, I read," said Williams, no whit perturbed. "I read printed books. Indeed, I am a great reader of printed books. But I have no great experience of handwriting." All the while his eyes were on that written sheet. "And this is a cursedly crabbed hand. Whatever rogue writ that should be sent back to school to learn his pothooks. Ah, I have it at last! Egad, I should have guessed it. Why, the name is Harry Latimer."

"Harry Latimer it is," said his lordship refolding the document and restoring it to his secretary. "It's at the head of the list; and the list is that of the men who were concerned in the raid on the King's armoury here two months ago, in Lieutenant Governor Bull's time. Latimer was the ring-leader. Robbery and high-treason both in one. That will be the indictment he will have to answer one of these fine days."

Dick Williams was staring at his lordship, a bewildered look in his eyes.

"But I thought he was away in Boston then?"

"So did a good many others. But he wasn't. He was here in Charles Town for three days. And that was one of the things he did."

Dick Williams looked gravely at his lordship.

"The man who wrote that list will testify, of course?"

"When the time comes."

"Then why don't you arrest Latimer?"

"Arrest him?"

"He's here in Charles Town," said Williams, whereupon Captain Mandeville interjected with unusual violence the question:

"How do you know?"

"We saw him this morning in Broad Street as we were on our way here, didn't we, Cheney?"

Cheney woke with a start from the uneasy dejection in which he had been standing.

"It's a fact," he stolidly attested.

Mandeville mused aloud as it seemed: "So he's come back, has he?"

"He has. This is your chance since you can bring forward your witness."

Lord William laughed, a little bitterly. "My good fellow, even if the sheriff's officers would execute my warrant, which I doubt, to bring forward my witness is not yet desirable. The matter must wait. But it will lose nothing by waiting. Be sure of that."

"I see," said Williams. "To disclose the witness would be to lose the services of your spy in the enemy's camp. I understand." He fetched a sigh. "Ah, well, I'll be patient, my lord, and meanwhile we may pile up the score against our gentleman." His manner became brisk. "I'll bear your messages to the back-country. I shall be setting out at once. There's nothing to be gained by stopping in Charles Town. If your lordship has any further word – "

"No. I think not. If you'll bear those I have given you, and report to me when you are next here, I shall be obliged. And now there's still to settle about you, Cheney."

"May it please your lordship," said Cheney.

But the mercurial Dick Williams settled it for him breezily.

"You come back with me, Cheney. You'll be safe enough beyond the Broad. And it's as easy to get out of Charles Town that way as by way of the wharves. Beside, up there with a musket in your hands you'll be more use to your king than stowed away aboard a man-of-war."

"Faith, I don't much care where I goes, so long as I doesn't stay in Charles Town."

"You ride with me, my lad."

"Ay, ay! We'd best be going," said Cheney, who seemed to have no mind of his own.

"Indeed, I think that's best," agreed his lordship. He turned to his secretary. "Innes, let them have ten guineas apiece."

But Williams recoiled. "My lord!" There was deep injury in his tone.

"Why, what the devil!" His lordship stared at him.

"I'm a spy, my lord. I don't mince words. I'm a spy, and I glory in it. But I don't take money for it. I do it as a duty and for the sake of the entertainment it affords me."

Looking into those humorous, dare-devil blue eyes of his, Lord William found no difficulty in believing the preposterous statement.

"Egad, Mr Williams," said Captain Mandeville, "ye've an odd sense of humour."

"I have. Haven't I, Cheney?"

"It's a fact," said Cheney, who was opening a receptive palm to the gold Mr Innes poured into it.

Thereupon they took their leave, and Lord William wearily resumed his place on the couch. "An interesting, attractive fellow that," he said, feeling for his snuff-box. "It's the first time I've found it possible to talk to a spy without feeling nauseated. But then he's not really a spy. He had very little to tell us, after all."

"He was very interesting on the subject of Harry Latimer," said Mandeville, who was brooding by the window.

"Interesting, perhaps. But hardly useful. If he had been before the Committee instead of that oaf Cheney we might have had something from him."

"Perhaps you might have had something out of Cheney if you'd questioned him."

His lordship yawned. "I forgot," he said. "And that fellow Williams talked so much. No matter. What use is information when you can't act upon it? And I thank God I can't. That way lies hope." He took snuff gloomily.

Chapter 4

Fairgrove

In an upper room of his handsome house on the Bay, Mr Harry Latimer was at his toilet with the assistance of Johnson. He was exchanging the clothes and the grime proper to Dick Williams for garments more suited to his real station. But when Johnson respectfully asked his honour what he would wear, his honour bade him lay out a riding-suit, and meanwhile give him a bedgown. Wrapped in this, he sat there listless and dejected before his toilet table what time his valet busied himself with the clothes Mr Latimer was presently to don.

When all was ready, instead of proceeding to dress, he dismissed the valet, and continued sunk in thought. Thus Julius the butler, found him when he came a quarter of an hour later with a silver chocolate service which he set down at his master's elbow. Julius, a short, slight, elderly negro, in a sky-blue livery, and with a head of crisply-curling white hair that looked like a wig, poured a cup of the steaming brew, and then, in obedience to a curt dismissal, withdrew again.

Mr Latimer sat on, alone with his thoughts. He had succeeded in his aims that morning beyond anything that you may yet suspect. Once he had seen that list which Lord William had shown him, there had been no need for any further questions. He had learnt all that he sought to know. And yet his success, far from bringing him elation, had plunged him into a dejection deeper than any he had yet experienced. For that list was in a hand that he knew as well as he knew his own. It was the hand of a man of his own age, a man named Gabriel Featherstone, who was the son of Sir Andrew Carey's factor at Fairgrove. This factor had been in Sir Andrew's service for thirty years, and not only himself but also his son were held by Sir Andrew in warm affection. So much had this been the case, that at one time when, as a boy, Latimer had been given a tutor, Gabriel Featherstone had been sent to share his lessons. For two years – until Latimer had gone to England to complete his studies – Gabriel and he had worked side by side at their school-books, and for some time afterwards they had corresponded. It was no wonder, then, that he knew the hand so well.

The discovery that it was Gabriel Featherstone who had supplied that list to Lord William and who was, therefore, the traitor in their ranks, had led Latimer straight to certain very definite and irresistible conclusions. And he was left wondering now at his own dullness in never having suspected these things which were suddenly rendered so appallingly clear.

From the moment that Gabriel Featherstone joined the Carolinian Sons of Liberty and procured his election to the General Committee of Provincial Congress, Latimer should have considered the possibility of some such purpose as he now perceived. Perhaps his own sudden conversion to the Cause had made him take the conversion of Featherstone too much for granted. Yet he should have known that self-interest must have restrained a man who, through his own father, was largely dependent upon Sir Andrew. He should have known that Sir Andrew's bigotry would have dictated the instant dismissal of a man who was the father of a rebel. Since this had not happened, it followed that he was a party to what had taken place. Possibly – indeed probably – it was at Sir Andrew's own instigation that Gabriel had been sent to act as a spy upon the doings of Provincial Congress.

And now Latimer found himself face to face with the clear duty to announce his discovery. The extemporaneous secret committee by which he had been empowered to make his investigation was to assemble again that evening at six o'clock at the house of Henry Laurens to receive his report. Make it he must at whatever cost. Of that there was no doubt in his mind. But the cost was heavy indeed.

It was not that he pitied or sympathized with Featherstone. Whatever tenderness he might have had for him was eclipsed by the fact that in spite of the past Featherstone had never hesitated to place a rope round Latimer's neck. The fellow was revealed to him for a venal scoundrel upon whom only a fool would waste his pity. But there was Sir Andrew. There was the breach already existing between himself and the man who had been his guardian and dearest friend, and who was Myrtle's father. That breach, the hope of healing which had been strong until this moment, must now be rendered utterly irreparable. For if he denounced Featherstone, there could be no doubt of what must follow. Whatever the feelings and hesitations of the others, Gadsden would see to it that the man be dealt with by mob-law. And if through Latimer's denunciation Featherstone should lose his life as a punishment for activities in which Sir Andrew himself had engaged him, it would be idle for Harry Latimer to hope that his adoptive father would ever forgive him. Myrtle would then, indeed, be lost to him irrevocably.

Yet denounce Featherstone he must.

There you have the two horns of the terrible dilemma upon which, as a result of his success, Mr Latimer now found himself. And it was a long time before there dawned upon him the possibility of a middle course, which, by removing Featherstone and thus putting a term to his espionage, might yet spare his life.

A man of quick decisions and of rather sanguine temperament, he decided to act at once upon the idea. Indeed, if it was to be acted upon at all there was no time to lose. He rose at last, and rang for his valet. When the man came, he bade him send a messenger to ask Mr Izard to step round to see him, and then return to assist him to dress.

Now at just about the time that Mr Latimer was beginning to make his toilet – which would be somewhere in the neighbourhood of noon – Captain Mandeville was setting out from Meeting Street, with intent to ride to Fairgrove, the imposing seat of Sir Andrew Carey on the Back River.

Seen on his tall black horse, in his scarlet gold-laced coat, white buckskins and lacquered riding-boots, the captain was a figure calculated to gladden the eyes of any maid that might happen to peep through one or another of the green jalousies veiling the windows under which he passed.

Charles Town had been planned by Culpepper a hundred years ago, at a time and in a place that admitted of generous spaces and regular lines such as were not to be found in the old world. Meeting Street in the European eyes of the Governor's equerry was a pleasant avenue, fringed with elms, and deriving a sense of width from the garden spaces between the houses on either side. Some of these, and mainly the more recent ones, of mellowing red brick, clothed in vine and honeysuckle, jasmine and glossy cherokee, were half concealed amid the luxuriance of their gardens; others, of wood, but very solidly built, mainly of the timber of the black cypress, stood sideways to the thoroughfare, presenting to it no more than a gabled end, whilst the long fronts with their wide deep piazzas faced inwards upon the gardens, which were enclosed behind high brick walls. The scent of late flowering bulbs, which early Dutch settlers had procured from Holland, mingled with the heavier perfume of jasmine and honeysuckle and the pungent fragrance which the sun was drawing from the pines.

The captain turned off into Broad Street, and rode past the Church of St Michael with its lofty steeple, so reminiscent of the work of Wren and so greatly resembling St Martin's-in-the-Fields. He crossed the open space at the Corner presided over by the statue of Pitt, which had been enthusiastically erected there five years ago to mark the province's appreciation of the Great Commoner who had championed the cause of the Colonies in the Stamp Act troubles.

And here the bustle of life and traffic was such that the captain found it in the main impossible to proceed at more than a walking pace. There were groups of seafaring men of all degrees from the ships in the harbour, standing to gape upon the sights of the town. Now it was a party of negro field servants in brightly-coloured cottons, shepherded by a swarthy overseer, that claimed their attention; now it was a file of three Catawba Indians, feather-crowned and mantled in gaudy blankets, each leading a pack-horse laden with the merchandise against which they had traded the pelts from their distant settlements beyond Camden. More than once Captain Mandeville was compelled to draw rein altogether to give passage to the lumbering mahogany coach of some wealthy planter, the tall phaeton driven by a young colonial macaroni, with his liveried negro groom sitting like a statue of bronze behind; or the sedan chair slung between its black porters bearing a lady of fashion on her shopping excursions.

For of all the towns in North America, this was the one in which the luxury and refinements of the Old World were combined in the highest degree with the wealth and abundance of the New. And, as was natural, their sybaritism governed their politics. There were, of course, firebrands, republican extremists such as Christopher Gadsden and this new convert to republicanism Mr Harry Latimer, and there was an unruly mob of mechanics and artisans and the like, who with little to stake were ready enough for adventure; but in the main the wealthy oligarchy of planters and merchants which had so long held undisputed sway in South Carolina, whilst sympathizing with the grievances of the North and the opposers of the oppressive royal rule, was restrained from overt action by self-interest. The security of person and property which they now enjoyed might be lost to them in an upheaval. And the same incubus of passivity sat upon the spirit of the avowed tories. In their ranks, too, there were extremists, like Sir Andrew Carey and the Fletchalls, who left everything but a fanatical duty to the King out of their calculations. But in the main they were as anxious as those on the other side to avoid an open rupture.

Thus it was the destiny of the Carolinians to follow, since follow they must, but never to lead, in this conflict with authority.

News of the skirmish at Lexington last April had rudely shaken them. But things had settled down again. Congress had met to frame a petition to the King, and the hope that all would yet be adjusted and that a reconciliation would be effected was held as stoutly as men hold the hopes of things they desperately desire.

Captain Mandeville's views on colonial matters were pessimistic, and it also happened that he loved antitheses as well as any man with a sense of irony. Therefore it was with mildly amused detachment that he returned the salutes of some of these ubiquitous blue-coated officers of the provincial militia – a body more or less constitutionally brought together against the need for unconstitutional emergencies – who doffed their black-cockaded hats to him as he rode by. He reflected that despite their superficial friendliness, they regarded his scarlet coat much as a bull might regard it, and that notwithstanding their friendly smiles of greeting – for many of them were men with whom he gamed and hunted and laid wagers on a main of cocks or a horse race – they might very possibly be cutting his throat before the week was out.

To Mandeville, it was all in the day's work. He had come out to the colonies in the service of his King, like the "poor devil of a younger son" as he was wont, more affectedly than accurately to describe himself. He was, in reality, the younger son of a younger son. He had run through the considerable fortune inherited from his mother – his father having married a wealthy heiress, in accordance with the best traditions of the younger sons of noble houses – and he was now in the position of dependency upon the State peculiar to British cadets, with the possible expectations that commonly delude them.

His uncle, the present Earl of Chalfont, had no issue, and Captain Mandeville was next in the succession. But as his uncle, now in his fifty-fifth year, was of a rudely vigorous constitution, and the Mandevilles were a long-lived race, the captain was not disposed to build upon expectations which might not be realized until his own youth was spent. Therefore, in coming out to the colonies to serve his King, Captain Mandeville had it also in mind to serve himself in the manner not unusual among his kind, the manner of which his own father had set him the example, and the manner in which Lord William Campbell – also a younger son – had served himself when he married Sally Izard and a dowry of fifty thousand pounds. The colonies offered a fruitful hunting-ground, and colonial heiresses afforded covetable prizes for younger sons who knew how to make the best of family glamour.

Apart from this, however, Captain Mandeville came out persuaded that in his own case the hunt need not be carried very far afield. Sir Andrew Carey, that wealthy and influential South Carolina tory, descended on the distaff side from that Mandeville who had been one of the original Lords Proprietors, was a remote kinsman of the captain's, and so passionately proud of his descent from so ancient and distinguished a stock as to be disposed to regard the kinship as much closer than it actually was. And Sir Andrew had a daughter, an only child. What, then, more natural than that this widower, with no son of his own to succeed him, should perceive in Mandeville the son-in-law of his dreams?

The only thing omitted from the captain's shrewd calculations was the existence of Mr Henry Fitzroy Latimer of Santee Broads and of the Latimer Barony on the Saluda. And this omission might entirely have wrecked those same calculations but for the dispensation of Providence by which Latimer was guided into the paths of rebellion.

The outraged Sir Andrew let it be understood that he saw repeated between himself and Latimer the fable of the woodman and the snake, and he swore that he would play out the woodman's part.

When Captain Mandeville's eyes, which missed few things, observed thereafter the disappearance from Myrtle's finger of a certain brilliant-studded hoop of gold, he accounted the battle almost over. Nor did he permit himself to be unduly concerned by the pallid listlessness that descended upon Myrtle in those spring days.

If he curbed himself, using a masterly restraint at present, while her grief endured, yet he envisaged the future confidently. He knew his world, and he knew humanity. He knew that there is no wound of the heart which time cannot heal. It was for him to contain himself until he was sure that the healing process should be well-advanced. The rest should follow naturally and easily.

There was no coxcombry in his persuasion. That he was agreeable to Myrtle she rendered evident. And in the quest for sympathy and affection which is natural to those who have been hurt as she had been, it was inevitable that her relations with her kinsman Mandeville should be strengthened in their intimacy. Add to this that he had now the assurance of Sir Andrew's entire favour and support. Sir Andrew had done more than hint it to him. There was an end to any thought of marriage between his child and the renegade Latimer, this ungrateful scoundrel to whom his house was closed, which the captain assumed – and not without justification – to mean that the way to his own suit lay open. That suit he now cautiously pursued, and it was in the pursuit of it that he was riding to Fairgrove, bearing a choice item of news which the interview that morning with Dick Williams had supplied him.

He turned up King Street, where the traffic was less brisk, and pushed on at a better pace towards the Town Gate. On a sandy waste beyond the unfinished fortification works, undertaken some twenty years before, but subsequently abandoned, he saw a considerable party of militia at drill. It was composed largely of young men of the working classes, the least responsible, and therefore the most inflammable material in the province. The sight of Mandeville's red coat provoked certain ribaldries, which they shouted after him, but more or less in a spirit of good-humour.

Paying little heed to them, he rode amain along the old Indian trail across the pine barrens, a desolate landscape of shallow dunes unrelieved by any vegetation beyond the clumps of pine trees that reared themselves black and fragrant in the sunshine. Anon as he drew nearer to the Back River, that branch of the Cooper on which Fairgrove had been built by the present Carey's grandfather, the road led across a swamp, at the end of which at last the country assumed a more fertile aspect.

It would be something after two o'clock in the afternoon when Mandeville brought his now foam-flecked horse to the tall, wrought-iron gates of Fairgrove, and the broad avenue bordered with live oaks, nearly a mile long, which clove the parklands about the stately home of Andrew Carey.

This house of Fairgrove was a noble four-square mansion of Queen-Anne design, with very tall, white-sashed windows equipped with white-slatted jalousies. It had been built fifty years or so ago, of brick, now mellowed by age and weather brought out as ballast by the ships from England. Emerging from the avenue on to a wide semi-circular sweep of gravel, you might have conceived yourself confronting an English country house of Kent or Surrey. Wide lawns were spread on either hand, under the shade of massive cedars, whilst a flight of terraces on the northern side broke the harsh slope by which the land fell away sharply to the river.

A negro groom led away the captain's horse. Remus, the negro butler, ushered him into the house, and into the long, cool dining-room, where Sir Andrew, who had just come in from the plantation, was refreshing himself with a morning punch. He was in riding-boots, and his gloves and long silver-mounted switch lay on the table where he had flung them a moment since. His daughter was ministering to him, but mechanically and listlessly. She had that morning received Harry's letter from Savannah, and so different was it from what she had hoped and expected that it left her with a feeling that life was at an end.

Sir Andrew, a big bluff man, looking in his grey riding-frock and buckskins like a typical English squire, heaved himself up to greet his visitor.

"Robert, my boy, we're favoured. Remus, a punch for Captain Mandeville."

The words were naught. The cordiality of the welcome lay in the ringing voice, the beaming countenance, the outstretched hand.

And Myrtle, slim, tall and ethereal in a hooped gown of lilac, a dark curl coiling on her milk-white neck, gave him as he bowed to kiss her finger-tips a greeting that was as frank and friendly as her listlessness permitted, whereafter she sought to busy herself with Remus at the great mahogany sideboard in the preparation of the captain's punch.

"Time hangs on your hands," Sir Andrew rallied him, "and it's plain the Governor and his council don't overwork you."

"They may be doing so before long, Sir Andrew. And, faith, the sooner the better." He paused to receive the punch, which old Remus proffered on a salver, and gracefully to thank Miss Carey for her part in its preparation.

"Confusion to all rebels," he said lightly, as he raised the glass to his lips.

"Amen to that! Amen!" boomed solemnly the voice of Sir Andrew, whilst Myrtle looked on with a face that was white and drawn.

They sat down, the captain and his host facing each other across the dark, glossy board on which glass and silver seemed to float, reflected as in a pool, Myrtle on a window-seat, perhaps instinctively placing her back to the light that her troubled coutenance might escape notice.

Sir Andrew filled himself a long pipe from a silver box, and Remus attended him with a lighted taper.

"No use to offer you a pipe, I know," the baronet mumbled, the stem between his teeth. And the fastidious Mandeville, who loathed the stench of tobacco-smoke, smilingly agreed.

"You miss a deal, Bob. You do so. And this is fine leaf of that scoundrel Latimer's own growing." His face was momentarily darkened. He fetched a sigh. "The fellow learnt the trick of curing it in Virginia. But he kept the secret to himself. A secretive dog in that as in other things. You should try a pipe, man. It's a great soother." But the captain merely smiled again, and shook his head. "And what's the news in Charles Town? We're out of the world up here. You'd be at old Izard's ball last night. I'd ha' been there myself, but

Myrtle wouldn't go. Moping over the black ingratitude of a damned scoundrel who isn't worth a thought."

"You must bring her to Mrs Brewton's ball on Thursday."

"Ay, to be sure."

"I don't think – " Myrtle was beginning in hesitation, when the captain gently interrupted her.

"Nay, now, my dear Myrtle. It is a duty, no less. The ball is being given in the Governor's honour. It becomes an official function. In these sad times Lord William requires the support of every loyal man and woman. Indeed, Sir Andrew, he desires me to say that he deplores your absence from Charles Town just now and that he would be the better for your presence."

Sir Andrew swore roundly and emphatically that in that case he would return to town at once, however much the stench of treason in it might turn his stomach.

It was not, indeed, usual for him to be on his plantation at this time of year, and he would certainly not have remained there since Lord William's coming but for the circumstances of his last departure from Charles Town and the oath he had then sworn that he would not return until the vile place was purged of its rebellious spirit.

He had fled from it in a rage in the middle of last February on the day following that 17th, appointed by Provincial Congress to be a day of fasting, humiliation and prayer before Almighty God, devoutly to petition Him to inspire the King with true wisdom to defend the people of North America in their just title to freedom, and avert the calamities of civil war.

To Sir Andrew it seemed impossible that anything more blasphemous than this lay within the possibility of human utterance. But when he heard tell that every place of worship in Charles Town was crowded with wicked fools who went to offer up that seditious prayer, when with his own eyes he beheld the members of the Provincial Congress going in solemn procession to St Philip's, with Lowndes the Speaker of the Commons House at their head in his purple robes and full-bottomed wig, the silver mace borne in state before him, Sir Andrew's indignation forbade him to remain in a place upon which he hourly expected some such visitation as that which overtook Sodom and Gomorrah.

He raged in impotent loyalty, and raged the more because there was little else that he could do to signify his execration of the event. That little, however, he performed. He made his protest, and it took the shape of closing his residence in Tradd Street, and shaking the rebellious dust of that place of treason from his loyal feet.

On his plantation he had since remained, and there he would have continued but for this viceregal summons, which he pronounced it his sacred duty unquestionably to obey.

"We'll be there by tomorrow Bob, dead or alive, to swell the muster of the King's friends." Dismissing the matter upon that, he craved for news.

He received from Mandeville, whose face was grave to the point of sadness, an account of the morning's interview with Cheney and Dick Williams, and the latter's accusation against Latimer of turpitude in his dealings with less powerful neighbours.

Sir Andrew's brows were scowling. But he thrust out a doubting nether lip. "That is not like Harry Latimer," he said slowly. And Myrtle rose abruptly from her window-seat.

"It isn't true," she said with heat.

"I scarcely could believe it myself," Mandeville agreed smoothly. "Men are not often dishonest without motive, and what motive could there be for such petty pilferings on the part of the wealthy Mr Latimer? And yet…" He paused a moment, a man hesitating between thoughts. "And yet, when a man practises the dishonesty of being false to his duty to his King…" He left it there.

"Ay, ay," assented Sir Andrew on a deep growl.

"Oh, you are wrong. Wrong!" his daughter insisted. "There is all the world between the two deeds. Whatever Harry may be, he is not a thief, and no one will make me believe it."

Captain Mandeville deplored to observe that time had not yet begun to do the work which he had been content to leave to it.

"No one could have made you believe him a traitor," her father answered her. "No one could have made you believe him secretive

and furtive – a fellow that comes and goes by stealth like a thief in
the night."

"Which reminds me," said Captain Mandeville, "that he is in
Charles Town at present."

Their startled glances questioned him.

"I had it from this same fellow Williams. He told me he had seen
him this morning."

"Then why in God's name don't you arrest him?"

"Don't, father!" Myrtle laid a restraining hand upon his shoulder.

"Pshaw, my girl! The fellow's no longer anything to you."

Captain Mandeville wished he could share the opinion. Meanwhile
he answered Sir Andrew's fierce question.

"Lord William would have signed the warrant already, but that – "
He checked.

"Well? But that what?"

"I persuaded him not to do so."

"You persuaded him?" Sir Andrew showed his amazement.
"Why?"

"For one thing, it would not be politic. We want to avoid strife
and any act that may lead to strife. Mr Latimer is something of a hero
with the mob; and we do not wish to provoke the mob into acts that
might call for reprisals."

"It's what they need, by God!"

"Maybe. And yet it has its dangers. Lord William saw that. Also,
Sir Andrew, I had other reasons. This Mr Latimer, after all, in spite of
what he has done, has thrust certain roots into your heart."

"I've torn them out," Sir Andrew protested vehemently.

"And then, there is Myrtle," the captain sighed.

"How good you are!" Myrtle rewarded him, her eyes shining
moistily.

"Good!" growled the baronet. "Good, to neglect his clear duty!"

"I doubt if I should ever do my duty at the cost of hurting either
of you, however slightly. You have become so very dear to me in the
months I have been in this exile that I could never leave your feelings
out of consideration in anything I did."

And then, before either of them could find the right words in which to answer that pledge of affection, Remus opened the door to make the dramatic announcement:

"Massa Harry, Sir Andrew."

It had never occurred to the old butler that there could be any doubt of admitting Master Harry, and so he had conducted him straight to the dining-room where Sir Andrew sat.

Chapter 5

The Rebel

Mr Harry Latimer, stepping briskly, his three-cornered hat and a heavy riding crop tucked under his arm, and drawing off his gloves as he came, advanced with a composure which Sir Andrew afterwards described as impudent.

Remus closed the heavy mahogany door, and silence reigned thereafter for some moments in that room.

Sir Andrew, Captain Mandeville and Miss Carey remained at gaze, three petrified figures, the two men seated, the girl, her breathing quickened, standing just behind her father's chair, her right hand resting upon the summit of its tall back.

You conceive perhaps the various emotions conflicting in the mind of each, and you certainly conceive that for the moment these emotions were dominated by sheer amazement. Deep as it was in all three, it was deepest in Captain Mandeville. He was not merely amazed. He was bewildered. For the tall, slim young gentleman who had entered, and who was standing now by the head of the table, was no stranger to him. He had seen and talked with him somewhere before, and the captain raked his wits to discover when and where that might have been. But only for a moment. Gradually the eyes of his mind metamorphosed the figure which the eyes of his body were devouring. The well-fitting, modish, long riding-coat of bottle-green gave place to a shabby brown coatee; the fine delicate hand, that was being withdrawn from its glove, became soiled and grimy; the rippling bronze hair, so neatly queued in its moiré ribbon, hung loose and unkempt about that lean, pale face with its keen blue eyes and humorous mouth.

The captain's fist crashed down upon the mahogany, so that glass and silver rattled, he half rose from his chair, momentarily moved out of his self-control in a manner foreign to him even at times of greatest provocation.

"Dick Williams!" he cried, and added: "By God!"

Mr Latimer bowed to him, his smile ironical.

"Captain Mandeville, your humble obedient. I can understand your feelings."

Mandeville made him no answer. His thoughts were racing over the ground covered that morning by the interview between Dick Williams and the Governor. He sought to recall how much had been disclosed to this audacious spy, who, thanks to the assistance of Cheney – whose unaccountable treachery was now also made clear – had so completely bubbled them.

Meanwhile Sir Andrew, too obsessed by his own feelings to give heed to the unintelligible exchange of words between Mandeville and this unwelcome visitor, was raging furiously.

"My God! Have you the impudence to show your face here, now that the mask is off it? Now that we know you for what you are?"

"You do not know me, sir, for anything of which I am ashamed."

"Because you're shameless," Sir Andrew choked, impatiently shaking off the trembling hand that Myrtle set on his shoulder to restrain him.

Mr Latimer looked at him wistfully. "Sir Andrew," he said very gently, "must there be war between us because we do not see eye to eye on matters of policy and justice? There is no man in all this world whom I love more deeply than yourself – "

"You may spare me that," the baronet broke in. "When I find a more ungrateful, treacherous scoundrel than you are, I may hate him more. But I don't believe that such a man lives."

Latimer's pallor deepened. Shadows formed themselves under his brilliant eyes.

"In what am I ungrateful?" he quietly asked.

"Must you be told? Could any father have done more for you than I have done? For years, whilst you were a boy whilst you were away in England on your education, I husbanded your estates, watched over them to the neglect of my own. Your father left you wealthy. But under my care your wealth has been trebled until today you are the richest man in Carolina, perhaps the richest man in America. And you squander the wealth I raised for you in attempting to pull down everything that I hold good and sacred, the very altars at which I worship."

"And if I could prove to you that those altars enshrine false gods?"

"False gods! You abominable – "

"Sir Andrew!" Latimer held out a hand in appeal. "Give me leave at least to justify myself."

"Justify yourself? What justification can there be for what you have done, for what you are doing?"

He would have added more. But Myrtle came to Latimer's assistance.

"Father, it is only just to hear him." Her plea sprang from a desire, deep down in her heart, to hear him herself. She hoped to find in his words something to mitigate the judgment she had passed upon him in a letter which had failed so miserably of its true aim – to recall him from his rebellious course.

Mandeville, inwardly alarmed at the memory of all that had been said that morning in the Governor's study, and quite undecided as to how to bear himself now, so that he might reconcile and serve conflicting interests, sat still and watchful, a player who waits until opportunity shall show him what line of play to follow.

"Sir Andrew," Latimer was saying, "you who live sheltered here in a province upon which the hand of the royal Government rests lightly, can have no more conception than I had until I went there four months ago of what is happening in the North."

But Sir Andrew did not mean to listen to a political harangue. "Can I not?" Contemptuous laughter brought the words out in a croak. "Can I not? There's treason happening in the North. That's what's happening. And that's what you've borne a hand in, plotting God knows what devilries against your King."

"That," said Mr Latimer, "is hardly true."

"D'ye think your seditious actions have not been reported to us!"

"Reported?" Latimer almost smiled as his keen eyes wandered to Captain Mandeville. He bowed a little to the captain. "I become important, it seems. I am honoured, sir, to be the subject of your reports."

"As equerry to his excellency the Governor, certain duties devolve upon me," Mandeville answered smoothly. "Perhaps, Mr Latimer, you are overlooking that."

"Oh, no." There was a gleam of that sedate amusement so natural to Latimer, and as irritating now to Captain Mandeville as it had been to many another who imagined himself to be the object of Mr Latimer's covert mirth. "I gratified this morning my curiosity on the score of your activities." The captain flushed despite himself. "But your reports – or, at least, the inferences you have drawn from them – have not been quite accurate. Inference, I believe, is not the strength of the official mind."

He turned again to Sir Andrew who was containing himself with difficulty, and who only half understood what was passing between Latimer and the equerry. "I have been plotting, perhaps. But certainly nothing against the King. By which I mean that I am not of those extremists who already utter the word 'Independence.' On the contrary, I am of those who are labouring to preserve the peace in spite of every provocation to support constitutionalism against all the endeavours to cast it aside for coercive violence."

The baronet restrained himself to sneer.

"It was out of your concern for peace, I suppose, that you planned the raid on the armoury last April?"

Latimer's eyes flashed upon Mandeville again.

"Your reports have been very full, Captain Mandeville."

This time the captain gave him back gibe for gibe.

"Inference, you see, Mr Latimer, is not always the weakness of the official mind."

But Latimer's counter whipped the weapon from his hand.

"That was not inference, captain. It was information. It is one of the things I ascertained this morning; one of the things I went to ascertain. For the rest" – and without giving the captain time to answer him, he swung again to Sir Andrew – "we desired to avoid here what was done in Boston: British subjects shot down by British troops. Si vis pacem, para bellum. It's sound philosophy. Since England, or rather England's King, acting through a too pliant ministry, chooses to treat this Britain overseas as enemy country, what choice is left us? We prepare for war that we may avert it; that we may prevail upon a ministry at home to receive our petitions, consider our grievances, and redress our wrongs, instead of brutally compelling us by force to submit ourselves to injustice."

"My God! You're mad! That's it! Mad!"

Captain Mandeville interpolated gently: "Did not Boston bring down upon itself this trouble by its insubordination?"

"Ay! Answer that!" Sir Andrew challenged.

"Insubordination?" Mr Latimer shrugged a little. "To what should Boston have been subordinated? The subjection of a free people to the executive authority of government is no more than a compliance with the laws they have themselves enacted."

"You are quoting Dr. Franklin, I suppose," said the captain with the least suspicion of a sneer.

"I am quoting from one of the letters of Junius, Captain Mandeville, one of the letters addressed to a king and a ministry who are so reckless as to threaten the liberties of Englishmen in England as well as in the colonies."

Sir Andrew's indignation blazed.

"Is that a thing to say of his gracious majesty?"

"That there should be occasion to say it is deplorable. But the occasion itself is not to be denied."

"Not to be denied!" Sir Andrew almost barked. "I deny it for one, as I deny every word of your trumped-up pretexts of rebellion! The damnable gospel of these Sons of Liberty. Sons of Liberty!" He snorted. "Sons of riff-raff!"

The tone stung Latimer to a momentary resentment.

"It was an Englishman, a member of the House of Commons, who gave us that name at which you sneer, speaking in admiring terms of our stand for liberty."

"I nothing doubt it. There are rebels in England, just as there are loyal men in America."

"Yes, and as time goes on there may be more of the former and fewer of the latter. For this, sir, I say again is no quarrel between England and America. That independency by which the North American colonies may be lost to Britain, desired at present by so few of us, may yet come to be the only issue. If it should come to pass, it will be the achievement of a besotted King who, although he glories in the name of Britain – "

But he got no further.

Sir Andrew on his feet, livid with passion, furiously interrupted him: "You infamous traitor! My God! You'd utter such words in my house, would you? You heard, Robert? You have a duty, surely!"

Captain Mandeville, too, had risen, and was obviously ill-at-ease.

"Robert!" It was a cry from Myrtle. In her distress – for she well understood her father's invitation to him – the ceremonious term of 'cousin' was omitted. Both Mandeville and Latimer remarked it, intent though they might be upon a graver issue, and both were thrilled, though each after a different fashion.

"Pray have no fear, dear Myrtle," the captain reassured her. And he swung to Latimer who was watching him.

"Here, under Sir Andrew's roof, I cannot take heed of the words you have used."

The tilt of Mr Latimer's nose seemed to become more marked.

"If you imply regret, sir, of that circumstance, I shall be happy to repeat my words in any place and time your convenience would prefer."

Again Myrtle distractedly intervened, yet never beginning to suspect that she herself, rather than any political consideration, was disposing these two in such ready hostility.

"Harry, are you mad? Robert, please, please! Don't heed what he says."

"I do not," said Mandeville. He bowed a little to Latimer, his manner entirely disarming. "I do not wish you to misapprehend me, sir. All I offer is an explanation of conduct in one who wears his majesty's uniform."

"It did not occur to me, sir, that you would offer more."

Sir Andrew turned upon him, his face now as purple as a mulberry.

"Leave my house, sir! At once! I had never thought to see you here again; but that you should come to offend my ears with your abominable doctrines of rebellion – "

Latimer interrupted him. "That, sir, was not my intent. I came solely that I might do you a service."

"I desire no service of you! Go! Or I will have you thrown out."

Myrtle stood behind Sir Andrew, white and distressed, passionately impelled to intervene, to seek yet to make the peace between her father and her lover – for that he was her lover still, her heart was telling her – and yet not daring to attempt to curb a passion so sweeping as that which now controlled the baronet.

"The matter that brought me," said Latimer, coolly fronting that wrath, "concerns the life of Gabriel Featherstone."

His ear caught the sharp intake of breath from Sir Andrew, and he saw the sudden movement of Captain Mandeville. But not even so much was necessary to announce how deeply he had startled them. Their countenances abundantly betrayed it. He paused a moment, looking squarely into the baronet's glowering eyes. "You would do well to bid your factor get his son out of Charles Town and out of the province before evening."

For the second time there was something akin to an explosion from that normally very self-possessed Captain Mandeville.

Mr Latimer smiled a little. "Captain Mandeville, you see realizes the occasion."

"What do you mean?" Sir Andrew controlled himself to demand. But Latimer observed that he was trembling.

"I mean that if Gabriel Featherstone is not beyond the reach of the Sons of Liberty by evening, he will very certainly be hanged, and probably tarred-and-feathered first."

"Gabriel Featherstone?" The baronet's cheeks had grown actually pale.

"I see," said Latimer, "that you are acquainted with his activities, Sir Andrew; with the particular form of service to the royal Government in which he had been employed by Captain Mandeville."

"By me, sir?" Mandeville demanded.

Latimer's ironic smile was momentarily turned upon him.

"Lord William Campbell," he said, "is hardly the most discreet of men. He is rather too easily drawn. And that without the lure of personal gain that dulled your own wits, captain. There are times when self-interest becomes a bandage to the eyes of caution. That, I think, was your own case this morning."

"You infernal spy!" said Mandeville with cold rage.

Latimer shrugged airily. "A thief to catch a thief."

"Will you tell me what it means?" demanded Sir Andrew. "What has this to do with Featherstone?"

"I'll tell you, sir," cried Mandeville. But Latimer stayed him. He dominated now, by the fear for Featherstone which he had inspired.

"I think it will come better from me, perhaps. Gabriel Featherstone is a member of the General Committee of the Provincial Congress, and a member also of more than one of its sub-committees. He has abused his position to keep the King's Council informed of our secret measures, and he has already woven a rope for the necks of several of us. The moment isn't opportune for hanging us. But should it come, as the King's Government confidently believes it will, Featherstone will be brought forward as a witness to swear away our lives. I gather that the royal council will be content with hanging me, the ringleader, as a warning and an example. It's a bugbear that does not greatly alarm me. Anyhow, I am prepared to take the risk, sooner than give you occasion, Sir Andrew, to mourn a valued servant, the son of one still more valued. But you can't expect the others concerned to be equally complacent. To remove the risk, they will remove Featherstone. And the manner of it will be as I have said."

Sir Andrew stared at him, his jaw fallen, the anger, which seethed abundantly within him, momentarily held in leash by dismay. And then at last Mandeville spoke.

"It's false," he said. "False! A silly trap to catch the name of the real denouncer. Featherstone is not the man. It was not Featherstone who supplied Lord William with his list."

"In that case it is odd that the list should be in Featherstone's handwriting," Mr Latimer mocked him. "You'll remember that I saw it, Captain."

Mandeville remembered not only that he had seen it but that he had very closely inspected it.

"When did you see it? How did you see it?" Sir Andrew demanded.

And it was Mandeville who answered him, and who, by his answer which related the whole of that morning's interview at the Governor's, explained to him several obscurities in what Latimer had just said.

"So that you're no better than a dirty spy!" cried Sir Andrew in disgust and fury. "A dirty spy! You and your friend Cheney."

"A spy, if you will. But the rest I disavow. Cheney's no friend of mine."

"And you've denounced Gabriel to your fellow-rebels?" Sir Andrew asked him.

Mr Latimer shook his head. "If I had already done that should I be here to warn you to get him removed? The moment after I denounce him he will certainly be apprehended, and then – " Mr

Latimer shrugged eloquently. "I trust, Sir Andrew, that you will place this at least to my credit: that out of my anxiety to spare you unnecessary pain – the pain of one who may feel himself in part responsible for the dreadful fate that overtakes another – I have been less than faithful to my duty."

Sir Andrew made him no answer. He looked heavily at Mandeville, as if for guidance. Mandeville's face, now a mask of complete composure, dissembled the activity of his mind. The dismay and anger at the prospect of losing so very valuable a spy – for whether Featherstone escaped or were hanged, he would be lost to Mandeville as a channel of information – was being dissipated by the knowledge that Latimer had not yet denounced him. In that case all might yet be well.

"And of course," he said acidly, "your regard for Sir Andrew will hardly go so far as to cause you to refrain from denouncing Featherstone."

Latimer did not conceal his rather scornful amusement.

"Such guilelessness, captain! Oh, the official mind! But I make you a present of the knowledge you seek. I shall go before the Committee at six o'clock today with the information you were good enough to give me this morning."

"You really think you will?" said Mandeville unpleasantly.

"I know I will. Which is why I must be taking my leave. Meanwhile, Sir Andrew, you are warned, and in good time to pass the warning on to Featherstone."

Sir Andrew, standing stiff and scowling, made him no answer.

Mr Latimer bowed gracefully, and turned to depart.

But he found that Mandeville had got between him and the door. The captain spoke, his voice cold and level but full of menace.

"Sir Andrew, this man must not be allowed to leave."

Chapter 6

The Deception

Sir Andrew roused himself at that summons. He reached out a hand to arm himself with the riding-whip that lay across the board.

Mr Latimer, midway between the baronet and the equerry, although arrested by the latter's words and clear purpose, did not appear to suffer any distress.

"You think to detain me by force?" he asked, and smiled.

The captain found himself admiring the young man's composure. And he was something of an arbiter in matters of deportment. He belonged to an age in which artificiality, the suppression of emotion, the histrionic affectation of nonchalance in all circumstances, was accepted as the outward mark of the man of quality. In England, where between Westminster and Oxford he had spent some six years, Mr Latimer had readily acquired this art of genteel conduct which, for the rest, sat easily enough upon a spirit that was naturally calm, detached and critical.

"You must see, Mr Latimer, that in the circumstances we cannot possibly suffer you to depart."

"Not only do I see it. I foresaw it. It was part of the risk I took."

"Lay hold of him, Robert," cried Sir Andrew. He sprang forward as he spoke, and Captain Mandeville did the like from Latimer's other side.

To avoid them, Latimer backed swiftly to the sideboard, and at the same time lugged from the pocket of his bottle-green riding coat a heavy, ugly-looking pistol.

"Not so fast, gentlemen!" he begged them, displaying that intimidating weapon.

It brought them up sharply in their advance, and Myrtle cried out at the same moment.

"You didn't understand me, I think," said Latimer. "I told you that I foresaw something of this kind. Praemonitus praemunitis." And he wagged the pistol. "It is the motto of my house. As Sir Andrew can tell you, I come of a singularly prudent family, Captain Mandeville. And now that you realize you are at a disadvantage, perhaps you will permit me to depart without doing violence to the proprieties."

"My God, you graceless blackguard," Sir Andrew railed at him. "D'ye dare threaten me? D'ye dare draw a pistol on me? On me?"

"Nay, Sir Andrew. It is you who threaten. I do no more than protect myself. Self-preservation is the first law of Nature."

Thus his cursed irony, which he could not repress, dug wider than ever the breach between himself and the man he loved, the man who because his erstwhile affection for Harry was now turned to gall, would, he knew, show him no mercy.

Sir Andrew measured him with eyes of unspeakable hate, the hate born of anger that is baffled and mocked.

"Let the dog go, Robert," he growled.

Mandeville had no intention of doing anything of the kind. He would risk being shot rather than lose the services of Featherstone. But because he preferred – self-preservation being the first law of nature with him, too – that Latimer should first empty his pistol into somebody else, he made a pretence of acquiescence.

He bowed a little, shrugged, and stepped aside.

"You win the trick, Mr Latimer," he said lightly. "But it is only the first in the game."

"Observe though that I've trumped the knave," Mr Latimer smiled back at him. He pocketed his pistol, but took the precaution of keeping his hand on the butt. As if perceiving this, and as if ostentatiously to show him that his way to the door was clear, Captain Mandeville turned aside and crossed the room to the mantelpiece at the other end.

Latimer paused a moment looking at Sir Andrew, and his eyes clouded with regret. He appeared on the point of speaking. Then, as if realizing that here words must be wasted, he bowed again and walked to the door. Even as his fingers closed upon its crystal knob, Captain Mandeville's seized the bell-rope by which he had gone to stand. Once, twice, thrice he tore at it, sounding in the servants' quarters a tocsin of alarm that must bring every lackey in the place at the double to intercept Latimer before he could leave the house.

But, out of the corner of his eye, Mr Latimer caught the violent pumping action of Mandeville's raised arm. He paused, his hand upon the knob.

"I ought to shoot you for that," he told the captain. "But it isn't necessary." He locked the door, withdrew the key, and crossed the room again, under their wondering eyes. "I shall have to follow the example of King Charles, and leave by the window." He unfastened the long glass door that gave egress to the lawn.

"It's an omen," Carey raged at him. "You go to the same fate."

"But in a better cause," said Latimer, as he pulled open the wing of the door.

"I warn you, sir," Carey flung after him, as he was stepping out, "that if any harm comes to Featherstone, I'll see you hanged for it. I will so, by God! though it cost me life and fortune. You graceless, treacherous hound!"

Mr Latimer was gone. Mandeville sprang to the window, and stepped out, to see him racing across the lawn to the gravelled drive, where his negro groom was waiting with the horses. At the same moment came clattering steps across the hall outside, alarmed beatings on the door and alarmed, plaintive, liquid accents of the black servants calling to their master.

Sir Andrew bade them cease and begone with a roughness such as he rarely employed towards those who served him. They departed chattering and wondering. To increase their wonder Mr Latimer from beyond the porch, already mounted, was calling Remus. He tossed the abstracted key to the old butler, then wheeled his horse about and rode off with his groom.

He was half way down the avenue before there surged out of the pain seething in his mind under the mask of nonchalance he had worn, the recollection of another matter with which he had hoped to deal whilst here at Fairgrove. And it was not until he had reached the gates that he conquered the anger that was driving him headlong away despite that recollection.

It had been his hope to make a very different impression, to earn some consideration in return for the service he went to do at some risk to himself. And he had also hoped from this to be given an opportunity to explain himself to Myrtle, to reason her into a gentler frame of mind, and to persuade her that because he loved his country was no sufficient reason why she should refuse to marry him.

It was Mandeville's presence at Fairgrove which had made shipwreck of his hopes, sweeping the interview into a course so different from all that he desired.

He drew rein, undetermined. He could not depart thus, leaving the situation between Myrtle and himself a hundredfold worse than before he came.

He paused, considering. From the distance came a plaintive chant, the singing of the negro slaves in the rice fields by the river, and the sound inspired him. He would write a note to her, begging her to come to him out here. A friendly slave – and he was well known to them all – should be his messenger.

He flung down from his horse, gave his reins to the groom, and ordered him to ride on for a half-mile or so, and there await him. Then he left the avenue, and plunged away through the live oaks and the tangle of vines in the direction of the chanting voices. But progress through the undergrowth of that leafy wilderness became more difficult the farther he penetrated. And at last he was forced to pause, and, in pausing, reconsidered. Better for his purpose than a plantation slave would be one of the house servants; and if he waited, some one of these would surely pass along the avenue before very long. They were all his friends, and any one of them would do his errand secretly.

So he retraced in part his steps until the flat stump of an oak that had been felled offered him a seat at a point whence he could, himself unseen, command a view of the avenue, dappled with sunshine and shadow. He sat down, and from an inner pocket he produced a notebook and a pencil, and hurriedly scrawled a brief but very earnest appeal to Myrtle. He tore out the leaf, folded it, and settled down to wait until chance should send him the messenger he needed.

And meanwhile up there at the house Sir Andrew was still storming, and Mandeville and Myrtle between them were engaged in soothing him, a task which brought them into a close alliance very pleasant and consoling to the captain. He felt that he had not conducted himself very well that morning. At first he had practised a praiseworthy restraint in the face of many difficulties and temptations. He had held aloof from all contention, refraining from the obvious quips and sneers at Mr Latimer's expense to which the young apostle of liberty rendered himself vulnerable. A less subtle man would never have missed those opportunities of displaying his own wit and consequence. But Mandeville knew too much of human nature. He had perceived that under Myrtle's indignation with Harry lay a real and deep, if momentarily numbed, affection for him. And he knew that avowedly to range himself on the side of Latimer's enemies, to harass and vex him with manifestations of hostility, might only serve to arouse that affection of Myrtle's into activity and provoke her indignation against himself.

Therefore, even at the cost of having his courage put in question, Mandeville had clung to the role of the unwilling and pained witness of a painful scene, until the circumstances had cruelly forced him to become an actor. The bad impression he feared thereby to have created he was now anxious to efface. And it was a relief to him to find Myrtle, in her ready understanding of the necessities, unresentful of the part he had played.

He was not the man to cry over spilled milk of however precious a quality. Latimer had got away, and therefore the utility of Featherstone as a spy was at an end. It still remained to save his life. But his life, shorn of its usefulness to Mandeville, was not a matter of much interest to the captain. He was infinitely more concerned to set himself right with Myrtle by assuming the role of tolerant, broad-minded peacemaker. When Sir Andrew, apoplectic with anger, protested that he should have said this, and answered that, Mandeville's calm voice laden with compassion for the object of the baronet's invective acted as a timely sedative.

"Mr Latimer, sir, is to be compassionated. A young man of such parts, of such agreeable qualities, to have been led away into such error!" He sighed his infinite regret.

And he had his reward, when presently he took his departure, furiously urged by Carey to lose no time in getting to Charles Town and placing Featherstone for safety aboard the *Tamar*. Myrtle came with him, not merely to the steps. She would walk with him to the gates. So, Captain Mandeville must go also to the gates on foot, leading his horse. And because of the impulse to express the increase of friendliness, almost the tenderness, which his selflessness and his alliance with her in that troubled hour had inspired, she thrust a hand through his left arm as she stepped along beside him. The captain was conscious of a slight quickening of his pulses. But ever master of himself, he conceived that here his attitude should be one of affectionate elder-brotherliness.

"My dear child, my heart bleeds for you." He sighed. "And I am angry with myself. To desire so intensely to lift something of this burden from your shoulders, and to be powerless! It exasperates me."

"But you have done so much already, Robert. You have been so good, so gentle, so patient, so generous!" She leaned a little more heavily and looked up into his face, almost fondly, so great and natural was the kindliness he inspired in her.

"Generous? If only I could think so. My every impulse is to give, and give – and, my dear, I am empty-handed."

"Oh, it is like you to forget. Didn't you persuade Lord William not to arrest Harry? Was that nothing?"

"Nothing at all. I would have saved him, yes. Not for himself, because I did not even know him. But for you, because he...because he has, or had, the inestimable blessing of your regard. I conceived that unless I did so, you might suffer; and so, even at the cost of duty, I... Oh, but what am I saying? For, after all, I have failed. I have betrayed a trust to no purpose."

"I shall never forget what you have done. Never."

"Then I have not altogether failed. It is a sufficient reward for me."

"But there is Harry. What – oh what – are we to do?"

His face grew overcast. "What can one do? One cannot argue with a passion. I had hoped that when he saw whither he was going, into what danger he was thrusting himself, he would have paused. But I might have known that if the thought of offending you could not act as a curb upon his conduct, personal danger would hardly have counted. At least, that is how it would be with me. And we are often misled in judging others by ourselves. Oh, it is all most damnable. If I could have detained him now, on the pretext of saving Featherstone, we could have put Mr Latimer under lock and key until these troubles are over, as over they soon will be once the troops arrive."

"Was that your intention?"

"What else? What other way was there of saving him from his own rashness? Perhaps...if you were to see him..."

"I? See him?" She looked up at her companion, her little face stern, her eyes almost flashing. And Captain Mandeville, who had made the suggestion by way of testing her, was now given a glimpse of the sturdy spirit that governed this frail body. He could not guess that much of it was begotten of resentment, because Harry had almost ignored her presence throughout the interview. Later when reviewing it more calmly, she would see that the occasion had been denied him. But at present there was only resentment. And this she expressed. "I do not think that I want to see him ever again. It is finished. Finished. Did you think I have no pride? What do you think of me, I wonder?" She halted him, and was confronting him, almost imperious.

"Does it matter, what I think?" There was a gentle wistfulness in his tone.

"Should I ask if it did not?"

They were, although they knew it not, in full view of Harry Latimer where he sat on the oak-stump, observing them with frowning eyes. And unfortunately they were out of earshot. So that, whilst he saw all yet he heard nothing.

And what he saw was Mandeville turn to her, and with the bridle over his arm, take both her hands in his, looking down at her with a face that was all tenderness. What he was left to, guess were the captain's words:

"And I, I dare not answer you," the captain said in tones that were an answer in themselves. "I dare not. And yet I am not a coward, although God knows I feared you might have thought so once this morning."

"Thought so? I? Robert, I thought you wonderful in your patience. Only a brave man could have borne himself as you did."

"My dear, you fill me with pride. And as for what I think of you…" He paused, he raised the hands he held, and stooped to kiss them, first one and then the other, and then because he felt a loosening of the grip of those hands which had been firm in his own, because he grew conscious of a shrinking on her part from that which she feared instinctively that he was about to say, he checked himself upon the brink. No man knew better than Mandeville the conquering power of patience. Indeed, in that knowledge lay all his strength. His tone grew light, robbing his words of all solemnity.

"Why, if I were to say that I think you adorable, you would laugh at me, I know." And himself he smiled, looking into her face which had grown very pale. "So, since you insist, I'll say you are the sweetest cousin ever a man discovered in the colonies. And I'll add that in Robert Mandeville you have a steadfast friend."

"A friend! A friend! Ah, yes!" Her grip of his hands tightened again, before finally releasing them, the colour came racing back to her cheeks. "I knew that I was not mistaken in you. How rarely can a woman find a friend, a true friend to depend upon in her need. Lovers she may have if she will. But a friend! Oh, God bless you, Robert!"

And as they moved on he, safe now in that elder-brotherly position to which he had retreated, went so far as to put an arm about her shoulder, hugging her momentarily.

"Count on me always, my dear Myrtle. In any trouble arising out of all this, command my help. You promise?"

"Why, gladly," she answered, looking up at him and smiling.

And that was the last that Latimer's scowling eyes saw of them; the soldier's scarlet sleeve with its gold-laced cuff about her shoulders, her little face upturned to his.

Mr Latimer realized that he had been too long away from Charles Town, and he conceived that all the cynical utterances of mysogynists with which he was acquainted fell lamentably short of truth. Slowly he tore up the little note he had written. And when presently Myrtle returned alone, Mr Latimer resentfully neglected the opportunity afforded him. He waited until she had passed, then went in quest of his horse and his groom, and rode straight back to Charles Town.

Chapter 7

Mandeville as Machiavel

Captain Mandeville got back to the gubernatorial residence that afternoon to find Lord William deep in the sociabilities of a reception which her ladyship was holding. The long drawing-room was a little crowded. There was an abundance of tories present, such as the Roupells and the Wraggs, and there were a few who, like Miles Brewton, her ladyship's brother-in-law, were so conservative in the method of their opposition to the royal Government as to appear – at least in the eyes of whigs – to stand somewhere between the two parties; but the remainder, and they made up the major part of the attendance, were members of families that Sir Andrew Carey would have described as rebel.

The discerning and rather scornful dark eyes of Captain Mandeville beheld here an epitome of the colony itself. Two parties secretly hostile, each arming against the other, and yet each anxiously straining to preserve the peace, since neither felt itself yet ripe for war, nor knew what war might bring it; each prepared for battle as a last resource, yet each intent not to precipitate battle, and each hoping that the ultimate need for it might yet be averted.

The captain made his way towards his lordship, and found himself presently confronting Lady William, a splendid, vigorous young woman between fair and dark who stood almost as tall as her viceregal husband and displayed an opulence of charms that compelled in the classical-minded the thought of Hebe. And it was not only her figure and movements that suggested vigour, but her countenance, too, which was boldly handsome.

"You are late," she rallied the captain. "And you bring the usual excuse, no doubt. Poor slave of duty!"

"Your ladyship's penetration spares my poor wit."

"Not penetration, sir. Compassion." She took him by the arm. "You are to come and talk to Miss Middleton. She loves a red-coat so much that it almost makes her loyal."

"Your ladyship must forgive me. I have to see Lord William at once."

He was grave; and, observing him sharply, there was a flash of apprehension from Lady William's eyes. For all her high and at times rather reckless courage, she dwelt in constant anxiety for the husband she loved who had been elevated to this position of as much difficulty as honour.

"Is it serious?" she asked.

"Not so much serious as urgent," he reassured her. "I have had a busy day."

She recovered the caustic humour that was natural to her.

"Nothing fills me with so much anxiety as your activities, Robert."

He smiled his acknowledgments, and passed on to draw Lord William presently from the ladies who had been engaging him. They were joined in the small adjacent room by Captain Tasker, his lordship's other equerry whom Mandeville had beckoned, and by Innes who had followed of his own accord upon seeing them withdraw. Mandeville wasted no words.

"The fellow who waited upon your excellency this morning calling himself Dick Williams, was Harry Latimer."

It was necessary for him to repeat the statement in other terms before it was understood.

"Good lack!" said his lordship, and proceeded to recall what had passed. When he had recalled it, he added: "My God!" and stared blankly at Mandeville.

Mandeville answered the stare with a nod. "I am afraid he got a good deal of information out of us. He was sent to spy out the land, to pry into your excellency's real feelings towards these provincials, and to discover the channel through which certain secret information of the transactions of the Provincial Congress was finding its way to you. I am afraid he has succeeded in all three aims."

"Oh, but it's impossible! There was Cheney," his lordship exclaimed.

Very briefly, Mandeville informed him of what had happened at Fairgrove. His lordship groaned.

You see with what a dangerous man you have to deal," said Mandeville. "He is resourceful, daring and a passionate rebel, and his wealth gives him extraordinary influence and extraordinary power."

"Yes, yes," snapped his lordship impatiently. "But Featherstone? Have you warned him?"

"That is not important," said Mandeville coldly. "Featherstone is a pricked bubble. He is of no further use to us since I was unable to detain Latimer."

"But, my God, man! We must save him."

"I wonder," said Mandeville in such a tone that the three stared at him in amazement.

"Didn't you say they'll hang him once Latimer has denounced him?"

"That or tar-and-feather him," Mandeville mentioned the alternative casually. And in the same level, well-bred voice he added: "If any such harm were to come to him, we should have a very clear case against Latimer. I, myself, and probably Sir Andrew Carey too, can bear witness that it was brought about by Latimer's seditious agency."

"And you would sacrifice Featherstone to obtain that?" The young voice was charged with horror.

Almost Mandeville looked surprise. "This is neither a case nor a time for sentiment." His tone was dry. "Better men than Featherstone have been sacrificed before now to policy. Myself, I am not very tender where a spy is concerned. A short shrift is the stake on the board with him. And consider what you stand to gain. You are afforded the means to rid the State of a dangerous enemy."

There was a long moment's silence before his lordship found an answer. His humane young soul was shocked.

"You're a cold-blooded Machiavel," he said at length, in accents of wonder.

Mandeville shrugged. "Your excellency is the Governor of a province that is rotten with sedition, and you must take what means you can to stamp it out. The ministry at home expects no less. Is the life of a poor creature like Featherstone to prove an obstacle in so great a work?"

His lordship clenched his hands behind his back, and took a turn in the room, a prey to very obvious agitation. Tasker and Innes looked on, saying no word, both of them a little appalled by Mandeville's soulless theories of statecraft. Mandeville watched his excellency almost in contempt. Was this boyish emotional young nobleman the sort of man to crush the hydra of rebellion? What hope, he wondered, was there for an empire, whose ministers gave such positions as these to younger sons all unequipped to bear them?

But Lord William, though humane and emotional, was not by any means as inept in statecraft as Mandeville supposed him. This his pronouncement now showed.

"Humanely speaking, what you suggest, Mandeville, is horrible. Politically it is mad. If we use Featherstone as a bait, how shall we afterwards dare to take Latimer? Before what court in the province will you bring him to trial? What court do you dream would convict him?"

"He could – indeed, he should – be sent to England for trial on such a charge."

His excellency crashed fist into palm to express his exasperation.

"You would make use of an enactment which is one of the present colonial grievances to deal with a man who is a hero in the eyes of the mob, and for an offence for which the province will acclaim him? Is that your statecraft? Don't you see that it would precipitate the very thing that we are at all costs to avoid? That it would bring open rebellion about our ears? That it would compel us to have recourse to violence on our side and so make an end of the last hope of conciliation between the colonies and the empire?"

"That hope is chimerical," said Captain Mandeville, with assurance. "It is the illusion that brings indecision, and the weakness of indecision into our policy."

But now Lord William asserted himself. "A matter of opinion, Mandeville; and not the opinion that I hold myself. However I may prepare for the worst, I still hope for the best. And I hope with some confidence."

"But if – " Mandeville was beginning.

The Governor held up his hand. " There is no more to be said."

Mandeville might dominate him upon all points but this, for upon this his lordship was dominated by his colonial wife and her numerous relatives in Charles Town, in all of whom the hope was confident – being firmly based upon their intense desires – that conciliation must yet prevail.

"I will thank you," his excellency concluded, "to waste no time in finding Featherstone. Let him join Kirkland aboard the *Tamar*. Thornborough will see to him, and he will be safe there. At need we must send him to England."

If mortified, Mandeville betrayed no sign of it. He bowed his acknowledgment of the Governor's commands.

"It shall be done at once," he said, as evenly as if there never had been any question of another course.

And Mr Innes, in relating the affair, offers upon it this comment: "His excellency called him to his face a cold-blooded Machiavel because he displays energy and determination, qualities in which Lord William is sadly lacking. If Captain Mandeville were the Governor of this province there would be a speedy end to its mutinous spirit."

Mr Innes little suspected that in this case the captain's determination went so much farther than his energy that, failing to discover Gabriel Featherstone at the house of the married sister with whom he dwelt

– and where of necessity he must inquire for him in view of the Governor's explicit order – Mandeville was careful to seek him nowhere else where there was the faintest likelihood of his being found. Captain Mandeville intended that the province should be governed according to his own ideas; and when these ideas were in conflict with the Governor's, it only remained for him to force the Governor's hand.

Meanwhile, Mr Latimer, too, had returned to Charles Town, and at just about the time that Mandeville was threading his way through the ranks of Lady Williams' guests, the young rebel was striding into the dining-room of his splendid mansion on East Bay.

It was a room of rather sombre dignity, panelled in dark oak, with portraits of bygone Latimers sunk into the panelling. Like most of the house, it was furnished mainly in walnut, imported fifty or sixty years ago from Holland, and of the character that in England is associated with the reign of William and Mary. From the wide overmantel the room was surveyed by a saturnine gentleman in a ponderous periwig, between whom and Harry Latimer a resemblance was to be traced. A still stronger resemblance might be traced – and has been traced rather maliciously by Lord Charles Montagu – between this portrait by Sir Godfrey Kneller of Charles Fitzroy Latimer, who was the founder of his house, and – in the actual words of Lord Charles – "that merry prince who was charged to his face by the Duke of Buckingham with being indeed the father of a good many of his subjects."

On a cane day-bed under one of the tall windows lounged a large, fair young man reading "The Vicar of Wakefield." He was the male counterpart of Lady William Campbell; but his countenance lacked a good deal of the force of hers, and his personality a good deal of her magnetism. Still, he remained a young gentleman of very amiable exterior whom it was impossible not to like. That he was indolent and good-natured you perceived at a glance. That the most serious business he knew in life were horse-racing, cock-fighting and fox-hunting, you would have no difficulty in believing at once. That he should be taking sufficient interest in provincial politics to be whole-heartedly on the side of the colonials was less obvious.

On Latimer's appearance, Mr Thomas Izard tossed aside his book and stifled a yawn.

"I was beginning to grow anxious for you," he said.

"Why, what's o'clock?" As he asked the question, Latimer sought the answer to it from the tall walnut clock standing in the corner. "Half-past five. Egad! I had no notion it was so late."

"The time will ha' been spent agreeably."

"Agreeably!" Latimer flung himself into a chair, to render a brief account of it. "You see," he ended, "I didn't overrate the risk to my liberty, although I hadn't reckoned on finding Captain Mandeville there."

Tom considered him with a gloomy eye. "I could ha' told you it would be long odds. The gallant captain rides out there almost daily."

"Why didn't you?"

"You'd ha' seen the inference and given me the lie most like. And, let me perish, I don't want to quarrel with you about any member of the faithless sex, Harry."

His bitter allusion to womankind derived from the fact that his wife had left him a year ago to run off with a young French nobleman who had visited the colony. Considering that she was a termagant and a schold who had given him two years of married torment, he should have been thankful. Instead, the human mind being tortuous, he was resentful, and prayed for the day when he might call out and kill the Frenchman who had really done him the greatest service of his life.

I mention the otherwise irrelevant fact that you may realise that he was about the unlikeliest counsellor Harry Latimer could have found just then.

"Ye-es," he answered slowly, his eyes troubled. And then he brushed the painful thing aside. His voice was almost casual. "Myrtle has discovered that she can't marry a man who doesn't believe that King George can do no wrong. And she has demonstrated to me her preference for a red-coat who has the honour to serve his gracious majesty. It's logical, I suppose."

"Logical!" Mr Izard sneered. "Who ever knew a woman to be logical? It's calculating. That's what it is, Harry. And so, let me perish, not worth a thought. I'm glad you take it so well. As I wrote to you, Mandeville may be Earl of Chalfont some day, if his luck holds."

But to his surprise Harry turned on him in sudden fury.

"What the devil do you mean, Tom?"

"Good Gad! Isn't it what you mean?"

"D'ye suppose I'd suspect Myrtle of being mercenary? Of selling herself for a title?"

"Never been known in the history of the world, has it?"

"Never with such women as Myrtle."

"It seems to me you've a lot to learn, Harry," said Mr Izard, as one speaking with the authority of experience. "Women are the most damned."

"I'll thank you not to generalize. Mr Thomas Izard, on Woman, isn't edifying."

"No. By Gad! He isn't! The subject don't allow it. But he's instructive."

And then the entrance of old Julius put a timely term to an unprofitable discussion. He brought a tray on which were glasses and a silver bowl containing a delectable punch of rum and pineapple and lemons, also a silver box of fine leaf and a couple of pipes.

Not until they were alone again did any word pass between the two friends, and then the interrupted subject was not resumed. There was a much more urgent matter.

"Since I require no deputy at the meeting, Tom, you may give me the letter that I left with you."

"Gladly enough," said Tom, and fetched the package from his pocket. "Egad, if you hadn't returned, and I had had to attend the meeting for you, I shouldn't have been there long. I'd ha' had a party of Sons of Liberty out at Fairgrove to fetch you away tonight."

"I was sure I could trust you for that," said Harry, smiling. "They little knew what they would be invoking when they thought to detain me."

The walnut clock struck the hour of six. Mr Latimer bounded to his feet.

"I must go," he said. "Six is the hour of the meeting. Stay to sup with me. I'll not be very long. Smoke a pipe meanwhile."

He was almost at the door when Tom called after him. "Look to yourself, Harry. Don't go abroad unarmed. You'll be a marked man, stab me, after what's happened."

Chapter 8

Devil's Advocate

It was but a step from Latimer's house to that of Henry Laurens',
where the special and self-elected committee of investigation was
already assembled to receive now the report which Latimer had
promised.

They came to business without loss of time. Briefly and lucidly,
Mr Latimer gave his account of what had transpired that morning at
the Governor's. Leaving, with true dramatic instinct, the more
sensational matter for the end, he began by relating all that had
passed between himself and Lord William, bearing upon Lord
William's correspondence with the back-country tories. And already
here, the first note of discord was sounded in that meeting.

"I formed the impression, gentlemen," he was saying at the end of
his plain narrative of what had passed, "that Lord William is in the
peculiar position of – "

He was unceremoniously interrupted by the elder Rutledge.
Turning to Laurens, who now presided, and speaking in the cold,
unemotional voice that was habitual with him: "I submit, sir, that
this is irrelevant. Mr Latimer's personal impressions are not evidence
for our consideration."

It was the lawyer speaking, and those who were not lawyers were
quick to resent it. In particular was Gadsden of these.

"Hold your tongue, John Rutledge," he snapped. "What you think of what Latimer thinks isn't evidence neither."

It raised a laugh against Rutledge which, outwardly at least, perturbed him not at all. As it subsided, Colonel Laurens – he had held the rank of lieutenant-colonel in Middleton's regiment during the war against the Cherokees – expressed the opinion that Mr Latimer should continue.

"If I were in a position to place before you an accurate and full report of what words were used by me and what by Lord William, then there might be some grounds for Mr Rutledge's objection. But as I am in no case to do that, and depending entirely upon my memory of what passed, the objection is frivolous."

"Frivolous?" Rutledge echoed the word, but coloured its utterance by no expression. Yet somehow he conveyed the sense that he sneered.

"Frivolous, because in such a case impressions are as precious as recollections, and possibly more accurate." There was a murmur of general agreement, and Latimer continued.

What he said amounted to an assurance that Lord William honestly desired – as was to be expected in a man of his colonial attachments – reconciliation, and that he would labour earnestly to prepare for the worst so as not to be taken unawares.

"But when all is said," Rutledge again interposed, "there remains the fact that he is in active correspondence with the back-country settlers, and that he is advising them to arm. Lord William, in fact, is running with the hare and hunting with the hounds."

Colonel Laurens took him up on that, his voice calm and gentle, inviting consideration.

"Are we not all doing that? Are we not indeed constrained to do it by the necessities of the case? Can we say to what lengths this or any other colony will be warranted by the voice of America in opposing the King's officers, though such opposition should be necessary for the very existence of the colony?"

The answer, as might be expected, came from Gadsden, harshly, impatiently: "That which is necessary for the very existence of the colony must of necessity be done. In such a case the consequences cannot matter."

And Drayton added, epigramatically summarizing Gadsden's pronouncement: "The worst should not deter us from action, since the worst is already assured us by inaction."

"That may be so," Laurens agreed regretfully. "But it is a matter to be determined by the future. And we are here to deal with the situation as it is at present."

The benign Mr Pinckney rapped the table. "Sirs, we are digressing. The matter is one for the Provincial Congress, when we lay before it the result of Mr Latimer's investigations. We have yet to hear Mr Latimer on the subject with which we are more immediately concerned: the leakage of information that has been taking place." And he nodded to Latimer to continue.

"In that matter," said Latimer, "my investigations were attended by singular good fortune." And he told them of the list which the Governor had shown him. "That list was in a hand with which I happen to be familiar. It was written by Gabriel Featherstone."

This created such a sensation as the disclosure of the identity of a traitor must ever create in any society of conspirators. Nor were all the exclamations hostile to the accused. Scoundrel though he was, Featherstone had known how to insinuate himself by flattery and other arts into the good graces of several leaders of the Colonial party, among whom were the Rutledges and Colonel Laurens. These were disposed to suspend judgment, and desired first to cross-examine the accuser. They were, however, anticipated in utterance by Gadsden, who bounced up as Mr Latimer, his report concluded, resumed his seat.

"This calls for action," he announced violently. "Immediate action. An example must be made. The blackguard must be arrested at once."

"Upon what grounds, sir?" Colonel Laurens asked him.

The question, especially coming from one who because of his moderation had long been in conflict with the uncompromising Gadsden, infuriated the republican.

"Grounds? My God! Hasn't Mr Latimer given us grounds enough?"

"Yes, yes. But I mean upon what actual charge is he to be arrested? What offence at law has he committed? My indignation against him is no less than Mr Gadsden's; but we must preserve the forms."

"To hell with the forms!" Gadsden roared. "The man's a traitor. For our own preservation he must be weeded out. And there's more to it than that. Haven't you heard? Haven't you understood from what Mr Latimer has told us that there's a rope about the neck of several of us, placed there by this scoundrel? And you talk to me of forms! What forms did you observe in the case of Cheney? What forms would you have observed in the case of Kirkland, if you could have got him? And what had they done compared with what this treacherous kite has done?"

Pinckney answered him: "Kirkland was a deserter from the militia. In that there was at least a technical offence upon which we could proceed against him. Featherstone, unfortunately for us, has done nothing which under the constitution would warrant so much as our expelling him from our midst, much less calling him to legal account."

"You'll sit and talk about constitution and legal forms until we are all destroyed. You spend your days in consideration whilst the other side is arming to crush us into submission."

Thus Gadsden began, and he was but gathering his forces for an oratorical onslaught upon his associates' scruples, when John Rutledge's cold incisive voice sliced into the outburst. Correct in all things and at all times, he addressed himself scrupulously to the chair.

"This heat, sir, in a matter asking calm deliberation is to be deprecated."

"Deliberate and deprecate and be damned," said Gadsden, and he sat down in a huff.

Rutledge pursued his even way, unruffled. "There are one or two points to be considered before we can regard Featherstone's guilt as established. At present it depends upon the evidence of a single witness; and his testimony again rests upon no better grounds than that of his recognition of a man's handwriting! Now those of you who have experience of courts are well aware that no evidence is more unreliable than that which depends upon handwriting alone. Nothing is more deceptive than the similarities or dissimilarities to be detected between one hand and another."

Less perhaps his argument than the deliberate manner in which he marshalled its points impressed his hearers. Therein lay the man's formidable strength as an advocate. He was never turgid, and seldom passionate. He convinced by the flattery of his calm, cold appeal to reason and intellect – often to reason and intellect not present in his audience. Even Gadsden a moment ago so impatient, now contained himself to listen attentively.

"Mr Latimer has told us," Rutledge pursued, "that he recognised the hand of Featherstone when shown the list of names by the Governor. I take it that in reality," and his calm full eyes turned slowly upon Featherstone's accuser, "this is no more than an expression of opinion on the part of Mr Latimer. I take it that it cannot possibly be more."

Latimer looked at Laurens, and Laurens nodded to him.

"It is much more," he said, his voice now as quiet and even as Rutledge's, and so invested with a note of finality. "It is a statement not of opinion, but of fact. My opportunities for becoming as intimately acquainted with the hand of Gabriel Featherstone as with my own are far greater than Mr Rutledge imagines." And he stated them at full and convincing length.

"Are you answered?" shouted Gadsden to Rutledge.

The lawyer's reply to the taunt was so full of dignity that it immediately placed Gadsden in the wrong and entirely vindicated himself.

"I am solely concerned that we should not do an injustice to one who has laboured for many months as our colleague. Beyond that I have no interest to serve. I regret that it should become necessary for me to state it." There was no heat in his words, no shadow of resentment. "Even now, even after this clear statement, which goes far to justify Mr Latimer, and with which he would have been well-advised to have begun, I should still deplore any action until we have obtained by tests – independent confirmation of his evidence."

"I have already applied a test and obtained independent confirmation," Mr Latimer announced.

"You have?" Rutledge's dark, level brows were raised a little in a surprise whose source was easily discerned. "May we know the nature of it?"

Mr Latimer realized, to his annoyance, that he was now constrained to go into matters upon which he would naturally have preferred not to have touched.

"But is it really necessary?" he said.

Rutledge answered him directly. "Surely you must see the necessity of putting forward all your evidence to substantiate so grave a charge as you are making?"

Latimer looked at him a moment. Then he turned to the president.

"I begin to wonder, sir, whether it is Featherstone or myself who is accused. It certainly appears to me that I am made to stand here on my defence."

There were cries of repudiation from Gadsden, Drayton and Moultrie, a friendly smile from Laurens, and another from Pinckney. Only the two Rutledges – the younger following the elder's lead – remained impassive. They dealt with evidence not with emotions.

"Before I continue, sir," Latimer resumed, "I invite you to place me upon oath – "

"Mr Latimer!" It was an exclamation of deprecation from the president. "You are a man whose honour no one questions. Your word is enough for all of us." And an assenting murmur ran round the table.

"Is it enough for the gentleman who constitutes himself the advocate of the traitor?"

"That's it!" said Gadsden. "He's named you rightly, by God!"

But the impeturbable John Rutledge disdained altercation.

"It is quite sufficient, Mr Latimer. You name me advocate for the traitor. I accept the office without shame. In commonest justice, it is necessary that the absent should be represented. I should do the same for you, sir."

"The need is not likely to arise," said Latimer curtly. "But let me proceed. The admission that the list was supplied by Featherstone came, if not from the Governor himself, at least from the Governor's equerry, Captain Mandeville, who procured Featherstone to act as his agent and convey to him intelligence of our deliberations and acts. And I had practically the same admission from Sir Andrew Carey, who was a party to placing Featherstone in our ranks for purposes of betrayal."

"Sir Andrew Carey?" Laurens questioned. "How does he come into the affair at all? "

"I had best be entirely frank, though you reproach me with indiscretion in the end." And now Latimer told them of his visit to Fairgrove, and of what had there transpired.

A silence followed the conclusion of his account, and after waiting a moment for any question that might be put to him, Latimer resumed his seat. It was only then that Rutledge spoke.

"In view of the energy employed by Mr Latimer, I deplore to be compelled to censure the lack of discretion by which it has been accompanied. It was a grave error to permit the other side to become aware of the discovery of Featherstone's treachery."

All eyes were turned upon him, and there was a heavy silence of disapproval in which all waited for some further explanation of his meaning. Since he made no shift to add anything, Moultrie took up the cudgels on behalf of Harry Latimer.

"Ye're a cursed curmudgeon, John, whom there's no satisfying."

"I confess," said Mr Latimer, "that the last thing I had expected was to be reprimanded by any member of this meeting."

"The meeting, Mr Latimer, is very far from reprimanding you," Colonel Laurens assured him.

"Which means, sir," Rutledge calmly replied, "that the meeting reprimands me. That is only because the meeting does not fully apprehend either the rashness of Mr Latimer's action, or the loss to ourselves which it entails. Let me make these clear. In the first place, Mr Latimer exceeded his commission, which is in itself a reprehensible matter. He was requested to visit the Governor to sound his real feelings and to endeavour, if possible, to discover by whom we are being betrayed. It was his clear duty to do nothing further until he should have presented his report to this meeting. And it was for this meeting to determine what steps should be taken to obtain confirmation of his report."

Moultrie impatiently interrupted him: "What better steps could the committee have devised than those which Mr Latimer took?"

"That is not at all the point." Rutledge was patience itself.

"Neither is that an answer," Gadsden taunted him.

"But I have no difficulty in supplying one. There are various ways of leading a spy into betraying himself. One of these – and it is the method I should have recommended – is to supply him with false information of intentions. If the opposite side is seen to act upon that information, it is very clear whence it was derived. Such a method would have had all the advantages of that adopted by Mr Latimer, without any of its disadvantages.

"What are these disadvantages?" Moultrie demanded.

Mr Rutledge looked round the table with those calm eyes of his, eyebrows raised to signify a faint surprise.

"Can it be possible that they are not as obvious to everyone here as they are to me? When a body such as ours discovers a spy in its midst, one of two courses is to be adopted. Either the spy is to be utilized as a means for supplying the other side with false information calculated to lull them into a sense of security and generally to mislead them as to intentions which it is desirable to mask, or else the spy is to be instantly suppressed. It is very probable that Mr Latimer's unwarrantable independent action has made either course impossible."

The faces about the board became grave. The hostility to Rutledge passed out of them, as the force of his reasoning sank into the minds of all. Latimer was conscious to his infinite vexation that a flush was slowly creeping into his cheeks. It was scarcely necessary for Rutledge to continue his elucidation. But Rutledge was merciless.

"That we can no longer make use of the spy for our own purposes is certain, since Mr Latimer has announced the discovery of him to the other side. That he will elude us, perhaps to work mischief against us on another occasion, is, for the same reason, now probable."

Gadsden heaved himself. "Then, by God! I am going to lessen that probability."

But Rutledge stayed him. "A moment, colonel! There has been impetuosity enough already. For Heaven's sake let us now proceed with some calm and forethought."

"And whilst you so proceed," cried Latimer, also rising, "you ensure this fellow's escape, and so make certain that I shall deserve your censure on both counts." Only the anger possessing him could have driven him to attribute to Rutledge motives so unworthy and so alien to his character. That imputation of dishonesty in one so rigidly honest lost him much of the sympathy in which the assembly had still been holding him. But Rutledge smiled again his inscrutable smile. Like Anthony, he carried his anger as the flint bears fire.

"Mr Latimer goes from rashness to rashness. Before action is taken against Featherstone, it is necessary that this meeting should determine what that course of action is to be."

"I have no doubt on the subject myself," Gadsden assured them.

Rutledge looked at him sternly. "The greater reason why you should wait." And the others, whom this forceful man was gradually subduing to his will, confirming him, Christopher Gadsden, though not without making plain his sullen resentment of the delay, resumed his seat. Mr Latimer, in a resentment still deeper, was forced to follow his example.

"There is apparent rashness on yet another score, which Mr Latimer might be well advised to explain to this meeting."

"Haven't you done with me yet?" cried Latimer.

"Unfortunately – in the interests of the cause we all have at heart – I have not."

"God give me patience!" said Mr Latimer wearily, and sank back in his chair.

Rutledge went inexorably on: "Mr Latimer himself has told us of the grave danger of detention at Fairgrove to which he was exposed. It is impossible that he should not have foreseen this risk."

"I didn't foresee that I should find Captain Mandeville there," Latimer defended himself.

"So much was not necessary. Sir Andrew Carey is a resolute, uncompromising man. And the risk existed. Mr Latimer must have known that it existed."

"Well! I took the risk," Mr Latimer answered. And he added the sneer: "What risks do you take?"

"None that I am not entitled to take," was the calm reply. "And you were not entitled to take this. Had you been detained at Fairgrove, had you disappeared, what then?"

"I should have been spared these impertinent questions."

"Not impertinent. What I require to know is in what case should we have been. Deprived of your report, we should not have known the result of your investigations, and Featherstone would have continued undisturbed to spy upon us."

Mr Latimer was very angry, and strive though he might he could not entirely keep the fact from appearing. He got to his feet again in a bound.

"Sir," he said to the president, "I do not know when I have been troubled by such a legal windbag or felt the blast of such asinine conceit. Mr Rutledge sweeps from conclusion to conclusion with a rashness far beyond anything with which he charges me. Let me say, sir, that I had provided for the emergency which he supposes. I left behind me a written report of what I had discovered from Lord William. Had I failed to return home by six o'clock this evening that report would have been laid before this meeting, and nothing would have been lost to it of my investigations."

The completeness of the answer and the degree of heat with which it was delivered won them all to his side again. He perceived the reflection of this on their faces, and swept on to follow up his advantage.

"Is Mr Rutledge sufficiently answered? Does he yet confess that it is himself and not I who want for prescience? I await the admission, and I shall accept it as a sufficient apology."

"With whom did you leave that report?" Rutledge asked him, hardily in view of the present temper of the meeting.

There was more than a murmur of disapproval. But it disturbed Rutledge no more than a breeze disturbs the oak.

"It imports to know," he insisted.

"My God, man! What do you imply now? Do you cast a doubt upon my word?" And white and wicked-looking Latimer leaned across the table towards his questioner.

But Rutledge remained cold, hard and clear as a diamond.

"I imply nothing. I ask a question.

"Answer him, for God's sake, Harry," said Moultrie impatiently.

And Harry answered: "I left it with my friend Tom Izard, who awaited at my own house my return from Fairgrove. Is that enough, or shall I fetch Tom Izard to confirm my word?"

"There is no need to bring Mr Izard into this," said Rutledge. "We all accept Mr Latimer's word."

"I'm glad of that."

"But may I ask him why he should have preferred Mr Izard to one of ourselves?"

"Because I did not wish to waste time in seeking any of you. Mr Izard is my friend, and he was conveniently at hand. Apart from yourselves, he was the only man who knew of my presence in Charles Town."

"Well, well, it is a trifle perhaps. But when men move as we are moving, trifles must be weighed and all risk avoided."

"I don't know what the devil you mean, sir," Latimer answered him. "But I gather that the avoiding of risks is your chief concern in life. You should not expect all men to be made on the same cautious pattern. Some of us have spirit, and can act better than we can talk, which is as well or nothing would be done; for believe me, sir, nothing is accomplished without taking risks."

"You may risk yourself all you please, Mr Latimer. I have no doubt you will do so abundantly. But you must not risk others with you, and you must not risk a cause." Significantly he added: "Mr Izard is the brother of Lady William Campbell."

Latimer's eyes flashed. "He is a member of the Sons of Liberty."

"So was Featherstone."

"Mr Rutledge, you go too far. I have said that Tom Izard is my friend."

"I heard you, sir. That, unfortunately, does not affect his other relationship to which I have alluded. I am not suggesting that Mr Izard is disposed to treachery. I mentioned Featherstone merely to show that no reliance can be placed upon the fact that he is a member of the Sons of Liberty. But it is to be remembered that he is constantly seeing his sister, Lady William, who is a very clever, enterprising woman; that he is constantly at the Governor's residence, and that he is a young man of light and pleasure-loving habits not by any means remarkable for discretion. That such a man should be acquainted in however slight a degree with any of our secret measures – "

He got no further. "You may spare me more of this," Latimer interrupted him. "I have allowed you to make havoc of my character, sir; but I'll be damned if I listen to you while you defame my friend. At least not in this place, where you shelter your impudence behind necessities of State."

"Mr Latimer! Mr Latimer!" the president endeavoured to restrain him. But he appealed in vain. Mr Latimer had unleashed his anger, and he let it run.

"If you have anything to say of Tom Izard, you may say it to me elsewhere, where I can horsewhip you if you are wanting in respect to him."

With the single exception of John Rutledge himself, every man present came to his feet on that. Rutledge alone continued to sit wrapped ever in that mantle of aloof disdain.

Moultrie caught Latimer's shoulder to restrain him. Angrily Latimer shook off the grip.

"Gentlemen," he said, "I take my leave of you. Since no word of thanks is forthcoming, since insult is my only recompense, I'll leave you to continue your deliberations without me. And while you and this windy attorney sit here, weighing straws and splitting offensive hairs, I'll act. Come, Gadsden, we know what's to do."

"By God, we do!" said the firebrand.

Drayton, too, ranged himself on their side. "I'm coming with you," he announced.

"Gentlemen! Gentlemen!" Colonel Laurens called after them, as they made for the door, which Latimer had already flung open.

"There's been talk enough," was all he got from Gadsden, who passed out.

Drayton shrugged in silence, and followed him.

Harry Latimer was going last, when Rutledge himself raised his voice to detain him.

"Mr Latimer, I warn you solemnly that the committee will require an account of the action you now intend."

"I'll render it with the Sons of Liberty at my back," Latimer answered him from the threshold.

"Mr Latimer! Let me prevail upon you to return and listen to us."

"Go to the devil!" said Latimer. And he went out and closed the door.

Chapter 9

Tar and Feathers

Outside, the evening breeze coming in from the sea with the flow of the tide cooled Mr Latimer's excessive heat, and brought him to consider one or two things to which in the last few moments his anger had blinded him.

It was idle, he reflected, to go in quest of Featherstone at this hour. By this time he must have profited by the warning which Mandeville would have borne him; and it was as certain as anything can be in this uncertain world that he was already safe from any vengeance that might be loosed against him. It was not a matter that admitted of doubt. The Governor's anxiety to remove him into safety would spring from the same source as Rutledge's desire to restrain Latimer and Gadsden from any violent measures against the scoundrel. If the Sons of Liberty took action, and dealt summarily with Featherstone, Lord William must feel under the necessity of asserting himself and demanding justice. He would have the clearest information that the person responsible for Featherstone's fate, directly or indirectly, was Harry Latimer; and he must choose between rendering himself and his rule ridiculous, and punishing the offender. If for the sake of his own and his royal master's dignity he took the latter course, he would probably precipitate in South Carolina the very troubles which both parties were striving desperately to avert. The American colonies were become highly combustible material, and a conflagration anywhere must spread in a blaze of revolt across the continent.

Latimer was under no delusion as to purpose for which Rutledge had demanded that he and those who departed with him should remain. And it was only his conviction that the thing Rutledge dreaded could no longer happen, rather than his own personal resentment of the cavalier treatment he had received at Rutledge's hands which had made him deaf to that demand.

The manner of his departure from the meeting, however, seemed to have committed him to joint action with Gadsden and Drayton, men who, as he well knew, were totally indifferent in their downright republicanism whether they precipitated a crisis or not.

He protested that Featherstone by now would have been conveyed to safety, and that therefore anything they could do was a sheer waste of time.

"Perhaps so," said Gadsden. "We'll hope not. And anyway I have called an assembly of my lads in the old Beef Market for this evening, against the chance of my being able to give them the name of the spy. You must come, Harry. You must tell them at first hand of your discovery."

Latimer shrank at first, protesting, from any such course; and but for his conviction that Featherstone was out of reach, nothing would have persuaded him to it. As it was, he ended by yielding to Gadsden's fiery insistence. Within a half-hour he was mounted on a stall in the Beef Market, addressing a crowd of young men, numbering perhaps a hundred, and composed almost entirely of mechanics and artisans – the lads to whom Christopher Gadsden had for months now been preaching the gospel of freedom under Liberty Oak outside his own residence. To these Latimer denounced Gabriel Featherstone for a spy, telling them of the infamous traffic the man had held with the royalist Government, and of the jeopardy in which he had placed some twenty patriotic necks.

When Gadsden in a few brief, hot, inciting periods had confirmed Latimer, those militant Sons of Liberty would wait for no more. With angry shouts of "Death to the traitor! Death to Featherstone!" they surged out, and away to do summary execution.

Up Broad Street and along King Street they swept in the direction of Fort Carteret, in the neighbourhood of which dwelt the sister with whom Featherstone was lodged. And as they went their numbers swelled, others joining them, attracted by the angry excited clamour.

"Featherstone! Featherstone!" was the cry. "Come and feather the stone! Come and tar-and-feather Featherstone! Tar-and-Featherstone! Tar-and-Featherstone!"

None of the three men responsible for launching the mob had any further part in the business. They were left behind in the now empty Beef Market. Gadsden, had he obeyed his instincts, would have placed himself at the head of his lads; and Latimer, too, would have thought it natural to lead a crowd which he had roused to this pitch of fury. But Drayton's legal, practical mind restrained them both.

"Let the mischief run," he advised. "No need further to implicate ourselves. We should be putting our necks under the knife without profiting the others."

Latimer was faintly indignant. "I am not by nature over-cautious," he said.

Instead of resenting the retort, Drayton explained himself. "Legal action cannot be taken against a mob. But it can be taken against an individual who leads it. And legal action must not be provoked because of the consequences that may follow out of it."

"He's right," said Gadsden, "although he reasons like John Rutledge."

"Who already has enough against you, Latimer," Drayton added.

Therefore, and because firmly convinced at heart that the mob must arrive too late, to accomplish its bloodthirsty aims, Latimer went home, accompanied most of the way by Gadsden who was a near neighbour of his own, residing also on the Bay.

He would have sat down to supper less complacently could he have suspected the infernal subtlety of Mandeville. Because he did not, because the happening was almost unaccountable in his eyes, he was shocked and dismayed when, an hour or so later Tom Izard came like a whirlwind into the dining-room whilst he was still at table.

"What's the matter?" Latimer had greeted him, seeing his startled face and agitated condition.

"Hell's the matter," Tom blazed out at him. "There's a mob of maniacs bent on devilry in the streets."

"Pooh! They'll do no harm. They'll seize an empty nest."

"Do no harm! Let me perish, it's the harm they've done already."

"They haven't got Featherstone?" cried Harry, his cheeks blenching.

"Got him, man? They've murdered him. They broke into his sister's house, and they've nearly wrecked it by their violence. Featherstone was sitting down to supper with her and his brother-in-law. There was no time to hide him. They got him. They dragged him out, screaming like a terrified woman. They tore the clothes from his back until they had him stark naked. A revolting business. They tarred and feathered him there almost under the eyes of his sister; then they dragged him, still screaming, through the streets to the Corner, and hanged him on the tree in front of the tavern. My God! I can't get the sounds of his screeching out of my ears."

Latimer sat there clutching the arms of his high-backed chair, staring straight before him, stark horror on his white face.

"They say," Tom informed him, "that it was you and Gadsden who set the mob on."

"Ay, ay!" It was an ejaculation of impatience, of exasperation, rather than assent. "But how came the mob to get him? What has Mandeville been doing? Didn't he warn him or didn't the fool heed the warning?"

"Nay, how do I know? Featherstone may have got no more than he deserved. But you should have kept your hand out of it, Harry. You'll have to look to yourself after this."

"What's that?" Harry considered him sharply, horror giving place to a sudden alertness. "Do you think – ?" he began.

"What?"

"Yes, by Heaven! That's it! That's it, Tom! This infernal Captain Mandeville has deliberately kept silent and let his agent Featherstone perish, so as to make a case against me so that I may be brought to account."

"Oh, you're mad!"

"Am I? What else is possible? Mandeville was in Charles Town two full hours before I denounced Featherstone to the Sons of Liberty in the Beef Market. In a quarter of that time Featherstone could have been placed beyond our reach. Why was he not? Why? Answer me that."

"But, if that was your belief, why did you trouble to denounce him?"

"Why?" Latimer stared at him for a long moment, whilst he sought within himself for an answer. "Oh, I was just led by the nose by my annoyance with Rutledge. A silly gesture of defiance to him. And it was unnecessary, because if I hadn't Gadsden would have set them on. But I give you my word Tom, I would never have done it, and had Gadsden done it, I should myself have gone to warn Featherstone, if I could have suspected the trap which Mandeville had baited for me." He paused a moment, then added in a dull voice. "Carey will never forgive me this."

And now came Julius, to announce Rutledge, Moultrie, and Laurens.

Harry tossed aside his napkin, and rose to receive them. All three, even Moultrie, who loved him, were stern and hostile. Rutledge was the first to address him, and this abruptly, uncompromisingly, his voice corrosively acid.

"So, sir, you have had your way in defiance and in despite of us all."

What was there that he could say that would be believed? He stood in silence to receive whatever reprimand Rutledge chose to administer, and he knew that Rutledge would not spare him. Outwardly he strove to maintain an air of impassivity, which the delegate mistook for insolence.

"The mob, sir, is acclaiming you its hero," Rutledge continued. "Therefore, you may be content, since that presumably is all that you desired, all that you wrought for."

"There, at least, you are at fault," Latimer answered him firmly. "Each of us carries in himself a standard by which to measure his neighbour. Out of your own vanity, I must presume, sir, you find in vanity the source of other men's actions."

"Excellent!" said Rutledge. "It is the very time for philosophic reflections. I'll ignore that insult with the rest."

"I am sure you will," said Latimer, conscious though he was that at every word he put himself further in the wrong.

Moultrie intervened. "You know what it means, Harry?"

"I know that I don't much care."

"But you must care," Laurens informed him gravely. "It is to make you understand that we have come. You have no time to lose. Your arrest may be ordered at any moment."

"My arrest?"

"What else?" Rutledge demanded. "You set a mob on to do a man to death, and think that nothing is to happen as a consequence. You would not listen to me this evening – "

"And I will not listen to you now," Latimer interrupted him. "It is your fault largely that I am where I am."

"My fault!" Rutledge looked at his companions to invite their consideration of this fantastic statement. "My fault? You are a little wild in your accusations, sir."

"Mr Rutledge, I do not choose to be more precise. This is my house, and if you must taunt me into insulting you, I prefer that you do it in some other place. Tom, will you be good enough to ring for Julius?"

"A moment, sir! A moment!" A faint colour was stirring in Rutledge's full cheeks.

"Indeed, you must listen to us," Moultrie added. "Don't ring, Tom. You are to realise, Harry, that we can't have you arrested."

"But who is to arrest me?"

"If the Governor orders it, we must submit. And if you are arrested you will be tried; and if tried you will certainly be hanged."

"If the Sons of Liberty permit it," countered Harry. "You say they are acclaiming me, and I said I was indifferent. I am not. I have changed my mind. I place my trust in the people, and so may you."

"But don't you understand, Latimer," Laurens explained, "that this is precisely what we desire to avoid – the explosion that must follow?"

"I am not at all concerned to avoid it. On the contrary, I shall welcome it. I shall welcome arrest and trial. It will enable me to expose the sly, deliberate villainy by which I have been driven into this corner."

The three looked at one another gravely. Then, in a firm tone of finality, Moultrie expressed what was in the mind of all.

"Harry, you must leave Charles Town tonight. At once."

"I don't perceive the necessity."

"But you'll go, nevertheless," said Laurens.

"Not a step."

Rutledge took up the attack once more.

"Are you so stupid that you don't understand, or so wilful and headstrong that you don't care? Are you concerned only to be acclaimed a hero by the mob. A pinchbeck hero! If you haven't the wit to see what must follow, then God help you! If you are arrested and brought to trial, there may be consequences that will inflame a continent. From Georgia to Massachusetts, from the Atlantic to the Mississipi, the brand of war is ready to the burning. Already it smoulders since that affair at Lexington, the least breeze of public feeling will fan it into flame. Persist in this mad defiance now and you may plunge your country into civil war. Can you stand there and calmly envisage even that so that you may pander to your monstrous vanity?"

"No, sir, I cannot." Mr Latimer was white and fierce.

"You'll go?" cried Moultrie and Laurens together.

"I'll stay."

"But – "

"If it were indeed a question of pandering to my vanity as Mr Rutledge says, I should bow now to your wishes. But it is not. I am moved by very different motives. To you, Mr Rutledge, I will explain myself no further. I am weary of your demands for explanations, weary of your questionings and cross-questionings. That you should ask me to go is enough in itself to determine me to stay. I do not recognise your authority over me, or your right to subject me to the questions and the veiled reproaches with which you have plagued me today. So I will beg you to spare yourself and me any further harangues. But if you will stay, Moultrie, I will open my mind to you, fully and completely. My mind and my heart for both are involved. And if Colonel Laurens cares to remain he is welcome to hear what I shall have to say."

Mr Rutledge bowed with stiff and formal dignity. "Mr Latimer, I will bid you good night. Colonels Laurens and Moultrie have the tranquillity of the province as much at heart as I have." He retired in good order.

Then, when he was gone, at last, Latimer unfolded heart and mind, as he had promised, to the two who remained, and to Tom Izard also. He showed them how he must now appear to Sir Andrew Carey, and how the trial, and the trial alone by bringing all to light, might put him right in Sir Andrew's eyes. It moved them strongly into sympathy with him.

"Damn Rutledge," swore Moultrie. "He has the manners of a curmudgeon. But he's the soul of honesty, Harry, and the staunchest patriot in South Carolina, and he has a mind."

"A mind, perhaps. But little heart. And a mind that is not supported by a heart has never achieved greatness for any man."

"It's no matter for that now, Harry. The fact is that if you remain you place not only yourself in danger, but the colony as well."

"It doesn't happen that I agree with you," said Latimer. "The Governor will never dare to move in the matter when he knows the part played in it by his equerry."

"But if you should be wrong in your assumption?" Laurens asked him in distress.

"If I am wrong, then the explanation is that, in neglecting to warn Featherstone, Mandeville was acting under orders from Lord William. That I cannot believe. But if it were true, Lord William should be more reluctant than ever to proceed against me. It may be an attempt to scare me away, to raise the very bugbear that you are brandishing. I don't know. But I mean to ascertain, and therefore I remain in Charles Town."

The end of it was that Moultrie and Laurens went off to report failure to Rutledge, and to receive in their turn his remorseless reprimands for their own lack of firmness. When they submitted to him the reasons which Latimer had given them, and actually manifested sympathy with those reasons, he was more contemptuous than ever, and wondered why he should be doomed to work with a party of emotional sentimentalists.

Rutledge went to bed that night persuaded that the colonies stood upon the threshold of civil war. Considering what was happening elsewhere in America, the conviction did not demand much foresight.

Chapter 10

The Mail-bag

Betimes on the following morning, Latimer received a visit from William Henry Drayton. With him came Tom Corbet, a member of the official Secret Committee.

"Put a pistol in your pocket, and come with me, Harry," Drayton invited him.

You conceive that Mr Latimer required explanations. He was afforded them.

A week ago a fairly full meeting of the Council of Safety, the executive body appointed by Provincial Congress and invested with the fullest powers, had been startled by Drayton's proposal that Lord William Campbell should be taken into custody.

This drastic proposal had found support at the hands of only two of his colleagues of the committee. The remainder, led by Rawlins Lowndes, the Speaker of the Commons, were solidly against it. They considered Drayton's assumptions based on insufficient evidence, and they would in no case be parties to so provocative a step as he advocated.

The end of a protracted debate was that further evidence should be sought of Lord William's real disposition. Latimer's subsequent visit to the Governor having added on this subject little or nothing to the information gained in the back country by Drayton, there remained the course secretly sanctioned by the Council of Safety, which was that the Governor's mails should henceforth be subjected to scrutiny. Thomas Corbet, mainly because residing upon the Bay, and therefore likely to be among the first to perceive the arrival of any packet from England, was entrusted with the business. And this morning Corbet, espying a new arrival among the British shipping, had gone in quest of Drayton to help him in what was to do. It had been thought well to reinforce themselves by including a third in the undertaking, and Drayton had proposed Harry Latimer.

"One reason is that you were convenient to our hand, your house lying on our way; the other that it is better to employ another man who, like myself, is already liable to arrest for last night's business than someone against whom there is as yet no charge."

"You mean that having taken one downward step, it cannot greatly matter if I take another," Latimer laughed.

And whilst Latimer with Drayton and Corbet went forth upon that further act of treason, Lord William Campbell, reduced almost to despair by last night's event, was listening to Mandeville's insistent counsel that action should be taken to avenge the murder of Featherstone

Already last night, when first the news of that outrage had been conveyed to the Governor by the mob itself, which had paraded under his windows, taunting him and defying him with threats to serve his other spies in the same fashion, there had been an acrimonious scene between Lord William and his masterful equerry.

Bitterly had Lord William upbraided Mandeville for a lack of diligence which his lordship suspected to have been deliberate. Calm, correct and dignified, Mandeville had defended himself with the assertion that he had gone straight to Featherstone's lodging, that the fellow being absent, he had sought him at the coffee house in St Michael's Alley, which was known to be a favourite resort of his; there he had learnt that Featherstone had gone to Goose Creek, and he had ridden all the way thither with a view to preventing him from returning into the town. He had missed him by minutes.

But this morning Lord William had received further details of Featherstone's capture. He had learnt that the fellow had been taken in his sister's house and dragged from her supper table, and this fresh information, reawakening his suspicions, led him to reopen the matter.

"How came you to leave no word with Mrs Grigg?"

Mandeville shrugged. "It would have been better had I done so, certainly. But I saw no reason to alarm the woman unnecessarily. I was confident of finding Featherstone myself."

Lord William looked at him with eyes in which suspicion still brooded; and it brooded, too, in the mind of Mr Innes, who was present at the interview in the Governor's pleasant study above the garden.

A bee sailed in through the open window on the warm air that was heavy with the perfume of the magnolias, and for a moment the drone of its flight was the only sound in the room. Then Mandeville, lounging easily on the Governor's day-bed, spoke again.

"What really asks your consideration is the action you are now to take."

"Action?" quoth Lord William.

"Action. You will not allow the deed to remain unpunished."

"One cannot punish a mob."

"No. But the mob's instigator is known. This man Latimer – "

Lord William interrupted him irritably.

"I told you yesterday what our position would be if this thing happened. Nothing has occurred to change that. We cannot now take proceedings without incurring the risk of a riot infinitely more disastrous than last night's."

"Yet if you do nothing there is an end to your authority."

"My God, man! If only you had got Featherstone away!" He strode to the window, and back again. He took a decision and halted by the writing-table. "Innes, please send a line to the Speaker of the Commons asking him to be good enough to wait upon me." Innes bent to the task. "At least I can save my face, as Governor Bull did when they raided the armoury. The Commons shall appoint a committee to investigate the outrage."

"That," said Mandeville, "is mere comedy."

"It's the alternative to tragedy, and that I am determined to avoid."

But an hour later came news which shook the firmness of the Governor's determination. It was brought by Stevens, who kept the post office. He was white and trembling, be it from the scare he had recently undergone, be it from natural indignation. He came to report that no sooner had the mail-bag from the *Swallow* reached his office that morning than the place had been invaded by three gentlemen of Charles Town who had demanded its surrender. Peremptorily he had refused, whereupon one of them had clapped a pistol to his head, and had held him motionless under the threat of death, whilst the other two had appropriated the mail-bag and carried it away. Only after their departure had their leader, as he was to be supposed from his action, withdrawn the pistol and gone his ways again.

Governor, equerry and secretary listened appalled to this narrative.

Mandeville, whose wits were less easily distracted from essentials than those of Lord William, and who permitted himself far less the luxury of indulging his feelings, proceeded almost at once to a pertinent inquiry.

"Gentlemen?" he echoed. "You said 'gentlemen,' Stevens?"

"I did so, your honour."

"That disposes of any idea of robbery. The thing acquires a political significance. Who were these gentlemen, Stevens? It's clear you knew them."

"Nay, captain. I name no names," cried the fellow in some excitement. "I've no mind to go the way o' Featherstone."

"So?" said Mandeville, and drew a bow at a venture, and yet not quite at a venture. "Latimer was one of them."

The assertion flung Stevens into terror. "I never said so. I never said so." He appealed almost wildly to the Governor. "Your excellency, I named no names. You, sir," he turned to Innes. "I take you to witness, sir, that I never said who done it."

Mandeville thought his panic said so. And at the same time he reviewed a picture in his memory of Harry Latimer, at Fairgrove, drawing a heavy pistol from the pocket of his bottle-green riding coat. So once more he loosed a shaft on assumption.

"Was Mr Latimer's pistol loaded, d'ye suppose?"

"To test it might ha' cost me my life..." Stevens had answered before he was aware of how much he was really saying.

"And the other two? Who were they?" asked Lord William.

"Don't ask me, my lord. They were members of the Provincial Congress, and it's before Congress or one of its committees the mails has gone."

They pressed him no further. Lord William indeed was too perturbed, too dismayed by the fact itself, to pre-occupy himself with the details of it; whilst Mandeville was so concerned with his discovery that Latimer was the chief actor in the outrage that he cared little who might have been the others.

"And what are you going to do now?" Mandeville calmly asked his lordship after Stevens had been dismissed.

"What is there to be done?" His excellency was reduced to a despair which he did not trouble to conceal.

"Nothing can be clearer than what should be done. But... I await your excellency's commands." And he tapped his snuff-box.

The Governor became peevish.

"Oh, damn your assumptions, Mandeville." His mind swung to what was no more than a side-issue. "Anyhow, I doubt if the mails they have seized contain any dispatches for myself. Mine came in by the *Tamar*, and there could hardly be anything to add to them."

Mandeville took snuff, and considered.

"Let us hope it is so. But even if it is, it makes the crime of tampering with his majesty's mails no less grave. It is a capital offence here as in England. If you take no action, faith, you will lose the respect and support of the few remaining loyal souls in the colony.

You may as well pack and quit, for you will have ceased completely to govern."

"And if I arrest Latimer – which is what you are really advising – the same will happen, and something more. I shall cease to govern, because I shall be flung out; and I shall leave civil war behind me."

"If Latimer continues free to pursue his rebel activities, civil war is assured. That is the other horn of your dilemma. You should perceive by now with what manner of man you have to deal. A desperate, reckless fellow, a revolutionist, the most dangerous man in the province. And every day he continues at Liberty he becomes more dangerous, for every day he establishes himself more firmly in the favour of the people. The thing to be done with him is clear, and there should be no delays about it. Put him aboard one of the English ships, and send him home to be dealt with."

The Governor stood considering a moment.

"If it was impossible yesterday," he said slowly, "it is, by what you have said yourself, more impossible still today."

"And will be more impossible still tomorrow," Mandeville countered, "when the need for it will be infinitely more acute. Hesitation to grasp this nettle has brought your excellency into your present difficulty. These scoundrels trade upon your scruples. They are cowards that abuse your generosity. You have been meek and conciliatory with them ever since you arrived. Show them the strong hand for once; show them that you are not to be scared by the bugbear of civil war which they dangle before you to cow you into inaction. That fear of yours is the foundation upon which they build. Strike it from under them at one blow, and you'll find them tumbling in dismay. The time for half-measures, for compromising and temporizing, has gone."

He infected the Governor at last with something of his own firmness. For firm Mandeville undoubtedly was and above intimidation.

"Yes," his lordship reluctantly agreed. "You are right, Mandeville. This man is too dangerous to be left at large in Charles Town. If I am to be trampled under the hooves of the mob, I may as well be trampled for getting rid of him as because he commands the mob to do it. At least I shall have done my duty by the State. Innes, if you will prepare a warrant for the arrest of Harry Latimer, and have it ready for me after breakfast, I will sign it. Mandeville will formulate the charge for you."

Mandeville permitted himself a smile. "I congratulate your excellency on the decision."

Lord William's young eyes considered him gloomily. "I hope there is occasion for it," he said, with a sigh. "God knows!" And he went at last to breakfast, a meal which he always took alone with Lady William in her ladyship's dainty little boudoir on the ground floor immediately underneath the study.

He was preoccupied and uncommunicative throughout the meal. His mind, as her ladyship perceived, was far from easy, a fact which she naturally attributed to the terrible affair of last night.

She waited patiently for him to unburden himself, too wise to attempt to force his confidence. But when breakfast had come to an end, and still he sat wrapped in his gloomy abstraction, she abandoned the ways of pure wisdom, and gave the reins to her concern.

Her questions drew from him the tale of the raid on the mails and of the warrant he was to sign in consequence of that and other things. It shocked her profoundly. Harry Latimer had been her friend – as he had been the friend of all her brothers and sisters and particularly of Tom – from childhood. Myrtle Carey, too, was her friend. And although she knew, being in Myrtle's confidence, that there was at present a cloud between the lovers, she also believed their affection strong enough to dissipate that cloud in the end.

"Is it…is it wise, Will?" she asked.

"I hope it is," he answered wearily.

"Ah! You don't know?"

"I know only that it is necessary. It is impossible that my authority should continue to be flouted and that Latimer should be left free to pursue what amounts to a career of crime."

"That sounds like Captain Mandeville," she said. "Has he persuaded you?"

Lord William had not the courage to admit it. In his soul he was ashamed of the weakness which permitted his equerry to dominate him so completely. His answer was an equivocation. "He tried to persuade me yesterday, and I refused to listen to him. Today, after Featherstone's terrible end and this outrage on the mails, I no longer need persuading."

"Have you counted the cost?" she asked him gravely.

"I have counted the cost of not doing it."

"Do you think there is any court in Carolina would convict Harry Latimer at present?"

His answer relieved her fears. "No. I do not."

"Then why make yourself ridiculous by arresting him?"

"He is not to be tried in Carolina. He shall go to England as by law prescribed for offenders in his class."

The announcement changed her gravity to panic.

"Merciful God!" she ejaculated. "Will, you can't do it!"

"Either that, or I must throw up the Governorship and sail for England myself. Charles Town cannot hold Mr Harry Latimer and myself at the same time. That has now been clearly demonstrated."

She was still staring at him in utter dismay, when her brother-in-law, Miles Brewton, was announced, and she welcomed his advent, persuaded that here was a very valuable ally.

A handsome modish man of middle age, Brewton was sincerely attached to Lord William Campbell, notwithstanding the fact that he himself belonged to the patriotic party. More than once already had he steered the Governor over shoals and evil passages, and Lord William had been glad to lean upon him, knowing he was probably as conservative and constitutional as any man on his side. Because of this and because of his genuine affection for Lord William, Mr Brewton spared no effort to maintain the popularity of his brother-in-law, and it was under his auspices and at his house that the ball in honour of the Governor was being organized for tomorrow night.

Her ladyship had at first imagined that this might be the occasion of this matutinal visit. But he soon made it clear that he was concerned with very different matters, and that he desired to be private with Lord William. And when presently they sauntered forth together into the garden, her discreet ladyship made no attempt to join them.

She was not destined to be long alone with her thoughts, for presently she had another visitor in the person of her brother Tom, who brought into the little room with him some of the careless boisterous high spirits with which his large person normally abounded.

He had resolved to spy out the land, and ascertain how far Harry might be justified of his estimate of Mandeville's deliberate endeavours to enmesh him. He approached the subject with the subtlety of a calf.

"What's this I'm told, Sally, of Harry Latimer's being blamed for what happened to Featherstone?"

She looked up from the couch on which she was seated, with the window immediately behind her.

"Where did you hear it?"

"Where?" Master Tom was nonplussed. He took refuge in the truth. "Why, from Harry himself."

"And how does he know?"

Tom stood over her, large and benign. "I came here to ask questions, not to be questioned," said he. And asked: "Is it true?"

"I'm afraid it is, Tom." She was suddenly inspired. "The best service you can render Harry is to go to him at once, and tell him to leave Charles Town without a moment's delay. Will is signing a warrant for his arrest, both because of the Featherstone business and because of his share in the raid on the post-office this morning. Hurry to him, Tom."

But Tom showed no disposition whatever to hurry. Instead he sat down beside her and smiled phlegmatically upon the sister whom his conduct was alarming.

"Not until I've seen Will," he said.

"What can you have to say to Will?"

"For one thing I can tell him to make out a warrant for my arrest at the same time. For I was with Harry at the Beef Market last night. All Charles Town knows I was there. And, between ourselves, I was also concerned in the raid on the post-office this morning."

"Are you mad, Tom? Oh, how could you? Have you no thought for me?" Her handsome opulent figure appeared visibly to swell with indignation. "How could you place me in this cruel position!"

"It isn't you that's in a cruel position. It's Will. He'll have to arrest his brother-in-law or change his mind about arresting Latimer."

Mr Tom Izard you see was, after all, not entirely without subtlety.

Chapter 11

Stalemate

Amongst them they shattered at least in part the Governor's resolve. For Miles Brewton's visit, too, was concerned with last night's business and the possible action Lord William might feel himself compelled to take in consequence. He came to impose caution upon his brother-in-law. Lord William an amiable weather-vane to turn obligingly with any wind that blew, was already wobbling undecidedly when he rejoined his wife to be faced by Tom Izard's ultimatum, and to be reminded unpleasantly that Tom's name was also on that list of rebels who had raided the armoury last April.

The distraction of his mind was suddenly pierced by a recollection of something that Mandeville had said: "Show them the strong hand...that you are not to be scared by the bugbear of civil war. That fear of yours is the foundation upon which they build."

If Mandeville were right, and of this Mandeville had persuaded him, then the threat of action should be as effective as action itself in ridding him of this pestilent Harry Latimer. If only this were achieved one way or another, his difficulties would be largely at an end for the present. Upon that he now took his resolve, and he announced it to them with some firmness.

"The warrant cannot be withdrawn. I shall sign it today. I have no choice. The Governor of South Carolina with evidence before him of acts of robbery and high treason all in one dare not refuse to take action. But the action shall be delayed. I will suspend the execution of the warrant for twenty-four...for forty-eight hours. And I shall formally communicate this to Mr Latimer today. Provided that he will leave South Carolina within the time I give him, I shall be content."

"An act of banishment," said Brewton, pursing his lips.

"It is the utmost clemency I dare show. More, indeed, than I have any right to show. If you are his friend, Tom, and mine, you will persuade him to take advantage of it."

The more Lord William considered this solution of the riddle, which had come to him with the suddenness of inspiration, the better he liked it. It assumed in his eyes the proportions of a diplomatic masterpiece. At a stroke, he saved his face, rid the country of a mischief-maker, and gave provocation to none. He was uplifted out of his despondency, exalted in fact when he retraced his steps to his study, and sent for Mandeville. When the equerry came, he found Lord William humming the refrain of a song.

"The warrant is signed," said his lordship airily. "But it is not to be executed until Friday morning – forty-eight hours hence. You are to intimate the same to Mr Latimer at once."

Mandeville thought him mad, and very nearly said so. His lordship explained himself, and Mandeville changed his mind. Almost he admired the nimbleness with which Lord William had dodged both horns of his dilemma, and since he could desire for himself nothing more than the removal of Mr Latimer, it did not very much matter whether that removal were effected in this way or another.

Content, therefore, Captain Mandeville sallied forth, and went on foot down Broad Street and then northward along the wide Bay Street with its bastions and courtine lines above the broad expanse of the waters of the Cooper River, here merging into the ocean. At anchor a mile away, beyond most of the lesser shipping in the bay, he discovered the black and white hull of the sloop *Tamar*, and reflected that with half a dozen such warships riding there it would be an easy matter to quell the mutinous spirit of these colonial upstarts. Past the crowded busy wharves he went, past the foot of Queen Street and on into the quieter region beyond the Custom House, where at last he came to the stately mansion of Mr Harry Latimer.

Julius in his sky-blue livery laced with silver ushered the captain into the library, that he might admire there, whilst waiting, the evidences of the culture with which the Latimers surrounded themselves.

And he was kept waiting some little time. It is possible that this was deliberate on the part of Mr Latimer. When at last the young master of the house made his appearance, he came clad in a coat of apricot velvet above black satin smalls and black silk stockings. The lace at his throat and wrists was finest Mechlin, a diamond of price flashed in his solitaire, and buckles of French paste adorned the red-heeled shoes that had certainly come all the way from Paris.

Whilst Julius held the door for him, he bowed gracefully from the threshold to his visitor.

"I am honoured, Captain Mandeville."

"Your humble obedient, sir." The captain made a leg in his turn. "I am sent by his excellency the Governor."

Mr Latimer advanced. Julius closed the door, and the two were alone together.

"A chair, sir?"

Captain Mandeville sat down. "I will come straight to business, Mr Latimer. You have been guilty, if you will forgive the liberty of the criticism, of a grave imprudence."

"Of many, sir, I do assure you." Mr Latimer was airy.

"I allude to your address last night to the mob in the Beef Market, as a result of which a man has been done to death."

"You are sure, Captain Mandeville, that it was as a result of that?"

"Of what else, then?"

"I have a suspicion that it is of your own deliberate neglect, sir, to take advantage of the warning you had at Fairgrove. It was not I who acted as Featherstone's justiciary, but you who acted as his murderer."

"Sir!" the captain was on his feet.

Blue eyes smiled serenely into dark eyes. Mr Latimer appeared to be mildly amused.

"Do you deny it? To me?"

The captain commanded himself. "I am not concerned to deny or admit. It is not I who am in danger of being put upon my trial."

"But that may follow," said Mr Latimer.

Almost the captain was taken aback. "How? What do you mean?"

"Oh, but does it matter very much? I am perhaps detaining you. And you will have, I take it, some communication to make to me?"

"Yes," said Mandeville. "I think it may be best if we keep to that. There is a warrant signed for your arrest, Mr Latimer. If that warrant is executed, you realize what must happen to you?"

"If it is executed?" Mr Latimer stared at him. "It is usual to execute warrants, is it not?"

The captain did not choose to deliver a direct answer. "In this case Lord William has been persuaded to deal leniently with you, and to spare you the full rigour of the law, provided that you will submit to the condition he imposes."

"That will depend upon the condition."

"His excellency will be satisfied if you will accept a sentence of banishment from South Carolina. He gives you forty-eight hours – a generous measure of time – in which to quit Charles Town. But he desires you to understand quite clearly that if you are still here by ten o'clock on Friday morning the warrant will be executed and the law will take its course."

Mr Latimer took a turn in the long room, considering his reply, but not his course of action. That required no consideration.

"Would it be impertinent, Captain Mandeville, or indiscreet to inquire by whom his excellency has been persuaded to so much clemency?"

"Chiefly, I believe, by Lady William."

"Ah!" Mr Latimer considered him very searchingly. "For a moment I almost suspected it might have been yourself."

"Myself?" Mandeville stared hard in his turn. "On my soul, Mr Latimer, you think too well of me."

"I was not thinking well of you at all when I thought that. Has it occurred to you, Captain Mandeville, that if I am brought to trial upon this charge, I shall urge in my own defence that I gave full and timely warning – to you and to Sir Andrew Carey – of what would happen to Featherstone if he were not removed from Charles Town?"

"What then, sir?" asked the captain, with the least hint of challenge.

"You will be required to admit it, and so will Sir Andrew Carey, and at need even Miss Carey, who was also present." Mandeville's eyelids flickered. Latimer watching him did not fail to observe that single flaw in the man's iron self-control. "You will all three be upon oath, and it is not to be supposed that all three of you will commit perjury."

"Where is the need? Such a statement will but further incriminate you."

"No, sir. It will incriminate you, and of a singularly heinous and atrocious deed. Why did you not take steps to save Featherstone! Why did you not even warn him? That you did not is clear from the manner in which he was taken – peacefully at supper with his sister and her family. You will be required to answer that question, and all the other questions, all the abominable implications, arising out of it." Mr Latimer uttered a short laugh. "You deliberately sacrificed Featherstone, your spy, your own man, that you might weave a rope for my neck." He came a step nearer, and smiled a little grimly into the soldier's set face. "Are you quite sure, Captain Mandeville, that you have not woven one for your own? Do you doubt that when your conduct is made clear yours will be the fate of Featherstone himself? That there will be tar and feathers for you, as there were for him? Can you really doubt it?"

Mandeville fell back a step. He had changed colour at last, and his eyes looked darker than ever in the pallor of his face.

"Your questions are impertinent, Mr Latimer." He changed his tone to one of utter formality. "I have had the honour to deliver the message with which I am charged by his excellency. I shall be happy to bear him your answer."

"You have it, Captain Mandeville. Tell him that he need not hold his hand until Friday morning. That I have no intention of obeying his decree of banishment, and that here in Charles Town I remain, for the pleasure of seeing you taken in your own dirty springe."

"Mr Latimer!" Mandeville's self-control gave out. "By God! You shall meet me for this."

"It is what I am suggesting." Mr Latimer smiled sardonically. "I shall certainly meet you. In the courthouse. But nowhere else, Captain Mandeville." And he pulled the bell rope.

Mandeville looked at him a moment, dark fury in his eyes. Then he turned, and strode to the door. On the threshold he halted again. Only the truth and his apprehension of the truth could have moved him to such a pitch of anger. He was caught, and he knew it. Latimer had proved too astute. He had discerned the vulnerable Achilles' heel, of which Mandeville himself had been unconscious. And so the captain now thanked Heaven from his heart that Lord William should not have listened to him when he had urged the immediate arrest of Latimer. That arrest he was now as anxious to avoid as Lord William himself. At all costs Latimer must be driven off, scared away. Therefore at the door, he played his last card.

"Mr Latimer, it is only fair to warn you that you build on sand. The consummation you imagine might follow if you were to be tried here in Charles Town. But if you are arrested you will be taken to England for trial as the law requires in the case of men charged with such an offence as yours."

For an instant that gave Latimer pause. But only for an instant, until his mind had surveyed the thing.

"Captain Mandeville, I do not believe that Lord William would perpetrate any such rashness. The law you invoke is one of the grievances that have caused the disturbances in these colonies. If you dared in the present state of things to attempt to enforce it you would provoke an explosion that would shatter you all to pieces. You say this to scare me. But even if it were as you say, I should apprehend as little as I do from trial here. There is justice in England. The English are just, and they are none too sympathetic with a Government that is endeavouring to curtail the liberties of Englishmen overseas. Whatever might happen to me, be sure that you would fare none too well at the hands of an English court, Captain Mandeville. And that, I think, is all I have to say to you."

Chapter 12

Revelation

Towards noon of that same Wednesday, a vast lumbering mahogany coach, with a coat-of-arms on the panel, and two liveried negroes maintaining themselves on the platform behind by their grip of a couple of broad straps, made its way down the comparatively narrow Tradd Street and drew up at the door of Sir Andrew Carey's town house. The coach contained Sir Andrew and his daughter. It was followed by a second one, almost as large, but of leather stretched over a wooden frame, and of more antiquated design. This contained Remus the butler, Abraham the valet, Miss Carey's mauma, Dido and a prodigious quantity of luggage.

Thus, more or less in state, Sir Andrew re-entered Charles Town, coming as we know, to lend by his loyal presence support to the King's representative in these seditious times.

Within a half-hour of his arrival, almost before the holland covers had been taken from the furniture, he was waited on by Captain Mandeville.

The equerry came spurred by panic. He realized that he had over-reached himself. Lord William had definitely committed himself to a threat, and retreat was impossible. Wherefore, upon quitting Latimer, Mandeville, had gone straight to Colonel Laurens with whom he had found John Rutledge.

Knowing their temperate views, their ardent desire for conciliation, their horror of anything that might precipitate a crisis destructive of all hope, he sought them in some confidence. He left them in despair.

Rutledge had summed up the brief discussion.

"We honour Lord William for his forbearance, and for this forty-eight-hours' grace. It is far more than we have any right to expect from him, and we are deeply sensible of the motives which inspire him. Inspired by the same desire to maintain peace, we will use with Mr Latimer what influence we have. But neither Colonel Laurens nor myself can be deluded by any hope of success. What you suggest that we should do we have already done. Already last night, before there was any question of a warrant, we urged Mr Latimer to depart at once. He was obdurate and obstinate in his resolve to remain."

Laurens who had received Latimer's reasons at first hand was even more chilling to Captain Mandeville.

"He is rooted in the persuasion that Lord William will not dare to proceed against him."

"That he is wrong there you should now be able to demonstrate," said Mandeville. "His lordship has signed the warrant, and he must perform as he threatens, or his authority is at an end and he renders himself ridiculous."

"We shall not omit to employ that argument. But for myself I have little hope that it will move Mr Latimer." He sighed, and shook his great head. "I wish I could think otherwise."

So Captain Mandeville took his leave, already persuaded that from this quarter, despite obvious goodwill, nothing was to be expected. Gloomily he took his way to Tradd Street, to ascertain if Sir Andrew had yet reached town. If Carey failed him he would have to study his position carefully. He might force a personal quarrel upon Latimer, and chance the issue. But he could not chance the effect of it upon Myrtle. If he were to be so fortunate as to kill Latimer in a duel he would, he knew – and the knowledge intensified the bitterness of his feelings – set up between himself and Myrtle a barrier which perhaps no subsequent patience could ever overcome.

That Sir Andrew would fail him seemed foreshadowed by the baronet's greeting.

"So that damned scoundrel had his way with poor Featherstone in spite of all that you could do! I'll never, never forgive him."

The words were simple enough. But the emphasis with which he uttered them supplied anything they may have lacked to express the full tale of his indignation and bitterness.

Mandeville was gently remonstrant. "Sir Andrew, I understand your feelings. But it is necessary to be just."

"That is what I intend to be. Just! And I'll see justice done on him for this. His black ingratitude, his loathsome treachery shall be brought home to him."

"And yet you must not forget that he came to Fairgrove yesterday to warn you, so that Featherstone might be removed, in t'me – "

"Did he?" Sir Andrew interrupted him. "Have you forgotten that we have his own admission that he came to spy, to obtain from us a confirmation of his suspicions. God in Heaven! The blackguard has made us parties in his deed of murder."

"No, no, Sir Andrew." The captain heard the door open behind him. But he went on without heeding it. "I am as much to blame as any man for what has happened. It was two full hours after my return to Charles Town before the mob moved to take Featherstone. If only I had not blundered, Featherstone could easily have been saved, as I honestly believe that Latimer intended. In judging him, Sir Andrew, you must lose sight of nothing that may tell in his favour."

He turned to face Myrtle, who had entered the room. She came forward now, a flush of excitement on her cheeks, her eyes bright.

"I am glad to hear you say that, Robert," she approved him, as he stooped to kiss her fingers. "It is what I, myself, have been telling father. But he is blinded by his anger and his grief."

"Blinded, madam!" the baronet retorted hotly. "I am seeing clearly for the first time in my life, I think. And I am perceiving what manner of black-hearted villain I took to be as a son to me."

"Sir Andrew, listen to me a moment," Mandeville begged. "Sit down, and listen quietly." And calmly he proceeded to expound the situation. "The warrant is signed, and unless he is gone from Charles Town by Friday morning it will be executed."

But there Sir Andrew interrupted him. "Why not until Friday? Why not at once? Why is this traitor and murderer to be given the chance to escape?"

"Lord William has been so persuaded."

"Who has persuaded him? Who?" And as Mandeville did not immediately answer him, he stared hard at the captain. "You did, Robert. You did. But will you tell me why?"

The captain sighed. "There were two excellent reasons. The first is your own affection for him – "

"I have told you it is dead. And I'll prove it at need. I am ready to give evidence that will help to hang him."

"To hang him!" cried Myrtle, and the flush of excitement perished from her cheeks.

Both men looked at her. But it was Mandeville who answered: "That is what will happen, Myrtle, if he remains here to await arrest. He will be sent to England for trial, and it is not to be imagined that any mercy will be shown him."

"He should have the mercy he showed Featherstone. More than that is shown him already in this quixotic delay – "

"Sir Andrew," Mandeville cut in, "are you quite sure that you do not deceive yourself? Are you quite sure that underneath your present indignation, the old love you bore him is not alive and vigorous, and that his death will presently prove to you a deep and bitter grief? You are the one man who might be able to save him. When I have told you that, can you be sure that hereafter you will be troubled by no remorse for having left him to his doom?"

"I shall be troubled by remorse if he escapes," was the fierce answer. "I am not the man to blow hot and cold, Robert. I know my mind."

"There is yet another point of view to be considered," said the captain. And, compelled to it, he now expounded the terrible consequences, the almost certain danger of open rebellion, that must attend the arrest of Latimer. It moved Sir Andrew no more than the other reason.

"Let it come," he said. "A little blood-letting is what is needed to make this colony healthy."

"But it will be the wrong blood," the captain argued.

"Surely, man, the Governor isn't powerless? There is a garrison at Fort Johnson."

"Less than a hundred men. If he were to bring them up, that would be the signal for the provincial militia to fall in on the other side. And then what would happen?"

"That which sooner or later must happen. Myself, I care not how soon. I want the air clearing of these poisonous mists. The royal Government has been too gentle, too timorous. Let it assert itself at last. There are enough loyal gentlemen in Charles Town to make a stand against this seditious rabble."

But the captain shook his head. "I don't share your optimism, Sir Andrew. Until the troops arrive we dare not provoke a conflict."

Sir Andrew heaved himself up in a frenzy of impatience. "But what in any case could I do?" he asked.

"Urge Mr Latimer to avail himself of the Governor's clemency."

"I?" Sir Andrew placed his hands upon his breast, and arched his eyebrows in amazement. "I urge him? My God, you don't know what you're asking, or else you don't know me. I'll urge him to hang himself."

"Oh father, father!" Myrtle put an arm about his neck. "Think what Harry has been to you. Think what he might be again, if you tried gentleness – "

"Gentleness? With a damned rebel? With a murderer?"

123

"Don't call him that, father. It isn't true. And in your heart you know it isn't."

"Didn't he set the mob on last night to murder Gabriel?"

"Was that like Harry? He must have been convinced that Mr Featherstone had been warned by Robert and had got away. He would never have done it else."

"He would never have done it in such a case, you mean. What purpose could there be in sending a mob to raid an empty nest?"

"I don't know. But I am sure that Harry will be able to explain."

"It is possible," Mandeville suggested, "indeed probable, that he simply obeyed the orders of his committee."

"But why, if he thought the man had gone?"

"Because he dared not tell them that. He dared not admit that he had been guilty of this breach of faith to those who sent him to Lord William. So he played out that comedy little thinking how it would turn to tragedy."

"That's it! That's it!" cried Myrtle, and her eyes thanked her cousin. "What else would have been possible where Harry is concerned? You know that he is generous, warm-hearted, impulsive. This would have been the act of a wicked man, and Harry isn't wicked, father. You know that."

"Do I?" he laughed his contempt of her plea. Then he shook her off and went striding away across the room, as if to relieve his feeiings by action. "By God! It's droll to have you two here pleading to me for Harry Latimer. And, by God! you waste your pains. Not a finger will I lift to save him from the rope he has earned himself! But my two hands are ready to help to hang him. If my evidence is wanted on what passed yesterday at Fairgrove, it is at the Governor's disposal."

"Sir Andrew!" Mandeville appealed to him.

"Not another word on that subject, Robert. If you have nothing else to say to me, I'll beg you to excuse me. My steward is waiting for his orders."

And he stamped out of the room in dudgeon.

Mandeville looked at Miss Carey with eyes that were full of regret.

"And so my last hope fails," he said, which was the literal truth.

She came to him and placed her two hands upon his arm.

"It was noble of you to try. Just as it was noble of you to persuade Lord William to give Harry these two days' grace. I shall never forget it, Robert. Never!"

"You mean that you'll remember my failure," said he, with a queer smile.

"No, Robert. Your generosity. Oh, but is there nothing we can do?"

"Nothing. I fear, in view of Mr Latimer's own obstinacy. I have done all I could. Perhaps it would have been better had I not gone myself, in the first instance. Mr Latimer does not trust me."

"Doesn't trust you? You?"

Mandeville shrugged. He was the big-hearted, tolerant fellow who forgives all, because he understands all. "What cause has he to trust me? In his place I should do the same."

When presently he took his leave, he left her more profoundly impressed than ever with his nobility and sterling worth. But he did not leave her considering those virtues of his.

One single fact bulked so largely in her mind that it permitted her to see nothing else at the same time. She was terrified, and out of that terror came presently a better understanding of herself than she had lately possessed. It had been necessary that the shadow of the gallows should fall upon her lover to make her fully realize that he was her lover still, her man, and that all the rest was vanity. What mattered his political opinions? What did it matter if he outraged the political religion in which she had been reared? What were politics to her, what was the King to her, by comparison with him? Something of the kind had stirred in her yesterday, when she had seen him abused and beset. But that had been a flash, a glimpse; no more. This was a flood of revelation. He was in danger of his life; in danger of ignominious death. The very thought almost stopped her breathing. He was her man, and if he died, if they killed him, hanged him, what would be left for her, what would become of her? She was answered by the memory of a line out of a forgotten play, a memory that arose impishly, mockingly, fiendishly. She would lead apes in hell.

She thought of the letters she had written to him when he was away, and how she had sent him back their betrothal ring. She saw it now as an act of vanity, stupid, silly, detestable. What did she know of these questions that were agitating the country so violently? Harry was not alone in his ways of thought. There were men of honour and position in the province – such men as Colonel Laurens and Arthur Middleton, Mr Izard, who was Lord William's own father-in-law, and a score of others whom once her father had esteemed as friends, and whom now he no longer admitted to his house, because their ways of thought were not his own.

Thus love and fear so wrought upon her jointly in that hour that for the first time in her life a doubt of her father's opinions entered her mind. It is thus, abruptly and in moments of crisis that conversions and apostasies take place.

And so it came about that in the early hours of that same afternoon, a sedan chair carried by two negro bearers in Sir Andrew Carey's liveries passed along the wharves, and swung through the gates of Mr Latimer's residence, to set down Miss Carey before the young rebel's door.

It was an outrage upon the proprieties. But proprieties had come to matter as little as political convictions.

Julius, a little confused by her appearance, conducted her across the wide hall, straight to the library where Mr Latimer was brooding. For Colonel Laurens and John Rutledge had but lately left him after a protracted and rather stormy scene at the end of which the young man had remained as defiant as at the beginning.

He leapt up in amazement as she entered, and in amazement stared at her across the room.

"Harry!" She held out her hands to him, pleadingly, almost piteously.

He advanced to her.

"Myrtle!" There was only wonder in his voice, and his next question was to explain the source of it. "You are alone?"

She nodded, then loosened and threw back her calash.

"But is this discreet?" he asked. He was about to add – "especially since we are no longer even betrothed." But he left that thought unuttered.

"Is it a time for discretion? Harry! What are you going to do?"

So that was it. He might have guessed it, he told himself. Here was another of Captain Mandeville's emissaries – for Laurens had admitted himself to be almost that – and he was to go through another scene perhaps more painful than the last.

"I won't affect to misunderstand you," he said gravely. "I am going to do nothing."

"But, Harry! You can't know – "

"I know all, and I am prepared for everything." And then he added: "Has Captain Mandeville sent you to persuade me to leave Charles Town, in case Colonel Laurens should have failed?"

"He has not."

"You surprise me. But no doubt he told you of my position and hoped that you would come to reason with me."

"He told me – yes – father and me. But he was very far from suggesting that I should come to you. What do you mean, Harry?"

His manner began to intrigue her. It was so aloof, so different from all that she had expected.

"You have, of course, become...attached to this kinsman from England who has descended upon Charles Town during my absence?"

"Robert has been very good, very kind. I...we are very fond of him."

He smiled, not quite pleasantly. "I have been afforded occasion to observe that for myself," he said.

She liked neither the smile nor the tone. "And he has been a very good friend to you, Harry," she asserted.

"To me?" He expressed amazement in his stare and finally in a laugh. "Oh! My dear friend Mandeville, how I have misjudged you!

127

I should have known it was friendship for me sent him carrying tales to your father of my association with the Sons of Liberty."

"Harry! How can you? It's not worthy of you. He carried no tales. He told father, so that father might reason with you, might rescue you before it was too late, before you got into the position of danger in which you now are."

"And in which your Captain Mandeville has been careful to place me."

"You don't know what you're saying."

"Don't I? Listen to me a moment. It is as well that you should know this man. Captain Mandeville desired to accomplish two things: the first was to drive me out of your father's house; the second, to drive me out of Charles Town. I embarrass the gallant captain by my presence. But I am also so accommodating as to afford him the means of disposing of me. His first wish was easily fulfilled. You saw it done."

"Harry " She was angrily reproachful. "This is infamous!"

"I quite agree with you. But wait until I have made all clear. To drive me out of Charles Town is not quite so easy. It asks more ingenuity. I am so unfortunate as to supply the opportunity, and to make quite sure of me, Captain Mandeville does not hesitate to leave a wretched creature of his own to be done to death." To dissipate her indignant disbelief, he advanced his arguments. But it was without avail.

"You are not mad enough, wicked enough, to say that of Captain Mandeville?"

"It sounds fantastic, I confess. But not when you have weighed the circumstances."

"See how your malice blinds you!" she cried. "It was Captain Mandeville who prevailed upon Lord William to stay the execution of the warrant for your arrest."

"He will say so to you, of course."

"Do you doubt his word! Perhaps you won't believe me when I tell you that he came to plead for you with my father? To urge my father to persuade you to leave Charles Town before the expiry of the respite he has obtained for you."

"That I can well believe, since I have shown him how unpleasant may be the consequences for himself if I am brought to trial. I find the situation interesting, and I don't mean to miss the remainder of the entertainment by running away." And then, abruptly he changed his tone, as a man tosses aside an instrument whose use is at an end. "But I am glad you came, Myrtle; glad to think that in spite of all that has happened, you still have some feeling, some concern for me."

That disarmed the anger kindled in her by his sneers at Mandeville. She came up to him, and set her hands on his shoulders, looking up into his face. "Harry! Harry, you mustn't remain. You mustn't! You must go, Harry. You must leave Charles Town."

He looked at her, and as he looked there came into his face that expression of sedate amusement, which at times could be so irritating.

"And leave a clear field to your new lover? Believe me, there is not the need. I am not one to prove importunate."

She recoiled as if had struck her.

"My new lover?" she echoed.

"This dear Robert, this gallant gentleman who serves his King so nobly, who was no doubt the first to show you that you could not possibly marry so wicked and abandoned a fellow as a rebel. This dear Robert who may one day make you 'my lady.' Oh, why not be frank and open with me, Myrtle?"

"Frank and open!" She was wild now with anger. It whipped the colour to her cheeks and lent a dangerous sparkle to her eyes. "How dare you... You insult me! How dare you suggest that I have ever been anything else!"

"Have you not? Oh, Myrtle! Myrtle! Why make pretence with me?"

"Pretence?" Her voice shrilled up. "I came to tell you –" She checked. "No matter what I came to tell you. Thank God I didn't. You have shown me what you are worth."

"But not quite all I know; not quite all that justifies me."

That brought her up, even as she was turning to depart. She looked at him over her shoulder, scorn and anger stamped upon her little face.

"Listen a moment, and judge for yourself, if I am still to be deceived. Yesterday when I came to Fairgrove, and after I had made my escape, I waited among the trees by the avenue for the chance of a word with you. In my wretchedness, in my dejection, I would have given all I had to have made matters whole between you and me. Perhaps if nothing else would have moved you – God knows – such was my need of you that I might have thrown my very principles to the winds, and been false to my beliefs. I wanted to beg you to take back the letters that you wrote me, to forget all that, and to accept again my ring."

She was facing him once more; the scorn had passed slowly from her face, and wonder was breaking on it. He paused now, and, breathlessly delivered, her question filled the pause:

"Why didn't you?"

"Do you ask?" His voice, his eyes, were wistful. "Do you remember nothing – in that avenue, yesterday? Whilst I waited there you came by in company with Mandeville, his arm about your shoulders, your face alight – "

"Harry!" There was indignant protest in the cry. She took a step towards him, to check him. But he went on:

"Then I understood indeed what had happened in my absence, why your letters had been so mercilessly uncompromising, how you must have welcomed the pretext I gave you for writing them."

"Harry! Oh Harry! To think that of me! Of me!"

He looked at her, and almost smiled.

"You'll tell me that my eyes deceived me – "

"No, no. But that was…nothing. Nothing!"

"Nothing! A man walks with you in a half-embrace, and it is nothing."

"But he's my cousin," she cried desperately, and thereby provoked only his scorn.

"Your cousin? Some thirty times removed at least; and two months ago you were not even aware of his existence. Yet on the strength of his kinship he drops from the clouds into the family lap. He is taken to your bosom – literally."

She controlled herself by an effort. She was white to the lips. She was very angry with him, and yet through all her anger beat the understanding that he sinned against her in thought because he loved her and was insensately jealous. Therefore she must have patience with him. At all costs she must disabuse his mind.

"Harry, will you listen to me?" she asked, and her voice was quiet, though her bosom raced. He bowed, still with a tinge of irony.

"I came here, Harry, to persuade you to go away. I came because... because I, too, wanted to say to you the things you wanted to say to me when you waited among the trees at Fairgrove. As ready today to make sacrifice to you of my beliefs, as you say that you were ready to sacrifice them to me yesterday."

"Myrtle!" His heart almost stood still. One half of his mind believed; the other laughed in scorn.

"Now do you believe that...that what you saw was...not what you thought it? I, too, was miserable and dejected. I had been unhappy ever since I had sent you back your ring. And your awful scene with father almost drove me mad. Robert was kind. He is kind, Harry, whatever you may say or think. He comforted me, and I stood so much in need of comforting, I felt so lonely and desolate that if Remus had put an arm round me in friendship I should have been glad of it. Harry, that is the truth. All of it. You do believe me!"

He took her in his arms.

"My dear! My dear!" He kissed the brown head that lay against his shoulder, and her tears flowed, to relieve a surcharged heart.

"You believe, Harry?" she said again.

"I believe you, dear," he answered her, and lied, for he was still struggling to believe. He wanted to believe, wanted desperately to believe. Because he was aware of this want he was the more distrustful, and ever at the back of his mind was that cursed picture

– the scarlet, gold-laced arm about the lilac shoulders, the woman's face upturned to the man's bowed head.

She looked up. "Harry, my dear, I have suffered so!" The stains of tears on that white face melted him completely. He bent down to kiss her, drawing her closer still. She sighed in his arms. She smiled at him, half-shyly, full tenderly. The vision of herself and Mandeville in the dappled sunshine of the avenue was at last extinguished.

"And now, Harry," her tone was coaxing, "you'll go away. You'll go away at once."

Through his brain crackled the laughter of the imp of jealousy. Back surged that cursed vision, and with it came a memory of words spoken once by Tom Izard in an excess of bitterness. "Women! The truth isn't in them. They'll wheedle and coax and lie to gain their ends, until I believe they deceive themselves as well as their victims."

He loosed his hold of her abruptly, and stepped back.

"So we come back to that!" He was sneering. "When we find the straight road closed, faith, there is always a way round. I might have guessed your aims."

"Harry!" she was affronted, wounded. "Harry! Do you...can you still doubt me? After what I've said?"

"No," he said, and it was like a blow. "I don't doubt you at all."

They stood considering each other in silence after that, whilst you might have counted ten, both faces bloodless. Then, still without speaking, she turned and made for the door, mechanically pulling her calash over her head as she went.

He sprang ahead of her. "Myrtle!"

"The door, if you please," she said.

He opened it, and let her go. Julius was waiting in the hall.

He closed the door after her, and stood a moment leaning against it.

Then, slowly, with bowed head, he crossed the room, and flung himself into a chair. He took his chin in his palms and stared before him like a sightless man, seeking relief in thought, but finding in thought only sharper and ever sharper torture.

Chapter 13

Dea Ex Machina

"I really believe," wrote Lady William Campbell in her diary, "that but for me, my poor Myrtle would have ended by marrying Robert Mandeville, than which I could desire my worst enemy no sadder end." And since I am quoting her ladyship, I may as well add this view of Mandeville, which immediately follows. "Mandeville is a monotheist, worshipping one only god, and that god is Mandeville. He requires not so much a wife as a priestess."

It is impossible in reading these diaries to escape the irresistible attraction of her ladyship's personality. You perceive her in these even lines of small well-formed characters, far more vividly than in the portrait which Copley painted of her a few months after her marriage. On his canvas you behold this boldly handsome woman, between fair and dark, with the generous mouth, the self-assured glance and the majestic carriage; and you gather something of her physical and mental force. But it is only the diaries that afford a complete revelation of her vigorous, uncompromising nature, the strength she could bring to her friendships and her enmities, her audacities of thought and action, her humour and her charm.

As she speaks to us with such complete self-revelation across the gap of a century and a half I feel that she is a woman I should like to have known, and yet by whom I am sure that I should have been overawed.

Without her intervention in the affairs of Myrtle Carey it is indeed probable that Myrtle's story would never have been worth the telling, and a beneficent deity it must have been that inspired Myrtle – in her craving for sympathy and comfort – to seek her ladyship's assistance.

It was done upon the impulse of the moment. The anger in which she had quitted Harry had by now been whelmed again in sorrow and in anxieties on his behalf. To excuse him there was ever the reflection that his harsh intransigence was the result of jealousy, that sour fruit that grows upon the tree of love. But in a measure as she excused him, her own trouble grew, and the need for relief, for sympathy, for help and practical guidance grew with it. In other circumstances she would have sought her father, although tenderness was not a natural quality with him. But in her present difficulties her father was the last person whose aid was to be invoked. And then as her chair, on its way up Tradd Street, was being borne past the corner of Meeting Street, she bethought her of her old friend Sally Izard. The very thought of Sally warmed her, and would have done so even had Sally not been the viceregal, and therefore all-commanding, person that she was.

She gave fresh orders to her chairmen, and obediently they swung to the left into Meeting Street, to set her down at Lady William's door.

The news she brought of Harry's obstinate refusal to leave Charles Town placed Lady William fully as much in need of Myrtle as Myrtle was in need of her ladyship.

The alarm evinced by Lady William and her brother, who happened to be still with her, was more than Myrtle could understand until Tom had made it abundantly clear.

Both announced that they would see Harry at once. There was a world of promise in her ladyship's tone, a world of self-reproach in Tom's for having so long delayed that duty.

"It will be useless," Myrtle told them with conviction. "Useless! Harry is persuaded that the whole thing is a plot of Captain Mandeville's to get rid of him."

"And I believe the same, myself," said Tom, regarding Myrtle with eyes of chill reproof.

Her ladyship, already on her way to the bell-rope, to ring for her carriage, checked and turned to stare from one to the other of them.

She remembered suddenly that if, from what she knew of it, the situation had not actually been engineered by Captain Mandeville, at least he had neglected to do the one thing that might have averted it.

"Why should you say that?" She addressed the question to her brother.

"Because in Harry's place I should have every reason to think the same," said Tom, and turned away.

Her ladyship understood. She came back to stand over the settle on which Myrtle was sitting. "What reason has Harry for thinking this?" she asked. "If I am to help you, Myrtle, you must tell me."

And Myrtle told her. At the end, reviewing Harry's hardness, Myrtle's indignation rose again. She was expressing it when her ladyship checked her.

"Why, what else is the poor man to think, Myrtle. He has your letters giving him his dismissal because you don't agree with his political views. He is distressed. But he doesn't despair because he knows, if he knows anything, that political obstacles are no great matter where there is love. There's no lack of tales like Romeo and Juliet to prove it, my dear. So he comes back to reason with you, and with his own eyes sees you in the arms of Captain Mandeville."

"Sally!" Myrtle turned upon her, flushing scarlet. "Not in his arms. I have told you the truth."

"That you were only half in his arms? But jealousy always magnifies a lover's vision, and in the eyes of Mr Latimer you will have appeared entirely in the arms of the gallant captain. What is the poor man to think? Exactly what he told you. That in his absence your affections had changed, and that you had seized upon his political convictions as a pretext for breaking with him."

"Sally!" And Myrtle was seized with sudden horror. "You don't believe that, too?"

"Not I. But, then, I'm a woman. Man, my dear is a logical animal. He reasons from evidence. And that's the source of all human error. Harry's reasoning is faultless. It's his intuitions that are deplorable."

"But Sally, what am I to do? He will not move. He will remain in defiance of the warrant. And if he remains…" She shuddered, and uttered a little moan, a picture of the gallows arising in her mind.

"I know, I know, dear." Myrtle was drawn to her ladyship's splendid bosom. "We must devise some way."

Her ladyship's mind worked briskly spurred by a necessity which touched herself – through her husband and her brother. At all costs Latimer must be sent packing, or a situation of peril would arise, a conflagration which must consume those she loved best.

"Can you think of nothing, Tom," she asked her brother. "You see how necessary it is that he should go – how necessary it is not only for himself, but for all of us? Could you persuade him do you think?"

"I?" Tom was moved to sarcasm, and out of his sarcasm pointed the way. "Yes, if he'd believe from me what he won't believe from Myrtle herself."

That fired the train. "You think he would go if he could be convinced of your love, Myrtle? If he could be convinced that he has no grounds for jealousy?"

Myrtle considered. "I think he might," she said slowly. Then, conviction growing with reflection: "I am sure he would," she exclaimed. "Jealousy is the only thing that keeps him."

"Then he must be convinced. You must give him proofs."

"But what proofs have I to give? How can I prove such a thing, if my word does not suffice?"

Her ladyship rose. She was in some agitation, struggling really with despair. "Proofs! Proofs!" she cried. "Oh these male fools that must be demanding evidence of what should be obvious. Tom, you're a man and you should know. What would a man consider final proof of a woman's love, short of her dying for him?"

"Sink me, how do I know?" growled Tom, and again it was his sarcasm that fanned the expiring match. "Marriage is sometimes accepted as a proof of affection."

"Marriage!" Her ladyship stared at him across the room, a sudden light in her eyes. He had said it. Out of his fatuity he had solved it. "Myrtle!" she came rustling back to the settle, and sank down beside the girl. Again her arm went round her and she looked closely into her face.

"Myrtle, you love – you really love – Harry Latimer?"

"Of course I love him."

"And you wish to marry him?"

"Some day, of course."

"No, not some day, Myrtle. That may be too late. Today. Tomorrow at the latest."

Myrtle was startled, almost terrified. She was beginning to advance reasons why this could not be, reasons of maidenliness and moonshine, which her ladyship peremptorily swept aside no sooner did she begin to grasp their import.

"Don't you see that it is the only way – the only proof you can give him, and so the only thing that will save his life, and God knows how many other lives as well? It's marriage or hanging for Harry Latimer. And it's for you to decide which."

She left her to think it over, and swept away to an open bureau set in the bay of a French window. She sat down and rapidly scrawled a note to Latimer begging him to give himself the trouble of waiting upon her ladyship immediately. "I have news for you," she wrote, "of the most urgent moment. If you do not come, and at once, you may have cause to regret it all your life."

She folded and sealed the note, and rose. Then she pulled the bell-rope. A woman of quick decisions and prompt action.

"Well?" she demanded of Myrtle. "Have you decided?"

Myrtle's distress was almost pitiful.

"But, Sally, my dear, there are other things to consider. There's father's consent to be obtained – "

"You can obtain your father's consent afterwards, when it's too late for him to refuse it." She handed the note to the servant who entered. "Let the messenger take that at once to Mr Latimer's on the Bay."

The man departed, and her ladyship, elated, triumphant, a little flushed, took up an attitude in the middle of the room.

"There, my dear!"

"Oh, but I am terrified," cried Myrtle, rising in her agitation.

"If it's the prospect of marrying terrifies you," said Tom, lounging forward from the background, "you may spare yourself, Myrtle. It just can't take place."

"What?" his sister demanded.

"Oh, it's like you to carry things with a high hand, Sally. You never see an obstacle until you fall over it. You've forgot the law. This isn't England. Myrtle's not of age, and can't marry without her father's consent. There's not a parson in the colony would tie the knot; and if he did, it wouldn't hold."

That staggered her ladyship. And it almost looked as if it staggered Myrtle, too, instead of affording her relief from the terror she had last expressed. She sat down again, limp and helpless

"Oh!" was all she said. But she couldn't have packed more dismay into a volume.

"We must obtain Sir Andrew's consent, then," declared her undaunted ladyship.

But Tom was so unfeeling as to laugh outright. "Blister me, Sally, it'd be easier to get the law altered."

And Myrtle confirmed him by a brief statement of the extent of the breach between Harry and her father.

This was checkmate, as even her ladyship was forced to admit. She sat down heavily, and for half an hour or more they talked round and round the subject, as trapped creatures go round and round an enclosure seeking a way out. And the only noteworthy feature of that barren conversation was the fact that Myrtle, who whilst no difficulties presented themselves had known only terror at the prospect of immediate marriage, was now as eager as either of the other two to discover a way into that estate.

And then Mr Latimer arrived, more promptly even than they could have hoped, now that they had no real proposal to lay before him. He came into the room, expecting to find her ladyship alone. He checked and stared at sight of her two companions. Then he bowed gravely.

Lady William went forward to receive him, and drove straight to the heart of the matter.

"Harry," she said, "you have been very cruel to this poor child."

"Madam," said he, "I have been under the impression that this poor child has been very cruel to me."

"That's because you have no eyes."

"On the contrary, ma'am, I have; and my sight's uncommon good."

"In your body, yes – in your great stupid obstinate head, Harry. But it's eyes in your soul I mean."

"Must we go into this?" said Harry, with elaborate calm. "If I had known – "

"You wouldn't have come. That's why I didn't tell you. But you'll probably go down on your knees tonight, and thank God that you did come."

You conceive what were now the arguments employed by her ladyship in the quality of Myrtle's advocate, and with what effect and overbearing force she pleaded Myrtle's case.

At least it startled him out of the sternness in which he had wrapped himself. He looked at Myrtle in amazement, and in something, too, of fear.

"You mean," he breathed, almost timidly, and could get no further.

"That since you demand proofs of her love for you Myrtle is prepared to afford you the only final proof a woman can give a man. In defiance of her father, at the cost if need be of breaking with him, she is prepared to marry you out of hand. That is the sacrifice to which this poor lamb offers herself so as to persuade you of her loyalty and devotion, and so as to save your life."

"Myrtle!" He advanced towards her, a great tenderness in his voice and his eyes. "Myrtle, my dear, is this really true?"

"Ay, humble yourself," her ladyship lashed him. "It will be good for your soul."

Myrtle rose to meet him, and took the hands he held out. "Yes, Harry. I swear that I would marry you at once, if it were possible."

"If it were possible?" he echoed, suddenly chilled again, already suspecting a trap.

"Ah!" put in Tom. "It isn't possible. That's the rub. But Myrtle meant it. Blister me, she did, Harry. The note was dispatched to you before we saw the obstacle."

Oh, there was an obstacle! Still holding Myrtle's hands but holding them mechanically, Harry looked round at the others, and thought he understood the trick. Myrtle was anxious to save his life, she had still sufficient affection for him for that, as indeed she had already proved. Having failed she had come to Lady William with her distress. And Lady William in her anxiety to rescue her husband from a very difficult position had conceived this very clever way of allaying his jealousy so as to remove the one insuperable obstacle to his departure. And she had fooled Tom into being a party to the deception. He was moved to contempt. Yet he commanded himself.

"But what is the obstacle?" he asked

It was Tom who explained.

"The law of the colony. Myrtle isn't of age. Her father's consent will be necessary, and in the present state of your relations with Sir Andrew – "

He got no further. Her ladyship interrupted him, crying out on an inspiration:

"But the law of the colonies doesn't run in England."

Harry's irony was not to be repressed.

"Your ladyship is proposing that we should go to England to be married?"

"Exactly!" She betrayed a faint excitement.

"Oh, rot me, Sally!" her brother protested.

"You need go no farther than the bay," she explained. "There's a British man-of-war at anchor there. There's a chaplain aboard the *Tamar*, and aboard the *Tamar* you will be in England under the shelter of the English law."

"By God!" said Tom, and it expressed their general amazement.

Harry stared at her ladyship a moment. So, she was sincere after all! He had done her an injustice. Then he turned to Myrtle, and Myrtle's eyes were veiled from his own by fluttering eyelids.

"You are willing, Myrtle?" He asked her softly, and even as he asked, he was drawing her towards him, his furiously suspicious jealousy laid to rest at last before this culminating proof that he was preferred to Mandeville.

"If – if you want me, Harry," she answered "and if it can be done as Sally says."

"You may leave the doing to me," said Sally. "I'll settle everything, even to the wedding-breakfast which shall be served aboard. And now, Tom, I think they'll contrive very well without us." And she swept her brother out of the room.

Chapter 14

The Solution

In the Council Chamber of the State House, sat Lord William Campbell and such members of his majesty's Council as still possessed the courage and the inclination to function. They were assembled to receive the Speaker of the Commons, whom his excellency had summoned, and who was punctual in his response.

Rawlins Lowndes, a man of fifty, who looked the planter that he was in private life, and yet conveyed also in his person some sense of the dignity and austerity acquired in the course of his activities first as Provost Marshal of the province and then as Speaker of the House, came accompanied by two members of the Assembly, the portly, genial Henry Laurens and the cold, aloof John Rutledge.

They stood to listen to the Governor's complaint of last night's riot, his censure of those responsible for keeping the peace in Charles Town, and his inquiry as to what measures it was proposed to take to punish the offenders and to ensure against the repetition of an outrage in which a loyal and faithful subject of his majesty's had been barbarously and inhumanly done to death, and the King himself affronted and insulted in the person of his representative, the Governor of South Carolina.

Rawlins Lowndes replied with calm that a committee should be appointed, and the matter investigated. At the same time he confessed the powerlessness of the Commons Assembly to avoid such outbreaks in times of popular excitement. He pointed out to his lordship that violent conduct by mobs was not peculiar to the colonies; that the same at that present time were to be seen with even greater frequency and violence in London itself; that it was the characteristic of Englishmen, whether at home in the heart of the empire or in one of its distant colonies to resent and rise against oppression and unjust rule.

"The fact, sir," he concluded, "that we reside at a distance of three thousand miles from the royal palace and the seat of Government does not alter our natures any more than it modifies our rights."

This was to diverge into a political side-track, and it was with reluctance that the Governor yielded to the compulsion to follow.

"Of what particular injustice do you complain, sir?"

"I allude, my lord, to the unjust policy of which this unfortunate man who lost his life was the tool and servant. He was known to be ministering to the unhappy design of the royal Government to endeavour to quell the American troubles by coercion of arms, instead of seeking to quiet them by the laws of reason and justice."

Thus Lowndes contrived to make of the case of Featherstone a vehicle for a re-statement of the colonial cause to the royal representative.

"It was known," the Speaker continued, "that this man, acting as a spy of the royal Government, had imperilled the lives of men who were honestly working to preserve the peace of the colony, and thereby the integrity of the British Empire. When that is understood, can you wonder that in their indignation the people should have risen in vengeance as they did last night?"

Lord William sighed wearily and dejectedly. "If I understand you aright, sir, you are conveying to me that no redress is to be expected. Is that your notion of how to conciliate the royal Government? You come to me with empty phrases of loyalty on your lips and treason in your hearts. I am growing accustomed to it. I am also growing accustomed to your accusations against the Government I represent of a conduct which is peculiarly your own. You speak of quieting the present troubles by reason and justice. Compare in this very business we are considering your own attitude with mine. The ringleader, the inciter of this mob is known to me, as he is known to you. I should be within my rights, indeed, it is my solemn duty, to arrest and punish him out of hand. Yet for the sake of peace, to propitiate the colony, to avoid any explosion of feeling which would justify my Government in that recourse to arms with which you reproach it, I have held my hand.

"I have contented myself with asking Mr Latimer to withdraw from the province, and I have accorded him forty-eight hours in which to do so. How does he meet my generosity? Captain Mandeville, here, informs me that he is utterly defiant. He asserts that he will remain to force my hand, to compel me to arrest him, confident that such an action will destroy the peace which I am so concerned to preserve. Would he do this, would he dare to do this, unless he had the support of authority behind him?"

"My lord, you wrong us there," Lowndes answered him warmly. "Mr Rutledge and Colonel Laurens here can both testify to that."

And upon his invitation, Rutledge stood forward, to state correctly and coldly that with Colonel Laurens he had used every endeavour of persuasion and of threat to induce Mr Latimer to depart.

"You threatened him?" the Governor questioned. "With what did you threaten him?"

"I told him clearly, my lord, that if he were arrested as a consequence of his obstinacy, the whole of such influence as I possess in this colony would be exerted against him and in vindication of your lordship's authority."

Some of the gloom was dispelled from his lordship's countenance. "Do you really assure me of that, sir?"

"As solemnly as I assured him," replied Rutledge without emotion. "If your excellency desires me I will undertake, myself, his prosecution. Judge from this, my lord, whether we are lukewarm in the cause of peace, whether we, too, are not prepared for almost any sacrifice to reach a settlement without being compelled to take up arms in defence of the common and unalienable rights peculiar to Englishmen."

Not until they had departed upon his lordship's friendly dismissal, and with them were gone, too, the members of the council, did the Governor give full expression to his satisfaction. His audience was made up of Captain Mandeville and a Major Sykes, the commander of the small garrison at Fort Johnson on James Island, at the harbour's mouth, an officer lately appointed to the council to fill one of the many gaps appearing in it.

Major Sykes, a loosely-built, red-complexioned Irishman with a freckled bony face and freckled hairy hands, cordially congratulated his excellency on this happy issue. His manners, like his morals, were those of a led-captain, and indeed the position which he held was one fit only for a needy military adventurer.

"Sure now there's an end to your lordship's perplexities about this blackguard," he laughed. He was free with his laughter, and boisterous.

His lordship pensively smiled as he lolled back in the great chair of state, set at the end of that big bare room with its rudely-carved wainscoting. Mandeville alone, sitting on his lordship's right, at the top of the long council table, remained glum and preoccupied. The solution of the Governor's perplexities was but the resumption of his own. For conscious of his vulnerability the very last thing he desired was that Latimer should be brought to trial in Charles Town. The exposure with which Latimer had threatened him would certainly ruin him with Carey, and might even cost him his life as well at the hands of an infuriated people.

"I wish I could share your lordship's optimism," he ventured presently.

"What now?" quoth his lordship, checked in the indulgence of his satisfaction.

"Can you trust these men?"

"Trust them? Why should they be dishonest with me?"

"I mean, can you trust their judgment? Rutledge may use his influence, as he says. But what will his influence be worth once he attempts to oppose the stream of popular feeling?" He shook his head. "Politicians, my lord, preserve their influence by following where they seem to lead. And Rutledge is a politician. Also he is vain, and his vanity deceives him. He attributes to the power of his own oratory the popularity he enjoys. His oratory succeeds because it tells his audiences the things they want to hear. The moment he tells something different, there's an end to his influence and his leadership. The people are like that in every land, and in every age. Pin your faith to Rutledge now, and you'll find him become a man of straw, to be scattered by the burst of popular indignation he'll provoke."

And Sykes approved him: "By God! Mandeville, it's right ye are, every word of you. Sure, don't I know it. And doesn't your lordship?"

Upon reflection, his lordship thought he did, despite his youth and inexperience. He stared from one to the other of them, his complacency shaken.

"Amongst the English races," Mandeville resumed, "it is ever the people who rule. They tolerate none but complacent masters who obediently perform their sovereign will. And amongst none of the English races is that trait more marked than among these independent colonials, as witness the things that are happening now. If we had the troops here it would be another story. But as we haven't, I make so bold as to say that I agree with Latimer in the confidence he reposes in popular feeling."

"Why here's a change, Mandeville!" cried his dismayed lordship. "First it was you who counselled proceedings against Latimer, and I who held back."

"Latimer's obstinate refusal to budge, his determination to remain and force the issue have opened my eyes. Would he do that if he were not very sure of where he stands."

"Then what am I to do? What? In heaven's name!"

Mandeville shrugged.

"I don't presume to advise," he said. "The situation bristles with thorns. But I think that in your lordship's place, I should get rid of Latimer with the least inconvenience to myself."

The Governor caught his breath, whilst from under white eyelashes the blue eyes of Major Sykes looked almost apprehensively at Mandeville.

"What are your suggesting?" gasped his lordship.

Mandeville rose, and leaned forward across the table. "I should have him quietly seized tomorrow night, and put aboard the *Tamar* for immediate conveyance to England to stand his trial there."

Sykes laughed in his noisy fashion. "Begad, I thought you were proposing to have his throat cut!"

"Faith so did I," added the Governor in obvious relief.

Again Mandeville shrugged, contemptuously this time.

"But where shall I stand when it is known?" Lord William asked him.

"It won't be known for months – not until news of it is brought out from England, and by then much may have happened."

"It'll be known the moment he disappears!"

"Not if it is done with proper care. Latimer will simply vanish, and the natural assumption will be that in the end he has preferred not to await arrest. That is why I suggest tomorrow night. That he should have gone secretly can be explained by reluctance to admit himself unequal to maintaining his bombast. Some may suspect us. But what is suspicion?"

"You are forgetting my terms to him. I gave him forty-eight hours grace: until Friday morning."

"Those terms he has rejected. He has announced his firm determination of remaining in Charles Town. What obligation of honour, is there, then, to await the expiry of the forty-eight hours?"

The Governor sank together in his chair, and brooded awhile.

"It would be an easy way out of the trouble," he said slowly, musingly. "But – " He broke off suddenly, and sat up again. "No. It is impossible. The first question asked me – and where there are suspicions, there must be questions – would lay the whole thing bare. If I ordered this, how could I afterwards deny knowledge of it?"

Mandeville did not immediately reply. He stroked his chin thoughtfully. Then, at last, he fetched a sigh.

"Ay! You've put your finger on the real difficulty." He paused before adding: "We'll say no more about it."

His lordship grumbled ineffectively, and rose to return home. Outside under the pillared portico of the State House, Mandeville, having seen the Governor depart, linked arms with Sykes.

"If you're for the wharves, I'll walk with you, major."

And arm-in-arm the two red-coated officers took their way down Broad Street, and came out on to the bay. At Motte's Wharf a wherry was drawn up manned by a dozen blacks in bright-coloured cottons, waiting to convey the major back to the fort. As he put out his hand in leave-taking, Mandeville, broached at last the matter in his mind.

"You have understood what is to be done, major?"

The Irishman's blank stare was a question in itself. Mandeville answered it.

"His excellency is to be saved in spite of himself."

Sykes caught his meaning; but no more than that.

"How is it possible at all?" he asked.

"Didn't you understand him? 'If I ordered this, how could I afterwards deny knowledge of it?' That was his question. Isn't the answer plain? He hasn't ordered it, and therefore he can deny all knowledge of it when he comes to be questioned."

"Oddsblud!" spluttered Sykes. "Was that his meaning, now?"

"You surely never doubted it! And he meant it for you, major. You've the only lads we could use for this, down at the fort. Bring half-a-dozen of them up to town tomorrow night, and net your bird."

Sykes stood a moment, considering.

"And if we should be mistaken, after all? If the Governor never meant it? Ye see it's impossible to ask him."

"You may leave the responsibility to me, Sykes."

Again Sykes considered. Then he shrugged and laughed.

"If you put it like that now, faith I'll certainly oblige." And then another doubt occurred to him. "But without an order from the Governor, how will Thornborough receive him aboard the *Tamar*?"

"He won't. And you needn't put him aboard the *Tamar*. The *Lass of Hale* should sail for Bristol with the evening tide tomorrow. I'll send a word to her captain to wait until the following morning. She'll serve our purpose. He'll go home in irons aboard her."

"Ay, she's convenient to the fort," Sykes agreed.

"And if the fellow should give you trouble," Mandeville instinctively lowered his voice, "don't be tender of him. An accident would be no great matter. I'm not sure that it wouldn't be the best solution after all."

It was not a suggestion upon which Mandeville would have ventured had he been less assured of the utter unscrupulousness of the man to whom he offered it.

Sykes closed an eye in token of intelligence; then he asked some further questions concerned with the means to be employed, to all of which the equerry smoothly supplied him with ready answers. Satisfied at last, Sykes stepped into the waiting wherry, and was pulled away across the sunlit water.

At supper that night, Mandeville found the Governor entirely recovered from the gloom in which last he had left him at the State House. The reason for this was presently disclosed.

"Mandeville, our riddle's solved. I have Mr Latimer's assurance that he will be gone from Charles Town within the time appointed."

And so taken aback was Mandeville that he uttered his thought aloud: "Now why the devil couldn't the fool have said so sooner!"

It raised a laugh, for there was something almost comical in the dismay of that usually imperturbable countenance.

"It remained for her ladyship to persuade him," the Governor answered, beaming upon Lady William. "What witchery she employed I can't guess nor will she tell me."

"Lady William's witchery is not of the kind that drives men away," said Captain Mandeville.

"La!" said her ladyship. "Here's unusual gallantry!"

"Gallantry, madam!" Mandeville affected grief at being so misunderstood. "I employed no gallantry. I but pointed to a mystery."

"And mysterious we'll leave it," she answered lightly. Adding nevertheless a jest whose meaning was clear only to herself. "I'll not have Captain Mandeville gnashing his teeth before he must."

But as a matter of fact, he was gnashing them already over the unnecessary measures he had taken, measures which must now be cancelled. So that Latimer went, the manner of his going was no great matter. If on the whole the captain would have preferred it to have been as he had concerted with Major Sykes, yet, on the other hand, Latimer's departure of his own free will would spare Mandeville the necessity of subsequent difficult explanations. Therefore, he was content.

Chapter 15

The Nuptials

Everything concerned with Myrtle's marriage fell out precisely as her ladyship promised and subsequently planned which was the way of things of which her ladyship had the planning.

To quiet Myrtle's grievous misgivings on the score of her father, her ladyship undertook that after the departure of the bridal couple she would, herself, not merely inform Sir Andrew of what had been done, but compel him to see reason and obtain his pardon for the runagates.

"And never doubt that I shall," said Lady William with convincing emphasis. "What men can't alter they soon condone."

Thus, out of her own splendid confidence, she allayed at last Myrtle's lingering fears and only abiding regrets.

So much accomplished, her ladyship unfolded the further details of her plan for getting the couple safely away. The Brewton's ball that same Thursday night, being of an almost official character, Lady William's viceregal position demanded that she should go attended by two ladies of honour. From the position of one of these she would depose her cousin Jane in favour of Myrtle. As a result, Myrtle would be expected to attend her throughout, and to facilitate this Lady William would arrange with Sir Andrew that Myrtle be allowed to spend the night at the Governor's residence. Thus the bridal couple would be ensured a clear and unhampered start whilst all Charles

Town was still entirely unsuspicious. For the rest, the real arrangement was that Harry Latimer should be at hand with a travelling carriage, and that as soon as Myrtle could conveniently leave the ball without being missed, she should join him, and they should immediately start for his plantation at Santee Broads, a drive of fifty miles, which would consume the whole of the night. Thence, after resting, they were to push on to a distant estate of Mr Latimer's in the hills above Salisbury, where for the present they were to abide. There in the cotton fields of North Carolina, their honeymoon might peacefully be spent without fear of pursuit from any save Sir Andrew, who would in any case be powerless to untie the knot which the law of England was so securely to tie aboard the *Tamar*.

And so, soon after breakfast on Thursday morning Myrtle departed from Tradd Street, on the pretext that her ladyship had bidden her come early. There would be a deal to do in preparation for the ball she casually announced in explanation.

"Not a doubt," said her father. And when he beheld the dimensions of the clothes-box that was being borne after her he raised eyes and hands to heaven. "Lord! The vanity of woman!"

But Myrtle was already down the steps and into her sedan chair, lest he should detect the tears that had suddenly come to fill her eyes at the thought that she was definitely leaving her father's home, and leaving it under cover of a deceit.

It needed all Lady William's stout cheeriness and confidence to dispel the black clouds that were gathering about Myrtle's soul when presently she came into her ladyship's radiant presence. Nor was she given much time for further brooding. Within a half-hour of reaching the Governor's residence, she was taking boat at the Exchange Wharf with her ladyship, a boat manned by four British tars and commanded by a pert boy-officer.

Out in the bay, as they drew near the *Tamar*, with her black-and-white hull, the snowy sails furled along her yards and the gleam of brass from her deck, they were joined by another boat, rowed by blacks in Linsey-woolsey jackets, and carrying Harry Latimer and Tom Izard.

In the waist of the warship they found a guard of honour drawn up, whilst Captain Thornborough, the handsome sunburnt officer in command of the sloop, came forward to receive them.

All was ready as her ladyship had predisposed. But to satisfy the pretext on which they came there was first a tour of inspection of the ship. When this was over, the captain invited the guests to a glass of Madeira in his cabin before leaving. He contrived unostentatiously to include in the invitation the chaplain who had, somehow, got in the way at the last moment.

In the cabin no time was wasted. No sooner had the steward retired after pouring for them, than with naval dispatch, Captain Thornborough made them come to business. The chaplain was brisk, and confined himself to the essentials of the ceremony. Within a few minutes all was accomplished and the captain of the *Tamar* was raising his glass to toast Mrs Henry Latimer.

"I'd fire a salute in your honour, ma'am, but it would occasion questions we may not be prepared to answer."

In the vessel's waist, where they had met scarcely an hour ago, husband and wife parted again for the present, and Myrtle and Lady William went down the steps to the waiting cock-boat.

Myrtle bore now on her finger the ring that had belonged to Harry's mother, the very ring that once, and not so long ago, she had returned to him. In her heart she bore perhaps the oddest conflict of emotions that has ever been a bride's. There was happiness in the thought that Harry now belonged to her, and that nothing could ever again come between them; there was happiness, too, in the reflection that thus she had conquered Harry's obstinacy and jealous doubts and prevailed upon him to save his life by leaving Charles Town. But there were regrets at the manner of her marriage, and infinitely more poignant regrets at the thought of what her father must suffer in his affection and his pride when he learnt of these hole-and-corner nuptials between herself and a man against whom he bore a prejudice that was amounting almost to hatred.

There were tears blurring her vision as she looked back over the waves on which the sunlight was dancing to that other boat at the foot of the ship's ladder into which her husband and his friend were stepping. And the boy-officer chatting briskly with Lady William gave her ladyship no opportunity to offer Myrtle any of the comfort of which she perceived the poor child to stand in need.

They reached at last the Exchange Wharf, and whilst a sailor held the boat firmly alongside by means of a boathook, the gallant stripling of an officer, standing on the wet slippery steps, handed the ladies ashore, to bring them face to face with Captain Mandeville.

Delayed until then by official duties, the captain was on his way to Fort Johnson to inform Major Sykes that his services that night would no longer be required. He was looking about for a wherry to convey him at the very moment that the cockboat from the *Tamar* containing her ladyship and Myrtle drew alongside the wharf.

Lady William, conscious as she was of being engaged upon a deed of secrecy, paused to stare at him, suspecting an excess of coincidence in his presence. Nor did his air of surprise allay her suspicions, as it should have done, for Captain Mandeville was not the man to show surprise when he actually felt it.

He doffed his black three-cornered hat and bowed.

"I did not know your ladyship addicted to water-jaunts."

Myrtle, esteeming him, persuaded of his sincere and selfless friendship, and detesting fraud beyond what was absolutely necessary to her safety and Harry's, would there and then have given him the real reason for her journeyings by water, had not her ladyship forestalled her.

"I am not," she told the equerry. "But Captain Thornborough offered to show his ship to Myrtle, and the child had never been aboard a man-of-war. But we detain you, captain," she added, bethinking her of the second boat that followed, and preferring that he should not stay to meet its occupants.

"No, no," he answered. "I am not pressed. I am only going to Fort Johnson. I was looking for a boat. I trust you found the man-of-war all that you expected it, Myrtle?"

"Why, yes," she said, and lowered her lids under his sharp gaze lest he should perceive the signs of tears about her eyes.

"But we have no enthusiasm," he faintly rallied her, smiling.

Her ladyship promptly rescued her.

"Come, Myrtle. The man will keep us talking here all day."

"Nay, a moment, of your mercy. This may be my only chance before the ball tonight."

"Your chance of what?"

"To ensure myself the dance I covet. The first minuet, Myrtle, if you will honour me so far?"

"But, of course, Robert." And impulsively she held out her hand.

He took it, and bareheaded as he had remained, bowed low over it. For an instant, as he did so, his eyes dilated; but his bowed head screened this from both the ladies. And then her ladyship whirled Myrtle away without further ceremony.

He stood watching them until they were lost in the bustling crowd about the New Exchange. Then, slowly resuming his hat, a deep line of thought between his fine brows, he turned his attention once more to that other craft which had already caught his eye.

He signalled to a wherry to stand by, but made no move to enter it until the boat he watched was alongside, and out of it sprang Latimer and Tom Izard. They exchanged bows formally, and without words, despite the fact that the equerry was – or had been – on easy terms with her ladyship's brother. Then Captain Mandeville stepped into the boat he had summoned, and sat down in the stern-sheets.

"Push off," he curtly bade the negroes.

The four men bent to their oars, and the boat shot away from the wharf.

"Where does yo' honour want fer to go?" the nearest negro asked him.

Captain Mandeville considered a long moment. Then he stretched out a hand to grasp the tiller.

"To the sloop *Tamar*," he answered.

When he reached her decks, her captain was below, but he came instantly upon being informed that the Governor's equerry had come aboard.

"Ah, Mandeville! Good-day to you," he greeted him.

Mandeville gave him a short good-day in return. "I want a word with you in private, Thornborough."

The sailor looked at him, mildly surprised by his tone.

"Come aft to my cabin," he invited, and led the way.

Mandeville sat down upon a locker with his back to the square windows that opened upon the stern gallery. On the table before him he observed a book, a decanter at a low ebb, and six glasses, in two of which a little wine remained. He could account for five of the glasses and assumed the sixth to have been for some other offficer of the *Tamar*.

Thornborough, standing straight and tall in his blue uniform with white facings, looked at him questioningly across the table.

"Well?" he asked. "What brings you?"

"Mr Harry Latimer has been aboard your ship this morning."

He had deliberately placed himself so that the light was on Thornborough's face, and his own in shadow. Watching the sailor now, he fancied that his eyes shifted a little to avoid his own. Also there was a perceptible pause before Thornborough answered him.

"That is so. What then?"

"What do you know of him?"

"I? What should I know? He is a wealthy colonial gentleman. But you should know more about him, yourself."

"I do. That is why I am questioning you. What was he doing aboard your ship?"

Thornborough stiffened. "Sink me, Mandeville! What's the reason for this catechism?"

"This fellow Latimer is a rebel, a dangerous spreader of sedition, and a daring spy. That is my reason. That is why I ask you what he came to do aboard your ship."

Thornborough laughed. "It had nothing to do with spying. Of that I can assure you. What should he have spied here that could profit him?"

"You are not forgetting that you have Kirkland on board?" Mandeville asked him.

"All Charles Town knows that. What should Mr Latimer discover by spying on Kirkland?"

"Possibly he came to ascertain whether he is still here. But if you were to tell me on what pretext he did come, I might be able to obtain a glimpse of his real reason."

It happened, however, that Thornborough's instructions from Lady William were quite explicit; and in nothing that Mandeville had said could he see any reason for departing from them.

"Mandeville, you're hunting a mare's nest. Mr Latimer came aboard with Lady William Campbell and one or two others so as to view a British man-of-war. To suppose that he could discover here anything of possible advantage to his party or of detriment to ours is ridiculous."

"You may find that you take too much for granted, Thornborough." Mandeville spoke mysteriously. As he spoke he rose, and proceeded to relate to the sailor how Latimer had visited the Governor only yesterday in disguise and pumped him dry on more than one subject. "If I had not subsequently discovered this, and ascertained the extent of the information he drew from us, I might have remained as unsuspecting as yourself."

Whilst speaking, he had idly picked up the book from the table, to make the surprising discovery that it was a book of Common Prayer. A book-mark of embroidered silk hung from its pages, and the book opened naturally in Mandeville's hands at the Marriage Service, which was the place marked. Idly he continued to turn its leaves. He even looked at the name on the fly-leaf, which was "Robert Faversham." It was odd to find such a volume on the captain's table. He set it down again, and assuming at last that Thornborough really had nothing to tell him beyond the fact which he had desired to ascertain – namely that Latimer actually had been on board the ship in Myrtle's company – he took his leave.

With a final admonition to Thornborough to be careful of whom he admitted to his sloop, the equerry went down the entrance ladder to his waiting boat, with intent to resume his voyage to the Fort. But within a dozen cables' length of the *Tamar* he abruptly changed his mind.

"Put about," he ordered, and added curtly: "Back to Charles Town."

He was obeyed without question, and the clumsy boat swung round to pull against the tide, which was beginning to ebb.

Ahead of them, drenched in brilliant sunshine, and looking dazzlingly white, the low-lying town appeared to float like another Venice upon the sea, the water front dominated by the classical pile of the Custom House with its ionic pillars and imposing entablature, whilst above the red roofs towered the spires of St Philip's and St Michael's, the latter so lofty that it served as a landmark for ships far out at sea.

Captain Mandeville, however, beheld nothing but a slender, woman's hand, with white tapering fingers protruding from mittens of white silk, and round one of these fingers a circlet of gold, gleaming through the strained silken meshes.

That in some mysterious way Myrtle and Harry had become reconciled was clear from their joint presence aboard the *Tamar*, whilst the discovery of that restored ring betrayed the fact that the reconciliation had gone the extent of renewing their betrothal.

That was reason enough to restrain him from going to Fort Johnson to bid Sykes hold his hand. At all costs, and whatever the consequence with which the Governor might afterwards visit him, Mandeville must allow the plan laid with Sykes to be carried out. He was in a difficult position. But he must deal with one difficulty at a time, and in dealing first with Harry Latimer he dealt with the more imminent danger to himself and all his hopes.

He sat there, elbow on knee and chin in hand, absorbed in thought, piecing together little tenuous scraps of evidence, and plagued to irritation the while by the obstinate association in his mind of the ring he had seen on her finger and the book he had found on Captain Thornborough's table. Those things and that visit of theirs to the sloop that morning forced a dreadful suspicion on his mind, a suspicion too dreadful to be entertained. He rejected it, as wildly fantastic; and yet the thought of the ring and the book persisted until he was landing on the wharf at Charles Town. Finally he shook it off. "What can it matter, after all?" he asked himself. "Sykes will make it all of no account tonight. I rid the State of a dangerous enemy and myself of a dangerous rival at one stroke. And I shall be treading a minuet whilst it is done."

Chapter 16

The Chaplain of the *Tamar*

That ball at the State House, given by Miles Brewton in honour of the new Governor of South Carolina, was of a piece with, indeed almost an epitome of, the ironic situation presented in those June days in Charles Town. If the spirit of tragedy gloomed upon the gay scene, the spirit of comedy was cheek by jowl with it, agrin.

Here, above smouldering passions and festering hates born of man's eternal misunderstandings and intolerance, and presently to find vent in war, was maintained an unruffled surface, reflecting only the amenities and courtesies of peace.

Actually the place chosen for the fête was itself the very nidus of the growing conflict. Above stairs were the chamber in which the representatives of the two contending parties met in conference; the room in which the Commons assembly, constituting itself into a Provincial Congress, debated measures for meeting the despotic oppression of the Mother Country; and the room in which the Governor and his council met for little purpose nowadays but to study how to subdue this transatlantic Jeshurun which, having waxed fat and lusty under the maternal aegis of the British Empire, was now kicking rebelliously against its parent.

Tonight one of those chambers was to concern itself with no strife of greater acerbity than the amicable contests proper to the green-clad card tables laid out for those who did not dance; the other was converted into a place of refreshment; a buffet ranged against one of the walls from end to end of the long room, laden with boned turkeys, game pies, jellied terrapins, gigantic sweetmeats in which sculptor appeared to have collaborated with confectioner, and a dozen other delicacies. And a troop of dusky servants paraded here, white teeth flashing in ebony faces that grinned already in anticipation of the feast's aftermath that should be their own. They were assembled to minister alike to loyalist and rebel, who as indifferently would presently take a punch or eat a quail in each other's company, exchanging quips as readily tonight, as tomorrow or the next day they might be exchanging pistol-shots.

Surveying the scene later that evening with Lady William, Captain Mandeville offered upon it an ironic comment which her ladyship thought it worth while to preserve for us in that diary of hers:

"There is this advantage in breeding, that until the moment when necessity bids men fight like beasts they may make things pleasant by conducting themselves like gentlemen."

The great hall below stairs was as gay as flowers and bunting and candle-laden chandeliers and girandoles could render it. At one end a gallery had been raised for the musicians, at the other a shallow dais, which was carpeted and furnished with gilded chairs for the Governor and his site.

Over the waxed and gleaming floor a throng as brilliant and fashionable as any that in a similar gathering the old world could show moved with well-bred and appropriate languor, with bows and curtsies, with slow waving of fans and nodding plumes set above powdered head-dresses, with flash of quizzing glasses and glitter of jewels.

It was a scene that would have amazed some of the gentlemen at home in Westminster who legislated condescendingly for these colonials under the impression that they were rude farmers at best and half-savages at worst.

And the irony which this function presented in general was still more keenly apparent in its particulars. There was Moultrie, square and sturdy in the blue coat with scarlet facings of the South Carolina militia, which was worn by perhaps a dozen others present. He was in easy talk with Captain Thornborough and a group of officers in the blue and white of the Royal Navy who had come ashore to attend this function; and with him, very gay and voluble, was the young republican Thomas Lynch. There was John Rutledge, handsome and impassive as ever, very elegant in an elaborately clubbed white tie-wig and a suit of violet taffetas with gold-laced buttonholes, deep in talk with the scarlet-coated, foppish Captain Davenant, who was Major Sykes' second-in-command at Fort Johnson. The Major, himself, for some reason unaccountable to Davenant, was not present. Miss Polly Roupell, the famous beauty, the toast of the Charles Town bucks and a white flame of loyalty, was gay and challenging to the equally gay and brilliant rebel William Henry Drayton; that other notorious and daring rebel, Captain MacDonald, in the blue and scarlet of the militia, was entertaining and clearly amusing the two daughters of the house of Cunningham, that most tory of all the back-country families; the youngest Fletchall, of that other ardent tory house, very spruce in pink and silver, spread his charms to dazzle the pretty rebel Miss Middleton, whilst the gaunt, stern-faced John Stuart, the King's Indian agent, himself looking like an Indian, was doing homage to the still beautiful Mrs Henry Laurens.

Had not nature rendered prominent as a frog's the eyes of George III – which looked down upon the assembly from the portrait by Sir Joshua Reynolds hung for the occasion above the daisset apart for his majesty's representative – well might they now have bulged to see rebel and loyalist rubbing shoulders there in such open amity.

But if the eyes of King George, being merely painted upon canvas, were incapable of emotion, those of Sir Andrew Carey were not. He kept himself aloof and apart with the elder Fletchall under the lintel of one of the French windows, which stood open to the garden and the cool evening air.

To a man of his narrow, uncompromising, almost fanatical outlook there was much here that was utterly incomprehensible and some things that enraged him. One of these was the sight of those militia uniforms – to him the very livery of treason – at a ball given in honour of his gracious majesty's representative. Another was that gentlemen of his majesty's navy should be passing the time of day with that detestable fellow Lynch, to whose ultimate hanging Sir Andrew looked forward confidently and pleasurably. And then these frivolous young women, whose minds went no deeper than a matter of powder and patches and the set of a French gown, chopping shallow wit with avowed rebels was to him a spectacle shocking and deplorable.

He was expressing himself to Fletchall in some such terms, and vowing that he would rather see his daughter dead than so lost to a sense of what became her, when above the rolling hum of talk and laughter and to subdue it, the orchestra suddenly crashed forth.

The solemn strains of "God Save the King" announced the arrival of the Governor. Instantly there was a shuffling of feet, and the gay confused throng ranged itself into some semblance of order, leaving a clear space by the entrance, and a clear way to the dais. Sir Andrew observed but did not permit himself to be deceived by the circumstances that the rebel militia officers present came to attention as readily as any, and stood so, in homage to the King, throughout the anthem.

On the closing bars of the music Lord William made his appearance, a handsome figure in ivory satin, a blaze of orders on his breast, his face looking almost boyish below his powdered head. Beside him stood her ladyship, radiant in cloth of gold over white brocade, an incarnation of regality such as – by one of life's abounding ironies – is rarely achieved by those of regal birth.

There was a sound as of wind in trees; a slither of feet and a rustle of silks, as, with billowing hoops, the ladies sank down to curtsey and each man bowed low over outward thrusting leg.

Then, to welcome their excellencies, Miles Brewton advanced with his comely wife, who had been Polly Izard and was her ladyship's sister. And here again was ubiquitously intruding irony. For Miles Brewton, the promoter of this ball in honour of King George's representative, the friend of Lord William and the brother-in-law of her ladyship was, himself, an open adherent of the colonial party and a member of the Provincial Congress.

His words of welcome were brief and graceful. They were expressed on behalf of "his majesty's faithful and loving subjects of Charles Town, here assembled," a description which provoked an audible snort of contempt from Sir Andrew Carey.

Lord William's reply was almost equally brief and fully as gracious. He thanked them on his own and Lady William's behalf, and took this opportunity of declaring feelingly that Charles Town might count upon him to labour earnestly to promote the real happiness and prosperity of the province he was sent to govern.

Thereafter, with nods and smiles of greeting as they passed up the room, the viceregal pair moved to the dais, followed by his excellency's equerries, Captains Mandeville and Tasker, and her ladyship's ladies of honour, Miss Carey and Miss Ravenell.

The band struck up an invitation, and the gentlemen sought their partners for the minuet. Lord William led forth, as his duty was, his sister-in-law and nominal hostess, and her ladyship followed on the arm of Mr Brewton, whilst the equerries paired off with the ladies of honour.

As they took their places on the polished floor, Captain Mandeville considered his partner with eyes of undisguised admiration.

"I do not think I ever saw you look more beautiful," he murmured. "How well your gown becomes you!"

It was true enough, and Myrtle knew it. Over a hooped petticoat of palest lavender, she wore a sacque of richly-flowered brocade. Her slim bust was set off by some old lace and jewels that had been her mother's, and at the last moment Lady William had thrust a blood-red rose into Myrtle's powdered hair, just below her ear.

"This is your wedding-dance, my dear," her ladyship had reminded her, between tenderness and raillery. "And you must look your best."

Her best she certainly looked. There was colour in her cheeks that were normally so pale, and an unusual sparkle in her eyes of so deep a blue that they seemed black in some lights and violet in others. Something of the excitement stirring in her lent her an unwonted radiance.

Aware of this, she found Captain Mandeville's compliment proper enough; yet she turned it off lightly. "Beauty we are told dwells in the eye of the beholder."

And Mandeville, impulsive for once, answered too quickly: "When I am he, then are you beautiful indeed."

She caught the throb of passion which escaped in his voice before he could control it. It chilled and startled her. Fortunately the figure of the dance, which was beginning, claimed their attention, and there was no occasion for words again until the end was reached, and each cavalier was bowing, hand on heart to his curtseying lady.

Nor was there occasion even then. For as the last note of the fiddles was being lost in the babble of loosened talk, Tom Izard, gorgeous as a peacock, upon whose colours he appeared to have modelled his own, came surging up to them to claim the next dance from Myrtle. Other gallants crowded after him, and as her ladyship sailed into the group to give Miss Carey the support of her countenance in this siege, Mandeville slipped away and went sauntering round the room indifferent to the raking fire of the dowagers' spy-glasses which a man of his figure and bearing could never escape.

Near the door of the smaller ante-room, in which, also, card-tables had been set out, without however having as yet found tenants, the captain was confronted by Sir Andrew, who had just separated from Lieutenant Gascoyne of the *Tamar*. Sir Andrew was obviously perturbed. Never the man to conceal emotion, his handsome countenance now plainly reflected feelings that could not be pleasant.

"D'ye know what I'm told, Robert?" he hailed his kinsman, and at once supplied the answer to his own question. "That Myrtle was with Harry Latimer aboard the British sloop this morning." His tone conveyed that he desired the announcement to be regarded as monstrous.

The manner of Mandeville's reply hardly fulfilled this desire. "They were in her ladyship's party."

"You knew!" Sir Andrew seemed amazed at this. "And you didn't tell me!"

"Why disturb you with it? Perhaps it was no great matter, after all."

"No great matter! If her ladyship has no more respect for her husband than to be seen abroad in the company of a notorious rebel, I mean that my daughter shall have more respect for herself and for me. It is known that I've forbid my house to Latimer. For Myrtle to be seen with him after that is to make herself and me ridiculous. Besides, hasn't she protested that she would never speak to him again. Is she playing a double game, Robert? Ye don't think that, do ye?"

"I am sure Myrtle is incapable of anything of the kind. You may be sure that she is quite single in her purpose."

"In what purpose?"

Captain Mandeville took refuge in philosophic vagueness. "Who can fathom woman?"

"Oh, damn your affectations!" Sir Andrew was undoubtedly irritable. "I want to understand this thing."

Mandeville reflected that so did he. But for him there was at least the measure of consolation that the inopportune Mr Latimer would trouble them no more.

He stood there in inconclusive talk with Sir Andrew, until the fiddles under the direction of Monsieur Paul, the French dancing-master who kept an academy in Queen Street, sounded a preliminary chord to summon the dancers to the floor. The chatter became a little less noisy and the movement of that throng of gaily-dressed men and women assumed a more definite character as the couples moved hither and thither to take up their stations.

A plump rather cherubic young gentleman in unrelieved clerical black, wearing a parson's bands and a white tie-wig, sauntered up to them. He was alone, he was obviously amiable, and he was to prove garrulous. Without ceremony he joined the captain and the baronet, and burst into an encomium of the fête, of Lord William, of Bady William, of Miles Brewton and Miles Brewton's charming wife, and finally of colonial life in general.

Mandeville thought him wearisome and scarce troubled to conceal the thought. But Sir Andrew, who honoured the clergy, was at pains to be pleasant in return. It had barely transpired that the gentleman was the Rev. Mr Faversham, the chaplain of the *Tamar*, and Sir Andrew was about to ask him certain obvious questions, when Tom Izard came by with Myrtle on his arm. She saw them, and smiled a smile that was mainly for her father and Mandeville, but which the parson, knowing nothing of the relationship between his companions and the lady, took entirely for himself. He bowed low. As he came up again, his face wreathed in a gratified smile, he turned to the other two.

"A delicious child!" he purred.

"To whom do you allude, sir?" the baronet asked him.

"To…ah…" The parson – unconscious instrument of Fate – made search for a name in his memory. The name he found in his haste was the name to which that very morning he had helped her.

"To Mrs Latimer."

"Mrs Latimer!" Sir Andrew's heavy brows were drawn together. Mandeville drew an audible breath. The ring and the book! He called himself a fool for having rejected the only possible inference from their conjunction. It should not have required the addition of the parson. But Sir Andrew, bewildered, was still questioning Mr Faversham.

"Mrs Latimer? Which here is Mrs Latimer?"

The parson did not quite like the tone of the question. It recalled him to his senses, and made him perceive the indiscretion he had committed.

"Per – perhaps I was mistook," he faltered. "Perhaps that was not the name."

"Oh, yes," said Mandeville at his elbow. And his voice was quiet, though his face was white. "That was the name. You have made no mistake. You married them this morning aboard the sloop."

The parson stared at him in sheer relief. "It is known, then," he said. "Bless me! I was fearful I had said too much."

He felt his arm caught in a grip that made him wince with pain. For Sir Andrew was a man of great physical vigour, and at the moment he was using it rather recklessly.

"Come in here, sir," he said in a voice thick as a drunkard's, and he all but dragged the unfortunate parson across the threshold of the untenanted little ante-room. Mandeville, following took the precaution to close the door. In any situation he could be trusted not to overlook essentials.

Leaning against one of the card-tables the cherubic Mr Faversham looked up in terror at the big handsome man towering threateningly above him, and heard in terror the deep voice that commanded him to explain clearly and without equivocation whom he had married and when.

"Sir...sir... I... I protest against the tone you take with me. You have not the right to...to – "

The baronet interrupted him, in a voice of thunder.

"Have I not, sir? I am Sir Andrew Carey. I am the father of Miss Carey, the lady of whom you spoke, I think. And you spoke of her as Mrs Latimer. Now, sir, be short and clear with me. I'll have no prevarications..."

"Sir Andrew!" the little fellow was indignant. "It is not my habit to prevaricate. I'll beg you to respect my cloth."

"Will you answer me?" roared Sir Andrew.

Mr Faversham stiffened. "No, sir, I will not. I dislike your manners, sir. I dislike them excessively. They are the manners of a boor...of a...a planter. Which is, I take it, what you are. I'll trouble you not to detain me." Thus in the dignity, which Sir Andrew's rudeness justified him in assuming, Mr Faversham now thought to take secure refuge. But never in all his life was he nearer having his neck broken than at that moment.

Sir Andrew, white with passion, and trembling, gripped the parson's arm once more, and literally shook the little gentleman.

"Sir, you trifle with me. You do not leave this room until you have answered me."

Mandeville came to the rescue. He was miraculously calm. "Is this insistence necessary, Sir Andrew? Can his reverence add anything to what already he has admitted? He has practically confessed that he married Myrtle to Harry Latimer this morning; and if I had not been dull of wit I should have known it without his confession. I had evidence enough, God knows."

Sir Andrew looked at the parson, wild-eyed, still maintaining that crushing grip. He was breathing heavily.

"Is this true?" he asked. "In one word, sir; is it true?"

And then the door was opened, and Myrtle stood on the threshold. She had seen her father's violent action in dragging the chaplain into the ante-room, and she had seen Mandeville thereafter close the door. It had required no more than that to tell her what had happened, and at the earliest moment she had disengaged herself from the dance, and with Tom Izard at her heels had come to intervene in a scene which so closely concerned herself.

She was pale, but quite calm and very straight. Her loyal, candid nature actually welcomed this occasion to make an end of the deceit she was practising.

"Father, what is it you require to know?" she came forward. Tom followed her, and closed the door again. If there was to be a scene, and he was quite sure that a scene there was to be, they could well dispense with witnesses.

Sir Andrew loosed the parson and turned on her, his great face purple, his eyes terrible.

"I have been all but told that you were married this morning to… to Harry Latimer. I… I can't believe it. I won't."

"It is quite true."

"True!" He stared at her for a long moment, his mouth open. "It is true!" Then he sat down heavily, and with his hand motioned away the parson who stood before him, whose very presence began to offend him.

Captain Mandeville tapped Mr Faversham's shoulder, and beckoned him towards the door. Glad enough to escape from all this mischief which he was overwhelmed to think that he had made, Mr Faversham obeyed the signal.

"I am sorry, Miss... Mrs Latimer," he faltered as he passed her. "I have been monstrous indiscreet."

"It is no matter for that, sir," she answered him and contrived to smile reassuringly.

"You may make amends by discretion now," the captain told him. "Do not mention a word of what has passed to anyone, not even to Lady William. Thus you will make it easier for us to...to repair the harm."

"Sir, you may depend upon me."

"Sir, I am much obliged. Your humble obedient." Mandeville bowed, and opened the door to allow the chaplain to escape.

Myrtle advanced another step towards her father, whereupon he stirred, and turned to look at her again with eyes that were now blood injected.

"You treacherous, hypocritical wretch," he growled at her in a voice that was dull with pain and rage. "You infamous jade! To hoodwink us thus! To cozen us with lies! To tell us that you had broken with this scoundrel Latimer, and all the while to be planning this dastardy?"

"That is not true, father. I have not been a hypocrite. When I told you that I had broken with Harry, I told you the truth."

"The truth! Do you still dare to stand there and lie to me after what you have done? Do you – "

"Sir Andrew!" Mandeville checked him, a hand upon his shoulder. "You are not being just. Things are not always what they seem."

"You'll tell me this marriage only seems a marriage! Don't be a fool, Robert. We have a fact here, not mere words. A damnable, scoundrelly fact." And he brought his great fist down upon the card-table. "Facts are not to be explained away by falsehood. They speak for themselves."

"Father, will you hear me?" she spoke intrepidly; pale it is true she was, but she showed no other sign of fear.

"What is there to hear from you? Can anything you may say alter this detestable fact? You are married. Married to Harry Latimer, an ingrate, a rebel, a murderer, a man who has only just stopped short of threatening my life. And you are my daughter! My God!" His hands raised a moment as if in appeal to heaven were lowered to his knees, and his chin sank into the lace of his bulging cravat.

She told him everything. Her self-deception in thinking that her love for Harry was dead. Her discovery of the fact when his life was menaced. Her attempt to combat his obstinate refusal to save himself.

"I discovered from him then that his reasons were concerned with me, and with my conduct towards him. To remove those reasons, so that he might depart while it was time, I gave him the only proof of my loyalty and devotion."

He turned violently to stare at her again.

"Your loyalty and devotion? Your loyalty and devotion to a rebel, a traitor? And what of your loyalty and devotion to your King? What of that?"

It seemed to him in his bigotry and fanaticism that he presented a crushing argument, an unanswerable question. But she answered it, a little wan smile at the corners of her mouth.

"What is the King to me, after all? An idea. Little more than a word. Harry is a reality. He is the man I have loved from childhood. What are political opinions to me compared with the danger to his life? How do I know that he is wrong, that you are right?"

"How do you know?" he asked her, and repeated it with rising vehemence of incredulity. "How do you know?" The blasphemy of the question appalled him.

"How, indeed? He is not the only rebel in America."

"No, by God!" said Tom from the background. But no one heeded him, for Myrtle was continuing:

"Here in Charles Town all that is best and ablest is already ranged in opposition to the royal Government. Are they all wrong? Are the few who think as you do so right that Harry is to be thrust out accurst because he has placed what he conceives to be his duty to his country above personal interest. That is what he has done. And when a man does that, it follows at least that his convictions are sincere. You protest your duty and your loyalty. But what have you done to assist the cause that you hold up to me as a religion? Harry has given ships, poured out his money and risked his life to serve the faith he holds, the faith which you account contemptible. Have you spent a single shilling to support the tottering cause which you account so sacred?"

"Stop!" he commanded her, in a strangled voice.

But she went relentlessly on. "A choice, a bitter cruel choice was thrust upon me yesterday. I did not know what to think, what to believe, until it came to me that the test of the worth of your opinions, yours and Harry's, lay in weighing what each of you had done for those opinions. After that, father, there remained with me only regret for the grief I might cause you by the step I was to take. Apart from that I had no single doubt, no single misgiving arising out of Harry's political views."

Carey was helpless, mentally battered in advance by the heavy guns of her arguments. Where he had thought to play the judge, the stern Rhadamanthus, it seemed that he was become the accused. He looked at Mandeville, whose mask-like face betrayed no emotion whatever.

"My God! He's bewitched her!"

Mandeville made him no answer. His dark, penetrating eyes shifted to Myrtle, who shook her head as she smiled again that almost pathetic smile.

"Harry has scarcely spoken to me about these things. What I have told you are no more than my own thoughts."

"And now, madam, you'd best hear mine," her father answered grimly. "I don't know how you planned this thing, or how far you were helped by your rebel friend Sally Izard and her brother there, who may tell her what I say. But I thank God for the merciful dispensation by which it has been made known to me in time."

"In time? In time for what?" she asked him.

"In time to enable me to take my measures." He stood up, calmer now that he clearly saw his way to checkmate the guilty pair and nullify their act. "There's one thing you've forgot. The marriage laws of the colony. You are not yet of age, Myrtle, and you cannot make a valid marriage without my consent." He smiled maliciously. Almost it was a leer. "You'd forgot that."

And then, even before she answered, Mandeville understood why a British sloop should have been chosen for the marriage.

"No, father," she answered quietly. "We did not forget it. But the law of the colonies does not run on board an English ship. By the law of England my marriage is quite valid, and no power on earth can cancel it. The deck of the *Tamar* is England at law."

Sir Andrew stiffened as understanding sank into his seething mind. For a moment he babbled furious incoherencies. Then he became intelligible again.

"It was that treacherous slut Sally Izard who contrived this. You'd never have thought of it for yourself. That damned she-cat!"

Tom stepped forward. "Control yourself, Sir Andrew. You are speaking of my sister."

"You –" In his fury words failed the baronet. Then Mandeville, ever calm, intervened.

"You are speaking also of the Governor's lady, Sir Andrew. If you are overheard – "

"Damme! I mean to be overheard. I mean to tell her to her face what I think of her, and Lord William may call me out for it. What's he, himself, but a doll on wires, a silly puppet in the hands of his rebel wife. A King's representative! By God! They shall hear the truth – "

"Sir Andrew! Sir Andrew! Calm, for God's sake!" Mandeville implored him, with something imperative and dominating in his voice. Pressing upon Sir Andrew's shoulders, he almost forced him down into the chair again.

"Leave me with him, please," Myrtle begged him.

But that was the last thing Mandeville desired just then.

"Not now, Myrtle. Not now," he answered quietly. "Indeed, you would be much better advised to leave him to me." He stepped close to her, and sank his voice. "I think I can quiet him – make him see reason. Go now, and trust to me." He pressed her hand and was conscious of a responsive pressure on his own.

She needed a friend, just such a strong calm friend as this. He drew her towards the door, and beckoned Tom Izard to escort her.

"Trust me," he said again, as she was passing out. "I'll make your peace with him. All will be well, Myrtle."

Trusting him she went, with Tom who did not trust him at all, but held his peace.

Alone with the baronet, Mandeville grew brisk.

"Now, Sir Andrew, the harm is done; and repining over what is accomplished never yet helped any man."

"I am in need of platitudes," Sir Andrew sneered. "They help a deal."

"What's to remember is that a thing done may be undone."

Now here was talk of quite a different kind. The baronet looked up sharply. Mandeville continued, his voice soft and low:

"Wives, Sir Andrew, can be widowed. And if Myrtle were widowed now, at this stage, scarcely wed as she is, the harm would be slight, indeed."

"If...ay – if." Sir Andrew was staring at him. He stared long and hard, and it seemed to him that although Mandeville's lips remained tight, his dark, unfathomable eyes were smiling. Gradually it was borne in upon him that Mandeville was offering a practical suggestion.

"What do you mean?" he asked at last, in a hushed voice.

Mandeville answered very slowly, a man measuring out words one at a time. "It is possible, Sir Andrew, that Myrtle is a widow already." He paused to sigh. "Poor Myrtle!"

Sir Andrew was trembling. "Will you be plain, man?"

"If she is not a widow already, undoubtedly her widowhood will follow soon; and it is certain that she will never set eyes on Latimer again."

He paused, and again he sighed, and made a little gesture of regret and helplessness. He would have preferred by much not to have been constrained to give Sir Andrew this news. But he saw no help for it if a terrible scene were to be avoided. For that Sir Andrew would, unless pacified, do as he threatened by Lady William, Mandeville could not doubt. Upon that must follow explanations which Mandeville had no desire to provoke. Therefore he took this the only means of quieting the baronet's fury.

"In view of Latimer's refusal to quit the province, Lord William has no choice but to proceed to extremes against him. But since to do so openly here in Charles Town might provoke a riot and bring about dreadful consequences to the royal Government which is not yet in case to assert its authority, Lord William has decided to have Latimer secretly arrested tonight and put on board a vessel to be taken to England for trial."

If any doubts had remained with Mandeville that Sir Andrew's affection for his adopted son had perished utterly they would have been definitely shattered now by the expression of savage satisfaction on the baronet's face.

"Yes, yes? And – ?" Sir Andrew asked him clutching his arm.

"By this time the thing should be already done. If he gives no trouble...he will live to be tried and hanged in England." Mandeville's tone was tinged with infinite regret. "In obtaining him a respite in which to quit Charles Town, I had done all that man could to save him... It was impossible that Lord William would further have heeded me if I had attempted to plead with him against dealing with Latimer in this fashion. Yet – for Myrtle's sake and even for your own – I have regretted it until this moment."

"There was no occasion," growled Sir Andrew.

"So I now perceive. Indeed, I am glad that he is put away in this fashion."

"It's a dispensation of Providence," said the baronet solemnly.

"Ay. Fate is not always quite so opportune. But you perceive, Sir Andrew, that there is no need for further trouble or excitation on your part. No need to embroil yourself by upbraiding Lady William."

"Oh! As to that..." Sir Andrew rose. "I make no promises. It is time, high time, someone spoke out. This woman in the position of a queen is a scandal in all loyal eyes. Her action today – "

"Sir Andrew, wait! Consider!" Mandeville laid a hand upon his shoulder, and looked squarely, gravely into his face. "You cannot make war on a woman without hurt to your dignity. But, further, you cannot bring her ladyship to task without publishing this...this adventure of Myrtle's. Do you wish to make it known that your daughter so far forgot her duty as to marry this notorious rebel? It is to put a blight upon her and upon yourself."

It was a shrewd plea, and of immediate effect.

"You're right. But then?"

"In view of what is happening to Latimer, this marriage will be as if it had never been, and no one need ever know of it. The few concerned in it are pledged to secrecy, and in a few days the only two men on the *Tamar* who are aware of what was done there this morning may have left these waters never to return. Why, then, injure Myrtle by a publication of...of – "

"Of this piece of infamy, you would say. Why, Robert, you are right, and I thank you for the warning. I'll hold my tongue."

Chapter 17

Grockat's Wharf

In the dining-room of his house on the bay – the only room that was not already muffled and swaddled against the imminent evacuation – sat Harry Latimer alone at supper, waited upon by Hannibal, a stalwart and devoted young mulatto in his service. Julius, his butler, together with Johnson, his valet, had already set out for Santee Broads to see the house made ready to receive the bridal couple. With them they had taken Myrtle's mauma, Dido, who had earlier accompanied her mistress to Lady William Campbell's.

Mr Latimer's travelling carriage stood ready in the coach-house, the luggage packed, and at eleven o'clock punctually, as he had ordered, the horses would be harnessed and they would set out to go post themselves by St Michael's, opposite the State House, there to await Myrtle.

As he was finishing his lonely supper, which is to say towards nine o'clock, Colonel Gadsden was announced. Gadsden had a ship that was sailing for England with the morning tide. He was on his way to her with letters, one of which from Henry Laurens was addressed to John Wilkes, that famous champion of the liberties of Englishmen wherever found.

"It's a forlorn hope," he confessed. "But Wilkes has a way of compelling petitions to be received, and he has already proved himself more than once the friend of America."

That, however, was more or less by the way. The real object of Gadsden's visit was to place the service of his ship at his friend's disposal should Latimer have letters for England.

Mr Latimer had not, but he was nevertheless grateful for the neighbourly offer, and he pressed the colonel to join him in a glass of port.

Colonel Gadsden took the chair that Hannibal proffered at his master's bidding.

"But I must not stay a moment. There's a wherry waiting for me at the wharf."

Hannibal poured for him a glass of the red amber wine, brought out in Latimer's own ships, which traded to Portugal the rice of his plantations on the Santee. The colonel held it up appreciatively to the candle-light, then sipped and commended it.

"You're not at Miles Brewton's ball?" Latimer asked him.

"Not I, faith. What should I do at a ball in honour of King George? For it's little less than that. The tories'll be there in full force. Here's perdition to them!" And he drank, whilst Latimer laughed at the vehemence of his toast. "And so you're leaving us, after all?" The colonel sighed. "Perhaps you're wise. But, egad! it needed some such Roman gesture as you threatened to put an end to this stagnation, to this eternal temporizing of both sides."

"Let us hope that we may yet temporize into a peaceful settlement."

"A stale delusion," Gadsden condemned it. "And a delusion that holds us spellbound whilst opportunity is slipping by. This letter of Laurens' to John Wilkes!" He shrugged contemptuously. "It expresses the hope of Laurens and some hundreds like him. They're lukewarm, which means neither hot nor cold. A detestable condition, fit for weaklings. Laurens loves his country, and he's loyal to our brother colonists in the North who have suffered. But he's loyal, too, to his own interests, like so many other of these wealthy planters. And he does not yet see how his own interests will best be served."

"You can't charge me with that," said Latimer.

"I know, lad. I know. Here's to our next meeting!" He finished his wine and got up.

"When will that be?" wondered Latimer.

"Sooner than you think, perhaps. For if the drums beat, Moultrie tells me you've promised to serve under him, and they may beat very soon now." He held out his hand. "Goodbye, Harry. Good luck!"

But Latimer, who had also risen, went with him to the door, and after the colonel's departure stood a moment under the stars that were appearing in the darkening sky. Slowly he retraced his steps to the dining-room, and sat down to wait. An hour or so later, after he had read the week's *Gazette*, and as he was considering seeking a book in the library, for it was yet a full hour before the time appointed to set out, Hannibal brought him a note that a messenger had just left.

He broke the seal, and unfolded the sheet. Hastily scrawled upon it in pencil were the lines: "Please come to me at the earliest moment. I have news of utmost urgency for you. Very important." And under this the signature, big and bold, "Henry Laurens."

He stood considering. "You say the messenger has gone?"

"Yessah," replied Hannibal.

Latimer thought it was odd that in such urgency as the note suggested Laurens should not have come at once instead of sending for him. But perhaps there was someone else concerned. Someone who might be with Laurens. Anyway, he had better go.

"Get me my hat, Hannibal."

Hannibal went out, and Mr Latimer set down his pipe and followed him. In the hall the slave proffered him not only his hat, but his gloves and sword as well. He took the hat and was waving the rest away when he remembered a warning Moultrie had yesterday given him not to go abroad unarmed. So, changing his mind, he took the small sword, and hooked it into the carriages which he was wearing under his silver-laced black coat.

179

"Order the carriage to follow me to Mr Laurens', and to await me there. I shall not be returning. Come with it, and bring me what I may require. Tell Fanshaw I have gone."

Fanshaw was Mr Latimer's factor, who, with his wife, would remain in charge of the Charles Town residence during Mr Latimer's absence.

Outside the gates, he turned to the right and went briskly along the Bay towards the Governor's Bridge. As he crossed the latter the advance of the making tide was gurgling up the creek which it served to span. There was not a soul abroad, and the only sounds seemed to be from the water, where odd voices were to be heard calling to one another and where lights dancing in the gloom indicated the positions of the ships at their moorings.

Mr Latimer passed Craven's bastion without meeting anyone, and he was just abreast of Wragg's Alley when abruptly from out of that narrow unlighted lane stepped a man, who hailed him by name.

"Mr Latimer!"

Before he could reflect upon the oddness of his being recognized in the dark across the width of the street by a man who was no more than a black outline in his own eyes he had halted and answered.

"Yes. Who is that?"

At once he realized his indiscretion, and something else besides. Behind him quickly-advancing steps became suddenly audible, and he guessed immediately that he had been followed. At the same moment, almost as if his clear reply to the stranger's hail had been a signal, four or five men came charging out of the blackness of Wragg's Alley and across the Bay Street straight towards him.

Mr Latimer did not wait. He was off along the courtine lines running like a stag. He was agile, strong and swift of foot, and he had the supreme advantage of being lightly shod. Away he sped, his feet scarce touching the ground, racing for Laurens' house, which was the first in the direction he was going and not above two hundred yards away. Behind him the blundering gallop of his heavy-footed pursuers was receding as was the cursing Irish voice that was urging them on, and Harry Latimer laughed as he ran, accounting the race already over, although he had not yet covered more than half the distance.

He was abreast of the dark and deserted custom-house with the next bastion on his left when suddenly the laughter perished in him. Two men who seemed to rise out of the ground, so sudden was their apparition, stood immediately ahead, and before he could check or swerve he was carried by his own headlong impetus straight into their waiting arms.

"Got him!" shouted one of his captors, but found breath for no more, for the captive writhing in their arms was not proving easy to hold. They swayed half way across the street in their struggles, and then, just as they imagined they were subduing him, he thrust violently and viciously upwards with his right knee into the body of one of them, and sent the fellow reeling back and doubled up with pain. Thus released on the right side, he swung round in the grip of his other assailant and broke the skin of his knuckles in a blow between the fellow's eyes that stretched him on the ground.

He was free of them. But the others were upon him in a bunch, and it was too late to resume his flight. At bay, then, he swung his shoulders to the wall of the custom house, to protect his back, whipped out his sword, and pinked the thigh of the foremost of those who beset him.

With a howl of pain the man fell back. His swiftly-dealt wound and the lithe blade gleaming lividly in the gloom gave his companions pause. But there was another coming up, who had followed more at leisure, and yet was not so easily intimidated.

"What's this, ye blackguards?" quoth that Irish voice. "How many more of ye does it need to take a man."

"He's armed, major," said one of them.

"Armed is he. Stand away there, ye good-for-nothing omadhauns."

There was the slither of a sword leaving its scabbard, a bulky figure advanced, and the next moment Latimer's blade was engaged by an energetic swordsman.

It was almost instinctive fighting, in which the eyes availed but little. But some little they did avail, and the advantage was heavily with Latimer, for such light as existed being behind his opponent, Latimer, by crouching, could make out enough to guide him, whilst himself against the background of the wall he must have been almost invisible.

For a moment he had feared that a pistol might end the matter. But since this had not yet happened he was now assured that they meant to do the business silently. He took heart at the reflection, and fought on, scarce daring for a moment to lose the feel of the opposing blade.

And as he fought he wondered who might be his assailants. The others had addressed his present antagonist as "Major," and the man's speech for all its brogue was of a quality that confirmed the title. Moreover Latimer could make out the gleam of the gold-laced cuff and buttonholes and the white of the man's small clothes.

Was this something that was being done by order of Lord William? It seemed inconceivable. And yet if it were not, how came a British officer engaged in it? They were questions that flitted in one second through Latimer's mind, to be dismissed in the next. The first thing to be done was to settle this major's account. The investigation of his identity and the rest could wait. To this first business Latimer addressed himself so aptly that it was done within a very few seconds of engaging.

Realizing his disadvantage in the matter of light, the major was in haste to be done. After a half-dozen groping passes in which the other's blade clung tenaciously to his own, following it round insistently, the major broke away with a violent forcing disengage, feinted high, and lunged. In the nick of time Latimer side-stepped, instinctively presenting his point to receive his antagonist. And receive him he did. The point of the major's unresisted weapon struck the wall. The sword bent double under the weight of his following impetus, and snapped off short, whilst impaled through the stomach on the antagonist blade the same impetus carried him forward until his body brought up against Latimer's hilt, and his face, a white mask in which the open mouth and eyes made three black holes, was within a foot of Latimer's.

Latimer was conscious, first of surprise, and then of nausea. Yielding to the latter, he thrust that body away from him so violently and impetuously that he loosed his grasp of the sword. Carrying it with him, still impaling him, the major toppled over backwards and lay there on the kidney stones writhing and faintly moaning.

Appalled and almost physically sick, Latimer leaned a moment against the wall. Then, as the voices of the men excited and objurgatory broke out about him, he roused himself to a sense of his increased peril, now that he was disarmed. He bounded forward to resume his flight, but one of the ruffians who had come up with him, thrust out a leg to trip him, and he pitched forward at full length. Instantly there was a knee in the small of his back with the weight of a whole body resting upon it, and two pairs of hands were busy about him. Whilst he was thus pinned down, his arms were wrenched behind him, and his wrists tied with a thong of leather.

Desperately he raised his head, and loosed one lusty shout for help. The next moment a muffler was wrapped about his mouth and nose so tightly that he could scarcely breathe. The two who had charge of him next tied his ankles fast together, then rolled him over on to his back, and left him lying there whilst they went aside to the others who were kneeling about their fallen leader.

One of the men whom Latimer had hurt was by now recovered, and had also joined that group, the other, on his feet again, was leaning still sick and faint against the custom-house wall.

If they had rendered Latimer helpless and dumb, at least they had not rendered him deaf, and their rough voices reached him where he lay.

"Is the major much hurt?" asked one of those who had been lately with Latimer.

"Hurt?" growled another voice. "Hell! It's killed he is. He's got it in the guts." Oaths followed, vicious and obscene.

All talked together explosively, until one who seemed to assume authority called them to some sort of order.

"Damn you, we can't stay here to be caught. Pick him up and carry him to the boat, and let's fetch that blasted tyke along as well."

Two of them came back to Latimer, and lifted him. Two others were doing the like by the major. The one in authority crossed the street to the side of the bastion. There he halted, at fault.

"Which way?" he asked.

"Straight on to the wharf where we landed, of course."

"Are ye sure the boat's waiting there?"

"Where else, Tim?"

"Hell!" swore Tim. "How do I know what orders the major gave the boatman? The boat, maybe, was to have come up for us."

They stood debating for some moments. It became clear that the major's insensibility left them in a quandary.

"God damn my soul!" cried one. "Even if we find the boat we don't know where to take him."

"He was to ha' been put aboard a ship for England," said Tim.

"Ay. But what ship. There's a mort o' ships to choose from yonder."

"Oh, heave him into the sea, and have done with it, damn him!" growled another.

"Wait, wait!" Tim admonished them. "It might be awkward afterwards, seeing what's happened to the major, and us with him. Who's to say we didn't murder him ourselves? Cap'n Davenant'll be asking questions when we gets back to the fort. Here, I have it! We'll take the blackguard to the fort, and let the cap'n settle it. Come on." And he began to move away down the street.

"But where's the boat, you fool?" one of them shouted after him.

"We'll go back to the wharf where we landed. And keep a sharp look-out the whiles over the water."

So they trudged on, bearing their two burdens, and without meeting a soul on the way, past Laurens' residence and on for a hundred yards or so until they came to Grockat's Wharf, around the piles of which the waves of the making tide were being whipped by a quickening breeze. They turned on to this, glad to be off the street at last. The leader went first, then the two who carried Latimer, followed by the others bearing the major.

"There she is!" cried Tim. "You see I was right."

Dimly at the far end of the wharf they could make out the lines of a wherry standing alongside, and the figures of one or two of the rowers were silhouetted in the light of a lantern glowing from the boat's bottom. On the breeze came a murmur of voices.

They hurried on towards the boat. In the stern sheets a man was standing, speaking to the crew. He paused as the newcomers advanced. And then the two of them that were handling Latimer, swung him forward to the man in the wherry.

"Here y'are damn you!" shouted one of them in exasperation. "Lend a hand!"

Three or four of those in the boat instinctively rose from their oars to receive the body that was almost being hurled at them. They caught it, and lowered it between thwarts.

"Fetch her up," Tim ordered at the same time. "The major's hurt. Let's set him down in the stern. Come on, there!"

The man who was standing in the stern sheets stooped and picked up the lantern.

"Now who the devil may you be?" he asked, and swung the light aloft to cast it upon their countenances.

What he saw was no great matter. What they saw by the light of that raised lantern was a gold-laced coat – a blue coat with scarlet facings and golden shoulder knots, the uniform of a colonel of the army of Provincial Congress. And above the stiff high collar they beheld a grim, grey hawk face that was entirely strange to them.

"Hell and the devil!" said the wooden-headed Tim, realizing the blunder they had made in the dark. And incontinently he turned and fled as fast as his legs could carry him up the wharf. After him, as if Satan were behind them, went his fellows, leaving the major's weltering body where they had dropped it in their sudden panic.

"What the devil...?" the man in uniform was beginning when he cropped the question, and bawled an order instead. "Up, and after them!"

In a moment his six negroes were out of the boat. But another shout from their master arrested them. He had lowered the lantern to the face of the man who lay almost at his feet. In a moment, he had removed the muffler from the captive's face.

"Latimer!" he cried.

And Latimer, lying there helpless, laughed up at him out of a countenance that was ghastly.

"It's lucky for me you had letters for England tonight, Colonel Gadsden," he said.

Chapter 18

The Pistol-shot

And this," said Latimer between scorn and amusement, "is how King George's representative keeps faith. On my soul, it's worthy of King George himself."

He and Gadsden were kneeling on the wharf beside the prostrate and inanimate body of Major Sykes, fully revealed to them in the light of the colonel's lantern.

"If Hannibal hadn't thrust a sword into my hand at the last moment, I suppose I should be on my way to England now." He got up. "I'm afraid the poor wretch is sped."

"Don't plague yourself about him," said Gadsden. "My men'll see to him. What of yourself? You were best away, I think."

"Yes, but not until I've seen the Governor. I owe him an explanation of how I killed a British officer, and perhaps he will offer me one of how this British officer came to meddle with me, when I had his lordship's word for it that no action would be taken until tomorrow morning."

"Ay," said Gadsden. "Ye're right. Ye don't want to be pursued for murder."

They set out. But they went on foot no farther than Mr Laurens' house, outside which Latimer's travelling carriage was now waiting with Hannibal in attendance. They climbed into it as eleven o'clock was chiming from St Philip's, and drove straight to the State House.

Latimer would have gone at once into the ball-room in his quest for the Governor. But in the hall, untenanted at the moment save by a half-dozen negro lackeys, who stared roundeyed at his dishevelled appearance, Gadsden stayed him.

"Look at yourself, man. D'ye think ye're a sight for the ladies?"

And only then did Latimer seem to become conscious of his condition. Stained almost from head to foot in mud and blood, his head unkempt, one of his stockings torn, and a rent in the back of his brave coat of black corded silk with silver lace and purple linings, he was a terrifying spectacle.

He remained, therefore, in the hall, whilst Gadsden went to find the Governor. A dance was in progress, and his excellency was engaged in it. So, of necessity, Gadsden must wait, whilst Latimer paced the hall.

But not for long was he alone. Down the stairs presently from the buffet above came Colonel Moultrie with Mrs Brewton, and then Lady William with young Drayton, and following almost immediately Myrtle herself on the arm of Tom Izard. Behind these there were two or three other couples, and all of them stood at gaze, appalled and terrified by Mr Latimer's appearance.

Myrtle ran to him in terror, Lady William and Tom Izard following closely.

"What's happened? Harry! Why are you like this?"

You conceive the bombardment of startled questions he was constrained to stand.

"It's nothing. A trifling accident."

"You're not hurt, Harry?" Myrtle cried.

He reassured her, and whilst doing so he perceived that her sudden advent, which at first had vexed him, was indeed most opportune. He drew her aside a little, and lowered his voice, so that his words were for her alone.

"My carriage is at the door, Myrtle. Hannibal is there. This is your opportunity. Slip into it, and wait for me. I'll join you in a moment, as soon as I have had a word with Lord William."

Momentary excitement and concern turned her pale. She had not seen her father since their interview in the little ante-room. Indeed, he had appeared to avoid her. But Mandeville had assured her that all was well; that he had pacified Sir Andrew and that she need fear no violent outburst. And she had thanked Mandeville from a heart that was full of gratitude for his concern and kindliness.

She nodded now to Harry, her eyes considering him with tender wistfulness. She would take her opportunity, she assured him, of slipping out unobserved. He should find her in the carriage when he came, and then he must tell her what had happened, who had attacked him.

The opportunity was not long delayed. Presently the music ceased, and a moment or two later Gadsden appeared at the door of the main ante-room, beckoning Latimer forward. He went, the others following. Myrtle lagged behind with Lady William until all had passed in, then Lady William hugged her an instant.

"Bless you, child! Be happy!"

She kissed her, and Myrtle was gone speeding out and down the steps, to the carriage into which Hannibal, grinning widely in welcome, assisted her.

And meanwhile, Lord William was advancing to meet Mr Latimer, and his eyes opened wide with astonishment as he surveyed the gentleman's disordered appearance.

"Mr Latimer, what is this?"

"The result of what appears, but which I cannot believe to be, a breach of faith on the part of your excellency. An attempt was made tonight to seize me and put me on board a ship for England."

There was a burst of indignation from Moultrie and Drayton who stood behind him, and a general murmur from others who were flowing into the ante-room and halting there at gaze. Amongst them, indeed in the foremost ranks, were Sir Andrew Carey with Stuart, the Indian Agent, and Anthony Fletchall, the back-country tory leader. Immediately behind Carey, and sharing his disgusted astonishment but manifesting it less freely was Mandeville. Others from the ballroom were pressing forward behind them, and it was with difficulty that a posse of lackeys in gorgeous liveries bearing trays of Sillery were able to circulate and draw attention to the refreshment which they offered.

Lord William fell back a step in sheer amazement at Latimer's words. Then he collected himself.

"I am relieved, sir, that you do not impute to any orders of mine an attack, whose object I imagine you are assuming."

"I am not assuming it, Lord William. Colonel Gadsden has seen enough to be able to bear me out in part. The intention was as I have said. I overheard it among the men who took me, and they were led by a British officer."

"That I cannot believe." The Governor's face flushed scarlet. Sternly he voiced a sudden suspicion: "Mr Latimer, is this an attempt to stir up feeling – ?"

But Latimer unceremoniously interrupted him.

"Your excellency, the body of that British officer will bear witness to what I say. It is lying now on Grockat's Wharf."

"Ay," said Gadsden. "I've seen it, and seen the men who carried it."

"You…killed him?"

"I had that misfortune. In my own defence."

There was hubbub now among the tories and among several officers of the *Tamar* who were present. But his lordship quelled it, raising his hand.

"Who was this officer? Do you know?"

Gadsden answered him: "Major Sykes from Fort Johnson. I had better tell your lordship what I witnessed of this affair." And he related how the men had brought Latimer bound and gagged, and had dropped him into the wrong boat. "But for that mistake, your excellency," Gadsden ended with a certain grim aggressiveness, whose significance there was no mistaking, "it is unlikely that Mr Latimer would ever have been heard of again."

The high colour remained in his lordship's face, but its expression grew troubled; almost he had a guilty look, for the mention of the officer's identity brought back to his mind the thing that had yesterday been suggested in Sykes' presence.

Into Carey's ear Mandeville whispered at that moment. "For his own sake he must disclaim all knowledge of it."

And even as he spoke, the Governor turned to seek him among the gaping crowd.

"Captain Mandeville!"

Mandeville stepped forward, graceful and unperturbed.

"Do you know anything of this?" the Governor demanded.

"I?" quoth Mandeville. "No more than your excellency."

But he was not to escape so easily. "That's an equivocal answer, Captain Mandeville," said Moultrie sharply.

A hand fell on the colonel's sleeve. He turned, and there beside him stern and impassive stood John Rutledge with obvious intent to restrain him from adding fuel to this already ample blaze. But Moultrie, indignant and concerned for his friend, for once shook off the arm of the lawyer with impatience.

And meanwhile Mandeville had drawn himself up, and was looking down his nose at the colonial officer.

"Colonel Moultrie, I have not the habit of equivocation."

"I know nothing of your habits, and care less," the colonel answered him. "But I know an equivocation when I hear it."

Lord William intervened. The atmosphere was becoming dangerously charged. "The equivocation will be removed, I think, if I assert to you on my honour, Mr Latimer, that it was by no orders of mine that this thing happened, and that I know nothing whatever of how it came about."

"Will your excellency go so far as to reprobate it?" Latimer asked him as courteously as such a question could be asked.

"Sincerely," was the prompt and emphatic reply. "And I shall not rest until I have discovered what is behind it."

Mr Latimer bowed. "I thank your excellency. I have reported the event, and rendered the immediate account of it which my departure from Charles Town makes necessary. If your excellency has no further questions for me, perhaps you will give me leave to withdraw."

"Assuredly, Mr Latimer." And his excellency slightly inclined his head.

Mr Latimer bowed a second time, and turned to depart. But departure was not quite so easy. There were friends behind him waiting to congratulate him on his escape, and there was Rutledge with a sharp reprimand.

"You see, sir, the perils into which your rashness is plunging not only yourself but all of us."

Latimer smiled. He was very weary, and suddenly conscious of his weariness now that the excitement sustaining him had passed.

"I hope that my departure will restore to Charles Town the peace of which, with the possible exception of King George, I appear to be the only disturber."

He passed on to be detained by others, and there was Moultrie assuring him that he would soon be back. "When you hear my drums there'll be a place for you, Harry. And don't bear Rutledge any ill-will. He's a curmudgeon. But honest."

Meanwhile behind him, at the other end of the ante-room where the crowd had melted a little, so that the lackeys with the Sillery were now circulating more freely, the Governor was finding himself beset by a knot of hostile tories led by Carey.

"Does your excellency really mean," the baronet was asking truculently, "that a British officer may be murdered in the streets and his murderer allowed to go his ways?" He was livid with anger and with something more than anger.

Lord William's manner was gravely, sadly tolerant. "The evidence is against you, Sir Andrew. No British officer has been murdered. Mr Latimer killed a British officer in self-defence. You heard the account of it from Colonel Gadsden."

"Your lordship accepts the word of open and acknowledged rebels against – "

"Sir Andrew, I think you are presuming," his lordship interrupted him.

"It is your excellency who compels it."

"I would, sir, I could as easily compel you to remember your manners." And his lordship turned his shoulder upon the baronet, to take a glass of Sillery from the tray a servant was proffering. Then deliberately he addressed himself to Laurens who was standing near.

Sir Andrew fell back a step, clenching his hands. He looked a mute appeal at Mandeville. Mandeville imperceptibly raised his eyebrows, and as imperceptibly shrugged. Sir Andrew understood that he must depend upon himself alone. Latimer was more than half-way across the room already on his journey to the door. Towards that same door the baronet now circuitously but quickly made his way. A servant approached him with a tray of wine. He was beginning to wave the man away when suddenly he checked the gesture. Inspiration gleamed in his full eyes. He took up a glass, and Mr Latimer turning at that moment came face to face with him. For a moment Mr Latimer stood, returning the baronet's intent regard. Then he bowed to him, and would have passed on. But Sir Andrew's words arrested him.

"You are leaving us, Mr Latimer?" the voice was smooth, and yet there was a note in it that stirred Moultrie and brought him in quick strides to the side of his friend.

"I am just going, Sir Andrew."

"But surely you will stay to drink first a loyal toast?" And Sir Andrew waved towards him the servant with the tray of glasses.

Latimer scented mischief, and for an instant hesitated, looking at Carey as if to fathom his purpose. Then, deeming that here unquestioning submission was the shortest and safest course, he took up a glass."

"A loyal toast?" he questioned. He added with a lightness he was very far from feeling: "With all my heart, or any other toast." And he quoted: "I warrant 'twill prove an excuse for the glass."

There was the slightest pause, in which Sir Andrew seemed yet again to be measuring the young man with his eyes. Then slowly, solemnly, almost pompously, he raised his glass. Lord William, across the room, upon which a silence had unaccountably fallen, stood very straight and stiff, considering the baronet. To him this seemed the prelude of some indefinable impertinence. Moultrie took a glass of Sillery from the tray that was thrust before him. The others, already supplied, stood waiting a little curiously for the toast.

"Gentlemen," said Sir Andrew, with the least suspicion of pompousness: "The King! God Save the King!"

Proposed at such a time and in such a place – with so many present who were actively engaged in opposing those measures for the subjugation of the colonies which emanated from the King himself – this was not so much a toast as a challenge. But all were concerned to keep the peace. And so, loyal and rebel alike, murmured in chorus: "The King!" and drank with Sir Andrew.

Under cover of that murmur, Moultrie had whispered imperatively to Latimer: "Drink!"

But even without that injunction it is unlikely that Latimer would have rendered himself conspicuous by refusing the toast. He had undergone enough that night to desire above everything the avoidance of further trouble. And so, after the least pause, in which he was questioning himself on the subject of Sir Andrew's purpose, he too, muttered "The King!" and drained his glass.

Sir Andrew lowered his own, still half full of wine, and looked at Mr Latimer with narrowing eyes.

"You had no compunction, Mr Latimer, in honouring that toast?"

Mr Latimer smiled, for all that by now the scent of danger was breast high with him. "None," he said lightly. "God Save the King, by all means. He stands in need of saving."

"From his enemies, you mean?"

"No, sir; from his friends."

It was a plain enough allusion to that party known as "the King's friends" through whom King George ruled the Empire in violation of the established system of placing the Government in the hands of the majority party in Parliament. And it is to be doubted if it was resented by anyone present, not excluding Lord William. It was sufficient, however, and more than sufficient for Sir Andrew's purpose.

"That," he said, "is a treasonable speech." And on the words, he flung the remaining contents of his glass full in the face of Mr Latimer.

"Sir Andrew!" It was Lord William who spoke, advancing, and almost thrusting himself between the two. His voice was charged with reproachful indignation, and of reproachful indignation were the murmurs that arose from every member of that company.

Some thoughtfully hustled the few ladies into the ballroom, and closed the door. Lady William, however, declining to be hustled, remained there with Miss Ravenell beside her.

Moultrie set a hand upon Latimer's shoulder to restrain him, to urge him at all costs to refrain from being entangled in a quarrel. It was hardly necessary. White and trembling, yet Mr Latimer preserved his self-command. He drew a fine handkerchief from his pocket and mopped his dripping cheek.

"You won't wipe that off with a handkerchief, my friend," Sir Andrew goaded him, rather coarsely.

He looked at Sir Andrew. Then half turned to the others present, and made them an inclusive bow.

"I take my leave," he said, and moved to depart, Moultrie making shift to go with him. But Sir Andrew resolutely, fiercely, barred his way.

"No, by God!"

"Sir Andrew!" Again it was Lord William who intervened, stepping up to Carey as he did so. "Are you out of your senses, sir? Deliberately you provoked Mr Latimer, and in the face of that provocation, Mr Latimer perhaps spoke foolishly – affording you the pretext you were seeking. But you shall push this matter no further. You shall respect his forbearance as we all do."

"Forbearance!" Sir Andrew laughed unpleasantly. "Here's a new name for cowardice. And do you make yourself a shield for cowards, Lord William, as well as for rebels and murderers!"

"Sir Andrew, you forget, I think, to whom you speak." Very dignified and stern the young Governor towered there beside him. But the tory fanatic and outraged father in one, flung off the last rag of restraint.

"Your lordship places me under that necessity. I did not invite your intervention in my quarrel. Nor do I think did Mr Latimer, though I've no doubt the cur will welcome it."

"Sir Andrew, you push things too far," cried Latimer, and there was no lack of voices to approve him.

"Please, please, Mr Latimer." His excellency raised a hand to restrain him, then turned again to the wrathful baronet "Sir Andrew, Mr Latimer has an engagement of honour with me, an engagement to be gone from Charles Town before morning. From that engagement I cannot, for reasons of high policy, release him, so that in no case would it be possible for Mr Latimer to remain to meet any…other engagement tomorrow."

"There is not the need to wait until tomorrow," Carey answered. "If Mr Latimer possesses the courage which he is so reluctant to display, let him meet me here and now."

Burning with shame and anger, Latimer turned to the faithful friend beside him.

"Moultrie, this is intolerable! He places me under the absolute necessity of proving my courage."

"He does not, Mr Latimer," his lordship answered him. "None present doubts your courage, rest assured."

"He'll be glad enough to rest in that assurance," mocked Sir Andrew. "But there again your lordship exceeds authority. I doubt his courage, for one."

The Governor looked at him a moment, sternly.

"Sir Andrew, you compel me to exercise my jurisdiction. In the King's name I forbid you to meet Mr Latimer."

Sir Andrew met the command with a burst of laughter, loud and offensively derisive.

"In the King's name! In the King's name! That's choice damme! In the King's name you forbid me to punish an insult to the King's majesty! I wonder what the King would think of his vicegerent in South Carolina." Then controlling his insolent mirth, he added, almost formally: "I must remind your excellency that you are a guest like myself, and that your warrant does not run here."

"You refuse to recognize my authority?" Lord William's head was haughtily thrown back, his face slightly flushed.

Sir Andrew bowed ironically. "With the utmost respect my lord, when that authority is exercised to shelter a rebel and a coward, I have no choice but to disregard it."

Angry voices broke from almost every pair of lips. But the old tory confronted them defiantly, scornfully, sure of his ground, upon which he was unassailable.

The flush deepened in Lord William's cheeks.

"I have not the power to order your arrest, Sir Andrew. You have given as yet no cause for that. But I warn you, sir, that if this quarrel, so wantonly provoked by you, goes forward, you shall feel to the utmost the weight of the law. Pray do not interrupt me. Since you have put upon me this affront, it is impossible for me to remain. Gentlemen," and he bowed to the company present, "I regretfully take my leave of you. Captain Mandeville will present my apologies to the assembly. A slight indisposition on the part of her ladyship has compelled us both to withdraw rather earlier than we had hoped." He turned to her ladyship proffering his arm. "My dear."

He was so dignified, so much the royal personage in that moment, that those whom he addressed realized fully that he withdrew to avoid embroiling himself in a vulgar dispute derogatory to his office; therefore no attempt was made to persuade him from a course announced with such utter finality. Even Lady William felt herself powerless to intervene despite every impulse to do so.

All but Sir Andrew, who remained erect in his defiance, bowed low in response, and remained bowed until, with Lady William on his arm and followed by Captain Tasker and Miss Ravenell, Lord William had passed out into the hall beyond. Then the men who were left behind, and they numbered close upon a score, loosed their anger upon Sir Andrew. But he remained disdainfully indifferent.

They might make themselves as hoarse as they pleased with invective and insult so long as he had his way with Mr Latimer.

When this was realized, those present resigned themselves to being spectators of a settlement now inevitable. But when it came to finding a friend to act for Sir Andrew there was only one man present who would undertake the office. This was Anthony Fletchall, and although as stout a tory as Carey himself, he undertook this office only after considerable pressure. There had been a little flash of anger from Carey when Mandeville had refused. But Mandeville had brushed this smooth.

"As your kinsman, Sir Andrew, it is almost my duty to stand by you. But as Lord William's equerry, it is my duty to hold aloof. I am in an impossible position."

Nevertheless it was Mandeville who dispatched the staring and startled lackey for a certain mahogany case in the keeping of Mrs Pratt, the custodian of the State House.

When the case, which contained a brace of duelling pistols, was produced it was taken by Mr Fletchall to Colonel Moultrie. The latter was standing beside Latimer who, in the background to which he had retired, had flung himself into a chair, where he sat, elbows on knees in an attitude of complete dejection. After what already he had endured that night, to be compelled to meet his father-in-law, and one who had stood to him in the past in the relationship almost of a father, was something altogether intolerable. He sat there sunk in misery, resolved that in spite of everything, and whatever might be thought of him, he would yet avoid this meeting. He was roused by the voice of Moultrie raised in sharp expostulation.

"But what is this, sir?" the colonel was exclaiming. "Pistols! We have not asked for pistols."

Latimer looked up, and spoke. "We have not asked for anything at all. We do not meet Sir Andrew Carey." He rose. "Mr Fletchall, if you will be good enough to ask Sir Andrew to step across to me, I shall hope to prove to him that we cannot meet."

"In the present position that would scarcely be regular," ventured Mr Fletchall.

"I care nothing for that. Something very much graver is involved."

Fletchall bowed and went his errand, and Sir Andrew came in answer to the request and stood in assumed calm before him.

"Sir Andrew," said Mr Latimer, for all to hear, "a meeting between us is impossible. You had better know the truth. Myrtle and I were married this morning."

He had thought to fling a bombshell and he had expected outbursts, rage, incredulity; anything indeed but the answer he received:

"That, sir, is but an added reason; I do not desire a rebel for a son-in-law, and even more," he raised his voice, "I do not desire a coward for one."

Latimer looked at him with eyes of despair. The stream of destiny was too strong for him. It was idle to continue to swim against it.

"Please conclude the arrangements, Moultrie. Let us get it over."

Sir Andrew withdrew again, and Moultrie renewed the discussion.

"But pistols – indoors! It is unheard of. It is monstrous, unthinkable. We demand swords."

One of his reasons for this insistence was that if swords were used he was sure that Latimer could contrive to take no harm himself and to do no great hurt to Sir Andrew. But Mr Fletchall had his instructions, and he clung to them obstinately.

"You are not in the right to demand. The choice of weapons is with us. We are the challenged side."

"I heard no challenge – " Moultrie was retorting, and then Latimer cut in.

"Oh, have done, William. Let us get it over."

"But they demand pistols!" Moultrie was reduced almost to frenzy.

"Then let them have pistols. What the devil does it matter?"

"Matter? Why there's the question of distance." And he swung to Fletchall. "What distance do you propose?" he asked, expecting to checkmate the other side.

Mr Fletchall, a short, stoutish man of forty with a phlegmatic countenance, was not even embarrassed. He measured the room with a calm eye.

"Considering the space, we suggest ten paces."

Moultrie laughed angrily. "Pistols at ten paces! D'ye hear that, Harry? At ten paces!"

"Across a handkerchief if they like," snapped Mr Latimer.

"But it's murder."

"Faith, have you only just discovered it?"

The music in the ballroom had been resumed by musicians in complete ignorance that anything untoward was taking place.

And then someone, whose nerves were being fretted, cried out that it should be stopped, and someone else would have departed to obey the demand, when Rutledge got in the way.

"By no means," he said. "The ladies must not be further alarmed. They will be alarmed as it is, soon enough." And he suggested, indeed, that if the affair was to go on, the parties had better remove themselves elsewhere. But Carey would not hear of it. He cared nothing, he announced, for the feelings of any rebel, man or woman, and none but a rebel could do other than rejoice in the punishment of a rebel. Here, where Mr Latimer had offended, let Mr Latimer expiate.

The end of it was that Rutledge turned the key in the door leading to the ballroom whilst the pistols were being loaded at a console by Fletchall and Moultrie acting jointly.

At the end of what seemed an age to Mr Latimer, Colonel Moultrie beckoned him forward to the middle of the room, whither Fletchall was also conducting his principal.

"We propose, gentlemen," said Fletchall, "to place you back to back. You will advance five paces, in a measure as they are counted towards the corner which each of you is facing." He turned. Thornborough, tall and elegant in his naval blue and white, stood immediately behind him. "Captain Thornborough, perhaps you will oblige by counting."

The sailor drew back a little, and a look of repugnance crossed his sunburnt aquiline face.

"I should prefer..." He was beginning. Then he shrugged. "Oh, as well I as another."

When the men were in position, back to back, their swords surrendered formally to their seconds, Captain Thornborough stepped forward.

"Gentlemen, as Mr Fletchall has said, you will pace your distance in a measure as I count. On the count of 'five' you will take your last pace, turn, and fire."

And whilst Colonel Moultrie advanced with the loaded pistols giving Mr Latimer the first choice as was his right, Captain Thornborough admonished the onlookers.

"Let me beg of you, gentlemen, to stand back, well out of the line of sight, and to guard against the slightest movement that might serve to draw the eye of either principal." He waited until all those present, including the seconds, were ranged far enough back to satisfy him. "Now, gentlemen, if you are ready..." He paused a moment, taking a couple of backward paces, and began the count: "One – two – three – four – five."

On the word, and at the end of the diagonal line in which they had paced away each from the other, the men swung round, face to face across the room. But only one of them, and that one was Carey, raised his arm. He raised it, slowly, deliberately, covering his opponent, who stood tense and straight to receive a fire which he was making no shift whatever to return. And then in the very moment that Sir Andrew drew the trigger, the door leading to the hall, which they had neglected to secure, was flung open with a crash, and Myrtle, in cloak and wimple, stood white and scared on the threshold.

In the same instant Sir Andrew's pistol spoke. But the interruption at the critical moment, whilst too late to arrest the shot, yet served to draw his eye and disturb his cold-blooded deliberate aim. His pistol jerked up by the fraction of an inch at the last moment delivered its bullet into the long mirror above the console at Latimer's back, and shivered the glass from top to bottom.

In two strides Captain Thornborough was at Myrtle's side. Rendered immovable by horror, she stood there, staring. But just as she made no attempt to advance further, neither did she yield to the captain's half-hearted endeavours to induce her to withdraw.

It was a situation more painful probably than any man present had ever borne part in before or would ever bear part in again.

And then the voice of Fletchall was sternly raised, and sounded oddly loud in the sudden silence which no one had until this moment perceived. For in the ballroom the music had ceased abruptly on the firing of the shot and was succeeded there by a momentary stillness of question and alarm.

"Mr Latimer, we are waiting for your fire."

"You need wait no longer," said Mr Latimer, whose pistol hand had remained hanging inert beside him throughout. "I do not intend to fire."

There was an outcry of protest from the men present, mingling with the din of voices swelling up now in the ballroom. Someone was beating on the door. But none present heeded that.

Mr Latimer addressed himself to the sailor who in some sense had acted as master of the ceremonies.

"Captain Thornborough, Sir Andrew's aim was disturbed by the opening of the door."

"The circumstance is unfortunate. But inasmuch as neither of you were parties to it, it does not affect your position. You must take your shot."

"I must take it?"

And it was Fletchall who answered him, the trembling of his voice betraying his nervous tension.

"You have no alternative. To have retained it so long...damme! it isn't decent."

"I suppose that I am within my rights, my strict rights, in retaining my fire as long as I please?"

There was a pause before any dared pronounce a decision that really demanded consideration by a court of honour. Then, since no one else attempted to reply, Captain Thornborough took it upon himself to give judgment.

"Within your strict rights, no doubt, Mr Latimer. But as Mr Fletchall has said, it is hardly decent. There are times when to stand upon our strict rights – "

Peremptorily Mr Latimer interrupted him. He was smiling, his head thrown back, completely master of himself again now that he was master of the situation. And Myrtle watching him, leaned her tortured spirit confidently upon his own, and felt her terrors lessening.

"I am concerned only with my strictest rights, gentlemen. Decency has had no part in this affair. Upon my strictest rights I intend to stand. Since I must take my shot, I will take it – "

He paused deliberately, smiled again and even inclined his head a little. "...some other day."

There was an echoing chorus of amazement dominated by Sir Andrew's voice:

"Some other day!"

"At my convenience," added Mr Latimer emphatically, and deliberately he stepped forward, abandoning the position to which he had paced, and proffering the unfired pistol to Colonel Moultrie. "It is a debt between Sir Andrew Carey and myself. A debt which I reserve the right to claim or not, like any other debt."

"You damned scoundrel!" thundered Sir Andrew, as a beginning to a torrent of invective, and reversing his pistol so as to convert it into a club he would have hurled himself upon Latimer but that Christopher Gadsden and three or four others restrained him by main force.

Someone had unlocked the door of the ballroom, conceivably to prevent its being broken down, and now on the threshold surged a crowd of gallants and ladies, arrested there by the spectacle of that burly man writhing in the arms of his captors and still uttering furious vituperation.

Mr Latimer, accompanied by Moultrie, crossed to the door where Myrtle stood. "My dear!" he said to comfort her, and laid a hand upon her arm.

Anthony Fletchall called after him:

"Mr Latimer, what you do is monstrous ill done. You cannot in honour leave Sir Andrew under the obligation to stand your fire whenever you shall choose to deliver it. If you intended to be generous – "

"I could have fired in the air," Latimer interrupted him. "I know that, sir. And I do not need, nor will I accept, instruction in matters of honour. But I'll explain myself, since almost you make it necessary. As you must all have seen, I had no intention of firing upon Sir Andrew. But if I had fired with deliberate intent to miss him, I should have cleared the score, and Sir Andrew would have been at liberty to begin all over again, either demanding another exchange of shots or forcing a fresh quarrel upon me. I have proved my courage once by standing to receive his fire. But I have no intention or wish to continue to be a target for him. So I retain my shot, and thus in honour I bind his hands from any further attempts upon my life."

They regarded him now with silent understanding, and with something of respect. Fletchall inclined his head a little.

"I beg your pardon, Mr Latimer."

Mr Latimer was not heeding him. Myrtle had clutched his arm, and was looking up into his face.

"Was that what he did?" she asked. "He forced a quarrel on you, Harry? And he fired to kill you? You?"

"My dear, what does it matter?"

"Matter?" she echoed, and she looked at her father. Her eyes were the cold eyes of a judge. "Why did you do this?" she demanded. "Why?"

He shook off those who held him, and they let him go. He advanced a pace or two, and stopped there, eyeing them both, his face white and distorted, his powerful body trembling with the awful rage that possessed him, the rage of the despot whose authority has been flouted and whose vengeance has been baffled. For baffled he knew himself, bound fast in the bonds of his own honour by an ingenuity that seemed to him nothing short of fiendish. And now his daughter, this jade who had been false to him, as he conceived it, who had played the hypocrite, disregarded his parental rights, and married the man who was become his enemy, dared to stand boldly before his face and question him.

"You false wretch," he reviled her before them all. "I did it to make a widow of you, to save you from the shame of this secret marriage…"

"To make a widow of me! Is that your love?" There was loathing and horror in her voice. Suddenly he seemed monstrous to her in his bigoted intemperate hate.

"Love?" he answered her, and laughed unpleasantly. "Go! Go! Out of my sight, both of you. I have done with you, Myrtle. I disown you utterly. Not a penny of mine, not a perch of land shall come to you from me living or dead. All I pray is that I may never see either of you again."

Her bridegroom put an arm about her. "Come, my dear," he urged her. He bowed silently to the company, and with the single exception of Sir Andrew Carey every man present bowed low in response.

Mr Latimer drew his wife into the hall, scattering a knot of negro servants who had collected about the door to listen. But the voice of his father-in-law still pursued him:

"You may escape me. But you cannot escape God. His vengeance will search out those who break the second commandment." And then someone mercifully closed the door.

Harry Latimer led Myrtle out and down the steps to the waiting carriage, the carriage which she had quitted in almost instinctive anxiety when he delayed so unaccountably in following her.

Thus, and in such a state of feeling as you can conceive those two set out upon their bridal journey.

PART TWO

Chapter 1

Marriage

This is, as you will long since have realized, no history of the Revolution in South Carolina, but simply an account of certain fateful transactions in the life of Mr Harry Fitzroy Latimer. If I am now to touch upon historical matters which may be considered to lie outside of that gentleman's story, these are introduced to supply the necessary and, I hope, elucidatory hyphen connecting the first act of this personal drama, upon which the curtain was rung down on the night of Brewton's ball in June of 1775, with the second and final act upon which it is to be rung up again in May of the year 1779, at the time of Prevost's Raid.

Mr Latimer's absence from Charles Town did not extend beyond three months. Far sooner than any could have imagined on the night of his departure did the drums of war beat a rally to all patriots. Long before he had reached his plantation of Santee Broads, indeed within a few hours of his setting out to journey thither, came express riders into Charles Town with the dreadful news that war was no longer an ultimate possibility but already an accomplished fact.

In the North a great battle had been fought on the heights above Boston between the insurgent colonial forces and the troops which the British Government had lately been pouring into Massachussets under Howe, Clinton and Burgoyne. And by this battle the colonies were definitely committed to that civil war which until the eleventh hour, even after the skirmish at Lexington, they had still looked to avert. The die was cast. All hope that the dispute might be settled by advocacy and argument was at an end. Only the arbitrament of arms remained.

The heralding throughout America of this fateful decision sent across the continent a wave of enthusiasm which few patriotic people have not known in the hour of war's declaration.

They were committed. Come now what might, they knew where they stood, and what remained to do. Where men perceive this clearly the rest matters little by comparison. So they girded themselves for battle, but still in the main with no thought of independence as the object of their strife. Like their ancestors Pym and Hampden they were making a stand not against sovereignty, but against the abuse of sovereign rights.

The Continental Congress had met at Philadelphia, and conscious of what was coming some weeks before the event itself carried conviction to the remoter provinces, it voted to raise an army of twenty thousand men. Two days before Bunker's Hill was fought Congress unanimously elected to the position of commander-in-chief "Mr Washington, the Potomac planter," as he was contemptuously designated by tories and British alike, but who, in spite of their ill-informed and misplaced scorn, was destined to become one of the great figures of all time.

In Charles Town there was a feverish activity of preparation, the reflection of which you will find in the collection of letters and general orders published by William Moultrie and designated his Memoirs. There was also an enthusiastic confidence which might have run less high could the Carolinians have suspected that the conflict upon which they were entering was to drag on with varying fortunes for seven years. There were skirmishes with parties of back-country loyalists, now frankly stimulated by Lord William. But the only immediate fruit of this was that in September the Governor, in imminent danger of apprehension, accompanied by Mr Innes and Captain Mandeville, took the Seal of the Province and went aboard the *Tamar* for safety.

Thus, furtively and ingloriously, closed the era of royal rule in South Carolina.

In view of the news which had so closely followed him, Harry Latimer had not considered it either necessary or expedient to go farther than Santee Broads. As long as Lord William was in Charles Town and nominally governing there, Latimer understood that his return would be a breach of faith, a violation of the parole given implicitly if not explicitly. With his lordship's departure, however, Latimer considered the parole extinguished, and he returned to offer his sword to Moultrie, who procured him a lieutenant's commission in the Second Regiment under his command. Soon he found himself promoted captain and attached to Moultrie's own person as an extra aide-de-camp during those early summer days of the following year when the fort on Sullivan's Island was feverishly building to defend the harbour.

Latimer brought Myrtle back with him, and they took up their residence at his mansion on the Bay. Thence, three times in the course of as many months, did he write to Sir Andrew Carey, who had now retired to Fairgrove, there to sulk over the black conduct of the country in which he had the dishonour to be born. Two of these letters remained unanswered. The third came back unopened, whereupon it was perceived that there was no hope just yet of healing the breach between themselves and that fanatical royalist.

But for this, there would have been no cloud to trouble the happiness of those two during that autumn and winter of 1775. As it was, Myrtle's conscience remained unquiet. Her affection for Harry was being relentlessly undermined by regrets at her estrangement from her father, by doubts of the rectitude of her own conduct. Hence a not unnatural reaction to the deeply implanted monarchist principles from which she had seceded in the time of panic and excitement produced by Harry's personal danger. With the aversion of that danger, so too had her spirit averted from the new faith which for a little while she had tolerated if not actually embraced.

There were times when she was disposed to regard herself as a victim, a sacrificial offering to procure Harry's immunity from the consequences of the evil course of rebellion upon which he had embarked. And where she might ungrudgingly have sacrificed her life, she grudged here the sacrifice of her soul which seemed entailed. For upon her soul she had taken the burden of the sin against the second commandment. Hitherto the constant hope, encouraged confidently by Harry and also in letters from Lady William, of a reconciliation with her father had thrust that parting denunciation of her father's into the background of her mind. But now that back in Charles Town, and in a Charles Town distracted by the preparations for war, this hope was proved at last idle, her father's words rang almost daily in her ears to bring her to something akin to remorse for the unfilial conduct of which she had been guilty.

It requires little imagination to perceive the inevitable fruit of this. Her manner towards Harry changed perceptibly. It became charged with irritability, and there were moments when because of the load upon her soul and mind she reproached him with a hundred matters that were but so many vents for her surcharged feelings.

She found herself detesting his military preoccupations in a cause whose unrighteousness had been inculcated into her heart by her parent, and she found herself expressing that detestation and uttering loyal sentiments which more than suggested that she desired the ultimate destruction of the colonials in the struggle to which they were committed.

There were scenes between them, in which each carried away by momentary resentment of the other's lack of sympathy and understanding said things that but served to widen the breach that was gradually but surely separating them.

"Why did you marry me?" cried Harry one day on a note of sheer desperation.

"I wish I hadn't," she answered him in her petulance. "I would give ten years of my life to undo that."

"You would give my life, you mean. For that is what was at stake. I wish you had thought of it in time. I wish you had known yourself better."

"Known myself better?"

"Why did you delude me with a tale of affection, which every day our life now proves had no real existence? Was it worth while to induce me to save myself only to be daily tormented through my love for you."

"Your love! Would you speak to me as you do if you loved me?"

"If I did not love I should not speak to you at all. I should let you go your ways, I should make no such desperate struggles to rescue my happiness from the wreck you threaten to make of it." And then in his exasperation he ran on: "Is it fair to blame me if things have gone other than you wished? It was your own fault. You chose your course. I made no attempt to persuade you. I left you free to follow your own bent. Why were you false to it? And why, having been false to it, do you now visit me with the blame?"

"What do you mean – my bent?"

"The path of loyalty on which your feet were set. You would have kept the affection of your father; you would have married your exquisite kinsman, Robert Mandeville; and some day you would have been 'my lady.'"

Swelling resentment looked at him furiously out of her lovely eyes. "Why must you sneer at Robert? He is a better man than you."

Stung by that in his turn he added words he was to regret as soon as uttered:

"You cannot more deeply deplore than I do that you did not marry him."

On that she left him to the conviction that he was brutal; and he was more than ever exasperated with her that she should make him so.

Of course there were passionate reconciliations. Momentary glimpses of the tragic reality beyond the control of either, of which these scenes were no more than the artificial manifestations! But the pendulum would not halt in its swinging between mutual love and mutual resentment; and the sad truth must be recorded that affection was gradually being worn away by the exacerbation of these misunderstandings.

In the early spring matters improved a little. Partly, this was due to the fact that military necessity drew Latimer away from home. The comparative idleness of the winter, when the news from the North was uncertain and depressing, had kept him moping a deal about the house. Thus husband and wife had been thrown together far more than was desirable in the existing state of feeling. But towards the end of February, as a consequence of certain intelligence that in New York the British were preparing an expedition against Charles Town, Colonel Moultrie was ordered down to Sullivan's Island to take command, and Harry Latimer went with him.

They were building there a fort large enough to contain a thousand men; and as this was looked upon as the key of the harbour, the news received set them feverishly to work with all the mechanics they could enroll and an army of negro labourers brought down from the country so as to complete the work in time to receive the British fleet.

There were as a consequence long absences from home for Harry, and since one result of these was a reduction of the friction between himself and his wife, he welcomed them. It happened, too, that Myrtle's condition urged him to subdue any irritation, and turn the other cheek whenever he found her disposed to scold. He did so the more readily and cheerfully since he now discovered a physical explanation for her impatiences.

For some two months before their child was born, their relations – thanks largely to his exemplary forbearance – had so far improved that Harry began to take a less despondent view of the future, and to trust entirely to Time to dull her pain at the estrangement from her father. With the birth of his son, it almost seemed to him that this time no longer lay in the future, but was arrived already.

There was between them in those days, in the hours stolen from duty, when he came to feast his eyes upon the swaddled bundle in the arms of the ever-faithful mauma, Dido, such a tenderness as had not prevailed even when first their troth had been plighted. They were lovers again, drawn close by this precious link, and the world to them lay in each other and the child. And because of this each was now yielding and generous to the other, each solicitous to fulfil the other's wishes.

One day in May, when the boy was a month old, and the mother in convalescence, she broached the matter of a name for him.

She was reclining on a daybed out of doors, set in the shade of the magnolias, watching with shining eyes the child gurgling idiotically in the arms of the black mauma. Harry, in the blue coat and white smalls of the Continental Army, leaned on the head of her couch contemplating her with eyes of entire devotion, and discerning as only lovers can a touch almost of holiness in her beauty. He observed the straight nose with its sensitive nostrils, the firm yet generous and tender mouth, and the deep mysterious eyes to which motherhood now brought a new and shining glory. His fingers were toying abstractedly with the long brown ringlet resting on that white slender neck when she looked up at him with a smile that in itself would have sufficed to make life glorious.

"We must christen the little heathen, Harry," she reminded him.

"Why so we must. What is he to be called?"

Now Harry knew his mind quite well. Since Charles Fitzroy Latimer had come to found their house in South Carolina, the first-born of the Latimers had ever been given one or the other of two only names – Charles and Harry – and they had borne these names alternately. It was a tradition he desired to see maintained; and in his mind he already thought of his son as Charles Latimer. But because of the complete amity prevailing now between himself and Myrtle, the more cherishable because of the storms they had traversed, his wishes were not to be expressed until she should make known her own.

"I had thought…" she began, and broke off, hesitating. "Nay. But have you no wishes in the matter? He is your son, Harry."

"Not more than he is yours. Therefore I'll wish whatever you may wish."

"It's very sweet in you." She caught the hand that was engaged upon her ringlet, and pressed it, holding it thereafter. "I had thought…" Again she paused, and looked at him, almost in apprehension. "If you do not like it Harry, you'll say so; and we'll think of it no more. But I feel that if I called him Andrew, the name would remain as a proof to my father that in spite of all that has happened I am still dutiful to him." She looked away again as she spoke, and then added: "But if you think other, Harry – "

"How should I?" Her submission to him would alone have melted any opposition even if he had been disposed to offer it. But he was not. He saw, and sympathetically understood her motives. Besides, he felt that he would have yielded to her even had she asked that the child be named Robert.

And so he swallowed lightly his regrets at this breach of a tradition of his house; was glad indeed to offer it up as a loving sacrifice to her desires.

Andrew the boy was christened, and the christening took place at St Michael's on the following Sunday, Colonel Moultrie being the rebel god-father provided by Harry, and Polly Roupel the royalist godmother of Myrtle's choosing.

In the peace and good understanding into which they were now come Harry and his wife continued until the first of June, when Captain Latimer, who was on leave at home, received an imperative command to return to duty in the more or less completed fort on Sullivan's Island.

A British squadron had appeared off Dewees Island, and it was clear that the attack for which they had been preparing throughout some weeks was at last about to be delivered.

When Harry bore the news to Myrtle she was filled with sudden terror for him and for the babe who might so soon be deprived of his father.

"Oh, Harry! Why, why have you espoused this dreadful quarrel?"

It shocked him a little. It was so different from all that in such an emergency he would have expected from Myrtle. He had known her from infancy, and had learnt to regard her spirit as of purest temper. She was not the weak, emotional, selfish woman to bring added pain to such a parting as this, or ever to allow considerations of herself to be thrust between her man and that man's duty.

Thus he had judged her, and thus indeed she was. What he was slow to perceive was that her resentment arose from the nature of the duty that was taking him away. Had he been riding off to fight the battles of that monarchist faith in which she had been reared, she would have hidden her grief in a mask of courage that she might strengthen and enhearten him; she would have blessed him at parting and prayed for him until his return. But he went to do battle on the wrong side, against ideals she could not cease from holding. Hence that disheartening almost petulant wail.

"My dear," he said, gently. "It is a sacred duty."

"A duty!" She looked at him, and her eyes were hardening. "Did I save your life by marrying you, to have you fling it away like this, in battle against the right?"

His face turned white. "Was that," he asked slowly "the only reason why you married me?"

Mutinous in her fierce resentment she stood, her shoulder turned to him, looking through the window of the dining-room where he had sought her, and giving him no answer.

He took it from her silence. His lip quivered a moment. A threat which was also a promise trembled for utterance. But he did not utter it. He would not have her afterwards troubled by remorse. He had done her a great wrong. He should have seen it at the time. How purblind he had been not to have understood her sacrifice, the sacrifice with which since he had actually taunted her.

He approached her. But still she did not turn. He took the hand that lay limply at her side, and raised it to his lips.

"Goodbye, Myrtle!" he said quietly, and let the hand fall again.

Still in her perversity she did not turn. There was a knot in her throat, and she would not have him see the tears that filled her eyes.

He moved away towards the door. There he paused a moment.

"I have left everything in order," he said quietly. "All is provided for. If anything should happen, all that I have will be yours. Yours and Andrew's."

"Harry!" It was the cry of a breaking heart. Suddenly she had spun round and was coming towards him, sobbing. He stood there, and she flung her arms about his neck, set her wet cheek against his. "Harry, my dear, my dear! Forgive me. I love you, Harry. I'm terrified at the thought of losing you. It is the thought of you and of the boy makes me...what I am. Why don't you beat me, Harry? It's what I deserve."

And so she ran on in a tale of repentance and self-abasement that was new in his experience of her, but which failed now to move him, because he did not believe it sincere. She was only repeating that which had happened when he was in danger of arrest by the royal Government. It was pity for him and fear for his life had moved her then. This she had now frankly acknowledged. And it was the same emotion that possessed her now. But not again could she delude him, even though she might delude herself.

Tender and considerate with her he was. To quiet her, he professed belief in what she said, but his professions rang false and hollow in her acute and straining ears.

And so in the end he left her.

Chapter 2

Fort Sullivan

The Executive of the General Assembly, which had by now replaced the old Provincial Congress, was in the hands of a legislative and privy council. John Rutledge had been elected president and invested with all the powers of Governor.

Despite a temperamental antipathy, which he believed mutual, and some lingering remains of that rancour provoked by Rutledge's hard unsentimental criticisms of his conduct in the Featherstone affair, Harry Latimer could not withhold his admiration of the sagacity, energy and strength with which the new president went to work to establish and maintain order, to levy troops and to advance the fortification of the town materially and morally against all emergencies.

In those first days of June there arrived in Charles Town that English soldier of fortune, Major-General Charles Lee, sent by Washington to command the troops engaged in the defence of the Southern sea-board. He was a man of great experience and skill, who had spent his life campaigning wherever campaigns were being conducted; and Moultrie tells us that his presence in Charles Town was equivalent to a reinforcement of a thousand men. But his manners, Moultrie adds, were rough and harsh.

The unfinished state in which he found the great fort of palmetto logs seems to have fretted him considerably. His correspondence with Moultrie in these days bears abundant witness to that, and we have a glimpse of the irritation caused him by the calm unexcited manner in which the stout-hearted Moultrie continued the works as if he still had months in which to complete them. Two things Lee was frenziedly demanding: the completion of the fort, and the building of a bridge to secure the retreat to the mainland of the force on Sullivan's Island.

If Moultrie was leisurely in the matter of the former, he was entirely negligent on the subject of the latter. He had not, he said, come there to retreat, and there was no need to be wasting time, energy and material in providing the means for it.

Lee's great experience of war had taught him to leave nothing to chance. Moreover, in this instance, he was fully persuaded that the fort could not be held – particularly in its unfinished state – against the powerful fleet under Sir Peter Parker standing off the bar. He reckoned without two factors: the calm cool courage of its defender and the peculiar resisting quality of palmetto wood, experience of which was not included in all his campaignings, extensive and varied though they had been.

Action by the fleet was delayed until the end of June, in order that with it might be combined the operation of a land force under Sir Henry Clinton. This had been put ashore on Long Island with the same object of reducing the fort, which was the key to the harbour. To this end Clinton erected a battery which should cover the transport and fording of troops across the narrow neck of shallow water dividing the two islands. But to defend the passage there was a battery on the east end of Sullivan's Island commanded by Colonel Thomson with a picked body of riflemen.

The defence of Fort Sullivan is one of the great epics of the war and few of its battles were of more far-reaching effect than this, coming as it did in a time of some uncertainty in the affairs of the Americans.

At half-past ten o'clock on the morning of June 28th Sir Peter Parker, on board the flagship *Bristol*, gave the signal for action, and the fleet of ten vessels carrying two hundred and eighty-four guns, advanced to anchor before the fort, confidently to undertake the work of pounding it into dust.

At eleven o'clock that night, nine shattered ships dropped down to Five Fathom Hole, out of range, leaving the tenth – the frigate *Actaeon* – crippled and aground to westward of the fort, there to be destroyed by fire next morning.

Throughout the action Moultrie's supplies of powder had been inadequate. Hence the need not only for economy of fire, but for greater markmanship, so that as few shots as possible should be wasted. And whilst the careful steady fire from the fort battered the ships and made frightful carnage on their decks, the British shot sank more or less harmlessly into the soft spongy palmetto or fell into the large moat in the middle of the fort where the fuses were extinguished before the shells could explode. It is said that of over fifty shot thrown by the *Thunder-Bomb* alone into the fort not a single one exploded.

But if these did not there were others that did, and although the casualties of the garrison were surprisingly small, yet throughout that terrible day of overpowering heat, the Carolinians in Fort Sullivan may well have deemed themselves in hell. Toiling there, naked to the waist for the most part, under a pall of acrid smoke that hung low and heavy upon them and at times went near to choking them, and amid an incessant roar of guns, with shells bursting overhead, they fought on desperately and indomitably against a force they knew greatly superior to their own. And amongst them, ever where the need was greatest, hobbling hither and thither – for he was sorely harassed by gout at the time – was Moultrie in his blue coat and three-cornered hat, his rugged face calm, smoking his pipe as composedly as if he had been at his own fireside.

Only once did he and his officers, who in this matter emulated their leader, lay aside their pipes; and that was out of respect for General Lee, when in the course of action he came down to see how things were with them, and to realize for himself that it was possible that with all his great experience of war he had been wrong in his assumption that the place could not be held.

The thing he chiefly dreaded had by then been averted. He had perceived that the fort's alarming weakness lay in the unfinished western side – the side that faced the main. Thence it might easily be enfiladed by any ship that ran past and took up a position in the channel. This vulnerable point had not been overlooked by Sir Peter Parker, and comparatively early in the battle he had ordered forward the Sphynx. the *Actaeon* and the *Syren* to attack it. But here fortune helped the garrison that was so stoutly helping itself. In the haste of their advance the three ships fouled one another's rigging, became entangled and drifted thus on to the shoal known as the Middle Ground. Before they could clear themselves the guns of the fort had been concentrated upon them, and poured into them a fire as destructive as it was accurate. The *Sphynx* and the *Syren* eventually got off in a mangled condition one of them trailing her broken bowsprit. The *Actaeon* remained to be destroyed at leisure.

And all this while, Myrtle in an apprehension which was increased to anguish when she remembered the manner of her parting with Harry, lay on the roof of the house on the Bay endeavouring thence by the aid of a telescope to follow the action that was being fought ten miles away, whilst the windows below rattled and the very world seemed to shake with the incessant thunder of the British guns and the slow deliberate replies from the fort.

Once she saw that flag – the first American flag displayed in the South; a blue flag with a white crescent in the dexter corner – was gone from the fort. And her dismay in that moment made her realize, as once before she had realized, the true feelings that underlay the crust of vain prejudice upon her soul. There followed a pause of dreadful uncertainty as to whether this meant surrender – the pause during which the heroic Sergeant Jasper leapt down from one of the embrasures in the face of a withering fire to rescue the flag which had been carried away by a chance shot. Attaching it to a spunge staff he hoisted it once more upon the ramparts, and when she saw it fluttering there again a faint cheer broke from her trembling lips and was taken up by the negro servants who shared her eyrie and some of her anxiety for the garrison among which was the master they all loved.

There she remained until after darkness had fallen, a darkness still rent and stabbed by the flashes from the guns, and until a terrific thunderstorm broke overhead and the artillery of heaven came to mingle with the artillery of man.

Then at last, unable to follow the combat with her eyes, and already drenched by the downpour which descended almost without warning, she allowed the slaves to lead her down from the roof, and went within to spend a sleepless night of anguish.

In the morning the news of victory filled Charles Town with joy and thanksgiving. It was a victory less complete than it might have been if Moultrie had not been starved of powder. With adequate ammunition, every ship of the British fleet would have been sunk or forced to surrender. But it was complete enough. The battered and defeated vessels were beaten off, and Charles Town was safe for the present.

Whole-heartedly Myrtle shared the general joy and thanksgiving. She knew herself now, she thought, beyond possibility of ever again being mistaken in her feelings. She had been through an experience of anguish which had sharpened the sight of her soul so that she had come to see her own fault in the discords that had poisoned her married life. It should never, never be so again, she vowed, if only Harry were now safely restored to her. That was the abiding anxiety. Was he safe?

But amid the general rejoicing how could she doubt it? It was known that the casualties had been few in the fort, only some ten killed and twice that number of wounded. Surely Heaven would not be so cruel as to include her husband among these.

She went actively about the house during that endless morning, stimulating all into preparations for welcoming Harry home, confident that he would come to her soon in the course of the day.

And come to her he did somewhere about noon, inanimate upon a stretcher borne by two of his men. The click of the garden gate and the sound of steps on the gravel brought her swift-footed eager to the porch, to swoon there under the shock of what she beheld, believing that it was a dead body those men bore.

When, restored to her senses, she was told that he still lived though sorely wounded, she would have gone to him at once. But they restrained her – old Julius, Mauma Dido and Dr Parker, the latter having flown instantly to Harry's side in response to the news borne him by Hannibal of his master's homecoming.

The doctor, elderly and benevolent, and an old friend of Harry's, very gently broke to her the news that although her husband's life was not to be despaired of, yet it hung by the most tenuous of threads, and that only the utmost care and vigilance could avoid the severing of this. He had been shot through the body in two places. One of these was a slight wound; but the other was grave, and Dr. Parker had only just extracted the bullet. He was easier now; but it would be better if she did not see him yet.

"But who is to tend and nurse him?" she inquired.

"We must provide for that."

"Who better than myself?"

"But you have not the strength, my dear," he demurred. "The very sight of him wounded has so affected you that – "

She interrupted him. "That shall not happen again," she promised firmly, and rose commanding her still trembling limbs. Although very white, she was so calm and so resolved that presently Dr. Parker gave way and permitted her at once to take up her duties by Harry's side.

He was delirious and fever-tossed, so that there was no danger of any excitement to him from her presence. She received the doctor's instructions attentively, displaying now the calm of an intrepid combatant preparing for battle. And save for one concession to her emotions, when she knelt by his bedside and offered up a prayer that he might be spared to her, she did not again depart from that stern rôle.

Down in her heart there was an instinctive knowledge that she, herself was in part responsible for his condition, even before Moultrie came, as he did later that day, to leave her by the admissions she drew from him no doubt upon that score.

It was like the kindly easy-going soldier to find time amid the many preoccupations of the moment to seek her, all battle-stained as he was, to offer comfort and obtain news of Harry's condition.

"It is precarious," she answered him. "But Dr Parker assures me that he is to be saved by care and vigilance, and these I can provide. Be sure that Harry shall get well again."

He marvelled at her calm confidence; marvelled, admired and was reassured. Here was the spirit in which the battle of Fort Sullivan had been won by his gallant lads, the spirit which conquers all material things.

He spoke of the fight of yesterday and of Harry's conduct in it, conduct of a valour amounting to recklessness.

"If I had not known him for a man with every inducement to live, with everything to make life dear for him, I might almost have suspected him of courting death. Twice I had to order him down from the parapet, where he was needlessly exposing himself in his zeal to stimulate the men. And when the flag was carried away a second time by a shot from the Bristol, before I could stop him, he had done what Jasper did on the first occasion of that happening. He was over the parapet and out on the sand under fire to rescue and bring back our standard. He was standing on the ramparts waving it to the men when he was shot. I caught him in my arms, and desperately wounded as he was, at the moment I really think my chief emotion was anger with him that he should so recklessly have exposed himself."

When presently he left her, and she went back to Harry's bedside, where her place had been filled in her absence by Mauma Dido, she took back with her the burning memory of Moultrie's words.

"If I had not known him for a man with every inducement to live, with everything to make life dear for him..."

And the truth, she told herself, was that through her he was become a man with every inducement to die. Deliberately he had sought death, that he might deliver her from a bond which had been forged by charity instead of love. For this was the lie she had led him to believe; this was the lie which, for a time, she had almost believed herself. Because he imagined that bond grown odious to her – and she had given him all cause so to imagine it – he had sought to snap it, that he might set her free.

How like him was that; how like the high-spirited selfless Harry she had always known. Impetuous and impulsive always, but always upon impulses to serve others. It was the service of others had made him a patriot, where a self-seeker of his wealth and prosperity under the royal Government would have striven to avoid all change. Whether his political views were right or wrong, noble and altruistic they certainly were. For that she must honour him, and for that, too, since she was his wife, she must make his faith her own.

Never again, if it should please God in His infinite mercy to spare him, would she give him occasion to doubt her, or to suppose that anything but love had brought about that precipitate marriage of theirs. And if he should not be spared, why then she would spend the wealth she would inherit, to the last penny, in forwarding the cause he had espoused.

In such a spirit did she address herself to wrestle with the Angel of Death.

Chapter 3

Severance

Harry Latimer did not die. For a fortnight, during the torrid heat of that July, he lay a prey to a fever that ebbed and flowed almost with the regularity of the tides, finally to sink down and leave him on the shores of convalescence.

Perhaps the greatest factor in his recovery was the will to live, aroused in him when he found that he owed the maintenance of his life during that season of greatest peril to the passionate, tireless and devoted battle which his wife had fought for him. Her tenderness and her solicitude during those first hours of consciousness, when she was herself worn to exhaustion, but sustained by her will and her determination to hold him back from death, convinced him as nothing else could have convinced him that she cherished him and desired him to live.

And presently as he grew stronger, in the days when at last under the insistence of Dr Parker she submitted to dividing with others her care of him, so that she, herself, might snatch some sorely-needed rest, there followed between them explanations that made an end at last to all possibility of further misunderstandings.

"If you had died, Harry," she told him, "life for me would have been at an end."

And with the proofs of her self-sacrificing devotion before him he believed her whole-heartedly now. He was thankful to have survived, and looked back with horror of himself and his own stupidity for having permitted a jealous doubt so to have wrought upon him as to send him in deliberate quest of death.

Meanwhile the tide of war was beaten back from Charles Town, and a sense of peace and security quickly restored to it, whilst elsewhere the American mind was inflamed with new ardour and the British mind cooled by dismay at the almost incredible disaster to Sir Peter Parker's fleet. But to avenge it another great fleet was already on its way to America, bringing additional forces amounting to some twenty-five thousand British troops and seventeen thousand German mercenaries engaged for the purpose by treaty with several German princes.

Since thus it had been rendered more than ever apparent that England would abandon none of her claims and accept nothing but the total dependency and servitude of the colonies, a violent change of feeling had taken place. The republicans who preached American Independence, hitherto a repressed minority, had raised their heads in force, and conversion to their doctrines ran like a wave across the thirteen provinces. So that when Richard Henry Lee of Virginia offered his resolution in Congress that "The United Colonies are and ought to be an Independent state" it was possible, although only by a bare majority, to adopt it. And so it happened that the thanks of the Continental Congress to the brave defenders of Charles Town, dispatched to them on the 20th of July, were from the United States of America to the State of South Carolina. The Republic had come into existence, and Moultrie's guns of Fort Sullivan had fired a salute that went far to establish the independent Government whose declaration was read a very few days later in Congress by Mr Thomas Jefferson.

In Charles Town the declaration of Independence was not read until the first Monday in August. By then, Harry Latimer, whilst still reduced in strength, was so far recovered from his wounds as to have himself carried in a sedan chair to Liberty Tree, the spot whence Gadsden in the old days had preached sedition to the people. It was thronged now by men and women, young and old, and thither came the military, marching with drums beating and flags flying. Hushed, they all stood in the sweltering heat, to hear the Reverend William Percy solemnly read the declaration, whilst his black boy held an umbrella over him with one hand and fanned him with the other.

The declaration was received with acclamations natural enough in the excitement of the moment. But not all present acclaimed it. Many even of those who had been most resolute in combating King George's rigorous methods of coercion were silent and uneasy, conscious of the heritage they were renouncing, driven to it by the intransigence of those who ruled the parent country.

Henry Laurens, who stood near Harry's chair, was observed by Myrtle to be in tears, and the usually expressionless face of John Rutledge appeared for once to reflect spiritual pain.

As they returned home from that function, it seemed to Myrtle that between the colonies and the mother-country was enacted something akin to that which had happened between her father and herself.

Chapter 4

Governor Rutledge

There followed now for South Carolina a period of peace and almost unequalled prosperity, what time the war with varying fortune was raging in the North.

The victory of Fort Moultrie – as Fort Sullivan had been re-named by the legislative in honour of its gallant defender – had earned the province this season of respite.

As one of the few open ports of America, Charles Town became the gateway into the colonies for all supplies. The bay, for the next two years and longer, was crowded with the shipping of neutral countries; the wharves hummed with activity; trade flourished.

Winter came and went before Harry Latimer was restored to his former vigour. To Myrtle these were perhaps the happiest days that she had known. She and Harry had come through storm into calm, and she had learnt that her world was made up of her husband and their boy, and that events happening outside that world should and could make no impression upon it.

If in the background of her mind there was ever the thought of her father, it was no longer attended by that sense of unfilial conduct on which her happiness had almost suffered shipwreck. She began to absorb something of the atmosphere in which she lived and views held at first out of a sense of wifely duty deliberately imposed upon herself to make amends, came in the end to be held out of pure conviction. Her father became in her eyes a moral reflection of the King whom he worshipped; and just as the intransigence of the latter was to blame for the rupture between the parent country and its colonial offspring, so was the intransigence of the former to blame for the breach between himself and his child.

They were as children, all three of them, during the spring and summer of '77. Harry had been promoted to the rank of major for his gallantry during the defence of Fort Sullivan, although Moultrie himself had privately expressed to him the opinion that he deserved to be shot for it. During his convalescence John Rutledge had come to visit him, to congratulate him upon his promotion and to honour him for the deed that had earned it.

"Sir," he had said in his stiff, formal way, "if once I blamed you for impulsiveness, I come to make you amends. If it is a fault, you have shown me that it can also be a virtue."

And presently, by the time that little Andrew was beginning to stand upon his own feet, Harry became immersed in affairs, which if not directly the affairs of war were at least very closely concerned with them. The whole of his considerable merchant fleet was now employed in the service of his country. Some of the ships were fitted out as privateers, others went upon voyages to the West Indies, to France and to Spain for war material and supplies, and in the lack of military engagements during that time he was able to devote the whole of his energies to the supervision of all the details connected with these shipping matters. Hence it resulted that South Carolina was better equipped in arms and munitions than any state in the Union.

And meanwhile in the North the fortunes of war fluctuated in amazing waves. At first the high hopes fired by the Carolinian victory over Sir Peter Parker steadily waned until that dreadful moment at the end of '76, when all seemed lost beyond the chance of redemption. Washington beaten back and back had at last retreated across the Delaware, his army reduced by casualties, sickness and desertions to a mere three thousand men and the river being now the only barrier between the British and Philadelphia.

The British, strong and well-equipped, sat down complacently to await the freezing of the river so that they might cross and make an end of that remnant of an army should it not meanwhile have completely melted away in panic. Cornwallis and his troops were already embarking in New York to return home. The war, from the British as from the American point of view, was at an end.

But it was not at an end from Washington's.

Suddenly the country was startled out of its gloom and despondency by the bold stroke of the American Commander-in-Chief in re-crossing the Delaware on that Christmas night and descending like a thunderbolt upon the advanced post of the enemy.

Hopes soared once more; spirits that had been drooping were again uplifted; men of the militia, whose time was expiring no longer thought of leaving the colours as they had been preparing to do, and recruits flowed in again to strengthen the American arm. And back from New York and his ships came the startled Cornwallis who had already counted the chickens that were never to be hatched; back to New Jersey to increase the British forces that were to deal with an enemy which yesterday had seemed not merely exhausted but annihilated.

Thus the war may be said to have recommenced. It dragged wearily on through '77 with the same varying ebb and flow as before, fortune in the main favouring the British arms, and American hopes gradually sinking, until suddenly from the very nadir they were lifted in mid-October to the zenith.

Burgoyne and the whole of the British North Army, surrounded at Saratoga by the Americans under General Gates, his supplies cut off and without hope of relief from Clinton, was compelled to the humiliation of complete surrender.

Such was the shock of the news in England that at last King George was constrained to put aside the obstinacy which had brought the empire this humiliation and to which he had sacrificed her finest colony. Under the pressure of outraged public opinion, which unable to endure more was manifesting a dangerous temper,

Lord North was compelled to come forward with two conciliatory bills. By these the King not only conceded now everything that had been the occasion of the controversy and over which already so much good red blood had been shed; he offered far more than America had ever asked. But he offered it too late. Congress would not treat with King George until he withdrew from America his armies and his fleets. Almost at the same time Franklin in Paris brought France not only to recognize the Independence of America but into a treaty of alliance defensive and offensive.

Thus Great Britain in the hour of dismay, found herself faced not only by her own recalcitrant offspring but by her hereditary foe as well. To this pass had the headstrong stupidity of a single man of foreign blood brought the great empire over which in his arrogance and vanity he must rule as well as reign.

It was evident to the ministry at home that the war in the North, which twice had been all but won, was now definitely lost. All was to be begun again, and it was now determined as a last resort to attempt the conquest from the South.

General Prevost in Florida was to be reinforced with troops from New York, so that he might open the new campaign with the conquest of Georgia; a comparatively easy matter this, for Georgia was indifferently disposed to war. So the last phase of England's struggle to retain her colonies opened in the autumn of 1778 with the invasion of Georgia by two expeditions of British troops supplemented by tory refugees from Georgia itself and South Carolina. And it opened disastrously for the American arms. The forces under General Robert Howe suffered a terrible rout, and Savannah was captured by the British.

After that Prevost had an easy task of completing the conquest of Georgia. So much accomplished, he made his dispositions to penetrate into South Carolina.

Rumours of this were already alarming Charles Town when Major-General Benjamin Lincoln arrived there early in December, dispatched by Congress to take command of the Southern department, and immediately preparations began under his orders to march the troops to the relief of Georgia.

Lincoln had been with Gates in the operations that had resulted in the surrender of Burgoyne, and some of the glamour of this the most glorious feat of American arms hung about him and lent him a prestige in the eyes of the Carolinians such as his own military merits were far from deserving. He was brave and patriotic, but he was without real experience of war and totally lacking in imagination which is able so often to fill the place of experience.

Harry Latimer, now acting as Brigadier-General Moultrie's chief aide and largely entrusted with all administrative matters, for which his conduct of affairs in the past year had shown him so admirably qualified, ate his Christmas dinner with his family and his brigadier in the big house in Broad Street that was now used not only as Moultrie's headquarters but also as his own and Harry's residence.

The reason for this claims a word of explanation, for in following the fortunes of the American arms we have momentarily neglected Latimer's own personal history.

Almost a year ago – in January of '78 – during Latimer's absence on an expedition against the Scovellites in the back-country, there had occurred in Charles Town the great conflagration, supposed to have been the work of tory incendiaries – for the place was honeycombed with traitors – which wrought such terrible havoc to property. Latimer's beautiful house, with all the choice furniture, plate and books, in which it was possible to trace his family's colonial history, had been burnt to the ground.

Moultrie had come to the rescue of Myrtle, who found herself homeless as a consequence, and he had offered her the hospitality of his house for herself and her immediate personal servants, Julius, Hannibal and Dido. As his own wife was away in Virginia at the time, the arrangement had proved mutually so convenient that when eventually Harry had returned to Charles Town it had not only been permitted to continue but had passed almost imperceptibly into a permanent arrangement. It suited the General to have the surveillance of Myrtle over the domestic side of his establishment no less than to have his chief aide, which Major Latimer became at about that time, immediately under his hand.

On the day after Christmas, the first and second regiments, some twelve hundred strong, were ordered to march to Purysburg, and on the 27th they set out, accompanied and reinforced by five hundred Continental troops. Purysburg was reached on January 3rd and the army sat down within sound of the British drums across the river, to watch the enemy, and challenge his crossing should he attempt it, whilst awaiting the reinforcements that should render them at need strong enough, themselves, to pay the first visit.

But for Howe's mismanagement of affairs and the rout he had sustained by his ill-judged action, the colonials would have been in sufficient strength to deal with Prevost without further waiting, and by seizing Savannah before he could fortify it, drive him to his ships. As it was not only did the reinforments awaited by Moultrie not arrive, but desertions began to reduce the forces already existing. This was the almost constant and inevitable result of the Fabian policy the American leaders were so commonly forced to adopt. The men of the militia did not lack spirit, but the absence of training and discipline rendered them insubordinate; unless quickly brought to action, camp-life wearied and fretted them and they became homesick. After that, since the public law by which they were governed could impose upon them no more than a small pecuniary fine for the greatest military crime, there was nothing to deter them from desertion.

At first things went well for the Americans at Purysburg. An expedition sent by Prevost to take post on Port Royal Island was sought out by Moultrie and defeated with great loss. This initial victory, coming almost immediately upon the heels of the arrival, on the last day of January, of General John Ashe with a body of twelve hundred North Carolinians, brought optimism and confidence.

In the middle of February came the victory over Colonel Boyd with his strong body of Carolinian and Georgian tories who were on their way to join the British forces at Augusta higher up the river. With characteristic intolerance and bigotry – just such a spirit as that which actuated Sir Andrew Carey – Boyd's green-coats had swept like a flail over the country, ravaging, burning and devastating as they went, until suddenly they were intercepted by the Carolinian force under Colonel Pickens, which cut them to pieces.

But by the time of these happenings, Harry Latimer was back in Charles Town with Moultrie, summoned thither by Lincoln to confer with Rutledge upon the state of affairs regarding the militia and to urge the necessity for reinforcements if a decisive action against Prevost were to be attempted.

John Rutledge was now invested by the new legislature with powers which transcended mere civil matters and gave him in military affairs an authority whose limits were scarcely defined. His re-election to the office of Governor was comparatively recent. He had resigned a year ago, upon perceiving that it was the aim to render permanent the emancipation from Great Britain implied in the Declaration of Independence, which at first in common with many others he had been disposed to regard as a temporary measure. For a year Rawlins Lowndes had held the office; but with the shifting of the war to the Southern provinces he had begged to be permitted to resign in favour of someone with greater knowledge of military matters, and Rutledge, whose scruples had meanwhile passed and whose mind had grown accustomed to the ideas that were henceforth to prevail in America, had accepted a position urgently thrust upon him by all those who rightly valued his great capacity for affairs, his energy, patriotism and uncompromising honesty.

Of the fact that his eyes missed nothing, Moultrie was to have a rather painful instance on the occasion of their second interview, held in Rutledge's house in Broad Street.

The Governor had disclosed the measures taken and the further measures contemplated so as to raise additional troops; and he had announced his intention of going, himself, to Orangeburg to form a camp for three thousand men, though he said nothing as yet of how these men were to be employed.

It is possible that already at this date Rutledge had conceived the great strategic plan by which he counted upon drawing Prevost's army to such an annihilation as had overtaken Burgoyne's, that at a stroke he might bring the war to an end. He guarded his secret so jealously that even today it is only by carefully weighing all that was written in the military correspondence and general orders of the time, and by scanning every word in them, that in glimpses, between the lines, the attentive student may perceive the inspiration and deliberate aim of all that was done. Since success was to depend upon misleading the enemy so that he might be subsequently surprised, secrecy was of the very first importance. And such secrecy did Rutledge observe that not even one so trustworthy and personally dear to him as Moultrie was permitted the least hint of his project, nor at the date of which I write did even Lincoln know what was so closely guarded in the Governor's mind.

But since presently one at least must share the secret, and since from inevitable actions of his own in Charles Town acute observers might draw inferences sufficiently near the truth to wreck his schemes, Rutledge was growing uneasy in the knowledge that the place still swarmed with traitors and with tories whose rancour had been increased by the appropriation of their wealth for the common weal. He was suspicious of all who were not avowedly and energetically on his own side, and he was, like all men who guard a secret fearfully, disposed to start at shadows.

It was of this that he now afforded more than a glimpse.

"There is another matter on which I wish to speak to you," he said at that second meeting. He spoke quietly, and yet in so odd a tone that Moultrie took the pipe from between his lips, and looked sharply across the writing-table before which he was seated opposite to the Governor.

He observed, perhaps for the first time, that Rutledge's face was rather grey and drawn from unremitting mental and physical toil; his features had lost some of their soft roundness, and the fullness under the chin was perceptibly diminished.

"Are you sure that you are wise in permitting Mrs Latimer to continue under your roof, in a house which is practically serving as your headquarters here?"

The General's stare became one of stupefaction. "What on earth can be the objection?" For the moment he almost wondered whether, considering the absence of his own wife, his moral character was being assailed.

"The objection there must always be to having a person of doubtful loyalty about headquarters. There are always in such places scraps of information to be picked up."

"My God!" ejaculated Moultrie, and such was his indignation that his manner of addressing the Governor became formal. "Is your excellency insinuating that Mrs Latimer is a spy?"

"If I thought so, I should not insinuate it. I should state it. No, William. I mean neither more nor less than my words convey. I think they are quite plain."

"Plain? Ay, damme, they're plain. What isn't plain is why you should utter them at all. Ye must have some reason. Or is it just panic?"

"I am not given to panic."

"But…but…" Moultrie was between amazement and exasperation. "Myrtle is the wife of my chief aide, a man as loyal and trustworthy as myself, as every action of his life goes to prove."

"I am not questioning Major Latimer's loyalty. But neither am I forgetting that his wife is also the daughter of Andrew Carey, the bitterest and most rancorous tory in Carolina."

Moultrie laughed, and resumed his pipe. He thought he understood.

"Here's a mare's nest," said he between puffs. "Your memory's failing, John. Mrs Latimer is completely estranged from her father. It is notorious that he bears her as deep a rancour as he bears Harry Latimer himself."

"Then why?" asked Rutledge, "does she visit him?"

"Visit him!" Again the pipe came from between Moultrie's lips, and having parted them to ask that question they remained apart a moment. He screwed up his rugged features as he added on a deeper note of incredulity: "At Fairgrove?"

Rutledge shook his head slowly. "Not at Fairgrove. Here in Charles Town at his house in Tradd Street. Fairgrove is in our hands. Military necessity obliged us to take possession of it at the end of December. Carey denounced the action in terms which under martial law would almost have warranted our hanging him. Whether it was from the rage he indulged, or from other causes, the gout from which he was suffering mounted to his vitals, and for a fortnight he lay at the point of death." Rutledge sighed. "He would probably have saved us a deal of trouble had he died. But you may have observed, William, that troublesome persons are commonly of an extraordinary and tenacious vitality.

"He recovered, and for the past month he has steeped himself in affairs, which he conducts through his factor, old Featherstone – another friend of ours. His ships trade hither and thither, exporting the produce of his farther plantations and other produce acquired by purchase. What they will import in return remains yet to be seen. Whether this commercial activity is being pursued in quest of oblivion of his surroundings or as a mask upon some other design of his, I am not prepared to say. But I have him under observation, William. His only visitors apart from persons known to be avowed tories are a few traders from the back-country and even farther afield – all of them natural objects of suspicion to me. And now his daughter – " He broke off, and sighed again, his rather owlish eyes, solemn and steady in their glance, levelled upon Moultrie. "If she were not residing in your house it would not give me a moment's thought."

Moultrie got up, so suddenly that a twinge of gout made him sit down again. "Nor need it give you a moment's thought as it is." He was contemptuously emphatic, and he rose again, more successfully this time. "If she visits her father, it means that they're reconciled at last, and for her sake, poor child, I'm mighty glad it is so. It isn't comfortable for a girl to have a father's curse hanging over her, whatever the father may be. As for the rest..." He made a broad contemptuous gesture of dismissal. "Moonshine! But I'll go into it. I'll question her." Abruptly, as if to change the subject he added: "Anything else?"

"Yes. Since you are going to question her, ask her if she can tell you anything about a man named Neild – Jonathan Neild."

"Who is he?"

"One of her father's visitors. He's been in Charles Town twice in the last month: once while Carey was ill, and once again since; three days ago, in fact. He calls himself a Virginian and a Quaker, and he looks like a backwoodsman. I should like to know more of Mr Neild."

"But, surely, men are not suffered to come and go here as they please?"

"Oh, no. Mr Neild's papers have been examined. They are quite in order. He bears a pass from Washington, himself."

"And his business here?"

"To sell tobacco from his plantations."

"Why in Charles Town?"

"Not in Charles Town. To Sir Andrew Carey for export. He claims to have traded for years with Sir Andrew, and that he has more cause than ever to do so now that Charles Town is one of the few ports open to trade."

"Faith, he seems to give a clear account of himself."

"He does, and yet... I distrust him. It's instinctive, I suppose. Non amote, Sabidi... You understand! So if you are questioning Mrs Latimer, ask her to tell you what she knows about him."

"I will. But it's improbable she knows more than you do." He got up.

"I'll be going." He stepped to the door, leaning heavily upon his cane to ease his gouty foot. There he paused and looked back at Rutledge. "Feeling as you do about Carey, why don't you relieve your mind by taking him into custody? You've enough on your mind these days without such petty worries as this."

Again, and very slowly Rutledge shook his head. "Not so easy as it sounds. The tories in Charles Town give me trouble enough as it is. I don't want to precipitate an outbreak. I don't want civil war in the town as well as in the province."

Moultrie found it humorous. "Gadsmylife!" he gurgled. "It seems the fate of Governors of Charles Town never to be able to do what they should do to keep the peace lest they break it. It's a quaint paradox, John."

"Too quaint to be amusing," said Rutledge, who was not easily amused.

Chapter 5

Jonathan Neild

If Rutledge's mistrust of Sir Andrew Carey's quaker visitor was as intuitive as he represented – and neither our faith in Rutledge's veracity nor our knowledge of what subsequently came to pass justify any other assumption – it is a proof that the Governor's intuitions were keen indeed.

The precise manner of Sir Andrew Carey's reconciliation with Myrtle may be briefly told. When he lay ill, immediately after his enforced return to Charles Town, Doctor Parker, who was summoned to attend him, almost despaired of his life. Because of this, and knowing how affairs stood between the baronet and his daughter, the good doctor, who was the friend of both went to her at once with news of his condition. He urged her, for the sake of her own future peace of mind, to put all rancour behind her now, and to render her father the loving care that might yet save his life, or, at worst, might soothe his end.

She required no urging. Her only doubt was whether her father would receive her. Upon this the physician reassured her. Her father was in no condition to refuse. And so, with the connivance of old Remus, who wept for joy at beholding her once more in his master's house, she installed herself at her unconscious father's bedside, to nurse him with a devotion akin to that which she had shown Harry some three years ago. For four days and three nights almost without intermission she remained at the post of duty until he was restored once more to consciousness and the crisis was overpast.

Then she had withdrawn, and she had left it to Doctor Parker and Remus to tell him what she had done, and to plead with him to receive her.

"But for her tender care of you, Sir Andrew," the doctor told him, "my physic could have accomplished nothing. She has saved your life."

"So, so," said that relentless old man on a note of mockery. "But who bade her do it?"

"I did," said Doctor Parker.

"You did? You did? Really, really! Hum! A damned liberty on your part, Parker."

"I desired to save your life, Sir Andrew. Perhaps you'll consider that was a damned liberty, too."

"Tchah! tchah!" Inarticulately the baronet expressed his irritability. His temper was so soured in those days that he was regarded by all the world as a perverse, intractable old man whom it was a thankless task to serve. "What you did was your business, and you shall be paid for it. But what Mrs Latimer may have done upon your invitation, as you tell me, was an infernal impertinence in you."

The doctor kept his temper.

"Your daughter, sir – "

"Damnation, man," Sir Andrew interrupted him with a fury extraordinary in one so weak, "don't you know that I have no daughter? Don't I speak English, or don't you understand the language? Which is it? There! You mean Mrs Latimer, I suppose. Well I do not desire the acquaintance of Mrs Latimer. That she should have thrust herself upon me when I was in no condition to have her turned out was an impertinence in her and an impertinence in you. I have nothing more to say about it."

There was a savage finality in the words, and not to excite him further, the doctor withdrew and came in sorrow to beg Myrtle to have patience.

"I shall prevail with him yet," he assured her with a confidence he was not dolt enough to feel before such unchristian obstinacy as Sir Andrew's. "But I must wait until he is stronger. Tomorrow or the next day perhaps."

She withdrew, to return upon the morrow. But both on that day and on the next the doctor put her off with the same tale of failure and the same hope for the future, and meanwhile she learnt that her father was gaining strength so rapidly that he actually insisted upon transacting business with a back-country trader who had come to visit him.

It happened, however, that when she came on the third day she was met by Parker with so joyous an expression on his face that it required no words to convey his news of the miracle that had been wrought. Her father consented to see her.

She found Sir Andrew sitting up in bed, propped by pillows; and she observed at once the change that less than four years had wrought in him. He had lost much of his earlier fleshiness, and his illness now had reduced him further, so that his face looked almost gaunt, its heavy bone structures starkly defined. There was no gladness in the pale blue eyes that were turned upon her, and the lips were twisted into a vinegary smile suggestive rather of cruelty than forgiveness.

She went down on her knees beside his bed.

"Father! Dear father!"

He spoke quietly, yet with the faintest bitterness. "Parker tells me that you have saved my life. Well, well! Odd that you should be at pains to save a life which you robbed of everything that made it estimable. But... I forgive you, Myrtle! I expected too much perhaps. I rated you higher than your worth."

"Father!" It was all that she could say. But her hand reached out for his, and when she had found it he allowed it to lie in hers.

That he should not more graciously express the forgiveness he professed to extend did not at all surprise her. She knew his hard unyielding nature, and was thankful at the moment to have his forgiveness on any terms. There was so much she desired to say.

Above all she wanted to tell him about Andrew, the grandson she had named after him. But his manner raised barriers to any tenderness, to any intimacy.

He asked questions. First he inquired more or less formally after her health and desired news of Mauma Dido. Next he spoke a little of the plantation which had been wrested from him, of the slaves who had been appropriated by the rebel Government for its seditious labours, and of other matters as far removed from the things that should lie between father and daughter. Almost he conveyed the impression that he was making conversation. Nor did even this continue long. Presently he professed himself tired, but desired her to come soon again.

She was almost glad to escape, and she went home wondering whether the old severance was not really preferable to this bitterly cruel make-believe reconciliation. For that was how she viewed it.

On the morrow, however, she found him much better disposed, just as he was clearly much better in health. He was up when she arrived, wrapped in a bedgown and occupying an easy chair. He had a smile of greeting for her, and his conversation today actually led the way to the very things of which yesterday she had desired to talk.

He wanted to know about the boy, and listened to her with a faint smile about his lips to the eloquence of her maternal pride. When he learnt that her son had been named Andrew, his smile broadened, and too readily she attributed this to tenderness. His next words disillusioned her.

"You thought by that to move me to make him my heir, eh?" And the fierce old eyes stabbed at her from under his beetling brows.

It was as if he had struck her with a whip. "Father!" she cried, and when his little crackle of laughter had spluttered out, she gave him a fuller answer:

"It is unworthy of you to imagine such calculation in me. Harry's wealth is far beyond our needs."

"It may not always be so," he warned her. "When this war is over, when these rebels have been whipped into submission, there will be a heavy reckoning for those who have borne arms against their King. But I am glad you are not counting upon inheritance from me. For I have disposed otherwise. It is as well that you should know. All that I may die possessed of goes to your Cousin Robert. That is an act of commonest justice. It at once rewards merit and punishes unfilial conduct."

Pain robbed her of all answer. The money was nothing. But to be disinherited by a parent is to be outcast.

"Well?" he asked her after a pause. "Have you nothing to say?"

"Nothing, father." She held herself bravely in control. "If that is your wish, I am content. And if you will consider the disinheritance as the end of our punishment I am more than content."

"So, so," he muttered. "There, there! I said it only to test you; to test the sincerity of your desire to be reconciled. I am glad you stand the test so well, Myrtle. Very glad." He turned to give her a smile, but she saw quite clearly through his poor attempt to deceive her. There was a false ring in his words. He was as a man who, realizing that his feelings have betrayed him into saying too much, seeks to retract. She imagined, being herself charitable, that he did so out of regret for having unnecessarily wounded her.

Then, to her increasing amazement, he actually desired news of Harry: how and where was he, and what particular activities engaged him. She answered his questions shortly, giving him no more details than were necessary, because of her feeling that her replies could not possibly do other than nourish his bitterness.

When he had drawn from her that Harry was with Lincoln's army guarding the crossings of the Savannah he laughed aloud. "And these ragamuffins think they hold Prevost in check, do they?" he scoffed. "Ridiculous! What are their numbers?"

"I am not sure," she answered. "But I believe at least five thousand."

"Five thousand!" It was an ejaculation of mockery, which brought a flush to her cheeks since it seemed to include Harry himself. To combat his contempt, to inculcate in him respect for the side her husband served, she made haste to assure him that Lincoln's army was soon to be reinforced. "They are enlisting militia in North Carolinia and elsewhere to go to their support," she assured him.

"Bah! A rabble. D'ye think such fellows can stand against trained soldiers – a pack of out-at-elbow ruffians ill-armed and probably without sufficient ammunition."

He seemed to wait for an answer. But she had none to offer, not knowing, indeed, what might be the truth of the matter. Her silence urged him to question her more directly.

"What artillery have they? For, after all, it is artillery that counts. What guns have they, that they should hope to hold the British? Tell me that?" It was an argumentative challenge, and had she possessed the information she would have advanced it to prove him wrong in the contemptuous conviction he suggested. As it was, her ignorance compelled her to confess that she did not know.

He turned peevish. "You don't know. You don't know! Bah! And you want to argue with me you pretend to tell me that Lincoln's riff-raff can stop a British army! Bah!"

"It was just such riff-raff stopped Burgoyne," she answered, stung by his mockery, and flung him by that reminder into such a passion that she bitterly upbraided herself for her momentary loss of temper.

But he simmered down again, and was gentle with her in the end, bidding her to come soon again to see him, even suffering her to kiss him at parting.

As she was descending the stairs, a man advanced along the hall, going towards the dining-room. His back was turned to her and he stepped quickly with a brisk martial step and the upright carriage of a tall well-knit figure, so familiar that she paused a moment in sheer amazement. The next moment she was speeding down the stairs, and after him. And as she ran instinctively she called to him:

"Robert! Cousin Robert!"

He checked and turned as she came breathlessly up with him. She shrank back in fresh amazement. The man's hair, long and black, hung like the ears of a spaniel about a face that was tanned almost to the colour of an Indian's. His countenance was of an odd and singular blankness. He wore an expression of perpetual surprise, resulting from a total lack of eyebrows. The lower part of his face, his mouth and chin, were lost in a dense black beard, whose incongruous and unusual growth gave him the air described by Rutledge – for this was that same Neild – as that of a backwoodsman. He was dressed in a suit of plain brown homespun of an old-fashioned cut, such as was affected by Quakers. Quakerish, too, was the round black hat he carried, the plain white linen bands at his throat and the steel buckles on his black, square-toed shoes.

He spoke, and his voice was nasal and harsh.

"Madam, my name is Jonathan, not Robert. Jonathan Neild."

She stared into the dark brown eyes that were stolidly regarding her out of that swarthy face. She was confused. She laughed a little. How could her fancy so have tricked her?

"Your pardon, sir. I see I was mistook."

He bowed in silence, and turned again to resume his way. But no sooner was his back towards her than the illusion returned. Rooted where she stood she watched him pass into the dining-room; she saw him still even after he had passed out of her sight, saw the swing of those square shoulders, the elastic step and an indefinable character in his movements that were unquestionably Robert Mandeville's.

On a sudden irresistible conviction she went after him.

About to take his seat at table, with Remus standing by his chair, he raised his eyes in mild enquiry when she plunged into the room. Again she checked. It was fantastic. This man was not Robert Mandeville. He was nothing like Robert Mandeville. And then the eyes of her memory beheld his back once more, the set of his shoulders, the characteristic walk.

"Leave us, Remus," she said shortly.

The negro's plain hesitation and his sudden nervousness were so much confirmation. He showed the whites of his eyes as he turned to the stranger, waiting obviously for commands from him.

"Do as thou art bid," said the harsh, nasal voice, and Remus in obvious uneasiness effaced himself.

248

When they were alone she came forward until there was only the table between them. She fought down her agitation, and strove to speak calmly.

"Robert, what does this mean?"

"I have told thee, madam, my name is Jonathan."

"There's not the need to repeat the lie," she answered him. "I know you. What you have done to yourself I can't guess. But that you are Robert Mandeville, I know – as surely as I know that I am Myrtle Latimer."

He revealed strong white teeth behind that black tangle of beard, as gently he smiled and shook his head.

"Thy fancy plays some trick upon thee, madam. I tell thee again, I am Jonathan Neild. A planter and a merchant and here to trade with Sir Andrew Carey."

"Ah! To trade in what?"

It was as if she presented a pistol, and the sneer that argues knowledge startled him a little. But this was barely perceptible in his manner.

"In tobacco, madam. I am a tobacco-planter from Virginia."

"From Virginia? With that accent?"

"I was not born in Virginia, madam."

"And that's the first true word you've spoken. I know well enough where you were born. And I know well enough what your trade is with my father." A flush of indignation was mounting to her cheeks. "I know now why he pretended so much interest in Harry, why he probed me with questions of the intentions of Lincoln's army, its numbers and equipment. You're here as a spy, Captain Mandeville. That is the trade you drive."

"Madam, thy insults touch me not, since 'tis clear they are intended for another whom you persist in supposing me to be."

She stamped her foot in exasperation.

"Very well, then. You shall be afforded the opportunity of satisfying Governor Rutledge of your identity."

The threat to her amazement discomposed him not at all. He spread his hands and spoke in a tone of mild protest.

"Madam, I have done so already. A stranger may not come and go quite freely in a land that is given over to the godlessness of war. Your Governor has challenged me already and my papers have been laid before him. I assure thee, madam, they have satisfied him."

She leaned forward. "That may be. But are they proof against the scrutiny that must follow when I tell the Governor that I know you for Robert Mandeville?"

"I trust so, madam. Thou wilt commit an idle foolishness."

"And if I bid them shave off your beard, and wash your face?"

There was silence for a long moment during which his dark eyes pondered her. They found her hard and resolute. Suddenly he shrugged and laughed, and it was almost as if he tossed aside a cloak.

"I surrender, Myrtle," he announced in his natural voice. "Your eyes are too sharp. Better surrender to you than to Governor Rutledge."

He had fatuously imagined that she but pressed him so as to force him to disclose himself, and thus satisfy her that her acumen had not been at fault. But there was no easing of her hardness.

"The one must follow upon the other," she informed him coldly.

"What!" It was a cry of sheer horror. "You would betray me? Me, Myrtle?"

"Isn't betrayal the purpose for which you are here?"

"No," he answered her with convincing emphasis. "It is not."

"What else, then?"

"What else?" He was almost indignant. "Can't you imagine it, considering your father's state? I had word of his condition, and I came at once out of solicitude for him, to do what I could. My solicitude was the sharper because I knew that he had no other kin at hand to stand by him, perhaps in his extremity. That is my offence, Myrtle."

If he thought to melt her with that story he was wrong. "You had word of my father's condition, you say. That is an admission that you had been in communication with him."

"Why not? We are kin, after all. What is there unnatural in our communicating?"

Remembering her father's announcement that he had made Mandeville his heir, she imagined that she held the explanation of his presence. But there was something else here that she did not understand.

"When did you learn my father's condition?"

"A month ago."

"Where were you at the time?"

"With Prevost at Savannah. I am serving with him now. I was with Clinton, but I exchanged when Prevost's army was ordered South."

She shook her head and smiled a little scornfully. "And you would pretend to me that you grew that beard in a month? Nay, in less than a month, for it must have taken you at least a week to get here."

"No. I don't pretend that."

"Then how do you reconcile it with the story you have told me?"

He looked at her between vexation and wonder. "You are too shrewd for me," he said.

"Shrewd enough to know where my duty lies, and so are you, Captain Mandeville."

If he was alarmed, he did not betray it.

"Your duty to whom? There is a duty to your father, to your family, and even perhaps a little to myself, Myrtle." He spoke quietly, almost humbly.

"And the duty to my husband? For you will remember that I am the wife of Major Latimer of the Continental Army."

His dark eyes grew wistful.

"If you feel it inevitably your duty to denounce me, I will give you the last proof of my regard by submitting. But it is to punish me a little heavily for the affection for your father which has brought me here into the lion's den. I knew that I was risking my life when I came. But I hardly thought that yours, Myrtle, would be the hands to destroy me."

That softened her. It brought back memories of the past, of all that she owed to Mandeville, of all, indeed, that Harry owed to him, although Harry, blinded by prejudice, would not admit the debt, and the subject had been a fruitful source of disagreement in the unhappy early days of their married life. For she had never abandoned the persuasion that Mandeville – out of concern for herself – had repeatedly shielded Harry, and that it was to Mandeville's influence with Lord William that Harry owed the respite which had enabled him to leave Charles Town after the Featherstone affair.

"What am I to do?" she asked, and clenched her hands. "If I could be assured that you have not come here to spy… But I can't be. My reason tells me that you have, and if I don't denounce you I become your accomplice."

"If you do, you are my executioner." Gently he smiled. "Poor Myrtle! The choice is difficult, I know. At least, I hope it is. I hope you would not lightly sacrifice the life of a man who is ready enough himself to sacrifice it in your service." And then he changed his tone to one of argument, as if all his purpose were disinterestedly to help her in the parlous choice with which she was confronted. "Listen, Myrtle. You say that I am here to spy. But to spy out what? What can I learn here that we do not already know? What information that I may bear back to Prevost can affect that which is inevitably to happen?"

"What is to happen?" she asked him breathlessly.

He made a little gesture of pity for a blindness that could not perceive what he had to tell.

"At Savannah Prevost is in sufficient strength now to drive through to Charles Town when he pleases. What is there to withstand him? A handful of steady continentals and a rabble of undisciplined militia led by an incompetent commander. Yet to make quite sure, Prevost awaits reinforcements. In a month perhaps, in two months at most, he will move. And then it will be a march. Nothing more. Within two months the British Southern Army will be in Charles Town. Be quite sure of that. For there is nothing to dispute our passage. Can anything that I might have gleaned here – assuming that I am indeed the spy you insist upon thinking me – alter or avert that fact? Answer the question for yourself, Myrtle. Ask yourself what advantage to your husband's side can result from handing me over to be shot or hanged. And ask yourself at the same time, if it might not be well in the hour when Prevost arrives that you should have in his immediate following a friend as devoted and loyal as myself. I have saved your husband aforetime, Myrtle, although you may little have guessed quite all that I was sacrificing when I did so."

"Sacrificing? What do you mean? What…sacrifice?"

He pondered a moment, then took the plunge. It could do no harm, and it might serve his desperate turn. His knowledge of humanity assured him that the woman did not live who could listen unmoved to an avowal of love.

"I mean, Myrtle, that you were, and still are, dearer to me than anything in all this world. In those old happy days here in Charles Town when first I knew you, when I was so often in your company at Fairgrove, the world became for Robert Mandeville a very different place from anything that it had ever been before or that it could ever be again. Yet I who would have given my life for you, loved you so devotedly, so selflessly, that I gladly gave life to another man so that he might rob me of you. That was because – "

"Don't Robert!"

It was like a cry of pain, and instantly obedient he ceased. The glow passed from his face as if he had put on a mask. Impassive once more, his head slightly bowed, he stood before her.

"Robert, I never knew… I never dreamed…"

"And I have done wrong to tell you now. I was carried away by an impulse I should have resisted. God knows I have resisted it often enough in the past. Forgive me."

"Oh, what am I to do? What am I to do?" She was white to the lips in her emotion and distress. She crushed fist into palm, and wrung her hands in an agony of doubt and indecision.

"Do?" he said. "Why that, at least, is simple. Repay the debt that lies between me and Harry Latimer. Give me the same respite that I gave him. Leave to depart. He had forty-eight hours through my intervention. Twenty-four will suffice for me. If I am not gone by tomorrow, then denounce me to your Governor. Am I asking too much. If so – "

"No, no, Robert." She faltered and paused, looking at him in distraction. "If...if I do this...if I let you go now, and say no word to anyone...will you, on your side, pledge me your word that you will not return to Charles Town or attempt to hold communication with my father while the war lasts? Will you do that?"

"Not to return, yes. I pledge you my word freely and sincerely. But as to holding communication with your father..."

"You must promise that, too. You must. It is the least, the very least, upon which I can concede so much."

He bowed his head. "Very well. I promise it. I will leave tonight."

This, you will remember, had happened a month ago, whilst Harry Latimer was with Moultrie at Purysburg.

Chapter 6

Prevost's Advance

Moultrie went home from his interview with Rutledge through a street that was seething with an activity very different from that of which it had been the scene in the old days. And it wore a different aspect in itself. The devastating fire of two years ago, which had devoured the houses at its foot, left a wide gap through which there was a clear view of the bay and its shipping.

Soldiers thronged the thoroughfare: raw recruits from the country on their way out to the racecourse to be drilled, trailing a brass field piece after them; men from the battery on Hadrell's Point, men up in town from Fort Moultrie, which was now garrisoned by Marion's force; rangers, infantrymen, artillerymen and engineers; a few continentals with the formidable, competent air of veteran soldiers, and a preponderance of militia, than whom no men could have looked less military.

And woven into this warlike pattern were the ordinary townsfolk: a few fine ladies, escorted by officers, and women of the humbler class escorting the rank and file, with here and there an elderly prosperous planter, too old or too loyal in principles to don a uniform and take the field.

Some wore anxious faces. But in the main the crowd was gay and light-hearted. The clouds of war were as yet remote. The invader's only attempt to set foot on Carolinian soil had been whipped back by Moultrie, and whilst it was already known to be Prevost's intention to march on Charles Town, yet it was also known that General Lincoln was in sufficient force at Purysburg to hold him. Moultrie's confident assurance that the British would have to ask leave to cross the Savannah had been communicated to the people, and was unquestioningly aceepted by them.

It was the dinner hour when the General reached home, and he found Myrtle and Harry awaiting him to go to the table.

Not until dinner was at an end, and the decanters, which Moultrie eyed fondly but from which his gout debarred him, were on the board, did he broach the matter, fatuous though he deemed it, that was agitating Rutledge.

"Myrtle, my dear, I hear that you are at last reconciled with your father."

She faced him, with a frank, open smile.

"Yes. I have just been telling Harry," and she looked fondly up at her slim straight husband standing immediately behind her chair. "And it has made me so happy, General. It has brought me a peace that has been absent from my heart for years. For although latterly custom was dulling the ache, still the ache was ever there, underneath all."

"I am glad, child, and so will you be, Harry."

"Indeed, I am. Nothing since our marriage has made me happier than this knowledge."

"But Sir Andrew has not yet made his peace with you?"

Myrtle did not give him time to answer.

"That will come, General. I am sure it will come. Down in his heart my father has always loved Harry, and it is my hope that presently, perhaps when this dreadful war is over, he will take him back into his affection."

Moultrie mumbled amiabilities, and dragged up a footstool to ease his foot that was particularly troublesome today. Then, rather ashamed of himself, and feeling singularly mean, but true to his promise to Rutledge, he set himself further to question her, a cloak of interest upon his prying intentions.

"Tell me how it came about, my dear: did you take your courage in both hands and go to him; or did he bend his stiff old neck at last, and send for you?"

With the same candour as before, she gave him the story of how the event had been brought about by Doctor Parker.

"I see," said Moultrie, when she had done. "Well, well! I am glad it should end so." He helped himself to leaf from the box Harry pushed towards him. Whilst filling his pipe, he went probing on with a skill in masking his approach which filled him at once with self-admiration and disgust. "Odd how the habits of a lifetime cling! No sooner has the old man recovered strength enough than his thoughts and such energy as he commands must be turning to trade again."

"Yes," she agreed. "And it has been a rare medicine to him. The occupation has restored him wonderfully."

"It must ha' done to enable him to be transacting business in person as I am told he is doing." Moultrie lighted his pipe from the kindled taper. Casually he asked: "Have you met many of his trader friends on your visits to him?"

"I have seen a few of them," she replied as casually.

"There's a Quaker who comes to sell him tobacco. A fellow from Virginia, I am told. Have you ever met him there?"

Was it mere chance that her eyes fell away from his own at that moment? And was it merely his fancy that the movement of her slight bosom became perceptible an instant later? Was there really a pause, or did it merely seem so to his ears that were straining so keenly for the answer? Those questions he asked himself with the instantaneousness of thought before she made reply in a calm voice.

"I may have done. I have met one or two. What was his name?"

"His name?" He searched his memory. "Neild, I believe."

"Neild?" she repeated slowly, and after a pause she answered slowly, like one who is not very certain: "Yes. I believe I did meet a man of that name." She admitted it reluctantly, fearing dangers in complete denial. Abruptly she added the question: "Why do you ask?"

He laughed good-humouredly. "They grow good tobacco in Virginia, and good tobacco is becoming very scarce these days. If this fellow should happen to be about and have any fine leaf to sell, I should be glad to know it. But you don't particularly remember him?"

She shook her head slowly, making pretence the while to be thinking. "No," she said at last. "Not...particularly."

"You never spoke to him?"

"I may have done. I think I did once, meeting him casually. But I cannot be sure."

"Ah well. It is no great matter." And Moultrie dismissed the subject and turned to speak of other things.

He did not think that she had prevaricated; chiefly because his easy-going nature – that one fault in a soldier which General Lee had deplored in him – preferred not to think so.

Myrtle was left uneasy, not so much lest the identity of Neild should be suspected, but because of the deceit which she herself had practised not only upon Moultrie, but upon her husband. More than once during those few days that Harry was in Charles Town she had sought an opportunity of telling him. But the fact that she had yielded to her hesitation and had not told him immediately on his return, made it impossible to tell him now. The very delay seemed to increase the tale there was to tell, burdening it with explanations which in themselves are always incriminating.

She had been foolish, to allow herself to be repelled by the thought of his own senseless jealousy of Mandeville, which he had more than once betrayed. That jealousy of his, were she to tell him now, would be more than ever fired by her silence on the subject since his coming. She was committed to a course, and to that course she had better keep. After all, what harm could follow now? Mandeville had pledged himself never to return to Charles Town whilst the war continued. Therefore what harm could her silence do? Or what good could be accomplished by her speaking?

And so when Harry departed once more from Charles Town a few days later in Moultrie's company it was still without any knowledge of his wife's interview with Mandeville at her father's.

They got back to the camp at Purysburg in a downpour of rain on February 26th, to receive the details of the rout of Boyd's forces and to find General Lincoln so encouraged by this success as to have determined upon more extensive operations against the British. He had detached two thousand men under General Ashe and sent them up the river to Augusta with orders to cut off a strong English force posted there under Colonel Campbell.

Campbell, however, did not choose to wait. Upon perceiving the massing of troops opposite to him and fearing a crossing below to cut him off from the main army at Savannah, he broke up his camp and marched briskly south, along the right bank of the river.

Ashe crossed in pursuit on the 25th, the day before Moultrie's return to Purysburg, and reached Brier Creek two days later. Here, just above the creek's junction with the Savannah, he took station, and thence on March 2nd he reported himself safe, being in a strong position and the enemy apparently afraid of him.

It must be assumed that he based his opinion of the enemy's fear of him upon the fact that no enemy showed himself before his lines. The reason, however, was very different from all that General Ashe supposed. At the very moment that he was sending off that complacent report, Prevost was making a wide detour to come round and take him in the rear, an event which happened on the morrow.

Scarcely indeed had his report reached the General at Purysburg, than on the heels of it came Colonel Eaton, who had swum the river with his horse, galloping into camp with the terrible news that Ashe was cut off and completely routed.

Never indeed was any army more utterly surprised, panic-stricken and broken than that army on Brier Creek. Appalled by the sudden and totally unexpected appearance of the British, the militia men had flung away their weapons almost without firing a shot, and had fled through swamp and flood, many of them perishing by water in their haste to escape from fire.

The effect upon the Carolinian army, which had thus at one blow lost nearly a third of its effectives, was a dejection easy to conceive. Fortunately recruits were coming in which raised their numbers once more, until by the end of the month they were almost at their original strength.

At the beginning of April, Lincoln was absent, summoned to Orangeburg by Governor Rutledge, there to confer with him upon the plan of campaign to be pursued. He returned, and word ran through the camp that they would very shortly be taking the field against Prevost. There was an activity of preparation and a feverish drilling of the new recruits that were sent hurriedly down to them. But before anything happened Lincoln was again summoned to Orangeburg by the Governor, and this time he took Moultrie with him, who in his turn went accompanied by Latimer.

Here in Orangeburg they found a considerable camp where some three thousand men were in training under Rutledge's own eye.

Lincoln had given Moultrie to understand that the Governor had conceived a coup which if successful should certainly end the war in the South, and might end it altogether. But he was not permitted to disclose any details. His own respect for Moultrie's opinion made him anxious that Moultrie should now be taken into Rutledge's confidence, so that he might contribute perhaps something to the plan out of his own military experience and acumen.

But a disappointment awaited Moultrie, the more keenly felt perhaps because of his relations of intimate personal friendship with Rutledge. He was admitted to certain of the conferences, but not to any of the vital ones. And when at last he departed again with Lincoln, to return to camp, he knew as little of what was afoot as when he had last left it.

One item of interest, however, he had gleaned from one of the few conferences which he did attend. Prevost had put forward a proposal for the neutrality of Georgia for the remainder of the war. Rutledge informed them of it, and that was one of the few occasions on which Moultrie heard him laugh.

"It is too absurd and ridiculous to require a moment's consideration," the Governor had pronounced. "Indeed, it scarce merits an answer. But an answer I shall send, to inform General Prevost of just that."

Once back in Purysburg, Lincoln made his dispositions as swiftly as it lay within his sluggish capacity to do anything. He was a stout slow-moving man, himself, slow of thought and slow of speech, and therefore slow in all things.

But at last by April 23rd he was ready, and, leaving Moultrie with a thousand men to watch Prevost, he marched away bag and baggage, horse, foot and artillery. He went north along the river, still swollen by the heavy rains but now settling under finer weather. His avowed design was to re-enter Georgia at Augusta, as Ashe had done, and to march down the southern bank upon Savannah.

From the orders he received Moultrie inferred that Lincoln was persuaded Prevost would not wait for him. Should Prevost attempt to cross, Moultrie was to delay him as long as possible, falling back when he must, but disputing every foot of the road to Charles Town should the British reveal the design of marching upon it. Meanwhile an express was dispatched to Rutledge at Orangeburg, to inform him that action was begun so that he might remove himself to Charles Town with the new forces he had raised.

As Lincoln had supposed, so things fell out. No sooner did Prevost obtain intelligence that the main body of Lincoln's army had moved off than he crossed the Savannah in force, and drove Moultrie back.

Above, Lincoln waited before crossing to Augusta until he had learnt that Prevost was on the left bank. Then over he went with his army, apparently to march upon the capital of Georgia, which was no longer defended. The explanation he gave out, so freely that intelligence of it reached Prevost, was that he regarded the British crossing as a feint to draw him out of Georgia. But that he was not so to be drawn, and that he meant to occupy Savannah.

Prevost will no doubt have laughed at the old sluggard and the notion of strategy which his pronouncement seemed to express. Well content to leave Lincoln's army in Georgia and out of account for all military purposes, he thrust forward as rapidly as Moultrie would permit him, to possess himself of the capital of South Carolina.

But at Pocotaligo certain doubts assailed him. Was Lincoln really as stupid as he represented himself, or was there here some subtlety at work which at present he did not perceive? That doubt kept him inert there for three days, until in the end the intelligences he received on every hand compelled him to dismiss it. The truth might seem too good to be true, but true it was. Lincoln, to possess himself of an empty nest, had removed the only barrier that might have retarded or even resisted the British. It was for the British to take full advantage, and press on.

Chapter 7

Rutledge's Nerves

Prevost now drove forward with an army that was between seven and eight thousand strong. But his progress being ever disputed by the retreating force under Moultrie a fortnight was occupied in covering the eighty miles of ground that lie between the Savannah and the Ashley. Having crossed the Savannah on April 25th, Prevost reached the south bank of the Ashley on Sunday, May 9th, and encamped there facing the peninsula between the two rivers on the point of which stands Charles Town.

Moultrie having fallen back across the Ashley some hours ahead had brought the weary remnant of his force – a bare six hundred to which rearguard actions had reduced his original thousand – safely into a town that was humming like a beehive with the activity of preparation, and quaking a little too in apprehension of the shock that now impended.

Rutledge had arrived the day before with his men from Orangeburg, and a small supplement of force had been added by the arrival of Count Pulaski, a gallant Pole urged by his sympathy with the cause of freedom to bear arms in defence of American Independence. He brought with him a hundred and sixty men of his legion.

Although the invader had the advantage of a force nearly twice as numerous as that of the defenders, yet the men of Charles Town were far from being without hope of holding their own.

Wonders had been wrought in the last nine days in the matter of fortifying the place, considering that when on May 1st, Major Latimer, sent forward by Moultrie for the purpose, had arrived in the town, he had found it utterly unprepared for an attack by land. The ferries of the Ashley were not then fortified and some weak defences were the only barrier across the Neck.

Latimer had gone to work at once, with the stout co-operation of Lieutenant-Governor Bee and the Senate, and having aroused the civil and military authorities to a sense of the danger, all those capable of labouring were at once impressed into service. An accomplished engineer, the Chevalier de Cambray, another of those distinguished foreign soldiers in the service of America, took charge of the works, and under his direction white men and black toiled day and night to throw up entrenchments. All houses in the northern suburb were burned down, and thanks to the retarding actions fought by Moultrie, before the red-coats appeared on the banks of the Ashley a strong line of fortifications had risen across the Neck, with abatis on which cannon were emplaced.

This in itself was encouraging to the inhabitants, and when presently the stout-hearted and capable Moultrie, whose epic defence of Sullivan's Island was not forgotten, rode in with his battered but cheerful troops, Charles Town's heart was lifted up by hope. The grimly-smiling, confident countenance of the easy-going General was in itself a moral tonic to all who beheld it.

Rutledge, now haggard and worn, the fullness under his chin entirely vanished, his elegant coat sagging a little about his body, which was shrunken by exertion, sleeplessness and anxiety, displayed an unusual nervousness. It was deplored by some of those who perceived it, and who could not know that it was the nervousness of the man who has laid a heavy stake upon the board and who awaits the turn of wheel or card, dreading the issue, however heavy may be the odds in his own favour. As the next day came and went eventlessly his nervousness increased, and on the evening of that Monday he betrayed it in a rather singular and in him entirely unusual display of irritability, as shall presently be told.

He was to sup that night with Moultrie and the Latimers. But both he and Moultrie were late in arriving. Myrtle and Harry in the dining room, where the table was laid and all prepared, awaited them. They were sitting together on the wide window seat, Harry with his arm about Myrtle's waist, her head on his shoulder and her eyes on Andrew, now a well-grown chubby lad of three who was astride his father's left knee, and at the moment deeply engrossed in unravelling one of the strands which he had detached from Harry's shoulder-knot.

These dear ones were Latimer's one deep pre-occupation in those days. But for their presence he would cheerfully have envisaged the coming assault. He had done his best to persuade Myrtle to withdraw from Charles Town. But Myrtle had manifested a positive dread of leaving him at such a time, and a horror of availing herself of either of the alternatives he proposed. She had represented that they would be infinitely safer in the town itself. Even should it fall to Prevost, the British did not make war on women and children, and they had little personally to fear. The worst dangers were those of bombardment. But if she were to put to sea in an attempt to gain the West Indies, one of his proposals for her and Andrew, she would have to face the peril of falling into the hands of some of the ships moving along the coast; whilst if she adopted his other proposal and went up-country to the Santee, she would know no peace from fear of the tory bands that still roved about the land, whose notorious ruthlessness and vindictive cruelty would keep her in a constant state of anxiety and dread. To this would be added anxiety and dread on the score of Harry himself who would be distant from her.

Thus in the end, however reluctantly, yet perceiving the justice of what she urged, he had yielded.

She had paid her father a visit that afternoon, and she had found him in a more fatherly mood than any he had yet displayed.

"It is his faith in the British arms," she was telling Harry. "He is so confident that Prevost will prevail, and that it can be only a question of days before Charles Town surrenders, that he is softened by exultation."

"There will be a reaction if Prevost does not prevail – as, pray God, he will not."

"In that case father's mood will not matter very much. But if Charles Town should capitulate, I think that father will stand our friend. In fact, he has as good as promised it. 'There's nothing for you to fear, Myrtle,' he told me. 'My loyalty is well-known, and I shall be there to welcome General Prevost when he enters. I shall have some influence with him; enough to make you safe.'"

"And to hang me," thought Harry, smiling to himself.

As if she had read his thought and were answering it, she said:

"I think such a consummation would so uplift him that he might be disposed at last to make his peace with you, Harry, and extend his protection over you as well. So that, whatever happens, there should be some gain for us."

"My dear!" He was a little aghast. "Much as I should welcome reconciliation with your father, you cannot think that I should welcome it at such a price."

And then Julius came in, ushering Lieutenant Shubrick, a war-stained but cheerful young gentleman on duty in the lines. With him came a large fair man who was bespattered with mud from his riding-boots to the collar of his full-skirted biscuit-coloured coat.

With an exclamation of surprise and pleasure, Harry set down the boy and rose. Myrtle rose with him.

"Tom!" she cried, and held out both her hands to the newcomer, who was grinning broadly as he advanced towards them.

Disregarding Andrew, who furiously embraced one of his legs, and more furiously still demanded his attention with shrill passionate shouts of "Daddy Harry! Daddy Harry!" Latimer too held out a hand to Tom Izard, who thus unexpectedly made his appearance after an absence of three years and more during which he had been campaigning with the Northern armies.

Tom shook hands with each of them, almost expressionless save for his laughter. Then laughing still he turned to the officer who had accompanied him, and whose erstwhile official sternness had now given place to a smile.

"Well, sir? Are you satisfied that I am known here? Tell him my name, Harry, like a good fellow, so that he may get back to his duty without wasting further time on me."

"But why? What's the matter?"

"I'm under arrest. That's all. You keep a devilish sharp lookout here. Having no papers I was very properly stopped at the outposts, and brought here under guard."

The lieutenant explained, holding himself stiffly at attention.

"Governor's orders, sir. Issued this afternoon. All attempting to pass the lines either coming or going to be detained and brought to headquarters. This gentleman describes himself as Captain Izard of the Continental Army. But..."

"That's right, Shubrick," Latimer interrupted. "Captain Izard is known to me. A friend of mine. I'll answer for him, Shubrick. You may go."

The officer bowed and went out, Julius following. Before the door closed again they heard his sharp order to the guard outside, and the tramp of departing feet.

Andrew had ceased his clamour for Daddy Harry's attention, and was now entirely engrossed in the big stranger. With eyes as blue as cornflowers and as round as saucers he pondered Captain Izard, who meanwhile had scarcely perceived him.

"What is it?" he was asking. "Is the Governor nervous?"

"He has cause to be," Harry replied. "The place is full of traitors, and with our strength considerably below what it should be and what Prevost should have every reason for supposing it, naturally Rutledge takes no risks of information leaking out. He suspects, perhaps with reason, that there's been enough of it already. But tell us of yourself, Tom. Where are you from?"

"Middlebrook, with secret dispatches for your omnipotent Governor. Gadslife! Rutledge has risen in the world since last we parted."

"He deserves it. A strong man."

"Oh, he's strong, and unpleasant, too, which is the way of most strong men. And who's this?" He bent over Andrew who had drawn quite close to him, and the youngster himself replied stoutly:

"And'ew Fitz'oy Latimer."

"Lord!" said Tom, and picked him up so abruptly as to scare him, which set him kicking and howling for "Daddy Harry!"

"Another strong man," protested Tom at the end of the struggle, setting down the youngster. Myrtle removed him to the care of Mauma Dido, and peace was restored.

Julius fetched the captain a glass of grog, and meanwhile the captain sprawled in a chair, his long legs stretched before him, and talked. He had nothing to add to their knowledge of American affairs, but a deal to tell them of Washington, whom he almost deified, descanting upon his fortitude, his genius, his patience and his indomitable strength.

He was still talking when the door opened, and the latecomers, Rutledge and Moultrie came in. Both were weary, and the riding-clothes of the Governor were as dusty as the faded uniform of the general, but whereas Rutledge's face had an anxious care-worn look the broad rugged countenance of Moultrie was cheerful as ever.

Myrtle would have rung at once for Julius to serve supper, but she was checked by Tom Izard, who rose and bowed to the new arrivals.

Rutledge was still considering him with a cold questioning eye, when Moultrie impulsively came forward holding out his hand and uttering a welcome. Then the Governor's voice came sharp and harsh.

"Why are you not in uniform, Captain Izard?"

"Because I am here on a secret mission. I bring you a dispatch from the Commander-in-Chief. I had the honour to be chosen for the service."

Rutledge's irritation was not appeased. Rather did it increase.

"What papers do you carry?"

"None, sir. Travelling as a civilian it was best that I should not."

"And you got through the lines, without papers and in those clothes?" It was almost an explosion of wrath.

Tom laughed freely and shook his head. "Let me perish! I did not, sir. I was arrested at the outposts, and brought here under guard."

"I see! Hum! That's better."

Moultrie raised his brows, and looked at Rutledge. "What else should you have supposed?" he asked.

"What I am justified in supposing," snapped the Governor. He was far from mollified, as was to have been expected. "You bring a dispatch," he resumed. "Where was the need to send a dispatch at such a time? If it had fallen into British hands..." He shrugged ill-humouredly.

Tom drew himself up, and spoke with chill dignity, unceremoniously interrupting.

"There could at no time have been any danger of that, your excellency. I had my orders."

"Yes, yes." Rutledge seemed to sneer. Possibly his old mistrust of Izard, on the score of his connection with Lord William Campbell, was an added irritant, although all reason for such mistrust had long since been removed. "The dispatch?" And he held out his hand.

Captain Izard turned down one of the gauntlet-like cuffs of his coat, cuffs that were normally stiffened with buckram, and proffered his arm to the Governor. "If your excellency will slice through the stiffening, the letter will pass straight from my hands to yours, as I undertook that it should."

Rutledge stared a moment. Then some of the gloom passing from his face, he took a knife from the table, and did as he was invited. The letter was found to replace half the buckram which had been sliced away.

"You think the British would not have found it? Well well, perhaps not. A British general wouldn't. I am sure of that. But I'd be less confident in the case of an officer of humbler rank."

He stalked away to the window with the letter, which was bound in silk and very lightly sealed. He spread and read it standing there aloof, his face expressionless. Then he asked for a taper which

Latimer supplied him, and in the flame of it he consumed the sheet utterly, dropping the ashes on the hearth.

Izard was amazed that he should thus destroy a communication presumably of military import without so much as showing it to the military commander of the place who was there in the same room. But he kept the thought to himself.

They sat down to supper. Throughout the meal, Rutledge was wrapped in thought, and his moodiness sat like a thundercloud upon the company, and even stilled the normal garrulity of Tom Izard.

When the Governor rose at last to take his departure, which was soon after the meal had been brought to an end, he desired a word apart with Moultrie and Latimer before leaving.

Moultrie would have ushered him into the office which he had established on the ground floor front for the dispatch of military business. But Rutledge stayed him.

"No, no," he said curtly. "I desire only a word with Major Latimer – a word of advice." And he turned gravely to confront Harry. He lowered his voice. "You would do well, sir, for the present, while this situation lasts, to discourage Mrs Latimer's visits to her father."

The Major stiffened, whilst even Moultrie made an ejaculation of impatience. Then Latimer controlled himself to ask quite steadily:

"Will your excellency tell me plainly what you mean?"

"I have told you, sir. If you want more you'll find it in the reflection that your father-in-law's sympathies are notoriously what they are, and that his house is a meeting-place for all manner of men whom I mistrust."

Moultrie intervened. "Since you are apprehensive in that quarter – "

"I am not apprehensive," Rutledge's denial was so testy as to make it quite clear that he was what he said he wasn't.

"Well, then, since you feel as you do, why don't you take a straight, simple course, and have Carey locked up until our present troubles are over?"

Rutledge's brooding eyes pondered him almost scornfully.

"Simple courses are for simple men. And I am not simple, William, as I mean to show." Abruptly he turned again to Latimer, who was frowning and breathing rather hard. "Once before, Major Latimer, you and I disagreed on the subject of a channel through which information was leaking to the opposite side. Your obstinacy, then, prevailed against my calmer and riper judgment. If that should happen again now, it will be very unfortunate for everybody, but most unfortunate for you."

"And now I think you threaten me, sir," said Harry, his bristles rising further.

"Tchah! Tchah! threaten!" Rutledge's contempt was withering. "This is not a time for airs and graces."

"Certainly not for graces. Your excellency makes that plain."

"I'll make something else plain, so that hereafter there may be nothing to excuse you. You shall not be able to say that I have withheld light from your mind. I told you four years ago, when Featherstone was sacrificed to your vainglory, that there is a better use for spies than to hang them or tar-and-feather them. They are ready channels through which false information may be conveyed to an enemy to his undoing. That is why I do not arrest Carey. He may prove just such a channel should I require it. If I do, God help him. He shall serve my purposes and betray his own active treachery at one and the same time. You understand? But in the meantime I must see that no grain of useful information should reach him. That is why I admonish you where your wife is concerned."

"I would have your excellency understand that I resent the admonition."

"Resent it all you please. But observe it."

"And that," Latimer continued coldly, "when our present engagements are over, and your excellency is of less moment to the State, I shall have the honour to ask for satisfaction."

Rutledge looked at him a moment in silence with an eye of dull contempt. "Sir," he answered, and now he was more like his normal emotionless self, "we may leave the future until it comes. My affair is with the present. In the present I am the servant of the State, and I have no thought or purpose that does not concern the State. If you think otherwise, why, sir, you are a fool, and there's an end on't."

Latimer hung his head in shame under that just rebuke. But Moultrie went to the rescue.

"We all know that, John; Harry knows it as well as I do. But, damme, it is possible to serve the State without insult to its citizens."

Rutledge gave him his hard cold eyes a moment. "Et tu, Brute!" he said. Then laughed shortly, turned on his heel, and stalked out of the house.

Chapter 8

The Spy

Early on the following morning, the vanguard of Prevost's army, composed of some companies of Scots Highlanders and Hessians, and numbering somewhere about eight hundred, crossed the Ashley, and advanced upon the town, under the command of Colonel Prevost, the general's brother. The general himself remained for the present in camp on the south bank of the river with the main army and the heavy baggage.

Within the lines Count Pulaski, who had ridden over from Hadrell's Point, paraded his legion, and having wrung consent from the Governor, rode out in a gallantly chivalrous but futile sortie from which he was speedily whipped back with shattered forces. The British pursued him to within a mile of the lines. There the Charles Town artillery which covered his retreat checked the advancing enemy, who halted and sat down out of range but well within the view of the defenders manning the trenches.

In the town behind them there was excitement and anxiety, but no panic, for the people had Moultrie's assurance that he was in sufficient strength to hold the place, and that the British should not enter.

It was a faith not shared by all. That afternoon a gaunt, keen-eyed man, whose faded uniform bore the epaulettes and badges of a colonel, came riding along the lines up to the abatis by the Town

Gate. Here were assembled Moultrie and a group of officers including Latimer, in consultation with the Governor.

Rutledge looked round at the man's approach. It was Colonel Senfo the State's engineer.

"Well?" Rutledge asked him. "What do you report?"

The colonel shook his head. "We are very weak," he answered. "Here on our left the lines are not above four feet thick, and the parapets are still far from completed."

"But work hasn't ceased?" quoth Rutledge on a rising inflexion.

"No. You can see them toiling yonder." And he pointed to a distant group of labourers actively wielding spade and mattock. "But the attack may come at any moment, and in what case are we to withstand it?"

It was Moultrie who span round, leaning heavily upon his cane, to answer him briskly.

"In better case than we were in Fort Sullivan. That was pronounced a slaughter-pen by General Lee – a soldier of great experience. It proved a slaughter-pen, indeed: for those who attacked it. We don't depend upon a few feet of earth, colonel. We've better than that to show these gentlemen when they ask our leave to enter the town." He turned again, pointing with his cane. "I think they suspect it. For you observe they are in no haste to taste our hospitality."

There was some laughing comment from the group, in which, however, Rutledge did not join. Aloof, glum of countenance, he stood, chin in hand, looking out towards the distant movement of men and the cloud of dust hanging above and about them in the sunlight.

"That is because they are not yet in sufficient force," he answered. He sighed. "If only it lay in our power to delay the crossing of the main army for twenty-four hours!" Almost as if thinking aloud, though Heaven knows that was far from being a habit with him: "Twenty-four hours!" he repeated.

But Moultrie belittled the importance of the time. "Pooh! We are as ready for them now as we shall be tomorrow."

"Are we?" Rutledge turned slowly to look at him. "I pray they may continue to think so. That they do think so now is plain. For if they had definite knowledge of our numbers they would not be delaying the attack."

Without waiting for a reply he stepped down from the abatis, and walked to his horse, which was being held for him by a groom. Moultrie and Latimer followed. At the moment of mounting, Rutledge turned again.

"Above all," he said, "see that a sharp look-out is kept along the lines, and that no one is allowed to pass out upon any pretext." The vehemence of his insistence was remarkable.

"But, of course," Moultrie answered. "It is being done. Also I have posted sentries along the water front."

"And let no military movement be undertaken without first consulting me," was Rutledge's last order as he rode away.

Moultrie was left frowning over that. He smiled crookedly as presently he looked at Harry.

"There's a despot for you!"

Harry did not smile back. He was warmed by indignation.

"Sometimes I ask myself who is the commander here."

"Sh!" Moultrie checked him. "Let be. He is acting upon some secret plan of his own."

"A secret from the general commanding!" exclaimed Latimer, and laughed. "I marvel you endure it."

"That is because I trust him, absolutely. He is patriotic, stout-hearted, and stout-headed. I am not sure that, myself, I possess all those qualities in the same degree. It's only fools, Harry, who don't know their limitations."

They mounted and rode back into town together, down Broad Street, through the wide gateway, at which sentries were posted, into the garden space about Moultrie's residence. The place wore now an aspect conforming more than ever with its temporary character of general headquarters. There was a guard before the door, and a couple of orderlies were on duty in the hall. In addition to the room which served as Moultrie's office, the library had been more or less cleared of superfluous furniture and was now also devoted to the business of war.

As a consequence, and excepting the dining-room, which had been left at their disposal, Myrtle and the boy were now confined to the upper part of the house.

Harry would have gone in quest of them at once. But in the hall they found in addition to the orderlies, two militia-men with a prisoner who had been brought in a few minutes before their arrival.

"We took him, sir, between the old Magazine and Lover's Walk. He was making his way towards the lines, and taking great care not to be seen."

Moultrie looked the fellow over with that keen small eye of his. He was a shabby, weedy young man in the garb of an artisan, and fright had reduced his countenance to the colour of clay.

Now Moultrie had not been out of his clothes for thirty hours, and with the prospect of another night in the lines, he was intent upon snatching what rest he could while opportunity served. It was a duty not only to himself, but to the State. So he left the fellow to Latimer, and went off upstairs.

With a sigh of weariness and of disgust at the task before him, Latimer turned to the door of the ante-chamber which now did duty as a guard-room.

"Fetch him along," he bade the guards.

They followed with their prisoner across the guard-room, where at that moment Lieutenant Middleton was explaining to a disgruntled ship-master the temporary harbour regulations with which he was desired to conform. Thence they passed into the quiet of the inner office. It was a spacious, bare room, well lighted by two windows in one of the walls, and by two glass doors in another, opening upon the garden, where all now was sunshine and fragrance.

Major Latimer crossed to the large, square table of plain oak, set sideways to one of these glass doors, which was closed and bolted. The table was equipped with writing-materials, and littered with papers, whilst a fragment of lead served to pin down a large map which trailed like a table-cover over one of the corners.

The major flung his hat on the table, pulled the wooden armchair half round, and sat down so that his elbow was on the board. The men brought their captive to a halt immediately before him.

"Have you searched him?" he began.

One of the guards stepped forward, and placed various objects on the table. They included a kerchief, a knife, a tinder-box, a purse and a pistol.

Latimer picked up the purse. Out of it on to the table he emptied eleven English guineas, in themselves almost enough to condemn so shabby a rogue as this.

"Gold, eh?" said Latimer. "What's your name, my man?"

The pallid lips parted, and the fellow's voice came in a croak of apprehension.

"Jeremiah Quinn, your honour. I swear to heaven I have – "

"Yes, yes. But wait. Just answer my questions. What is your trade?"

"I'm a carpenter, sir."

"Where do you usually work?"

"Here in Charles Town, your honour. I've a shop in Middle Lane."

"How long have you been here?"

"All my life, sir. I were born in Charles Town, as plenty folk can swear to your honour. My brother was gard'ner to Colonel Gadsden, and – "

"Not so fast. One thing at a time. What was taking you to the lines?"

The answer was delayed by a tap on the door, followed by the entrance of Lieutenant Middleton.

"His excellency the Governor is here, sir," he announced and before the announcement was quite uttered, Rutledge had unceremoniously brushed past him into the room.

Latimer rose. The lieutenant disappeared, closing the door.

Rutledge's harassed eyes conned the spy an instant malevolently.

"I was told of this arrest," he informed Latimer without looking at him. "But you are examining him. Please continue."

He dragged a chair over to the glass door, a little beyond Latimer, and sat down with his back to the light.

The major also sat down again, marvelling that at such a time a man in the position of the Governor should be concerned with the examination of a wretched spy.

He resumed his questions.

"I was asking you what was taking you to the lines."

The prisoner moistened his dry lips. His terror appeared to increase now under the cold eye in the Governor's pale inscrutable face that was so unwinkingly fixed upon him.

"I... I was seeking to get out o' the town."

"So much we perceive. But with what intent? Why did you want to leave the town?"

"For fear o' the British, of what they'll do to us when they come in. They're terrible cruel."

"So that fear of the British was leading you straight towards their camp?"

"I weren't going to their camp. I swear before God I weren't. I wanted to get out into the country, where a man may lie hid until this fightin' be o'er."

"I see. You represent yourself as just a coward. Are you married?"

"No; sir. Widower. No children. I'm all alone with nobody to care for me. So what for should I stay to be murdered?"

"Where did you get this gold – this English gold?"

"They're my savings, your honour; my savings from better days. All I have in the world. 'Tweren't natural I should leave it behind. 'Twas all I was taking with me."

"That's to be ascertained," said Latimer, and turned again to the objects on the table.

He picked up the handkerchief, and held it up to the light, scanning it closely, and running his fingers along the hem. Satisfied that it was entirely innocent, he turned his attention to the knife.

Watching him the prisoner's face grew leaden, his eyes almost glazed. He looked like swooning when a sudden question from Rutledge roused him.

"Whom do you know in Tradd Street?"

The question startled not only Quinn, but Latimer as well. Yet neither of them betrayed it. Latimer continued apparently engrossed in his task, but his ears were intent upon the reply.

"Nobody, your honour."

"You don't know a Quaker named Neild?"

Latimer was relieved. Considering that Carey dwelt in Tradd Street, he had expected a very different question. The prisoner hesitated a moment.

"Neild, your honour?" he echoed. He was playing for time to collect his wits and consider his answer. Yet in the very endeavour blundered upon that answer: "Will it be Master Jonathan Neild?"

"I see that you do know him. He's lodged in Tradd Street, isn't he?" The prisoner nodded. "Then why say you know nobody in Tradd Street?" And without giving him time to answer, he passed to the next question: "What is your business with him?"

"He engaged me, your honour, to make some boxes for him, for shipping his tobacco. I'm a carpenter, your honour, as I've told the major."

"When did he so engage you?"

"Two days ago. Day before yesterday."

"Did you take him the boxes when you went to see him today?"

"No, your honour. I went to tell him I shouldn't be able to make them, as I was leaving Charles Town."

"Why did you tell him something it was against your interests to make known? Something that must have procured your detention here?"

The prisoner was startled. Grimy fingers fumbled nervously at a grimy neckcloth, for a moment. "I... I didn't think of it."

"What did Neild answer you?"

"Nothin' much, sir. Said as he were sorry. That he must find another carpenter."

279

"He didn't say he would lay information of your intentions to leave a town from which none is permitted to depart at present?"

"No. He said nothin' more'n I've told your honour."

The Governor turned to Latimer. "If you've followed my questions, and this man's answers, I think you'll see we've every reason to detain him."

"I had already seen that, your excellency," Latimer answered. He had finished with all the other objects from Quinn's pockets and was now examining the last of them, the pistol. He lifted the cock and opened the pan. There was no priming. "Whilst you were putting a pistol in your pocket against emergencies, why didn't you take the trouble to load it?" he asked.

Quinn's lips parted but it was some seconds before he replied. A sort of paralysis seemed suddenly to have overtaken him. At last his answer came:

"I… I…had no powder."

Latimer looked at him, and slowly nodded, as if satisfied with the answer. Then he dismounted the pistol's ramrod and thrust it into the barrel. It went home. The barrel was empty. Watching him with terrified eyes, Quinn saw him turn the ramrod in such a manner that the end of it must scrape against the inner side of the barrel. Suddenly Latimer looked at the prisoner, pausing in his probing. Then he removed the ramrod, pulled open the table's drawer, searched there a moment and found a probe, long and slender as a knitting-needle.

Rutledge came to stand over him whilst he was at work with this. A musket crashed to the ground, and there was a sharp movement of feet from the group of guards and prisoner. Turning, startled by the noise, Latimer and Rutledge beheld Quinn's body sagging loosely as an empty sack in the arms of the soldiers. He had fainted.

"Poor devil!" said Latimer, who guessed readily enough the panic which had laid him low.

"Come, come," rasped Rutledge impatiently. For the major had interrupted his work.

As the soldiers eased that inert body to the ground, Latimer's probe brought a cylinder of fine paper from the inside of the barrel. He spread the little sheet on the table. Rutledge leaned heavily upon his shoulder as he lowered his head to read it with him. But the message was in cipher.

"No matter," Rutledge grumbled. "It's enough. Give it to me. I'll have it deciphered presently."

This was of course irregular. But the despotic Rutledge, invested as he was with more than sovereign powers, was fast becoming a law unto himself. Latimer surrendered the document, and the Governor pocketed it.

He turned to the guards. "Take him away," he curtly ordered. "Let him be closely confined under guard until we take order about him."

He paced the room, hands folded behind him, until it was done and for some moments afterwards. Latimer, worn and weary, and even a little stricken at the thought of the fate awaiting that wretched spy whom his own wits had tracked to his death, sat waiting for the Governor to depart.

Rutledge came presently to halt before the table. "That was shrewd of you, Major Latimer," he said without warmth, and Latimer well knew to what he alluded. "But don't imagine that we have caught the real British agent."

"I don't," said Latimer. "There remains here the writer of that letter."

Rutledge nodded. "That is the man we want. You don't suspect his identity, I suppose?"

Latimer looked at him without answering. For the second time in the half-hour he imagined that he was to hear his father-in-law's name. But again he was mistaken.

"Neild," said Rutledge. "This Quaker, this tobacco-planter. That is the man I suspect."

Again, as when first the name had been mentioned, Latimer sought to remember where he had last heard it. Suddenly he succeeded. Rutledge meanwhile was continuing:

"He has suddenly appeared here again, three days ago; the day before the British reached the Ashley. It's vastly coincident. And the very fact that he lodges with Carey, on the pretence of trading with him, is in itself suspicious."

"Shall I order his arrest, sir?"

"Hum!" Rutledge considered, stroking his long chin, which from its loss of fullness seemed to have grown longer. "If he is what I suspect him to be, you'll not find him as easy to unmask as that poor wretch who was here just now."

"Don't you think, sir, that if this Neild had anything to hide, he would choose some other lodging than Carey's? That is to draw suspicion and attention at once, considering what is known of Sir Andrew's sentiments. Surely, sir, no spy would wish to do that."

"A shrewd bold man might count upon our arguing just as you are arguing. Would draw suspicion flagrantly upon himself that thereby he might disarm it. But it would need a bold man; a very bold man. And to trap such a man one should proceed with cunning. So you had better not yet order his arrest."

"I could have him watched."

"Yes. Wait." He paced away again, and back to the table once more. "The thing would be to examine him so that he does not suspect that he is being examined. But how are we to accomplish that?"

"He's a tobacco-planter, you say?"

Rutledge nodded. Latimer considered still a moment. "I might send for him on the pretext of desiring to buy tobacco."

"You might. And he would know exactly what you meant. You've other things to think of at the moment; and he knows it as well as we do."

"Once here, I might disarm his suspicions."

"How?" The word was nothing, the tone everything in its implied contempt.

"I should have to depend on my wit for that," said Latimer, piqued by the other's question. "If you bid me do it, I will see what I can accomplish."

"It's that, or nothing, I suppose," said Rutledge. "Very well."

He stalked away to the door, his head bent in thought, and went out. A moment later, he was back again.

"Major Latimer, whether you unmask him or not, after you have examined him you'd better have him detained."

"Even if I am satisfied that there is nothing against him?"

"In any case. I'll take no risks of having messages sent to Prevost just at present. No risks at all."

Chapter 9

The Lie Confirmed

An orderly left a message at Tradd Street a couple of hours later, desiring that Mr Jonathan Neild should give himself the trouble of calling upon Major Latimer at General Moultrie's headquarters. Mr Neild, the orderly was informed by Sir Andrew's butler, was not then at home. But upon his return the message should promptly be delivered.

His return must have taken place soon thereafter for in less than an hour you behold Mr Neild stepping into the hall of Moultrie's house on Broad Street, and announcing in a nasal whine, but with all the calm of an untroubled mind, that he was there by the major's invitation.

Lieutenant Middleton, who had received his instructions, put him in the library to wait, and stationed a guard unobtrusively in the garden under the library windows. This may seem supererogative precaution. Considering that the man had come of his own free will, it was hardly to be imagined that he would now attempt to run away. But the lieutenant understood that no risks were to be taken, and that the bird being safely caged, however willingly, it would be as well to make quite sure that the door of the cage was shut.

That done young Middleton went upstairs to inform Latimer. But he was confronted by Myrtle, who checked him just as he was about to rap upon her husband's door.

"What is it, Mr Middleton? Is it very urgent?"

She asked the question anxiously, yet on a muffled note. Clearly she desired not to disturb the sleepers. Influenced by this, Middleton tiptoed towards her, away not only from the door of Latimer's room but also from the door of the general's which was near it. She beckoned him down to the half-landing, and there by the tall window that looked upon the wider space of garden at the back, where they could allow their voices liberty, she informed him that her husband was asleep, worn out, and begged that the lieutenant's message unless very pressing should be delayed for an hour or two.

"He will be in the lines again all night, sir, as you know," she ended.

Middleton was perplexed. "I scarce know what to do. There is a Mr Neild here – "

"Who?" She interrupted him so sharply as to startle him.

"Mr Neild," he repeated. "A Quaker tobacco-planter."

At first he thought that her face looked scared. But in the next moment he imagined that this must have been due to a trick of the light. Her voice when now she questioned him was composed and level.

"But what does Mr Neild want with my husband?"

She spoke of this Neild as of someone known to her, which seemed nowise odd to Middleton, considering that the Quaker was lodged and traded with her father. It was possible that she had made his acquaintance in the course of one of her visits to Tradd Street. Therefore, Middleton experienced a certain hesitancy in telling her what was the exact position.

"Possibly to sell tobacco," he evaded.

"Oh, but in that case…" She paused, and then on a fresh resolve she added: "I will go and tell him that Major Latimer is not to be disturbed at present."

Already she was descending the stairs, and Middleton was in a quandary. How far was he right in permitting Mrs Latimer to see a man who was virtually a prisoner?

He went after her. "No, no, Mrs Latimer. It is not necessary. Mr Neild can wait."

"But he may have to wait an hour or two. A discourtesy."

"Pray do not give yourself the trouble, madam. I will tell him."

"But I should like to explain the circumstance. I know Mr Neild, and I should be glad of a word with him. I haven't seen my father for a day or two, and he may give me news of him."

Thus, ever increasing the young officer's perplexities, she moved on into the hall, Middleton following. His military instincts told him this was wrong. On the other hand Mrs Latimer was the wife of his superior officer, of the general's chief aide. What harm could follow from her being allowed to speak to Neild, who, after all, might be innocent enough of all evil intentions?

"Where is Mr Neild?" she asked.

"In the library, madam. But – "

She waited for no more, but walked straight into the library and closed the door. Having closed it she leaned against it for a moment in prey to the emotion she had so spiritedly suppressed.

The tall brown-clad figure of Mr Neild, exactly as she had last seen him, was standing by one of the windows, looking out upon the garden. He continued thus a moment after the sounds of the opening and closing of the door had reached him. Then, very leisurely in his movements, a man completely at his ease, and neither afraid nor to be frightened, he turned to see who had entered, presenting that singular countenance with its heavy beard and lack of eyebrows that was so unlike the face of Captain Mandeville. Upon beholding her he took a sharp step forward, and the gasp by which it was accompanied was audible across the room. Then he recovered, and bowed, master of himself and resuming the part he played.

Myrtle, too, commanded herself once more. She went forward, outwardly self-possessed. But the voice in which she spoke, came harsh and strained.

"What do you want here?"

For a long moment his piercing eyes considered her. Then, as if the scrutiny had answered some question in his mind, he spoke, in the nasal voice of Neild and in the submissive attitude his rôle demanded.

"Madam, I trust I do not incommode thee. I was bidden to wait here for Major Latimer."

She uttered a cry of impatience, of anger.

"Oh! Are we to play this comedy again? What of your word to me, your word of honour that if I kept silence and allowed you to depart, you would never return to Charles Town or hold communication with my father while the war lasted? You lied to me in that, and you have lied to me in all else. It was a pretence that you came here then solely out of concern for my father who was ill. You were what I supposed you. Your return proves it. A spy. And you have made me your accomplice. The accomplice of a spy!"

"Myrtle! For God's sake!" He spoke in his natural voice at last.

But she went wrathfully on. "And my father has connived in all this, without regard for my honour, or my feelings."

He bowed his head a little. "Your father is a loyal subject of the King," he answered softly.

"But loyal to nothing else, to no one else." She had reached a chair, and she sat down rather helplessly. "Oh God! How you have used me between you. Poor fool! Poor fool! I see it now. That is what I have been!"

He approached her, and set his hands — stained brown like his face — upon the back of her chair. A moment he hesitated, then he touched her shoulder gently. She shrank, shuddering under his touch, in a disgust that was not to be mistaken, and instantly rose again to confront him.

"Why have you carried audacity so far as to come here — to this house! What do you seek?"

Again she was subjected to that curious scrutiny before he answered her; and his answer took the form of a question.

"Have you no knowledge of why I am here? Is it by no contriving of your own?"

"My contriving? Are you mad?"

"Have you said nothing to your husband of the true identity of Jonathan Neild?"

"I?" She was amazed. "I would to God I had!"

"Are you sure that no unconscious word of yours – "

"Oh, I am sure. Sure!" Indignation and impatience were blent in the assertion. "Once, indeed, I lied, I was forced to lie, to General Moultrie in my husband's presence. He asked me if I had ever met you – met Neild, that is – at my father's house, and whilst I admitted that I had, I pretended no suspicion of your true identity. Oh!" She clenched her hands in shame and anger. "And you have the effrontery to come here to – "

"The effrontery!" he interrupted, and uttered a little laugh. "That was not the driving force, I assure you. I come because I am bidden to come. It is not an invitation that I dare refuse. And if I did, compulsion would have been employed to bring me."

"By whom?" she asked breathlessly.

"By your husband. The invitation was from him. I imagined... But no matter what I imagined. If you will look from that window you will see the reality. A sentry is pacing there with bayonet fixed, to make sure that I do not escape that way. It is very plain that I am suspected of being something other than a tobacco planter. But I am reassured since you tell me that you have not denounced me. For I know of no other evidence against me, and I think I can trust myself to play my part."

"To play your part?"

"The Quaker Neild."

She laughed quite mirthlessly. "And you think you will be allowed to play it? You think that now that you have violated your word to me I shall continue to hold my tongue? That I shall continue this lie to my husband?"

"What else?"

"What else?" she echoed.

"Yes. What else? Dare you denounce me now? Dare you? Don't you see that in doing so you will denounce yourself? That you will be proclaiming yourself my accomplice." Very quietly he made his meaning plain. "You have already admitted, you say, that you met Neild at your father's house. Will your husband and the others – for others will be concerned in this – believe that you did not recognize me then? What inference will they draw from your silence? What is to be thought of your constant visits to your father since? Your father's loyalty is a little too well known. Myrtle, my dear, think well of what you do before you destroy us both to no purpose. For you will certainly destroy yourself with me, and perhaps drag your husband down as well in the general ruin. And what shall you have gained? If no other considerations weigh with you at least do not disregard these. Ponder them well before you take a step so terrible to yourself."

"God of Heaven!" she burst out passionately. She fronted him, white and fierce. "You have me in a trap!"

His shrug and his melancholy little smile deprecated the description. "My dear!"

"That is the evil you return for the good I did. That is how you repay me for having kept silence and spared your life."

"I thought," he ventured to remind her, "that you did that in discharge of an old debt between us; that you realized it was the least you owed to me. Are you quite sure that you have paid the debt in full?"

"Quite. As sure as that I will enmesh myself in no further lies."

"It is not necessary," he said quietly. "You are already so enmeshed that escape is impossible either for you or for your husband."

"For my husband? You're mad, I think!"

"Am I? Consider a moment. If I am arrested, your own arrest will follow."

"Why! Will you denounce me in your turn?"

"In denouncing me, you will have denounced yourself. Keep that in mind. You will be asked to explain how long you have known this identity which you now betray. I shall be asked the same. Can you expect mercy if you show me none?"

For a long moment amazement left her dumb. Then she broke into speech, hot and passionate: "Oh, you are vile! Vile! I think I begin to know you. Harry was right about you from the first; and I would never listen to him. I have been under a delusion that you were noble, chivalrous, generous. Poor fool, again! Poor fool!"

She saw him wince, perceived the sudden quiver of his lip, saw him turn white under the stain on his cheeks. But he mastered himself.

"I am," he said firmly, even with a certain dignity, "a man fighting for life. If I lose my life through your agency, Myrtle, I shall sting your husband to death before I face a firing-party, and since I cannot reach him save through you, I shall have to drag you with me. That is the price you will have to pay if you persist in being merciless. Spare me; say no word of what you know, and if the worst befalls me, I vow to God that I will hold my peace in my turn, and go to my death without a word to hurt you or Latimer. Those are my terms."

She collected her scattered wits to answer him. "Me you can hurt, I know. But how can you hurt him? You can't! You can't! You say this to frighten me. You coward!"

"Ah, wait! Consider further. If you are charged with complicity, what do you think must follow? It will be assumed that this complicity is a very full one. You have been freely visiting your father. I, at your father's have been collecting and dispatching to the British, information that is of use to them. Whence have I derived this information? From you, of course. That will be the clear assumption. And whence have you in your turn derived it? Whence could you derive it but from your husband?"

"Do you think any man will believe that Harry Latimer consciously betrayed anything that would help the enemy?"

"No. But so much is not necessary. He may have been – he must have been – indiscreet. And in war indiscretion is a capital offence; in its consequences as serious as conscious betrayal."

It was a disarming stroke. It left her limp and cowed. And when she rallied, it was only weakly to upbraid him.

"I am repaid for setting my trust in your word!"

He sighed, and turned away. "It is my fate ever to be misunderstood by you. I have served you with a devotion such as I have paid no other man or woman living. I saved your husband's life not once but half-a-dozen times in the old days here; saved it, when his death might have left my way open to the thing I desired above all else. And now, at what may be the end of the chapter, all I have earned is your contempt. God pity me!"

It was a crafty appeal. It touched her, despite herself. "You broke your word," she repeated, but now almost in self-defence.

For once he betrayed heat. "Do you think I do not hate myself for that? But what choice had I?" And bitterly he added: "You cannot even do me the justice to perceive that I am not my own master."

"You are not the master of your own honour?"

"No." His voice rang out full and clear for the first time in the course of that interview. Instantly it was muted again as the explanation followed. But although muted, it was still fraught with dignity, and his tall figure seemed to grow taller as he spoke. "My honour is my country's. She disposes of it. Had I kept faith with you, I must have broken faith with England. I was ordered to return to Charles Town. I have obeyed. That is all. For the rest, I have said that I am fighting for my life. So I am, that I may continue to devote this life to the service of my country. It is all that is left me to serve." And very softly and sadly he added: "You made it so when you married Latimer."

To the distraction with which his earlier pleas had afflicted her mind he added now by this touching apologia. Undecided she stood before him, whilst, deeming no doubt that he had said enough, he awaited with bowed head the decision which it was now hers to make.

And then, suddenly, both became conscious of a brisk step approaching the door, a step which she knew for her husband's, and which converted her distraction into panic. As in a dream she heard the nasal voice of the Quaker, Jonathan Neild, and yet the make-believe sentences he uttered were to remain graven on her memory when she could no longer recall the words in which he had said things of vital import. As she began to speak, he circled quickly and

291

silently, so that his back should be turned to the door, and he should not directly see it open.

"And so, Madam, thou'lt understand that I am anxious to be returning home to my plantation and I am vastly exercised by all this godlessness hereabout which may have the effect of delaying me on my travels."

The door had opened, and Latimer stood under the lintel at gaze, but without surprise, for Middleton, uneasy under the responsibility thrust upon him by Mrs Latimer's action, had gone at last to rouse him and inform him of the situation.

Myrtle, controlling herself by an effort, directly faced him. Her companion, full conscious now of his presence, yet able by virtue of the position he had taken up to feign not to perceive it, droned steadily on, without having made the least perceptible halt.

"At this season of the year the young plants, as tender and delicate as new-born children require all a planter's care. Although I have done a good trade with friend Carey, yet had I known how I should be delayed I would not have made this last journey, I should be on my plantation now to take advantage of the first warm rains for the transplanting, or I may yet pay for the trade I have done by the loss of a whole season's crop. I tell thee, madam..."

He half turned as he spoke. Out of the corner of his eye he permitted himself to catch sight of the open door. Abruptly he checked, and turned completely, so as to face the man who stood there. He waited a moment, then:

"Friend," he said, and bowed a little, "art thou Major Latimer, whom I await?"

"I am," said Latimer. He came forward, leaving the door wide behind him. He turned to his wife, speaking gently but none the less reprovingly. "Myrtle, this was hardly prudent – "

The Quaker interrupted him. "I prithee do not chide the lady for having compassionated me, coming hither to beguile the tedium of my waiting."

"Mr Middleton told me only that Mr Neild was here," she found herself saying. "He did not add that you had sent for him. So I imagined that perhaps he had brought some message for me from my father."

The slight cloud cleared entirely from Latimer's brow. He smiled.

"It is no great matter, after all. But you knew that Mr Neild was again in Charles Town?"

"Not...not until Mr Middleton brought word that he was here."

"Well, well, my dear. I think that you may leave us together now."

And he went to hold the door for her.

Committed thus to the perpetuation of her falsehood, and more deeply enmeshed than ever in its tangles, she passed out, bearing in her breast a heart of lead.

Chapter 10

Concerning Tobacco

Major Latimer asked his wife no questions, because he was persuaded that she would know of Neild and of Neild's association with her father no more than was known to the world at large. If other association there was, and if Neild's presence in Charles Town had aims other than that of trading in tobacco, Myrtle would have been kept as much in ignorance of it as he was, himself. Indeed, the very words he had overheard the Quaker uttering during those seconds in which Neild had, as he conceived, been unconscious of a second listener, confirmed this view. Nevertheless, when all was considered, he would have preferred that his wife should not have held her interview with the Quaker. Such things touching a man under suspicion, if divulged, give rise to thoughts and questions from which he must wish to keep his wife aloof.

He came forward now and past his visitor, deliberately, so as to compel the latter to turn. Thus Neild's face was brought into the full light from the window and Latimer's was placed in shadow. The major scanned his visitor's countenance with interest. He found it odd, but was hardly able to explain its oddness. It was invested with an air of perpetual surprise that was unlike any face that Latimer remembered ever to have seen on any man. The beard he considered a loathsome affair; but he could not imagine it assumed for purposes of disguise, since no beard in this world would have sufficed to disguise such a countenance as that.

Mindful of his instructions, he addressed the Quaker with scrupulous courtesy. "I am sorry, Mr Neild, to put you to the inconvenience of visiting me here, and sorry to have detained you on your arrival."

"Nay, friend, nay!" The other was genial in his dismissal of the apology. "The inconvenience is naught. If I can serve thee in any way, I prithee command me."

"Sit down, Mr Neild... It is Neild, is it not?"

"Jonathan Neild, friend." The Quaker took the chair to which he was waved, the chair which Myrtle had lately occupied set beside a heavy Louis XV writing-table. Carefully he placed his round hat on the floor, his face composed but wearing ever that look of almost disconcerting astonishment.

Latimer drew another chair to the table, and sat down almost opposite.

"You realize that in these times, sir, it is necessary to guard ourselves most scrupulously from enemy agents – "

"What have I, friend, to do with enemy agents, as you call them? To me all are alike, all being engaged in war, which is an abomination in the eyes of the Lord."

Latimer waited until the pious interruption was at an end, then resumed.

"The officer who inspected your papers made a satisfactory report. But the Governor has ordered a further examination of the papers of all strangers at present in Charles Town, in consequence of the apprehension this morning of a spy inside our lines."

His eyes never left the Quaker's face, watching for some sign of discomposure. But not so much as an eyelid flickered in that permanently surprised countenance. Calmly, Neild carried his hand to the breast pocket inside his brown coat, and produced thence a folded sheet.

"If it is my pass thou desire to see, friend, why here it is." He unfolded the sheet, and proffered it. "I make no protest, friend," he droned on. "So long as men commit this wickedness of war, so long must the innocent suffer, and the righteous be tormented."

Latimer laughed as he took the paper. "You shall not be tormented, sir. That, at least I can promise."

He scanned the pass, which was issued from Washington's camp at Middlebrook. "This is quite in order." He folded it again, but did not yet return it. "How long have you been in Charles Town, Mr Neild?"

"Since Saturday evening, friend. Three days."

"And before that? When were you here last?"

"Close upon three months ago I was here for a week."

"Your business being?"

"The sale of tobacco, friend. I am a planter of tobacco."

"With whom has your business here been conducted?"

"With thy father-in-law, Andrew Carey."

"And no one else?"

"No one else. Andrew Carey, as thou wilt know, owns many ships and does a great trade. He is able to take all the tobacco that I grow and all that I can purchase for him from other planters at present, his own plantations having been perforce neglected as a consequence of the war."

"His own plantations?"

Carey had no tobacco plantations, and the tone of Latimer's question all but betrayed the fact.

Neild made for safe ground at once.

"Either his own plantations or the plantations hereabouts from which he was in the habit of buying aforetime. I know not which for certain."

"Your acquaintance with Sir Andrew is a recent one, then?"

"Oh, yes."

"When, exactly, did you first become acquainted?"

"On the occasion of my last visit here in February when I made my first sales to him."

"Yet you lodge with him? Or so I understand."

"Naturally, friend, since he is my only buyer. It is at his invitation that I come."

"Do you think, sir, that having regard to Sir Andrew's political convictions, it is prudent for a stranger to lodge in his house at such a time?"

"I do not perceive the imprudence, friend."

"Himself he is suspect, as he well knows. That, you will understand. A stranger lodging under his roof must perforce become also an object of suspicion. That, too, should be clear to you."

"Nay, friend, it is not clear at all. His convictions are naught to me; nor yet are thine. Since both these convictions have led to strife, it follows that both are wrong. But I am not concerned with that. I am concerned," and he smiled faintly for the first time, "to sell tobacco. Here friend is some fine leaf of my own growing." He drew a leather bag from his pocket as he spoke, untied the neck, and proffered it. "Make essay of it, friend. Thou'lt find it choice if so be thou knowest tobacco."

Latimer took the bag, conned the leaf, then smelt it. He smiled appreciatively. "Choice, indeed," he said, returning it.

"Nay, but smoke a pipeful, friend."

Latimer shook his head. "I know something of tobacco. I do not need to smoke that leaf to judge its quality. It is superior to any that ever I have produced."

Neild shrugged a little. "As thou wilt," he said regretfully, and pocketed the bag.

Latimer rose, and proffered him his pass. Neild got up, too, to take it. Watching him intently the while, Latimer could detect no shade of relief or of any emotion whatsoever upon that stolid face. Save for his one trivial slip in the matter of Carey's plantations, he had answered all questions satisfactorily. And that one slip might be the result of an ignorance that afforded no ground for suspicion. And yet it was an odd thing that a tobacco planter who had lodged with Carey for a week on one occasion and for three days on another, for the sole purpose of selling him tobacco should not have elicited the fact that Carey himself had never grown the plant. Tobacco would be their natural topic of conversation.

"Ay," said Latimer almost in a sigh, and as if pursuing his own thoughts. "You Virginia planters can teach us a deal. We Carolinians can produce nothing that can compete with your leaf for flavour. Is it true that you use cider in the fermentation, as I have heard?"

There was a moment's pause before Neild answered him. For the first time in that enquiry his reply to a question did not come prompt and pat. A broad smile expanded his bearded mouth. He shook his head.

"That, friend, is a secret that we guard most jealously."

It was a clumsy way out, though the best that any man in Mandeville's case could have adopted. But from that moment Latimer suspected him. He betrayed, however, nothing of this suspicion. He smiled agreement, appreciation even, of the humour of the Quaker's closeness.

"Naturally, naturally. And you guard as secretly the methods of your sweating process."

"Oh, yes," the Quaker agreed, still smiling.

"Of course. But there are other matters that are common knowledge I imagine. At least knowledge of them may easily be obtained. For instance – and this is a point upon which I have often been curious, yet oddly enough, have never had occasion to satisfy my curiosity – how many plants do you allow to the acre in Virginia?"

Again the Quaker hesitated whilst he made rapid mental calculations. Desperately he plunged at last.

"Somewhere about three thousand, I believe."

"Three thousand!" Major Latimer seemed slightly surprised.

"A...as nearly as I can remember," Neild made haste to add.

"But planting so closely as that, what weight of tobacco do you look to get from each plant?"

"Why...er...the merest trifle less than the average."

"But what is the average in Virginia?" asked Latimer, and almost at once, added the suggestion: "A pound?"

"A pound, yes. A pound."

"Ah." There followed a pause, during which Latimer thoughtfully considered him. "I wonder what weight of seed you allow to the acre?"

Neild pondered. He was faced by the necessity of more desperate calculations, and found himself hopelessly without any guide. "I don't recall the exact amount, friend," he replied, at last. "I leave such details to my overseer. Myself, I am more concerned with the sale of tobacco than with its growth."

"Yes, yes," Latimer persisted, smiling. "But you must have some notion of the amount – approximately."

"Approximately? Well, I should say…" He took his nether lip between finger and thumb, and a frown of thought corrugated his brow.

In his heart was the desperate hope that if he delayed, Latimer might prompt him as before. But all that Latimer did was to utter an inviting: "Yes?"

The wretched man plunged desperately there being nothing else left him.

"About five pounds," he blurted out.

He found Major Latimer's stare deepening in intensity.

"To the acre? Five pounds to the acre?"

"As nearly as I can recall."

And now the soldier was smiling again; but it was a smile very different from his last; a smile that the Quaker did not like at all.

"It is extraordinary," said he, "how methods may vary between one province and another. Now here in Carolina we cannot plant more than half the number of plants to the acre that you tell me are usually planted in Virginia. Our plants yield only half the weight you tell me is yielded by yours. That is remarkable enough, but when we come to this question of seed, the difference is more remarkable by far. You allow five pounds to the acre, you tell me. Do you know what we allow? Of course you don't, or you would not have answered me quite so foolishly. We allow half an ounce, my tobacco-planting friend. Remarkable, isn't it?" Latimer's smile was broadening.

"Almost as remarkable as that a spy who comes here masquerading as a tobacco planter should not have taken the precaution to make himself master of these details."

The Quaker stared at him a moment, then, to his infinite amazement, gave way to laughter in which amusement was blended with contempt.

"A spy! Ho, ho, ho! A spy! Verily, friend, they who engage in war will for ever be starting at shadows, and perceiving an enemy in every bush. A spy! And thou'rt assuming that upon no better ground than my ignorance of some details of tobacco planting. Faith, friend, if every man in like case is to be deemed a spy, there must be a mort o' spies hereabouts."

"But every man in like case does not pretend to be a tobacco planter," said Latimer, no whit deceived by the other's easy assurance.

"To be a tobacco planter does not mean that a man must plant tobacco with his own hands, but rather one who owns plantations, which is my case. I leave the planting, as I have already told thee, to my overseer and his men. Myself I am concerned to sell the leaf."

Latimer shook his head. "It won't do, my friend."

The Quaker became serious, slightly annoyed and very dignified. "Have thine own way. Because I do not know how much seed will go to the acre, it follows that I am a spy. Excellent reasoning, friend. But I venture to trust it will hardly suffice even for men who are besotted by war."

Major Latimer moved back towards the window behind him.

"Come here," he said sharply. "I want to have a look at you."

The Quaker started. The perpetual astonishment of his face seemed to increase.

"Friend, I do not like thy tone. Civility – "

"Come here. At once!" Latimer's voice was hard and peremptory.

Mr Neild shrugged, and spread his hands in resignation. Then he shuffled forward, his air faintly sullen.

"Stand there, in the light."

Not merely in the light, but directly in a shaft of the afternoon sunshine did Latimer place him, what time he closely scanned that swarthy face, which impassively submitted to this searching examination. It revealed to Latimer at last the reason for that odd, surprised look with which the Quaker's face was invested.

"Why have you shaved your eyebrows?"

"I have no eyebrows, friend."

"You had when last I saw you, wherever that may have been. I begin to find something familiar in your face, Mr Neild. I wonder what you would look like without that beard. Take off your neckcloth, and open the breast of your shirt."

"Friend, I must protest against this – "

"Open the breast of your shirt; unless you prefer that I call the guard to do it for you."

Again the Quaker shrugged ill-humouredly, but finding resistance vain, he slowly obeyed with fingers that certainly did not fumble.

Almost Latimer found himself admiring the man, of whose real trade he no longer had a single doubt. His nerves were certainly of iron.

"So," he said, as he surveyed the white breast bared to his view. "As I thought. You have stained your face."

"It is written that we are to suffer fools gladly," said the Quaker, in tones of weary resignation. "My breast being covered hath escaped the sun, by which my face and hands are burnt."

Abruptly, from between the fellow's fingers, Latimer plucked the neckcloth which he had removed but was still retaining. He looked at it in the light, and laughed.

"Sunburn that comes off on your neckcloth! I could tell you of a better dye than walnut juice." He looked him squarely between the eyes again. "Now, Master Spy, shall we put an end to this play acting? Will you tell me who you are, and what is your real name?" And then, even as he asked, he found at last the clue he sought in that face he had been studying so intently. "Egad!" he ejaculated on a note of intense surprise. "You need not. I know you, Captain Mandeville."

The man before him quivered; a spasm crossed his face, like a ripple running over water. Then he was composed again as before. Very faintly he smiled. He bowed his head a little.

"Major Mandeville," he corrected. And added with a tinge of irony: "At your service."

After that for a long moment they remained staring each at the other, each grave faced and suppressing whatever emotion he may have felt. Then at last Latimer spoke, and what he said, all things considered, was odd.

"I always thought your eyes were blue. That is one of the things that most deceived me."

"It is one of the things upon which I counted," said Mandeville easily, as if discussing something in which he was not so perilously concerned. And he stated no more than the fact. Blue eyes are readily associated with the fair complexion and hair that were Mandeville's; therefore the possession of dark eyes was of enormous value in such a disguise as he had adopted.

Latimer moved past him, and came forward towards the table. Mandeville half turned to follow him with his glance.

"I don't think," said the American, "that we need prolong this interview."

"It means a firing party?" quoth Mandeville in the same cool tone of detachment.

"What else? You know the forfeit in the game you play." He reached for a hand-bell as he spoke.

Sharply came Mandeville's voice to check the intention: "I would not ring that bell if I were you."

Latimer rang nevertheless.

Mandeville spread his hands. "You realize that my arrest must be followed by that of your father-in-law?"

"What then?"

"Consider well all that may follow upon that."

The door opened, and Middleton appeared.

"Call the guard," said Latimer shortly.

Middleton went out again, leaving the door wide.

"You fool!" With passionate vehemence Mandeville hissed out the word. "What of your wife?"

"My wi…" Latimer's jaw dropped. His eyes dilated as they stared at his prisoner. "My wife knew? Knew that you are not the Quaker you pretended to be?"

But it was less a question than an exclamation of bitter conviction. In a flash, at the mere mention of Myrtle by Mandeville, he had seen the terrible truth, and swift on the heels of that came an array of memories marshalled out of the past to fill him with horror and dismay. It did not need the shrug and quiet smile that were Mandeville's only answer, to make him perceive how fatuous had been his momentary assumption that Myrtle had been as deceived in Jonathan Neild as at first he had been deceived himself.

Came firm steps outside, a word of command and the ring of musket-butts that are grounded. Middleton reappeared.

"The guard, sir."

Latimer commanded himself. "Let it wait," he said. "Until I ring again."

Middleton went out. And this time, assuming naturally that the examination was not yet over, he closed the door.

And now, white faced, almost vicious, Latimer turned upon the sardonically smiling Mandeville.

"Now, sir," he said, "perhaps you will make yourself quite plain, so that there may be no misunderstanding. What do you imply against my wife?"

"But is it really necessary to ask? Does not your own wit tell you? I think it must, or you would not have changed your mind about the guard."

"Nevertheless, sir, I am concerned to hear from you the precise danger that will threaten her, when you and Sir Andrew Carey come before a court-martial?"

Mandeville's hand dropped to his pocket. Instantly Latimer covered him with a pistol which he snatched from his own breast.

"Put up that hand at once!"

Mandeville laughed. "It is only my snuff box," said he producing it and tapping it composedly. "I need a sedative. My nerves have been jarred a little." He raised the lid, and holding a pinch of tobacco between finger and thumb, he resumed: "Reassure yourself. I have no weapons about me such as would justify you in pistolling me in self-defence." He applied the snuff to his nostrils. Thereafter, having pocketed the box, and as he was dusting the fragments of tobacco from his fingers, he added with a smile: "It would be a convenient way of disposing of me, I know."

"Mandeville, you will answer my question – or – by God! – you'll find yourself against that garden wall inside the next ten minutes with a firing-party before you. I'll shoot you out of hand, and take the risk of it."

"Risk is hardly the word. Certainty, my friend. Certainty. The Governor would have something to say to you. An awkward man, Rutledge. He would probe for the reason. And where do you think he would probe for it? He would have Andrew Carey haled before him and precisely that would happen which must happen if you persist in sending me before a court-martial. Besides, even if he did not, be sure that all my measures are taken. You do not imagine that I came here in answer to your summons, whose probable object I could not possibly misunderstand, without making due provision for the worst. I am too old a soldier, my dear Latimer, not to make quite sure before going into action that my lines of retreat are clear. You should remember that. In the old days I gave you credit for some wit. Your present attitude hardly appears to justify me. But perhaps you are unduly agitated. Let me exhort you to be calm, and calmly to consider whither you are driving."

Latimer made the effort, not because he was thus tauntingly invited, but because he realized the need to keep his temper that his wits should remain unimpaired. He pocketed the pistol and sat down again at the table. By an effort he spoke calmly.

"When my wife was here with you just now, she knew who you were?"

"But of course. She has known it these three months, ever since we first met in Tradd Street, when you were away at Purysburg with General Moultrie. Any inquiry must bring that fact to light. Andrew Carey will see to that."

"You tell me that Andrew Carey desires the ruin of his own daughter?" Latimer's tone was, properly, incredulous.

"He desires your ruin, Latimer; and to encompass it he will not hesitate to destroy his daughter. With her you, yourself, become of necessity involved. You must perceive that."

Latimer had not perceived it. He did not perceive it now, nor was he concerned to perceive it. There was something far more horrible here to engage his perceptions. Whilst he pondered it, Mandeville continued.

"She has been regularly coming and going between Moultrie's headquarters here and her father's house. Her father will swear, what it will require no oaths to establish: that she has brought information which has been passed on to the British."

"That at least is a lie!"

"Is it? The matter is not worth argument. False or true it will be very readily believed; it will be the preconception of the court."

And miserably Latimer realized the truth of this, remembering the offensive recommendation he had received from Rutledge to forbid his wife's visits to Tradd Street, a recommendation which he had indignantly disregarded.

Calmly Mandeville resumed: "If her father swears that as swear it he will, it follows that such information as she has conveyed can have been obtained only from yourself. Where shall you stand then, Latimer?"

"Bah! I don't care!" Latimer was obviously in torment.

"For yourself, perhaps not. But there is Myrtle. Do you think I care for myself? Do you think it is to save my own life that I am troubling to caution you? It is because if I am brought to trial, so inevitably will Myrtle be; and because whatever my fate, she will be made to share it. Whether you are involved or not, I care not a farthing rushlight."

Latimer leaned his elbows heavily upon the table, and took his head in his hands. His face seemed to have aged in the last few minutes. The youth had all gone out of it. It was drawn and haggard.

Mandeville looked at him from under lowered eyelids, and again went on, speaking slowly now. "I wonder whether you have ever gauged the depth and ferocity of Carey's hate, for the wrong you did him – the intolerable wrong of baulking him – his revenge by legitimate means. You bound him hard, when you withheld your shot that night at Brewton's ball. Do you conceive how he has writhed in those bonds? How his hate has grown and grown by contemplation of his incapacity to call you out, and deal with you as one man with another? To reach you, he suffered himself to be reconciled with Myrtle. A cruel comedy. He regards her with a detestation only a degree less than that with which he visits you. In his eyes, she is an ingrate, an unnatural child who has turned against her parent, joined his worst enemy. Call it mad, if you will. On my soul I believe he is mad where you are concerned. But do not, for Myrtle's sake, make light of the power for evil that lies in that madness of hate by which he is afflicted."

He ceased at last. Still Latimer did not move. Still he sat there grey-faced, staring straight before him. There was a long pause, during which Mandeville composedly buttoned his shirt and resumed his neckcloth before a mirror on the overmantel.

"Well?" he asked, at last. "What are you going to do? You cannot without danger long delay your decison."

Latimer was as one who awakens. He stirred and rose.

"I cannot let you go. I would not if I could. My duty there is clear. I cannot shield myself at the expense of my country."

"As to that," said Mandeville, "you need have no apprehension that any action of yours now can avert what must be. Tomorrow, or the next day at latest, Prevost will enter Charles Town. Here I am his agent; but not his message-bearer. I have several of those. One of them, as you told me, and as I already knew, you caught this morning. But there are others whom you did not catch, nor will.

Others who will convey any information of importance up to the last moment. Charles Town is doomed, sir. Whatever you may do by me cannot affect that."

"It may be. But – and I thank God for't – I have my orders, and they are to detain you in any case."

"Detain me all you please. But if you have any regard for Myrtle, to say nothing of yourself, you will do no more than that."

"I must think." It was almost a groan. Then controlling himself Latimer announced his decision. "Meanwhile you shall be detained as I am bidden."

No gleam of triumph in his eyes revealed Mandeville's relief. But he checked Latimer as he was about to ring again.

"A moment, please! May I send two lines to my lodging, to announce that I shall not be returning just yet, and…to avert what must happen if they have no news?"

Latimer frowned, clearly hesitating.

"Consider," said Mandeville, "how natural would be the request in the case of my simple detention upon suspicion, and how natural must be your acquiescence." He paused, and as Latimer still did not answer him, he added: "Unless you can do that, you may as well denounce me out of hand, for Carey will act as was concerted between us in the event of my not returning."

A moment still Latimer stood undecided. "Very well," he said at last conquered by his dread, and by something else vaguely stirring in his mind. "There is what you need for writing."

Mandeville sat down and rapidly scrawled some lines on a sheet of paper. As he was folding it Latimer held out a hand across the table.

"Let me see it."

The spy looked up in surprise. Then surrendered the sheet.

He had written: "I am detained on business, and I may not return tonight. – JONATHAN NEILD."

"This is a code, of course."

"Of course," said Mandeville. "It explains my position, but allays alarm."

"Very well." Latimer folded the sheet. "Superscribe it."

When that was done, Latimer pocketed it. "It shall be delivered before nightfall, whatever may happen to you."

"What!" Mandeville bounded to his feet. "You are breaking faith!"

"No. But I must consider my course. I must have time to think." He rang the bell abruptly.

Mandeville drew a deep breath. He even smiled a little.

"You have tricked me," he complained, but without bitterness.

"Perhaps not," Latimer replied, "At best I may have obtained a respite. You shall be informed."

To Middleton who came in: "Remove the prisoner," he said. "He is detained pending further inquiry."

"Come, sir. By the right. March!"

Mandeville was the Quaker Neild once more, shuffling a little in his steps, and speaking through his nose.

"Nay, friend, nay! I know naught of thy military orders."

But he went out, and Latimer was left alone with his misery.

Chapter 11

Via Crucis

Little imagination is necessary to follow the path by which the mind of Harry Latimer now journeyed to the Calvary of all that he held dearest in this life.

Forgotten by him in that hour of agony was the war upon which he was engaged; forgotten the enemy at the gates and the imminence of the peril by which Charles Town was threatened. In his own past, as he went over it in anguished review, he found that which blotted the present from his mind, making it a thing of no account.

Seated there alone in that partly dismantled library, he went back to the beginnings of his married life, and to the quarrels that had poisoned it until on that day when the battle of Fort Sullivan was fought, he had deliberately sought euthanasia in death. Again he heard Myrtle denouncing their marriage.

"I wish I had not married you. I would give ten years of my life to undo that!"

And he remembered her tacit admission that she had married him only to induce him to depart from Charles Town; that she had married him out of pity, to quiet her conscience which told her that it was because of her, and of what he had discovered between her and Mandeville, that he was so obstinately determined to remain in Charles Town even though he should hang for it.

Back beyond that his thoughts ran on, to that day at Fairgrove when with his own eyes he had beheld evidence which only a fool could subsequently have been brought to disregard.

Oh, it was all plain; most damnably plain. His entire married life had been a miserable lie; her love had been a shameful make-believe; their child...oh, God! Their child, born in a wedlock that was a mockery of all that wedlock should be. Again he leaned his elbows on the table, and took his head in his hands, closing the eyes of the flesh so that the eyes of the soul might review again and recognize at last this fool's paradise which he had so complacently inhabited.

It was Mandeville whom she had loved. Himself she had married for the reasons he had reviewed already, and further perhaps not only to save him but to save Mandeville, too. For he remembered now how he had pointed out to her in what peril must Mandeville and Lord William stand if they dared, indeed, to attempt to hang him. Either that or else her impulse of pity for himself had been the only spur. And this impulse had afterwards been repented as must be all impulses that are to involve in their consequence the whole course of subsequent existence. That repentance she had expressed more than once and in terms so unmistakable that again he was a fool to have allowed them to be thrust aside by fresh lying protestations of affection made at a time when he was almost at the point of death.

It was Mandeville whom she had loved throughout. He should not have needed the bitter proofs that lay now before him. Her reconciliation with her father had taken place at a time when Mandeville was in Charles Town. What did that prove but a continuous correspondence between them? The story of her father's illness was but another lie wherewith to dupe him. And whilst Mandeville had been there in disguise, she had been meeting him daily at her father's; meeting a man who was her husband's enemy. And was meeting him the whole extent of her treachery? Might it not be true, as Mandeville had more than hinted, that she had conveyed to him information gleaned here at Moultrie's headquarters? If she was false in one thing why should she not be false in the other? Indeed, of the two, considering the faith in which she had been reared, betrayal of the Colonial cause was a light offence compared with her betrayal of the fond fool of a husband who trusted her so completely.

Did he lack proof of this? Was there not her own admission to Moultrie that she had met Neild at her father's? An admission made – as he now perceived – because denial would have been fraught with danger. And was it possible, was it for a single moment to be supposed – as for a moment in his blind faith he had supposed – that she should have been deceived in Mandeville's identity? Why, even assuming that Mandeville and her infernal father had been in league to lay a trap for him through her, would they not have begun by disclosing Neild's true identity? So that one way or the other, she must have known. Yet knowing it, she continued to visit Mandeville at her father's house. Had she been honest, she would have denounced him at once to the Governor; or if merely some old tenderness remained, at least she would have told her husband the truth on his return to Charles Town. Instead she had lied by her silence; and once indeed by her speech, when Moultrie questioned her. For what but a lie was the answer she had made? And that very day, an hour ago, when he had found them together in this room, she had lied to him again by her attitude and her very words. She had proved herself then to be Mandeville's accomplice. Would she be his accomplice in such work as he was engaged upon, work that threatened Harry's life and honour as it threatened the lives and fortunes of all in Charles Town, unless at the same time she were something more?

The evidence was complete, and the truth that leapt from it stark and inexorable filled him with a shuddering horror.

Still seated there as the daylight was fading, Myrtle found him when she came, wondering, in quest of him.

"Harry!"

He sprang up abruptly at the sound of her voice, startled like a man who has been suddenly awakened. Corrosive reproaches and recriminations were surging to his lips. But they remained unuttered. In that little moment in which she approached him across the room, he took his decision to employ guile, to question craftily, to discover at all costs the whole truth. The truth! He heard a devil laughing in his soul. The truth! Had he not fed himself to a surfeit in the past hour upon the vile nauseating truth? Not, then to test these abominable irresistible convictions, which required no further test, but to plumb the depths of her infamy and turpitude would he question her.

"Harry, what are you doing here? It is almost dark." There was a straining note of anxiety in her sweet voice, the voice that he had loved best in all the world. He guessed the source of her uneasiness.

He yawned and stretched himself. "I... I must have fallen asleep," he explained drowsily through his yawn.

He caught the sound of the deep breath of relief she drew, and knew how she would be arguing. If he had been able to fall asleep after his interview with Mr Neild, it must follow that nothing had transpired to disturb his peace of mind.

"My poor Harry!" Her voice was a caress of tenderness and concern. "I know how weary you must be. I am glad that you slept a little."

"Yes," he muttered. "Yes. If that cursed Quaker hadn't been brought in this afternoon, I might have had a little rest. God knows I need it."

"What have you done with him? With Mr Neild?" She spoke evenly, almost casually, and in his heart he damned her for a traitress.

"Detained him," he answered shortly.

"Detained him?" Her voice was casual no longer. It was startled. "Detained him? Why?"

"Rutledge's orders. That is all."

"But what is there against him?"

"Nothing that I could be certain of. But Rutledge desired him to be kept in custody for the present, until our troubles here are over, on the chance of his being a spy. Rutledge will take no risks of having information sent to the enemy." He sat down again. Myrtle remained standing, leaning rather heavily upon the table. "Unsupported," he thought, "her trembling would betray her."

"But…do you…do you think he's a spy?"

He laughed easily. "Why, I vow your voice shook then. No, no. The fellow's papers are in order, and he seems to be what he pretends. We shall have to keep him until his being at large can no longer matter in any event. That is all. And yet…"

"Yes?" she asked. He did not answer, but sat as one thinking deeply. "And yet – what?" she demanded.

He feigned to rouse himself, and looked at her. In the dim light her face was indistinct.

"I cannot quite escape the conviction that the fellow is not what he pretends, however much appearances may be in his favour. D'ye know, Myrtle, there's something oddly familiar about him. Something that eludes me. But I shall find it yet, I hope. He reminds me of someone. But so vaguely that I cannot think of whom it is. Tell me, did you notice anything of the kind?"

"I? No." She was emphatic. "No."

"And yet you must have seen a good deal of him, and talked with him often."

"I?" she cried again, and this time it was almost as if she were about to deny it.

"Why, of course," he answered. "At your father's."

"Yes. I have seen him there once or twice."

"And you've talked with him, of course."

"Not…not very much."

"No? Well, at least, you were in here with him this afternoon for a quarter of an hour or more before I arrived. You must have been talking to him then, observing him."

"Yes, of course." Her voice was becoming strained and unnatural. She could no longer command it as she would.

"And in all that time you observed nothing in the man that reminded you of anyone else?"

She uttered a nervous laugh. "Why, no. It is some fancy of yours, Harry. It must be."

"Ah well!" He sighed and rose. "Perhaps it is." And very casually, almost as if rallying her, he asked: "But what on earth did you find to talk about with such a dullard in all that time?"

"I?" she paused perceptibly, then abruptly answered: "Oh, I forget."

"Forget?" His tone expressed astonishment. "Oh, come Myrtle. You must have had some reason for seeking him when Middleton told you he was here. What was it?"

"Why…why are you questioning me like this?"

"But…" He paused, a man amazed by her sudden demand. "Is there anything surprising in my questions?"

"No, no. But…well, if you must know, I wanted news of my father."

"But you saw your father only yesterday."

"Yes, but when Mr Middleton told me Mr Neild was here, I imagined that he came with some message for me from my father. I didn't know that you had sent for him."

"Oh, I see. And then, of course, you would be staying to discuss with him the matter of this summons?"

"Of course. He thought it strange, and wondered why you should want him."

"And after that? You see, my dear, I am anxious to see if anything that passed between you might give us a clue to go upon. Try to remember what you talked about."

She made a pretence of trying, then impatiently, almost irritably, burst out: "Oh, I can't. It was all so…so trivial. He talked of tobacco. It is his only subject. He's a tobacco planter."

"You're sure of that? That he's a tobacco planter?"

"Well, isn't he?"

"That is what he represents himself. But I have my doubts. You know nothing of him beyond that?"

"What should I know?" Her petulance became more marked. "Don't be ridiculous, Harry. I came to fetch you to supper. General Moultrie is waiting."

"Forgive me, my dear. I am a little harassed."

314

They went into the dining-room together, she with terror in her heart, he with hatred in his. He had given her a chance to speak, to confess; and she had fenced with him, and put him off with answers every word of which was a lie in its suppression of the truth. And this was the woman he had taken to his heart, this was his wife, the mother of his boy! This perfidious liar! It but remained to consider what course he must pursue.

During supper he mentioned casually to Moultrie that the Quaker had been there, and that his papers were in order, but that in accordance with Rutledge's instructions, he was having him detained.

Moultrie laughed. He regarded the Quaker's plight as comical, and Rutledge's fears as more comical still.

Myrtle, whom Harry was covertly watching, was deathly pale, and did no more than make a pretence of eating. But he was to startle her yet more.

Abruptly towards the close of the meal and making his voice as casual as he could he asked a question that flung her into panic.

"Myrtle, do you happen to know what has become of your cousin, Robert Mandeville?"

Her knife clattered to her plate. Terror looked at him out of her eyes, under which he saw the shadows deepen as he watched her.

"Why…why do you ask?" Her voice came hard and rasping.

He raised his eyebrows. "But…" He seemed perplexed. "Now what is there extraordinary in the question that it should startle you like this?"

She attempted to smile. But the attempt was pitiful.

"It…it is…that I am not very well," she said weakly. "I am easily startled. My…my ears," she added on a sudden inspiration, "keep straining for the guns."

"Poor child, poor child!" Moultrie murmured sympathetically.

"I know, dear, I know." Nothing could have been more soothing than her husband's voice. "I asked the question because Mandeville has been oddly in my thoughts this evening. Heaven knows why. I'm not given to thinking about him. You know nothing of him I suppose?"

She shook her head. "Nothing," she said.

Moultrie thrusting back his chair and rising put an end to the matter. But it was ended already, for Latimer had no intention of driving her into further falsehoods.

"Come along, Harry," the general urged him, "there's work to do. I had a message from Rutledge a half-hour since. He's in the lines."

Lest he should arouse her suspicions Harry went to kiss his wife. She rose, and clung to him a moment. He patted her shoulder encouragingly, assured her that they would not be long away, that there was no danger of an attack that night, and followed Moultrie, who had already departed. As he reached the door, her voice, rather strident in its suddenness, arrested him:

"Harry!"

He turned. She was standing leaning against the table, and looking straight before her and away from him. She was obviously in prey to some inward struggle.

"I... I...want to – " She broke off. There was a pause. Then she resumed. "I want you to take care of yourself. I shall not get to bed until you return."

But he knew that this was not what she had desired to say and he went out with the assurance that for one moment she had attempted to draw back from the morass of falsehood into which she was sinking.

Chapter 12

The Test

The whole of that night was spent by Latimer in the lines, where the men stood to arms in the lurid light of an array of flaring tar barrels which partially dispelled the darkness and provided in some small measure against surprise.

Early in the evening there had been some heavy firing which had startled the town, conveying the impression that an assault was being attempted. It resulted from an unfortunate incident, which had, however, the immediate effect of delimiting the too vague powers of Governor Rutledge. Hitherto the Governor had claimed to himself the control and command of the militia which he had brought in with him from Orangeburg. Discovering that night a breach in the abatis, he had ordered up a body of these men under Major Huger to repair it. Their movements before the lines had alarmed those who guarded them, and whose orders from the general to fire upon any persons approaching the fortification in the darkness were quite explicit. Imagining that they had to do with a party of the enemy a few hopping shots were loosed at the moving figures, which were taken by the entrenched men as a signal. A rapid fire of musketry and even of some cannon ran swiftly along the lines to rake the open ground beyond.

The excitement was soon allayed; but in the meantime Major Huger and twelve of his men had been killed. And the result was a sharp encounter between Moultrie and Rutledge, in which the former demanded that an end should be made to this dual control of the military forces, which if continued would end in ruining them. Rutledge, dismayed by the event, gave way more promptly than was his custom in disputes.

Another result of the unfortunate death of the gallant and widely esteemed Benjamin Huger was that Tom Izard, who was more or less without occupation and anxious for employment during his enforced sojourn in Charles Town at such a time, was placed in command of a company of militia.

It would be towards three o'clock in the morning, when as Moultrie and Latimer were riding along towards the Town Gate from an inspection of the fortifications to the south which the sappers were still actively labouring to strengthen, they were challenged out of the gloom. As they drew rein an officer rode forward to inform the general that his excellency desired to consult with him at once.

They found Rutledge with a half-dozen officers, of whom Christopher Gadsden, and at least three others were also privy councillors. The Governor was seated on a pile of rubble by the gate, the officers standing about him, and the group was lighted by the ruddy blaze of a tar barrel. Half assimilated by the darkness in the background, on the very fringe of the wide wheel of light, their waiting horses were being held for them.

Moultrie and Latimer dismounted, and leaving their horses in the charge of a militia-man, they advanced towards that gathering, which had all the air of a council of war.

A negro was serving out Antigua rum from a jar which had been fetched from Gadsden's house. The newcomers were given each a cup, which was very welcome to them both, for at this hour before the dawn there was a chilling sharpness in the air. Moultrie took further advantage of the respite to fill and light himself a pipe.

Then, when the negro had departed to carry the jar to the officers on the abatis with General Gadsden's compliments, Rutledge broached the matter upon which these men had been summoned.

He was seated on the rubble in an attitude of some dejection his elbow on his knee, his chin in his palm, and his face revealed by the ruddy light looked more grim and careworn than ever.

"Information has reached me that Prevost has made all preparations to bring over the main body of his army as soon as it is daylight. The British number between seven and eight thousand men, which is more by at least a thousand than I had hitherto supposed. They are well-equipped, well-armed, in good order and strongly supported by artillery. At what number do you put our own strength, General Moultrie?"

"Somewhere in the neighbourhood of three thousand," Moultrie answered him.

Rutledge sighed wearily. "Too generous an estimate by a thousand, I fear."

This, however, Moultrie would not admit. He went into details to prove the Governor wrong, and partially succeeded.

"Even so," Rutledge rejoined at length, "we are very far from being in sufficient strength to withstand the formidable army arrayed against us."

Moultrie laughed. "We never have been, even in the opinion of men of wider military experience than your excellency's. General Lee spoke just so to me when I commanded the fort on Sullivan's Island. His only preoccupation was that I should have a sound bridge for retreat. I trust your excellency will not push the parallel as far as that."

The grim humour of his words drew a ready laugh from some of the others whom previously Rutledge had been infecting with his gloom. It was characteristic of Moultrie, with his easy ways and his indifference to danger, obstinately to refuse to estimate strength by numbers only. He was not merely brave in himself, but he inspired bravery in others.

"I have to remember, sirs," Rutledge answered in his cold, formal voice, "that should the British force the lines there will be great loss of life and great suffering in the town itself."

Gadsden interposed almost irritably. He was the same downright extremist in military matters that he had always been in politics.

"That is not the thing to remember at such a time as this, Rutledge."

"Not for you, perhaps, who are soldiers and have plain soldierly duties to perform. But certainly for me, who am responsible for the welfare of those over whom I am placed to govern. You know what are the horrors that attend the storming of a town. Will you expose Charles Town to that? Dare you do it, knowing the weakness of our defences?"

Moultrie took the pipe from between his teeth. "By God!" he cried out, "You are not proposing that we should surrender before ever a blow has been struck?"

"I am not in a position to make proposals of any kind until I know what terms the British might be disposed to offer."

He was interrupted almost angrily. Several of them spoke at once, sharp and excitedly. Moultrie best expressed their general amazement.

"My God, man, what's come to you? Is the situation more desperate than at Fort Sullivan? Yet then, when Lee advised its evacuation – and Lee was neither a coward nor a fool – you wrote to me, while the battle was raging: 'I will cut off my right hand before I sign the order to retreat.' Those were your words then. I treasure the memory of them. And yet now you – the man who could write that at such a time – "

He was drowned by the uproar of the others who made chorus to him in their upbraidings of the Governor. Rutledge waited until the storm of protest had abated.

"This, sirs, does more credit to your valour than your judgment. You cannot deny the weakness of our earthworks."

"But they still remain earthworks," Moultrie countered. "And it is for the British to attack them. I know which side has the advantage in such a contest."

"If you had not a town behind you I should agree, general."

"There was a town behind me at Sullivan Island," cried Moultrie in exasperation.

Rutledge preserved his calm. "There is an obvious difference between the situations. There will be a bombardment, and in the bombardment the town will suffer horribly. That same bombardment can render our trenches untenable. It were best, general, as a preliminary, to send a flag, and ascertain what terms General Prevost is disposed to grant us."

Moultrie swore with unusual vehemence. "I shall certainly send no flag," said he. "The defence, not the surrender of the place has been entrusted to me. I hold it can be defended, and I intend to defend it."

Rutledge rose. "And if I order you to send a flag?"

"Before you can order so grave a step as this, you must have the authority of your council. If the council decides to support you, I must do as you wish. But short of that I will not take the responsibility."

The others present were as fiercely and unanimously of Moultrie's mind that Rutledge was compelled to bow to their will.

But if he could not prevail upon them, he certainly could and did prevail upon the council assembled at his house soon after daybreak. The result of it was that in the light of early morning, ill-humouredly and burning with shame the defender of Charles Town penned the following lines, which the council itself dictated to him:

"General Moultrie perceiving from the motions of your army that your intention is to besiege the town, would be glad to know upon what terms you would be disposed to grant a capitulation should he be inclined to capitulate."

He had insisted upon the last clause, claiming that the question of capitulation was yet to be weighed again whatever the terms that Prevost offered.

As the sun rose it was Major Latimer, as Moultrie's chief aide, who rode out of the lines under a flag of truce borne by one of the two troopers who escorted him, towards the British camp.

Away to the south-west they could perceive the masses of scarlet and the glitter of arms and accoutrements of the main army which was already beginning to cross by the ferry.

It was not until an hour before noon that Latimer returned, and upon being informed that General Moultrie had gone home to await the British answer, he followed at once. News of what was happening had leaked out, and there was a dense crowd in Broad Street when Latimer and his troopers came riding thither. They were hemmed in by it before Moultrie's own door, and Latimer found himself bombarded by anxious questions, which he would not have been authorized to answer even had he been qualified. As it was he was in ignorance of the contents of the letter that he bore.

It was only with difficulty that he could break his way through the throng, largely composed of men and officers relieved from the lines, who, instead of using the respite to snatch the rest of which they stood in need, were driven by anxiety to besiege in this fashion the general's door.

At last Latimer reached the quiet haven within the garden gates, and dismounting went straight in quest of Moultrie, who, roused by the uproar outside, met him in the hall. They passed into the library together, and there Moultrie opened the letter which was not from General Prevost, but from his brother, the colonel commanding the advance guard. It ran as follows:

"Sir,
"The humane treatment which the inhabitants of Georgia and this province have hitherto received, will, I flatter myself, induce you to accept of the offers of peace and protection which I now make, by the orders of General Prevost; the evils and horrors attending the event of a storm (which cannot fail to be successful) are too evident not to induce a man of humane feelings to do all in his power to prevent it; you may

depend that every attention shall be paid and every necessary measure adopted to prevent disorders, and that such of the inhabitants who may not choose to receive the generous offers of peace and protection, may be received as prisoners of war, and their fate decided by that of the rest of the colonies.

"Four hours shall be allowed for an answer; after which your silence will be deemed a positive refusal.

"I have the honour to be, sir, your obedient servant,

"J M PREVOST

"Colonel commanding the advance camp at Ashley-Ferry."

"Damn his impudence," said Moultrie, as he finished reading. "And damn the Governor for giving him the chance to put it upon us. Unconditional surrender. That's his demand in plain terms. And a four hours' truce is all that accompanies it."

He handed the letter to Latimer, who had barely finished reading it when Rutledge arrived, driven by his impatience to know what answer the British had made.

He looked more hollow-eyed and haggard than ever this morning. But he had changed his clothes, his wig was well curled, and he seemed to have recovered his erstwhile calm which latterly had been deserting him. He read the letter in silence, standing by one of the tall windows to do so. When he had read, he slowly folded it, his brows rumpled in thought. His lips moved. But all the comment he offered was to exclaim: "Four hours!" as if that trivial detail were the only thing that mattered in a letter demanding unconditional surrender.

"You realize what he means?" quoth Moultrie.

Rutledge looked up. He manifested neither impatience nor anger.

"Entirely," he said, and pocketed the letter. "I must lay this before the council at once." He began to cross the room towards the door. "You had better come to the meeting also, Moultrie; send word to Pulaski and Laurens to be there as well, as soon as they can contrive."

He opened the door, then paused, and turned again. "Major Latimer," he asked, "what have you done with the Quaker Neild?"

"I have detained him, as you commanded me."

"You found out nothing about him?"

"Nothing definite," Latimer lied. "His papers were in order."

"I knew that. Another matter: I have already warned you to discourage your wife's visits to her father. Have you done so?"

Latimer flushed a little. "I have already had the honour to tell your excellency what I think of the order."

"I care nothing, sir, what you think of my orders. But I do care that you obey them. Mrs Latimer visited her father again late last night. I know because I am having the house watched. If this should happen once more I shall be constrained to measures which will be as distasteful to you as to myself."

He went out without waiting for a reply.

Moultrie looked at Latimer and shrugged. "You'd better do as he wishes. The man is obsessed by his terror of spies. Gad! I don't know what's come to him." Then with an abrupt change to a brisker tone: "And now if you'll –" He checked. The sight of Latimer's drawn white face gave him pause. "No, no, you're worn out already, and you must rest, my lad. Whom have we got here?"

And Moultrie walked out into the hall, Latimer following with dragging feet. He felt that he could have borne his physical weariness cheerfully but for the wound that was gnawing at his heart, a wound which the Governor's last words had set bleeding anew.

Three orderlies waited outside, and one of them in reply to the general informed him that Mr Middleton was in the office. The subaltern was fetched and received his orders.

"Find Count Pulaski and Colonel John Laurens, and bid them attend the Governor at once at his house. That first. Then find Colonel Cambray, and tell him to push on with the work on the left of the lines – he knows the place – as fast as possible. Then my compliments to Colonel Finlay and order him to have all the ammunition taken up into the lines immediately. When I left this morning some of the men had not more than three rounds. That is all, Mr Middleton. Please lose no time." He turned, as Middleton went off, and thrusting an arm through Latimer's, he uttered a short laugh. "You see what I think of Prevost's offer. We don't capitulate on such terms as those, or on any terms, if William Moultrie can prevent it. And if it were not for this confusion of the civil and the military authorities, there would never have been any question of it. That's where the mischief lies, Harry. If each of us had kept to his own business this situation would never have arisen. Lincoln, who is Commander-in-Chief in the South, is, himself, under instructions from Rutledge, who is not a soldier. Look at the result. Lincoln with a strong army is wasting time capturing Savannah which is practically without defences, and not worth capturing. While he is doing it Prevost may reduce Charles Town and destroy an army. That is what the civilian mind can never understand. That to capture cities or whole provinces is a waste of time and energy so long as the enemy armies remain in the field. In my heart I am sure that it is entirely through Rutledge's damned meddling that Lincoln is idling in Georgia. It all resulted from that visit to Orangeburg and the secret consultations held between them."

It was unlike Moultrie to express himself so freely; and it was the first time in Latimer's experience of him that loyalty to Rutledge had not made him take Rutledge's part, even when Rutledge was manifestly mistaken in his course. From this he judged the bitterness in Moultrie's mind at finding himself in a difficult strategic position when if he, or any other experienced soldier, had been consulted, the advantage might have been entirely on the other side.

"It almost drives me mad," he concluded, "to think of what might be, and of what is. But, by God I'll deal with what is, as a soldier should deal. I'll be ridden no further by any civilian, and I don't surrender to Prevost any more than I surrendered to Parker."

Abruptly he added:

"Now go break your fast, lad, and get what rest you can until I need you again which will be all too soon."

Latimer stood hesitating a moment after Moultrie had departed. And it was none of the things that Moultrie had said that now engaged his mind. The thought of coming face to face with Myrtle was repellent to him just then.

With leaden feet and a dull ache in his mind he went towards the dining-room. Myrtle was standing by the window, with little Andrew at her side when he entered. Both turned, and whilst Myrtle gave her husband a wistful smile from out of a wan white face, Andrew came bounding towards him, with joyously excited cries, to embrace his dust-stained knees.

Never in his life had Latimer felt nearer to tears than at that moment as he lifted his little lad up until the chubby laughing face was level with his own.

More slowly Myrtle crossed to his side. "Set him down, Harry," she urged gently. "You are scarce fit to carry your own self, my poor boy."

Knowing what he knew, her solicitude was almost an insult in its insincerity. He kissed the child, and set him down, then suffered himself to be drawn to table, and sat there his chin on his breast while Myrtle ministered to him, poured him coffee to which she added a tablespoonful of rum, deeming him in need of the stimulant, and piling a plate for him with slices of venison and ham.

Urged by her he began to eat, mechanically, whilst she gave attention to keeping Andrew from tormenting him. It was characteristic of her not to intrude with any excessive solicitude such as that with which a less thoughtful woman might have plagued him, nor yet to trouble him with her own deep distress at his condition. She knew that he was already shouldering a sufficient burden. His haggard face and dull eyes bore witness to it, as did his stained and dusty uniform and his rather dishevelled head which dust had rendered almost fulvid.

Quiet she sat there, quieting their son, making no attempt to disturb him, not even attempting to address him. And he eating mechanically and stealing ever and anon a glance at her pale, finely-featured, spiritual face, was indulging thoughts that at first were very bitter, but into which gradually there crept a doubt. A trite old saying to the effect that appearances are deceptive and not to be trusted had occurred to him at first as he contemplated her own gentle, almost angelic countenance. Who, he asked himself could believe that one so fair and sweet to behold could be so canker-hearted as was she? And then, just as he persuaded himself that here was proof of the truth of that old adage, its other application to her case also occurred to him. What if, in spite of all appearances, she were innocent, at least of part of that which he imputed to her? What if, after all, her love for him were no such pretence as he had yesterday been persuaded?

Then he remembered the lies into which he had led her last night, and the glib smoothness with which she had uttered them. Oh, she was false, through and through; false to him, false to his cause, a shameless betrayer of both. It was no wonder Rutledge bade him see that her visits to her father ceased. For that insult he had all but struck Rutledge, had warned Rutledge he would require satisfaction when the country's present demands upon them both should be at an end. There was an apology due to Rutledge, who out of mercy and compassion had no doubt said far less than he actually knew.

Latimer pushed away his plate, drained the cup of hot coffee, with its stimulating addition, and sank back in his chair with a sigh of utter weariness and dejection. She was instantly at his side with a pipe already filled with tobacco. He took it with a word of thanks mechanically uttered, and not perceiving that she also brought a lighted taper, he groped in his pocket for his tinder-box. His fingers closed upon a folded piece of paper, and it was almost as if they had touched a coal of fire. For instantly he knew this for the letter Mandeville had yesterday written; the letter which was to prevent Carey from carrying out what had been concerted between Mandeville and himself in the event of the former not returning. In the turmoil of mind that had subsequently been his own, Latimer had forgotten that letter until this moment. It had remained undelivered, and yet Carey had made no move. Why was that?

Asking himself the question, he took the taper Myrtle proffered. Still asking it, he lighted his pipe, and smoked awhile with knitted brows. Very soon the answer, the only possible answer, came to him.

Carey had not moved, because Myrtle had conveyed to him what he himself had last evening told her: that Neild was detained as a precautionary measure, but that in reality there was nothing against him. Naturally, then, Carey dared not move, lest by doing so he should destroy Mandeville.

That was the entire and the only possible explanation of Carey's inactivity. And it was also a proof that she carried news from headquarters to her cursed father. Rutledge was more than right, Latimer's wife was a spy in his own household. It amounted to no less than that.

"Have you been out today, Myrtle?" he asked her as a test.

"No, dear. The streets are so crowded, and the people so excited. I would rather not go amongst them."

He took a pull at his pipe, and then with his eyes upon her, he asked her abruptly: "When did you last see your father?"

That the question startled her he must have perceived even had he been watching her less closely.

"Why do you ask?"

"From interest, of course. I'm wondering how he's taking the present situation."

"Oh! Why, just as you would expect him to be taking it." She seemed relieved. "He is confident that Charles Town cannot stand against the British."

"And jubilant in that confidence, I suppose?"

She sighed. "I suppose he is."

"But you haven't said when you last saw him."

"Two or three days ago." Her tone was casual.

"Then you haven't seen him since Neild's arrest?"

After a momentary pause she answered: "No," and at once asked: "Why?"

He shrugged. "I should have thought it natural that you should wish to reassure him about his friend; to tell him that the Quaker has

come to no harm and is really in no danger. But it doesn't matter."
He lapsed into thought again, and pulled steadily at his pipe.

She not only lied, she lied unnecessarily, from which he argued
that her conscience must be uneasy indeed. And how calm she was,
how brazen with that hypocritical saintly look of hers!

He roused himself from the train of thought following upon this
to answer a question she was putting him.

"Harry, is father right in his persuasion?"

"I hope not," he answered grimly.

"But what do you think? What do you believe? Are we strong
enough to repel the attack? Have the reinforcements arrived?"

"Reinforcements?" he stared at her. "What reinforcements?" He
had uttered the question before the dreadful suspicion crossed his
mind that she was pumping him for information.

"I thought you were expecting reinforcements."

"Oh, those," he lied in his turn. "They came in yesterday. Last
night."

"Many?" she inquired.

"A thousand, or so."

Her face lighted. "You infernal hypocrite!" he thought.

"That's a great many, isn't it?"

"A goodly number."

Again there was a pause at the end of which she asked him: "Are
our numbers very inferior to the British?"

For a moment he smoked in silence, deliberating his reply.

"You are asking me State secrets," he said at last, with a touch of
sternness.

"Oh, but Harry!" her tone was one of gentle remonstrance.
"Surely you can tell me. You understand my anxiety."

"I think I do," he said, and she thought his tone was curious.
Then he lapsed again into his gloomy abstraction without giving her
any further answer. Repelled by his manner, she fell silent.

Resentment of her impudent attempt to draw information from
him smouldered in his heart. He was within an ace of rising,
denouncing her for a treacherous faithless creature, and taking her

by the throat to make an end for all time to her deceit and lying. Then again there came a doubt. After all, if she were loyal, such questions would not be unreasonable at such a time. If she were loyal! Inwardly he laughed in wicked mockery. If she were loyal! What a fool he was, after all that last night he had learnt beyond possibility of doubt, after all the lies he knew her to have told him, still even for a moment to suppose a possibility of her loyalty. All that remained was but to ascertain the extent to which she was disloyal, the extent to which she would betray her husband's, that she might serve her lover's cause.

Into his mind floated in that evil moment the substance of words spoken long ago by Rutledge – words of which Rutledge had lately reminded him – uttered in connection with Gabriel Featherstone. When a person is suspected of spying two aims may be served at once. That person may be lured to complete self-conviction, and the side for which he spies into defeat, by false information given him under the cloak of a complete faith in his integrity.

Inspiration stirred in him. Abruptly he put down his pipe, pushed back his chair and rose.

"I must be going," he said. "There is no rest for me just yet."

He took up his hat and sword from the chair where he had placed them. He went over to Andrew, who presented for his kiss a face that was smeared with honey.

Myrtle had risen. She was agitated, on the verge of tears which she bravely strove to repress until he should have departed. To the anxiety of the time was added an anguish of doubt regarding Harry. Did he suspect her? His manner had been so odd since yesterday. And yet, since clearly he had not discovered Neild's identity, what was there he should suspect? Relief could lie only in complete confession. Yet this confession must trouble him, and how could she trouble him at such a time? Thus her unselfishness, her very regard for him, drove her at every step to tangle herself still further in this hateful coil.

"My dear!" she said, and put her arms about his neck.

Had Andrew been older the gleam in those eyes of his father, that looked at him over his mother's shoulder, the mocking set of that mouth might have given him something to think about.

Harry's hand stroked his wife's dark hair.

"You are full of fears, Myrtle, I know. But you have been very brave. Be brave a little longer; only a little longer. Listen, dear. I'll tell you something...something that you must forget as soon as you have heard it. It is a secret known only to myself besides Moultrie who is responsible for the plan. It's success depends upon utter secrecy. If it were known all would be destroyed."

"Ah, don't tell me, then, Harry. Don't! I can be patient."

She was afraid, he thought, as indeed she was, but not for the reasons he supposed.

"Nay, but I want you to know. It will allay all your fears. We have Prevost's army in a trap. He believes that Lincoln is beyond the Savannah. But the truth, the tremendous truth, is that Lincoln is close upon his rear. By tomorrow Prevost will find himself between two armies where he thinks to deal only with one. Let him but remain where he is for another twenty-four hours, and his destruction is as certain as that the sun will rise tomorrow. Now, my dear, a little more patience, and all will be well. I tell you this to give you peace. I shouldn't. But...well, I know how true and staunch you are, and how discreet."

He kissed her, and was gone, leaving her reassured and happy in that tremendous proof of his implicit trust and love.

Chapter 13

The Strategy of Rutledge

It was no later than eleven o'clock that morning when Latimer rode out by the Town Gate into the lines, and there met Moultrie returning from an inspection of the works at the point where he had ordered Cambray to see them reinforced.

The general's rugged bony face wore a sly smile as he greeted his aide.

"The Council did not sit very long," he informed him. "Though, damme, they might still be talking if I hadn't shown my teeth. I told them they might save themselves from debating surrender, because I'd never consent to terms so dishonourable as those proposed by Prevost. There were enough of them on my side. As for the others, they knew that if it came to open rupture between us the town would be solidly behind me in my determination to defend it."

"We are to fight it out, then?"

"Sooner or later. Meanwhile at the instance of Rutledge we are still temporising. I've sent another message to say that whilst I cannot possibly accept the terms proposed I shall be happy to discuss less rigorous conditions if Prevost will appoint officers for the purpose."

"Then if less rigorous conditions were proposed – "

"No, no. We do not surrender on any terms. Not as long as I am in command. But whilst we are parleying time is gained."

"To what purpose?"

Moultrie permitted himself a wink. "To strengthen the lines. We continue meanwhile our preparations, and every hour gained is an advantage."

They had come abreast of the tent of Colonel Beekman who was in command of the artillery. Standing by this they beheld a knot of men, most of whom wore the blue uniform of the continental army, whilst a few, and of these was Rutledge, were in civilian dress.

A mounted officer rode forward to halt, hat in hand, before Moultrie.

"A message, sir, has been sent in by Colonel Prevost, that unless work on the lines is suspended during the passage of the flags, he will march in his men at once."

For an instant Moultrie's face turned glum. Then he laughed outright. "They've seen through the trick. Faith, there are moments when the British almost display intelligence. My compliments, Captain Dunbar, to Colonel de Cambray, and will he order his engineers to cease work."

Captain Dunbar saluted, and rode off upon that errand.

Moultrie would have continued on his way, but an officer of foot now advanced from the tent.

"His excellency's compliments, sir, and he will be glad to have your presence at a meeting of the Privy Council in General Beekman's quarters to discuss the reply from General Prevost."

"It has arrived already? Egad, they lose no time." Moultrie at once dismounted. "Come along, Harry. On my life it should be an interesting meeting."

They left a man from the trench tethering their horses to one of the projecting beams of the abatis.

Within the tent they found the eight Privy Councillors already assembled, and with them Colonel John Laurens, the son of Latimer's old friend, Henry Laurens. He was an accomplished and enterprising young officer, widely beloved: by the men for his conspicuous gallantry, but rather mistrusted by Moultrie for his almost equally conspicuous want of discretion. His recklessness in exceeding his orders had been the occasion of a severe and unnecessary loss of life in an engagement undertaken at Coosohatchie in the course of Moultrie's retreat from the Savannah.

Nevertheless, Moultrie was glad enough of his presence now, assured that here was a stout ally against the unaccountable pusillanimity which Rutledge was displaying.

The general sat down on the edge of Beekman's camp bed. Rutledge already occupied the only chair, at a square deal table furnished with writing materials. Three or four others had found seats of various descriptions, Gadsden being perched on an ammunition box, whose contents were not more explosive than his own humour.

Calmly Rutledge read the letter received from the British by general in which he announced his willingness to hold the conference proposed by General Moultrie, and that for this purpose he had the honour to appoint two British officers, one of whom should be his own brother, Colonel Prevost. They would be glad to receive the two commissioners General Moultrie should send to confer with them, and the British commander suggested that the conference should be held at some point between the British and American lines.

Rutledge laid down the letter, and with his grave owlish eyes looked round the little assembly. "In the absence of General Moultrie, I accounted it my duty to open the dispatch, which is addressed, of course, to him." He paused. No one said anything. Moultrie, himself, merely nodded. "It is something that General Prevost should consent to parley. It now remains for General Moultrie to tell us what are the terms that he has in mind to propose to the British, so that we may take a decision upon the matter."

"Terms of what?" barked Gadsden.

"Terms of surrender, of course," said Rutledge gravely. "Nothing else is in question here."

There was complete silence, a silence of dismay and stupefaction, which endured some moments, to be broken at last by one of the civilian privy-councillors, John Edwards, a merchant of Charles

Town. In a quavering voice, with tears in his eyes, he made his feeble protest.

"What! We are to give up the town at last!"

"Give up the town?" echoed Moultrie, and his hard laugh rang through the tent. He looked at Rutledge. "Will your excellency dare to go back and tell the people that?"

And Gadsden supported him. "They are as firm and calm as can be expected of men in this extremity, and ready to stand to the lines and defend their country." He looked Rutledge squarely, almost menacingly, between the eyes. "The man who tells them we must surrender will be torn in pieces for a traitor."

And a general growl of agreement and of hostility to Rutledge showed how every man present was of Gadsden's mind.

But Rutledge was as unmoved as if made of granite.

Calm of glance and of voice he marshalled the arguments that already he had used that morning to the council at its earlier meeting. He painted the horrors of a storm, the destruction of property and of life and of more than life at the hands of an infuriated and excited soldiery. He reminded them of the women and children in there behind the lines, reminded them, too – although that was unnecessary – that he had neither wife nor child of his own in the town, so that it was not for his own kin that he pleaded, but for theirs. Then he passed on to point out to them that there is a point in warfare at which the bravest may surrender without loss of honour, where indeed valour and honour demand surrender for the sake of others.

"You talk boldly of dying for your country in the trenches; and you conceive that to be the highest expression of courage. You are wrong. Death is often a welcome avenue of escape for men who are confronted by a terrible choice, such as that which confronts us now. And I tell you that it requires more courage for me to sit here where I sit and say the things that I am saying to you, than to go out there and receive a British bullet which would end my own personal responsibility."

His eloquence, which was seldom exerted in vain, wrought upon them now; the magnetism of his stern personality subdued them at last, all but Moultrie whose nature if easy was shrewd and calculating, and who preferred arguments of solid fact to mere appeals of rhetoric.

"All this is words," he said. "Wind, damme! I heard the like when I was put to defend Fort Sullivan. That, too, was a slaughter-pen into which I was leading my countrymen. But on that occasion, I'll remind you again, I had the support of John Rutledge, as strong then as he is weak now. Supported by him, I prevailed and gave the British their first defeat in this war. What I did then, I can repeat now. I am neither in better case, nor in worse."

Thus, at a blow, he struck out the effect of Rutledge's oratory. Men believe what they desire to believe, and this they got now from Moultrie. There was a spontaneous outburst of approval, and Rutledge, sitting there like a sphinx, was bound to wait until their acclamations had subsided.

Then at last his level voice was charged with bitter contempt of them.

"You would do well to remember what is the British force and what is ours. Prevost has more than twice, indeed, nearly three times our numbers."

"At Fort Sullivan," Moultrie answered him, "the odds were nearer ten to one."

"There is no parallel!" Rutledge raised his voice to dominate the others. The fierce, unusual vehemence of his tone instantly quelled them. "There your men were behind a fort made of soft palmetto wood, whose power of resistance was unsuspected an opponent without experience of such material. Also fortune was on our side. You know, Moultrie, that but for the fact that two of the battleships fouled each other in the channel as they were manceuvring to attack you from the West, the day might have ended very differently. I do not say this to decry your valour and the valour of the men who fought with you on that occasion, but to remind you of the difference of the conditions. You must remember the state of our fortifications now, the paltry earthworks sheltering our men, which may be carried by the first vigorous assault. Half the defenders of the town are raw militia, who have yet to stand fire. Opposed to them you have an army of almost three times their number of seasoned soldiers, with a preponderance of Highlanders and Hessians and a weight of artillery that nothing can withstand."

"For that statement, at least, you have no warrant," cried Gadsden. "Only actual engagement can prove what we can and what we cannot withstand."

"I know. And in the end we may have to put it to the test, much though I desire to avoid it. I am not saying that we should accept any terms that Prevost may dictate. I am urging that our commissioners should confer with his, and ascertain what are the utmost terms that can be extracted. When we know those we can determine what is to do. But to put an end to the passage of flags at this stage, and to invite the British to attack us before we have tested every avenue of compromise, is a thing I cannot countenance and to which nothing – nothing! – could induce me to consent."

Mr Ferguson, another of the civilian councillors, now interposed.

"That being so, are we not wasting time in talk that is too general, vague and inconclusive? Would it not be better if General Moultrie were to tell us what alternative to unconditional surrender might be proposed by the commissioners we are to send?"

"I, sir?" demanded Moultrie. "I have no alternative to propose save this." And he brought his hand down upon the hilt of his sword.

"Your excellency, then?" said Mr Ferguson. "You will have considered the matter, surely."

"Ay," said Rutledge grimly. "I have considered."

"What do you say, then, should be proposed?" John Edwards asked him, and all grew very still to hear the answer.

Rutledge paused a moment, and for a moment his eyes fell away from those of the assembly which were all focussed, and most of them in hostility, upon himself. Then, as if commanding himself, he raised his bold glance again, and slowly expounded what he had considered.

"When in Georgia, and desiring to ensure the peace of that province, so as to leave his army free to invade South Carolina, General Prevost proposed to the Georgians that they should enter into an agreement of neutrality with him, leaving their ultimate fate to be determined by that of the other colonies at the conclusion of the war."

He paused, and there followed a silence of consternation growing to horror and anger, in which men looked at one another. It was young Colonel Laurens, advancing a step towards the table as he did so, who voiced the general thought.

"My God! Are you suggesting that we should signify our willingness to accept any such proposal as that if he will make it?"

"A proposal," Moultrie reminded the Governor, "which, in the case of Georgia, you, yourself, denounced as too ridiculous to merit even an answer."

"Nevertheless," said Rutledge, intrepidly in the face of that general resentment, "that is what I propose that our commissioners should now offer Prevost."

His boldness and their own amazement struck them all dumb. Presently, however, Moultrie found his voice.

"But, stab me, have you weighed all that your proposal will entail?" His tone was incredulous. "You tell us that you have considered the matter. Have you considered that such a proposal means not only the surrender of Charles Town and the army defending it, but the surrender also of the army in the South under General Lincoln?"

Rutledge's glance faltered a moment under the stern blue eyes of Moultrie. But it hardened again immediately. "I have," he answered.

Gadsden smacked his thigh, and bounded to his feet, shaking with anger.

"Then here's my opinion on it, and on you," he roared. "In plain words, you're a damned traitor, Rutledge. A damned traitor," he repeated, "and you deserve a rope."

Rutledge sat quite still, but what little blood there was in his face receded from it, leaving it to the very lips of the hue of lead. There was a muttering about him that was ominous and full of menace. He rallied his strength to withstand it.

"Hard words will not serve our need," he said with a calm he was very far from feeling.

"Hard words!" young Laurens retorted. "No words are hard enough for what you propose. We are to be disloyal not only to ourselves, but to the sister colonies that trust us. Damn me, Rutledge, are you a traitor, or a coward? Which? Charles Town is to save its skin by betraying the whole American cause. That is what you ask us to assist you to do. You leave me wondering—" He broke off, repressed perhaps by the Governor's cold, unfaltering gaze. "No matter. I for one will have no further part in this debate. I am going. Back to my post in the lines, to prepare to receive the attack."

And with a final snort of contempt, the tall handsome young colonel swung on his heel, and was striding out of the tent, when Rutledge's voice detained him.

"A moment, Colonel Laurens!" There was something minatory in the tone. "You are at liberty to depart if you choose but you will remember that the deliberations of the Privy Council are secret. I invited you to attend this meeting, partly that we might have the benefit of your military experience, partly because your English education and English ties commended you to me as one of the commissioners I may have to appoint."

"You flatter me, sir," sneered Laurens.

"I am concerned only to warn you, sir."

"To warn me?"

"To practice discretion – a quality I have not yet observed to be conspicuously developed in you."

Remembering the affair at Coosohatchie and the deserved reprimand he had received, young Laurens flushed scarlet.

"Sir," he said, "it is a compliment I cannot return."

Rutledge disregarded the taunt. Coldly, firmly he proceeded.

"I will not have you talk out there of what has happened here in private. Should you do so, you may find the consequences more serious than on the last occasion when you disregarded the orders of your superior. I will have no disorders provoked in the lines or in the Town."

Laurens drew himself up to the full of his fine height.

"When this present business is over, Mr Rutledge, I shall have a word to say to you in answer to that insult. For the moment, I am your obedient servant. You need not add the fear of my indiscretion to the other terrors that already distress you." And he went out.

Rutledge's chin sank to his breast. Gadsden, who was warm-hearted, found his own resentment tempered by a certain pity. He began to talk, to reason with the Governor. But he was harshly interrupted at the outset.

"I will not enter into the arguments again. With the consent of the council, or without it, I intend to go forward with the proposal, as I have announced."

Gadsden's pang of pity changed instantly to a rage that almost choked him.

"Why, you damned traitor… Do you say you'll dare do this thing without the consent of the council?"

Rutledge stood up. His face was set and hard. "God helping me, I will. I know what I am doing. You may call me traitor, or what you please. Your opinions leave me indifferent. I have a duty to perform by the people of Charles Town who have invested me with sovereign powers. And that duty I will perform in spite of insult, abuse and even threats." There was a dignity about the man that awed them, that compelled them to bridle their anger.

Gadsden bowed. "You will perform your duty without my assistance, then," said he drily; and he turned to depart as Laurens had done. But coming face to face with Moultrie, who had also risen, he halted, and clapped a hand upon the general's shoulder. "You are in command here, remember," he sternly admonished him.

Moultrie smiled grimly back. "And as long as I am in command," he answered, "be quite sure that Charles Town will not surrender. If

Mr Rutledge insists upon sending to the British any such proposal as he has mentioned, he sends it in his own name, not in mine. And should General Prevost accept it, he will make the discovery that any agreement made by him with the civil Governor of Charles Town is not binding upon its military commander."

"Ay, ay!" Gadsden nodded his approval, and went out. He was followed by two other of the officers present, who saluted Moultrie almost ostentatiously as they passed him, but took no further notice of the Governor.

John Edwards with a curt announcement that he disclaimed all responsibility in whatever the Governor might do, invited Ferguson and the third civilian present to come away.

They obeyed him promptly enough, but not before Ferguson had expressed himself.

"Have a care how you tread, John Rutledge, or you may find your feet leading you to the gallows. If you've sold us to the British... Have a care, I say!" And he swung round to follow the others who were already leaving.

Rutledge, standing there, impassive to the end, made him no answer. But, Latimer, who watched the Governor intently saw his pale lips curl in a smile of terrible contempt.

And then Ferguson paused confronting Moultrie.

"Act according to your judgment, general," he enjoined, and be sure that we will support you."

Three only now remained, and of these two were members of the council, and they were men upon whom Rutledge had particular claims – of kinship in the case of one, of many years of good friendship and co-operation in the case of the other. Of these, his brother-in-law, Roger Smith, who commanded one of the militia regiments, was the first now to abandon him. He stood scowling, undecided a moment after the others had gone; then shrugging aside his hesitation he looked at Rutledge.

"I am sorry, John that you should have taken this decision. I would support you if I could do so in honesty. But I can't. It is better to die out there... Anything is better than disloyalty to the other provinces that trust us and depend upon us." And he, too, went out.

Be it that he felt this desertion by his relative more keenly than he had felt the others, or else that the breaking point of his endurance had been reached, the Governor sat down heavily and resting his elbows on the board, took his head in his hands.

Moultrie touched Latimer on the shoulder. His face was set; the habitual bonhomie had entirely departed out of it.

"Come," he said quietly, and turned to leave.

Rutledge's voice arrested him. It uttered Moultrie's Christian name on a note of supplication such as Latimer himself had never yet heard, and could not believe that any other had ever heard, from those cold lips.

The general turned, and the two men looked at each other across the width of the tent. Latimer had the uncomfortable sensation of being an intruder.

"Shall I go, sir?" he asked his general.

To his surprise it was Rutledge who answered him.

"By no means, sir. I may need you in a moment." Then he turned his eyes slowly to Moultrie again. "Do you, too, believe the damnable things in the minds of those men who have left me? Do you believe me capable of such a betrayal?"

"Believe it?" echoed Moultrie. "What else am I to believe since you yourself propose the betrayal?" He paused. Rutledge did not answer him. He just looked at him with eyes that were full of pain. "You have heard what I shall do," Moultrie resumed. "And you have seen enough to know that I shall be supported. The rest now is your affair. I wash my hands of it, John, as did the others."

Rutledge brought one of his hands down upon the table in a gesture of exasperation.

"Very well," he said. "Do as you have said. Do it, whatever happens. If Prevost should accept my proposal, send him word that you and the army defending Charles Town will resist in spite of any agreement between him and your Governor. Let it be understood between us that you shall do that. But for the present, appoint me two officers to be my commissioners in this conference with the British, and to bear them this proposal of neutrality."

Moultrie drew himself up, indignantly. "I'll cut out my tongue first."

Rutledge looked at him sadly. "And you are my friend, Will! You know me better, perhaps, than any living man, and I dare swear that not in all the years of our acquaintance has your trust in me ever been deceived. Yet all that is to count for nothing with you." He uttered a little laugh of bitterness.

"It's no question of trust, John. Even if I consented, where should I find me two officers to carry such a message? You heard what Laurens and Gadsden had to say. It is what every man who wears the American uniform would answer me if I invited him to go on such an errand."

"Roger Smith would go for one, if he had your orders. And there is Latimer, there, whom I have detained for this, so that he might hear the assurance I have just given you. Perhaps he would now consent to go for another?" His eyes questioned Latimer as he spoke.

Considering the long antagonism between them, Latimer found a certain cruel humour in the situation. It was almost as if Fate avenged him upon Rutledge for all the mistrust which he, himself, had suffered at Rutledge's hands. There was something of poetic justice in the fact that Rutledge in the hour of his need, distrusted by all, should stoop from his high office, almost humbly for once, to beg the trust of Harry Latimer.

Because Latimer was gifted with some vision, he was unable to believe Rutledge guilty either of cowardice or treason, as had been so freely and recklessly implied. To him, not only Rutledge's whole life, but his very demeanour at that council, gave the lie to any such charges, rendered them fantastic and grotesque. Perhaps his recollection of the harsh judgments Rutledge had passed upon him more than once, and his reflection that these had been justified by externals, made him now doubly wary of externals where Rutledge was concerned; determined him to judge Rutledge's present action by his knowledge of the man, rather than the man from the appearance of this action.

Therefore his answer was not only prompt, but uttered with a deference that in all the circumstances was eloquent indeed. Bareheaded he bowed.

"I have the honour to be at your excellency's service."

Rutledge's stern face was suddenly softened by surprise, and the glance he flashed on Latimer was almost one of gratitude.

But it was Moultrie who spoke, his tone harsh.

"You are at my service, sir," he reminded Latimer. "You will take your orders from me. And I will never order you on such an errand. Neither you nor Smith, nor any other."

"And yet," said Rutledge in a hard, firm voice. "It must be done, or we perish."

"You have been answered upon that," Moultrie reminded him.

Rutledge made a gesture of impatience, of distraction, with his fine hands.

"It is not what I meant. I scarcely know what I am saying." He passed a trembling hand over his moist and pallid brow. "What I meant to say was – " He paused and dropped his voice. "It must be done that Prevost and his army may perish."

"What!" Moultrie stiffened with amazement as he rapped out that single word.

With forefinger erect, Rutledge beckoned them nearer by a broad repeated gesture. Resolution and despair were stamped on his white face.

"Sit down, both of you. Draw close. I have dreaded this. Dreaded it beyond everything. It is a secret so formidable, so far-reaching, that I was prepared almost for anything sooner than its disclosure. For if a breath of it leaks out before the time, this war which may be ended tomorrow at a blow, will drag on and on perhaps for years."

They sat still, Moultrie on the ammunition box, Latimer on a keg, both of them stricken by the vehemence of his almost whispering voice and the enormous thing that he suggested.

"If all that I have planned works out as I have planned it, we shall hold Prevost here as Burgoyne was held at Saratoga, and we shall burgoyne him as completely. Think what that would mean today. The British campaign in the North has come to nothing. If the campaign now opening in the South should thus, at the outset, be shattered at a blow, what heart for war would there be left in England?

"That is the terrible secret that I carry. That is the secret your mistrust, Moultrie, your insubordination, compels me now to disclose before you will carry out my orders, before you will afford me the one thing necessary for success – delay." He had spoken with bitterness; to this he added now a touch of contempt. "Why, do you imagine, have I had these flags coming and going? Why did I ask you to send to ask for terms, and swallow the insult with which you met the request? Why did I constrain you to send yet again to propose a conference? Why? For the same reason that I am asking you now to send this proposal of neutrality. Delay, delay, delay! Time! Another twenty-four hours, that is all I ask. I am branded a traitor, a coward! I tread the road to the gallows I am told. I am to be called to account for this later on, as Laurens threatened me. For what?" He laughed softly but savagely.

"God! What it is to have to handle fools! Fools, who think a man whose courage and loyalty have been proved a score of times, can turn coward and traitor all in a moment. Would a coward have born their insults as I bore them? Pshaw!" He sank together in his chair, as if worn out by the fury which he had suddenly unleashed.

Moultrie began to wonder had the Governor's mind given way under the strain of the last few weeks, whether these were not the ravings of a madman's nightmare.

"The only evidence before them was that of your proposal itself, and of the fears you manifested," he answered very quietly. "From the one and the other what could they conclude but what they did. They were without this explanation…this half-explanation which you have given me."

"Half-explanation?" cried Rutledge. "Ay, ay, you must have it all, all to the last drop, before you'll help me. Very well, you shall have it. But, I warn you, both of you, that if a word of it leaks out, if this thing should miscarry through indiscretion, your heads shall pay for it. Listen, then. Just now, Moultrie, you implied that in military matters I am no better than a fool and a muddler. You voiced the opinion of me which is held by every one of your thick-skulled fellow-soldiers. I knew what was thought of me, and I have allowed it to be thought. I perfectly understood your 'ne sutor ultra crepidam.' Oh, yes! If I had kept to the management of civil affairs, and left General Lincoln to control the army of the South, he would not now be idling in Georgia, and we should not now be in this position. His army would be with us here, and, daunted by superior forces Prevost would have been compelled to hold back from Charles Town, would never have attempted its reduction. Very true! Very true! But Lincoln is not idling in Georgia. He is not in Georgia at all, as you and as Prevost, to his undoing, suppose him. He should be now between Coosohatchie and the Ashley with all his forces."

To Moultrie – this was a blow between the eyes.

"God of Heaven!" he cried. "How do you know that?"

"How?" The dark eyes gleamed. "Because that is what was concerted between him and me at Orangeburg. His expedition into Georgia was a feint to lure Prevost to destruction. His orders were to march down the right bank of the Savannah, as if to capture the defenceless capital of Georgia, to reap an easy empty victory. But at Purysburg he was to cross again, and follow Prevost, so as to keep within a two days' march of him. Before tomorrow dawns he will be here, and Prevost will be burgoyned. Now do you understand at last?"

Moultrie stared at him with gaping eyes and fallen jaw. It was all so simple, so obvious now that he was told, and it had been left for a civilian mind to evolve this master-stroke of strategy.

"And, and Prevost doesn't suspect?" was all that he could ask at last.

"Would he be where he is if he did?"

"My God!"

"Now you begin to see why I have played for time. If I had not made you send that flag at three o'clock this morning, the bombardment would have opened at dawn. By this time Charles Town would be half in ruins. Perhaps the attack would have been delivered, and considering their numbers, they might very well have carried the place by now. Then, Lincoln would have come too late. Possibly, once masters of the Town, the British could have held the place against him, as we could never hold it against them. But what matters more is that the chance to end this war at a blow would have been lost.

"That is why, Moultrie, you must support me now. This parley must be held and this proposal laid before them. It is not likely that Prevost will accept it believing that he has us at a disadvantage. But neither will he peremptorily dismiss it. It is too weighty for that, and it demands some consideration. While they are considering, ruin creeps upon them."

Moultrie got up. "John, humbly, I beg your pardon, and so shall the others, every one of them when all is known."

Rutledge dismissed the notion by a contemptuous wave of the hand. "That is of no importance. While I am writing my letter here, find Roger Smith and give him your orders. Say that I have satisfied you that it is a wise measure."

"And if he refuses?"

"He will not refuse. I know Roger. For our other commissioner we have Latimer here..." He broke off. "What ails you, man?"

For now that his eyes fell upon Latimer for the first time since his disclosure, he beheld him pale to the lips, leaning back against a tent pole with every appearance of utter exhaustion.

Fear galvanized him into collecting himself under that question and that sharp scrutiny.

"It is nothing, sir," he muttered. "I... I am a little faint."

Moultrie was instantly at his side, tenderly solicitous.

"Poor lad! He is worn out. He has hardly rested in these last two days and nights."

"Alas! That is the case of most of us. He must command himself for this. You may rest all you please on your return, Major. General Moultrie will have to give you leave."

Moultrie meanwhile had produced from his pocket a flask of grog.

"Take a pull," he commanded peremptorily. Latimer obeyed him, and the spirit steadied him. But it could not calm the torture of his mind at the thought of the test to which he had submitted Myrtle.

If she were faithless indeed, then all was lost, unless he could at once return and take his measures to prevent her from conveying to her father the lie he had told her, the lie which by cruellest irony was now disclosed to be the truth. If news of it were to reach Prevost, the British general must send his scouts afield for confirmation, and then...

Latimer groaned aloud. "I... I am not well. I am afraid I cannot go."

"Command yourself!" Rutledge spoke sternly. "You understand that I cannot further publish this thing. Go, you must, dead or alive. Your country demands it."

"And then my rank," Latimer faltered. "For such a conference as that none less than a colonel should be sent – "

"If that is all, you shall be made a colonel on the spot. But go you must. Make up your mind to it, and it will become possible. Come, Latimer!" He turned to Moultrie again. "Send for Roger at once."

He took up a pen, dipped it, and began to write as Moultrie went out.

Latimer sat there in the silent tent within which there was no sound beyond the scratching of Rutledge's quill. From outside came an occasional order, the tramp of feet of marching men, the thud of hooves, and at moments snatches of song from the men in the trenches. Latimer heard nothing of all this. His body only sat there, the legs straight and stiff before it, the chin sunken into his black military cravat, stark horror in his soul.

Chapter 14

The Arrest

It would be a little before two o'clock in the afternoon when Colonel Smith and Major Latimer returned from the conference held within a half-mile of the lines. They presented their report to Rutledge in Beekman's tent, where since their going he had sat dispatching business.

Colonel Smith announced that Colonel Prevost, whilst holding out no hope that the proposal of neutrality would be accepted, yet considered it much too important to be dealt with out of hand, and must refer it to his brother the general. The British commander's decision would be made known to Governor Rutledge at the earliest moment.

Rutledge smiled a little, well content. Whenever the reply came now, his object was served; the delay necessary to the success of his plan was obtained. If, as he supposed, the British refused the proposal, they must intimate it and send with it yet another demand for surrender. In this way the remainder of the afternoon would be spent, with the result that it was unlikely that they would now open the attack before dawn tomorrow. And under cover of night Lincoln would make the last stage of his advance, which should bring him upon the enemy's rear before daybreak.

Gravely Rutledge thanked and dismissed the officers, with a kindly word for the obviously exhausted Latimer, to whom he conceded leave to go home and rest until his general should send for him again.

There was a throng outside the tent, attracted by the news of the return of the commissioners; and several, amongst whom were Gadsden and Laurens, beset the two officers with questions as they came forth. Latimer wasted some little time in answering them, then at last got to horse, and rode home.

When, jaded, worn and sick at heart with anxiety and fear, he staggered into the dining-room, he found Myrtle there in walking dress and wide-brimmed straw hat, with Tom Izard, who had been relieved from his duties in the lines an hour ago, and was voraciously appeasing a hearty appetite. Julius, who was waiting upon him, made haste to set a chair for his master, considering him with a look of affectionate concern.

Covered with grime and dust, his face haggard and drawn, his eyes blood-injected and glazed, Latimer dropped into the chair, a limp sagging body that seemed half-bereft of life.

Myrtle came to put an arm about his shoulders.

"Harry, my dear!" In her concern for him she forgot the situation of the town. "You are worn out! You must go to bed at once."

"Presently, presently!" His speech was thick and slurred. "I must have food, first." It was more or less of a subterfuge, for food was the last thing in his thoughts.

He ate nevertheless what was placed before him by Julius, ate absently, without knowing what. And he drank copiously of the fine claret Julius poured for him. And all the while Myrtle stood beside him in tenderest solicitude to anticipate his slightest possible wish.

Presently, whilst still eating, he dismissed Julius from the room, then raised his dull eyes to look at Myrtle.

"You have been out, I see."

"Yes," she answered, after the slightest hesitation.

"Where did you go?"

Her glance avoided his stare. "I went to see father, this morning." And at once she added the explanation. "I went to tell him about Mr Neild, in case he should be anxious as you suggested."

"Ah!" Here again she was lying to him, for as he was persuaded she had already told her father yesterday of this. So that whatever the business that had taken her today, it was other than she represented it. He turned cold at the thought of what it really might be. He rose abruptly, and seized her fiercely by the shoulders. "Myrtle, answer me truthfully, in God's name: Did you tell him anything else? Did you say a word of what I told you this morning?"

"Harry! Are you mad?"

"Answer me! And answer me truthfully for once. Did you?"

"What do you mean?"

Flushed and indignant, she struggled in that grip of his. But he held her firmly despite his weariness.

"I mean that you have lied to me again and again in the last twenty-four hours. You have answered with falsehoods my every question." She turned white under the accusation. "But if you value my life and your own at a straw – if you have any thought for Andrew, and what may become of him – tell me now the truth about this. What did you say to your father today?"

She was panic-stricken by his knowledge. Yet before seeking to probe the extent of it, before uttering any of the terrified questions that rose to her lips, she answered him as he demanded.

"Nothing that I could not have said in your presence." And after a pause, she added passionately. "That is the truth, Harry. I swear it. The rest... I can explain."

"Not now, not now." He let her go, and turned to Tom, who was looking on with a startled countenance, uncomfortable at witnessing a scene of this character. He controlled himself by an effort.

"Tom," he said quietly, "I need your assistance on an urgent matter. May I count upon you?"

"Of course." Tom was on his feet at once.

"Come, then." He beckoned him, and moved towards the door.

Myrtle attempted to delay him. "Harry! Harry!" She was distraught.

Firmly he put her aside. "Not now. Later on." He pulled the door open. "Come, Tom."

They went out into the hall. "Wait for me a moment, Tom," Harry requested him, and turned to go upstairs.

Deeply intrigued and uneasy Tom paced the length of the hall, where the two orderlies were on duty.

Presently Harry came downstairs again carrying a mahogany case under his arm. Myrtle, overwhelmed, almost stunned by what Harry had said, and wondering distractedly how much he really knew, and how she could ever make him understand the motives that had driven her along that abominated path of falsehood, sat limp and stricken in the dining-room where they had left her, daring to make no attempt to follow him.

Tom's jaw dropped at sight of the mahogany case.

"Stab me! What the devil's afoot?"

"I have something to do which I should have done yesterday if I had had my wits about me. God send it may not be too late now!" He looked at Tom, and an odd smile broke on his white face. "It's very opportune your being here, Tom. You were a witness of the first shot in the duel that is to be finished today. I desire you to witness now the end of it."

"My God, Harry!" he cried, his face blank with amazement. And he added "Carey?"

Latimer nodded. "Yes, Carey, that black-hearted monster. I owe him a shot at ten paces. I am going to discharge the debt. I pray I may be in time. But if I am too late to prevent him from betraying us, at least I shall not be too late to punish, and to rob him of the chance of gloating over his evil work."

"But Harry...your father-in-law...!" Tom was bewildered and horrified.

"That's why, Tom. Ask no questions now. I'll tell you all afterwards, and you shall give me reason. On my honour you shall. Take my word for that, if you're my friend, and ask no more questions. But come and see the thing done."

"If you put it so," said Tom gloomily, and shrugged a reluctant consent.

"Thank you, Tom. Come along. I shall require another witness to make all correct." He had moved forward, and was now abreast of the orderlies, who came swiftly to attention. "Is Mr Middleton in the office?" he asked, and upon receiving an affirmative answer, he threw open the door on his right, and called the lieutenant.

Middleton came out very quickly. "You're back, sir? I didn't know, or I would have come at once. Something has happened that I think you should know." He paused, hesitating, obviously a little uncomfortable.

"Yes?" demanded Harry, impatiently. "What is it?"

"Sir Andrew Carey, sir – "

"What about him?"

"I arrested him today on a warrant of the Governor's."

Tom in the background sent up a prayer of thanks to Heaven. Latimer stood quite still, not knowing yet whether this should suffice to make the secret safe, and not daring to hope.

"On what charge?" he asked presently.

"No charge, sir. He is detained as a precautionary measure. He was one of several, half a dozen or so, who have been so detained by the Governor's orders."

Latimer considered. So that was all. Rutledge was yielding to his fears of information reaching the enemy which might yet put him on his guard, and he was detaining all those whom he had reason to know attached to the British cause. In fear lest the answer should dash his sudden hopes, he almost hesitated to put the next question.

"At what time did you arrest him?"

"At noon precisely. A messenger rode in from the lines with the warrant and the list of persons covered by it."

Latimer understood the motives that had impelled Rutledge to take that step, but unfortunately he had taken it an hour and a half after he himself, had told Myrtle his cock-and-bull story which by an incredible irony turned out to be the truth. The arrest had been made too late, he feared. And yet there was a chance that it might be otherwise.

"Does Mrs Latimer know this?" he asked.

"I don't think so, sir. I haven't told her."

Latimer took his chin in his hand, and the subaltern observed that hand to tremble. "Mrs Latimer visited her father today," he said. "Do you know whether she visited him long before he was arrested? Did you see her come or go?"

"I saw both, sir. Mrs Latimer left here just half an hour before I did. I met her returning, as I turned into Tradd Street with my men on my way to arrest Sir Andrew."

Latimer's face perceptibly lighted. "So that you arrested him almost immediately after Mrs Latimer left him?"

"Within ten minutes of her leaving certainly."

"Thank you, Middleton," said Latimer in dismissal, and the subaltern went back to the work which the major's summons had interrupted. Latimer stood there in thought a moment after he had gone. Hope began to revive within him. The arrest must have been made in time. It was impossible that in those ten minutes Carey could have communicated with anyone. Rutledge's secret was safe from betrayal. But on the other hand, he would never know now the full extent of his wife's duplicity, to question her would be worse than futile. Considering the lies she had already told him, he could not now believe a word she said.

Tom Izard stood helplessly at hand, thankful that circumstances should have prevented Harry from carrying out his dreadful purpose. Harry looked at him, and suddenly laughed aloud.

"That second shot will have to wait," he said.

He turned and went reeling down the hall and up the stairs, the sinister mahogany box tucked under his arm, a man in the last stage of exhaustion, craving nothing but sleep now that the only spur to continued action had been withdrawn.

Without so much as removing his boots that were caked with mud and white with dust, he flung himself on his bed, and was asleep almost before his body had come to rest upon it.

Chapter 15

The Awakening

From somewhere about four o'clock on the afternoon of that Wednesday, and throughout a night in which scarcely an eye in Charles Town was closed in slumber, Harry Latimer lay in a lethargic sleep until peep of day on Thursday.

Then, as the first faint light of dawn made a grey oblong patch of the window of the room he occupied, he sat up suddenly, wide-awake as if summoned; as summoned, indeed, he had been by his sleepless inner consciousness.

Before his eyes had considered that grey patch of window, he knew that it was the hour of dawn, the hour in which Prevost's army realizing itself caught between two fires, must lay down its arms and surrender, unless...

There was no unless. That sudden dread that came to haunt him was but the ghost of an earlier dread, a dread of yesterday which he had proved unfounded before committing himself to the sleep whereof he stood so desperately in need.

It was the hour: the hour of victory; the hour perhaps which should mean the deliverance of his country.

Strange how still it was. But at any moment now the guns would be shattering this stillness, unless indeed Prevost should decide to surrender without ever a shot fired.

He swung his feet to the ground, making the discovery that whilst he had slept someone had removed his boots, his sword and belt, and eased his clothing.

"Are you awake at last, Harry?"

It was Myrtle's voice, the voice he loved and hated. She had kept vigil beside him, and rose now, a shadow faintly visible against the gloom.

"It is the dawn," he answered, uttering the dominant thought in his mind, the thought that had pierced the lethargy of his senses to arouse him. "It is the hour. My place is in the lines. I must be in at the death. My boots! Where are my boots?"

He was groping for them even as he spoke. He found them, and was already pulling them on when she kindled a light.

He stood up buckling on his sword, his eyes questing for his hat, which presently he perceived and snatched up from the chair on which it lay.

She asked him questions, which he scarcely heeded. Did he think that all would be well, that all would fall out as he had told her yesterday? He answered her mechanically, and was going without another word.

"Harry," she called to him. He turned, and saw her in the soft candle-light, her face sad, her eyes red from weeping. Even so the beauty of her touched him, moved him to pity for her and pity for himself. "When you come back I shall have something to tell you, something I could not, dared not tell you before." She paused, faltering. He made no answer. But stood there looking at her with eyes that to her were inscrutable. "You have reason to think badly of me, Harry. I have been a fool and a coward. But nothing more than that. Be sure I have been nothing more than that. When you come back I will tell you all. All!"

"Ah!" He drew a breath. She could tell him nothing that he did not know. There was a test, then, after all. The test should be the measure of her frankness later. "Very well," he said, and so departed.

There were lights in the hall below, and orderlies drowsily on duty. The officer in charge was Ensign Shubrick, who informed him, whilst his horse was being fetched, that the general had been in the lines all night, and was there still.

"It is expected that the British will attack at daybreak," the officer concluded.

"I know, I know," said Harry, and laughed, which the officer thought odd.

The light was growing rapidly, and when he came out into the chill of the garden, objects were clearly visible and already beginning to assume colour. Faint lines of vermilion streaked the sky to the east over the sea.

Latimer mounted and rode out into the street, in which he discovered as much traffic and movement as was normally to be found there at noon. It had been thus all through that night of suspense. The restless anxious townsfolk had roamed the streets, coming and going towards the lines, eagerly questing for news of what was happening and what was likely to happen presently.

He rode up Broad Street, past St Michael's and the State House, and then away to the right, up King Street. As he came level with Moores Street, he became conscious of loud sounds of cheering among the people who made a dense throng ahead towards the Town Gate. Suddenly the throng broke, and men came racing towards him shouting wildly in a frenzy of excitement that was obviously joyous.

They were abreast of him, a scattered crowd of runners, young and old, military and civilian, laughing and shouting as they ran. Along the street, windows were being thrown up, and doors opened to emit half-clad men and women who came in fear and trembling to seek the reason of this sudden uproar.

Latimer checked a man, a wheelwright of his acquaintance named Sampson, to ask him what had happened.

"Where ha' you been, major?" the fellow crowed. "The British be going. Going! They be in full retreat. Ferrying theirselves like mad over the Ashley as if the devil were after them. Charles Town's rid o' them! Charles Town's free. Free!" He roared it all at the top of his voice that others besides Latimer might hear him, and without waiting for question, sped on with the other bearers of glad tidings.

Latimer in prey to mingled fear and hope, went on at the gallop, scattering the people to right and left in his reckless dash for the Town Gate.

Long before he reached it, his ears were assailed by a terrific roar from the lines. It was the cheering of the men in the trenches venting their relief at the end of the strain of their long anxious vigil.

The noise of it was still reverberating along the lines when he mounted the abatis to join the crowd of officers clustered there about the guns, and to look for himself in the direction in which all were gazing.

At that moment the rising sun sent its first low shafts of light across the dreary landscape. It struck upon scarlet coats, and flashed back from arms and accoutrements, away over on James Island across the Ashley River. And on the near side by the ferry there were no more than the last detachments of the rearguard, which yesterday had been the van, waiting to cross in the wake of the rest of that fast retreating army.

Latimer's heart sank like a stone through water. There could be one only explanation to this sudden flight. The British had been warned in time, and at the eleventh hour they were escaping from the trap. They had been warned! Warned! The word boomed, like the note of some gigantic gong, through his tortured brain. And his senses suddenly sharpened, showed him something that yesterday in his sleepiness he had overlooked. Not ten minutes only, as he had so fondly imagined, had elapsed between the time of Myrtle's going to her father and Sir Andrew's arrest; but forty minutes. He had left out of account the half-hour that she had been with him.

With those deafening cheers still ringing in his ears, the cheers of men who beheld here only deliverance, knowing nothing of what else should have been added to it, Latimer descended from the abatis, and regained his horse. Several spoke to him, but he answered none. He mounted, drove home his spurs and felt the infuriated beast bound forward under him. Back, at a break-neck gallop he went by the road he had come. There was one only thing remaining to do. In justice and in mercy he must do it, and do it quickly before they arrested him, as arrest him they certainly would. He remembered what Rutledge had said yesterday on the score of what must happen to Moultrie or himself should this secret of Lincoln's approach leak out prematurely to wreck the plan, the secret which until constrained to it by sheer necessity Rutledge had hugged so jealously to his soul.

In the garden, as he flung down from his foam-flecked horse, he found Tom who had ridden in but a moment ahead of him with the joyous news. And Tom was barring his way, his face alight, babbling idiocies of thanksgiving for the town's safety.

Latimer thrust him aside, and sprang into the house. Startled by his manner and the evil look in his face, Tom followed him after a moment's pause of sheer amazement.

"Where is your mistress?" Latimer demanded of Julius who was amongst a crowd of servants in the hall; and upon being answered that she was in her room, he went up the stairs two at a time.

As he burst in upon her, she turned from the open window by which she was standing. His well-known step had warned her a second earlier of his approach, and there was an eagerness in her sweet face as she turned to greet him now, an eagerness which at once gave place to terror at sight of him. For rage and grief had distorted his countenance into an evil mask.

A hand on her bosom to repress its sudden heave, and slim and sweet she stood there, her face as grey as the grey morning gown she wore.

"You traitress!" he said. "You soft, white, lovely treacherous thing. I told you that secret yesterday to test you. You had lied to me so much, you had betrayed so much, and yet still doubting like a fool I must plumb the very depths of your treachery. And I have plumbed them, by God! You have ruined us. You have saved your British friends, the people of your father and your lover and you have doomed me to dishonour and a firing-party." He pulled a pistol from his breast. "If you survive, you share my fate, for clearly I could have betrayed this thing, this tremendous thing, only through you. In mercy then as much as in justice, I must spare you that!"

She stood white and tense, her eyes dilating as she watched him slowly raise the pistol. And then through the wall from the adjoining room to which his raised vehement voice had penetrated came a glad hailing shout:

"Daddy Harry! Daddy Harry!"

It gave him pause. His eyes dilated in horror. A sob broke from his lips. "Oh God! The child!" He lowered the pistol. "What is to become of him?"

And then a strong hand gripped his shoulder from behind, and another clutched his wrist. The pistol was wrenched from his grasp. He wheeled in speechless fury, and found himself face to face with Tom Izard.

The two men stared long at each other in utter silence. The situation was one that baffled words. Beyond them in the room stood Myrtle, her face in her hands, and for a moment the sound of her sobbing came to mingle with the joyous crowing of the child in the next room and the glad cheering of the townsfolk moving along Broad Street. Then came another sound from immediately below; brisk steps in the hall, accompanied by the jingle of spurs and the clank of swords, and a voice, the voice of General Moultrie, raised and sharp in tone, issuing an order.

"My God, Tom, you don't know what you've done!" cried Harry in bitter reproach.

Steps were ascending the stairs.

"I know what I've saved you from doing," said Tom gravely. "You are surely mad, Harry!"

"Am I? Ask her. Ask Myrtle if she has any cause to thank you."

"What!" Tom's voice was suddenly hoarse.

Shubrick appeared, halted and came to attention.

"The general's compliments, sir, and he will be glad if you will step below at once."

Latimer nodded wearily, and Shubrick departed. A moment Latimer stood there looking back at his wife, whose sobbing had suddenly ceased, whose soul had been gripped by a terror even greater than before. Then he smiled wistfully, broken-heartedly into the eyes of Tom Izard.

"Look after her, Tom," he said, and went downstairs in answer to that summons. The voice of his son, calling him in tones that were growing peremptory, followed him down into the hall.

Chapter 16

The Inquiry

Shubrick was waiting for him by the door of the library, and opened it for him when he arrived.

He went in to find four men assembled there: Moultrie, Gadsden, Colonel John Laurens, and Governor Rutledge. All four faces were of a preternatural gravity. The three soldiers were old friends of his, men by whom he had been honoured and esteemed. Two of them had been his father's friends. Rutledge was a man whose temperament had persistently jarred his own, between whom and himself there had ever been a certain indefinable hostility. Yet, behind this, each held the other in a certain respect, and until this moment neither could have reproached the other with anything that touched his honour,

These four, he perceived at once, were gathered there to judge him, to hold the brief, more or less informal preliminary inquiry which must prelude the court-martial before which he would presently have to answer – unless he could now satisfy them that he was clear of the guilt they were already imputing to him.

Rutledge was, naturally enough, the first to address him. And whilst he could well imagine the inward rage consuming the Governor's heart to see the shipwreck of the plan which he had cherished, to see lost through treachery a chance not likely to recur, yet never had he known Rutledge outwardly more cold, self-contained, and correctly formal than he was now.

"I told you yesterday, Major Latimer, when I was constrained against my judgment and my will to impart to you the plan of campaign I had concerted with General Lincoln, that it would go very hard with you or with General Moultrie – the only two in Charles Town who then knew the secret besides myself – if this thing should be prematurely divulged. The situation that I dreaded has arisen. Warned in time, the British have escaped the trap; and the consequence to our unfortunate country must mean a prolongation of the war for months or perhaps years with all the uncertainty, misery and horrors attending it. That warning must have reached them either from General Moultrie or yourself."

"Is it quite impossible that General Prevost's own scouts should have perceived the approach of General Lincoln?" asked Latimer, and the calm of his own voice surprised him and gave him confidence. He had come to this ordeal in terror. Now that he was faced with the necessity to answer questions, the terror fell from him, he recovered his mastery of himself and his wits grew keen and sharp.

"It is not impossible," said Rutledge. "But in all the circumstances highly improbable, and in this instance it is not what happened. This we know. The British had with them a score or so of continental prisoners, whom in their precipitate retreat they abandoned. These men I have examined, and they positively assure me that at one o'clock this morning the British camp was aroused from sleep as a consequence of the arrival of a messenger for General Prevost with news of what was preparing for him. The matter was freely discussed in the British camp, and these men overheard it and were themselves mocked with it. The British began to break camp immediately after the arrival of that messenger."

There was a tap at the door, and Shubrick appeared.

"Mrs Latimer, sir, begs insistently to be allowed a word with your excellency."

"Desire Mrs Latimer to wait a moment. We may require her presently."

Shubrick retired, whilst Latimer breathed a prayer of thanks. His aim now, his only aim, at all costs, was to spare her, to save her, for the sake of the boy. His heart was suddenly moved to an infinite pity. Standing, as he believed himself to stand, upon the brink of eternity – for that this could end other than in a bandage and a firing-party he had little hope – the things of this world by which, in common with other men, he had set such store whilst life was strong within him, shrank now to proportions more in relation with that eternity upon which he was about to embark. He was given the acute, all-embracing mental vision of men in extremity, the knowledge, which, all-knowing, is all-forgiving. In the light of this he beheld Myrtle no longer as the traitress he had dubbed her, the false deceiving wife who at once betrayed himself and his cause. Rather did he behold her as a poor, weak human soul in the grip of forces against which it had not the strength to prevail. She had loved Mandeville. There was, no doubt, much in Mandeville to compel a woman's love. Her first mistake had lain in not being true to herself in that emotion. But this mistake had been a mistake of pity. Nobly she had sought to sacrifice the desire of her life to loyalty to the friend of her childhood and to the troth she had plighted him before she had come to fuller knowledge of herself. All had gone well until Mandeville had appeared in her life once more. That and the filial piety which likewise for his own sake she had immolated had proved too strong for her. And to this was yet to be added the faith of toryism in which she had been reared. All these made up forces against which she could not struggle.

That now was his view of her. Hence this infinite loving pity – such a pity as that which he was persuaded had induced her to marry him that she might save his threatened life – swayed him to save her for her own sake and for the sake of their child who must otherwise be left without a protector in this world. His one dread was lest under examination she should betray herself before he could have made her safe.

As Shubrick closed the door, Rutledge again addressed him.

"It lies, you see, between yourself and General Moultrie. You will not, I suppose, wish to suggest that he may have been our betrayer."

"That I certainly do not."

Rutledge inclined his head. "Colonel Laurens," he said significantly, and the tall, youthful colonel advanced grave and sad of face.

"Your sword, Major Latimer."

But there Moultrie intervened. "No, no! You go too fast altogether. You take too much for granted. Surely there is no need to deprive him of his sword until his guilt is really established."

"Oddslife!" said Gadsden. "Can it be more fully established than it is already. It's either Latimer or yourself, Moultrie. And to suppose that it is you will be as ridiculous as to suppose that it was Rutledge."

Latimer had already unbuckled his sword. He delivered it to Laurens, who went to place it on the library table.

Moultrie with an ill-tempered shrug pulled up a chair and sat down beside this same table. Gadsden followed his example. Both had been in the lines all night, and both were tired. Laurens remained standing, but moved away a little into the background. Rutledge set himself to pace the room between Latimer and the others.

"The assumption is, Major Latimer, that you imparted the news to your wife. We are persuaded that you are guilty of no worse betrayal than that. You desired very possibly, and perhaps not unnaturally, to allay her anxieties. We sympathize with that as far as we are able, but it is not a plea that will greatly avail you before a court-martial."

"I realize it, sir. But what is the further assumption? For a further assumption there must be. To whom did my wife betray this secret in her turn?"

"To her father, whose attachment to the British cause is scandalously notorious."

Latimer smiled. "That, sir, is very easily disproved. It is within your excellency's own knowledge and General Moultrie's that after you imparted this secret to me, I did not leave the lines until I set out with Colonel Smith to meet the British commissioners. I did not return until just before two o'clock in the afternoon, and from the time that you told me of Lincoln's advance I did not see my wife until then – over two hours after her father had been arrested by your orders."

"What's that?" cried Moultrie.

Latimer repeated his words, whilst Rutledge stroked his chin thoughtfully, obviously puzzled.

"How do you know the hour of Sir Andrew Carey's arrest?" Gadsden asked him suspiciously.

"From Middleton, the officer who effected it. He was on duty here in the afternoon, and it was natural that he should tell me this."

Rutledge, still very thoughtful, rang the bell, informed himself from Shubrick that Mr Middleton was on the premises and desired him to be called.

"If Middleton confirms him, that knocks the bottom out of the charge, John," said Moultrie.

Rutledge made no reply. Middleton came, and did confirm Major Latimer's statement. He had arrested Sir Andrew Carey at noon precisely, within ten minutes of receiving the Governor's order.

"I congratulate you on your promptitude, Mr Middleton," said the Governor. "You may go, sir, unless…" He turned to the others. "Perhaps you would like to question him."

Laurens took advantage of the occasion.

"When you arrested Sir Andrew Carey, how was he occupied?"

"He was writing – just finishing a letter, or what looked like a letter."

"Did you seize it?" Rutledge asked him sharply.

"Certainly, sir. That and his writing case. They are in the general's office."

Rutledge smiled a little. "Mr Middleton, I congratulate you on your thoroughness. Please fetch me this writing-case. You may sit down, Major Latimer, if you choose."

Latimer availed himself of the privilege, and waited in fear for the production of the writing-case.

It was brought and opened, and Middleton indicated the letter upon which Sir Andrew had been engaged when arrested. Rutledge thanked him, dismissed him, and went to sit down at the table, between Gadsden and Moultrie, with the case before him, the particular letter in his hand.

"It is in cipher, of course," he said, "which at once marks its character."

"However that may be, sir," ventured Mr Latimer, "it is clear that if my wife conveyed the news of Lincoln's approach to her father, she must have conveyed it before she actually knew it, assuming that I was the only possible channel of information – which is the assumption upon which you are charging me."

"Damme! that seems clear enough," Moultrie agreed.

"Nothing," added Mr Latimer, "could be more clear, and in view of it I think you may safely leave my wife out of this."

"On the contrary," said Rutledge, "I think it is time we had her in." And again he tinkled the bell.

Appalled, Major Latimer exerted himself to avoid it. If Myrtle were brought before these men it was unthinkable that she would not implicate herself. He appealed to the oldest of his friends present.

"General Moultrie, is this necessary? Must my wife be harassed by questions on such a matter as this – a matter on which," he added desperately, "I accept full responsibility."

"Mrs Latimer, herself, has begged to be allowed to come before us," answered Moultrie ill-at-ease.

She was brought in, and Tom Izard who accompanied her was permitted at her own request to remain. Colonel Laurens went to set a chair for her immediately facing Rutledge at the table. She accepted it with a murmured word of thanks. She was pale, but wonderfully composed. From Harry's fierce, almost brutal accusation, and from what else Tom had told her in answer to her questions, she had realised completely what had happened, and the terrible thing of which her husband stood accused. The tangle, she saw, was an appalling one; but knowing herself innocent, and equally confident that however the betrayal had come about, it was not her husband who was guilty, she had the shrewd sense to realise that here nothing but a full statement of the truth could avail him. By laying all the facts before them, surely the truth must reveal itself.

Tom Izard took his stand beside her. Moultrie and Gadsden who had risen when she entered, resumed their seats and Laurens went round to stand behind Rutledge. From where she sat, by turning her head a little to the right, she could see her husband, seated with an outward composure that was very far from reflecting what was passing in his soul.

Rutledge's level voice expounded very briefly the situation: the plan by which it had been hoped, in his own phrase, to burgoyne the British, and the fact that the British forewarned had evaded the trap.

"It follows, madam, that we have been betrayed. And as, besides myself, only General Moultrie and Major Latimer shared the secret, it follows that the betrayer is one or the other of these two. Since we are satisfied, from reasons with which I think you will not require me to trouble you, that General Moultrie is not the traitor, it follows that the guilt of this terrible betrayal attaches itself inevitably to your husband."

She would have interrupted him at this stage, but he restrained her by raising his hand.

"All that I require of you, madam, is that you will answer one or two questions. First of all: Did Major Latimer at any time yesterday inform you that General Lincoln was secretly advancing upon the British rear?"

She did not immediately reply. Here at the very outset she found all her firm resolve to tell the truth and nothing but the truth shattered by the very first question asked her. She looked in terror at

Rutledge and almost in equal terror at her husband, sitting there so stern-faced and seemingly impassive.

"Answer, madam," rasped the voice of Gadsden.

She bowed her head: "He did," she said scarcely above her breath.

There was a gasp from each of those judges, which in itself revealed the fact that despite the almost conclusive appearances they had resisted until this moment the acceptance of Latimer's guilt.

"Hell!" exclaimed Gadsden.

And Moultrie, his good-humoured face suddenly darkened by wrath, swung round to Latimer: "God! You smooth-faced traitor!" he ejaculated, and to Latimer it was like a blow.

"No, no!" Myrtle cried, and there was more anger than dismay in her voice now. "You know that he is not that, General Moultrie. You know him; you know what his life has been, how he has risked it again and again in this cause. You know that if he told me, there was no thought of betrayal in his mind. He told me out of affection for me, out of compassion for my anxieties, to allay the fears that were troubling me."

"No one who considers Major Latimer's service to the cause of freedom can suppose anything else, madam," Rutledge answered her, and by that answer administered a rebuke to Moultrie.

To Latimer it was an odd thing that whereas the man upon whose friendship he would chiefly have counted in this hour should turn against him, whilst one whom he regarded almost as his enemy should be at pains to hold the scales of justice level. And level Rutledge continued to hold them in what he added.

"Indiscretion and imprudence," he continued in the same passionless voice, turning now his sombre eyes upon Latimer, "have marked his actions from the outset, and have spoilt much of the good service that he has been privileged to render. That is the most with which we charge him now. In such a case, however, indiscretion is almost as grave a fault as active treason, and it exacts the same penalties."

He saw her face twitch and her body stiffen in terror. He paused a moment to allow her to regain her self-control before asking his next question.

"And you, madam, although realizing out of what motives he imparted to you this tremendous secret, did not scruple to carry it immediately to your father?"

"That I most certainly did not." She was vehement. "I am ready to make oath as to that, and as to every word I may say, Mr Rutledge."

"Mrs Latimer, oaths will not dispel facts, facts that can be firmly established. Your father's arrest yesterday took place within a quarter of an hour of your leaving his house. At the time of his arrest he was just completing a letter which I have here, a letter written in cipher. That alone stamps it as a communication to be conveyed to the enemy, a communication akin to one taken on an enemy agent the day before."

"I know nothing of that, sir. Nothing. I said no word to my father or to anyone of what I had learnt from my husband, either yesterday or at any other time."

"Surely, sirs," broke in Latimer, "her assertion is enough in default of proofs to the contrary. And you can prove nothing beyond the fact that I am your betrayer. For that, I repeat, I will accept full responsibility. But do not, I beg of you, subject my wife to further torture."

She turned to look at him, and trapped creature though she knew herself there shone in her eyes a light of tenderness and wonder, as if this defence of her, this readiness to sacrifice himself to save her, blotted out every other consideration. She knew what her act must seem to him; how in his eyes the betrayal of which he supposed her guilty was confirmed by all the lies which he had discovered that she had told him, lies which he believed – and was justified in believing – were intended to screen a double betrayal. And yet, in spite of all, he would immolate himself in her place, take upon his loyal steadfast soul the guilt and shame of a deed for which he must atone with his life, and die in the contempt of all men of honour.

It lent her strength to the task before her, strength to tell the whole truth at whatever cost to others, so that he might know it at last.

It was the voice of Moultrie, their friend, which came to rouse her, with its sinister bitterly hostile note:

"You are forgetting, sir, that Mrs Latimer has already admitted that you told her."

"But not that she told her father," he answered fiercely. "As I told her, I may have told others. Why not? Mr Rutledge knows my capacity for indiscretion. Why should I have confined it to my wife alone?"

"At present," Rutledge answered him, "we are concerned with what Mrs Latimer informs us you did confide to her." And he turned again to Myrtle. "Mrs Latimer, will you tell us what was the object of your visit yesterday to your father?"

"Is it unusual for a daughter to visit her father?" sneered Latimer.

Rutledge rapped the table with a pencil he was holding

"Please, Major Latimer! Unless you can restrain yourself, I shall examine the witness in your absence. Now, Mrs Latimer."

She began to speak in a low, composed voice. "So that you may understand, I shall have to go back to the beginning. When I shall have done, it is probable that you will not believe me. I can only protest again, and upon my oath that I shall tell you all the truth."

It impressed them oddly with its foreshadowing of disclosures perhaps beyond the scope of this informal inquiry.

"In February last, when my father returned to Charles Town and lay dangerously ill, I went to visit him, for the purpose of being reconciled, and further that I should perform a daughter's duty by him in his extremity." And now came the story of her first meeting with the Quaker Neild and her discovery of his identity, a story whose details startled them all, and Harry more than any. For to him it was as if she were giving her own lover to a firing-party.

Moultrie would have interrupted her, but Rutledge restrained him, his legal mind insisting upon regularity of procedure.

"Presently, presently! Let Mrs Latimer continue her story."

"Conceiving him a spy, I would at once have denounced him. But he persuaded me that the reason of his presence here in disguise was entirely my father's condition. My father, as some of you may know, had made Robert Mandeville his heir after he disinherited me for marrying…a rebel. It was natural in the circumstances that interest as well as solicitude should have brought him to my father's side at a time when my father's life was almost despaired of. Because of that, I believed him. Because I believed him, and because he swore that if I held my tongue he would depart at once and never return to Charles Town as long as the war lasted, I… I kept the matter a secret." She paused, and then continued. "The day before yesterday, whilst my husband was snatching a brief rest, Mr Middleton came to say that a Quaker named Neild was here to see him. I was angry and terrified. I came down at once, and I saw this man here in this room. I came to upbraid him with his broken faith, the deceit he had practised upon me – for that I now believed it to be – before denouncing him to my husband."

"You denounced him to your husband, do you say?" ejaculated Moultrie, incredulous.

"No. It is for that that I am now being punished. If I had done so none of this could have happened, for upon his arrest must have followed immediately my father's. But he made me afraid, afraid not only for myself but for my husband. He showed me that my father's reconciliation was no more than a cruel comedy, played for the purpose of entangling my husband sooner or later and bringing him down in shame and ruin."

She enlarged upon this, going into the causes of her father's hate, explaining how he had chafed in the bonds which his unfinished duel with Latimer had imposed upon him.

"Captain Mandeville showed me that I could not now denounce him without denouncing myself. That by saving him once before, I had rendered myself his accomplice. That even if he were silent as to that, my father would drag the fact into the light to damn me, and my husband with me.

"I know now that I should have been strong, that I should have told my husband at once, and taken the risk of the rest. But there was more than that. There was a debt between Captain Mandeville and myself. In the old days when my husband's life was in danger it was Captain Mandeville who, by interceding with Lord William Campbell, out of kindness and affection for me, had prevailed upon him to give my husband the alternative of banishment."

"You believed that?" cried Gadsden, with memories of the night when bound hand and foot by Mandeville's contriving – as he more than suspected – Latimer was about to be flung by mistake into the barge in which the merchant was returning to the wharf.

"I believe it still. Because of that debt and because of my fears, again I consented to hold my tongue. Circumstances forced it upon me. My husband came into the room whilst I was still talking to my cousin. My courage failed me in that moment. Afterwards, when I would have told him, it was too late. He informed me that acting upon his orders to detain the man in any event, he was keeping him under arrest for the present."

She paused, and taking advantage of the pause, Rutledge touched the bell on the table.

"It is your wish, I assume," he said, looking round at the soldiers, "to see this man?"

They started out of the absorption into which one and all had been plunged by Myrtle's story. Hastily they assented.

Shubrick came in, and Rutledge beckoned him forward.

"Have the man who passes as a Quaker named Neild brought here at once," he said, "then send a guard for Sir Andrew Carey, and put him in the ante-room until I require him. As you go, ask Middleton to bring me the letter found upon the man Quinn who was shot yesterday."

Shubrick went out, bestowed in passing a half-scared look upon Major Latimer, who was sitting back in his chair with half-closed eyes reviewing in his mind the confession that he had just heard from Myrtle.

There was a new pain in Latimer's heart now. This was the woman whom he was persuaded had betrayed him, whom less than an hour ago he would have shot if he had not been mercifully prevented. Whatever else her clear straightforward narrative might accomplish, it had accomplished his own conversion to the truth, scattered the last hideous doubt in his mind, and made all clear that hitherto had been troubled and confused. It had revived in him the will to live, if only that he might make amends and earn forgiveness for vile assumptions that dishonoured only him who entertained them.

Then her voice roused him. She was speaking again, in the same quiet self-contained tones.

"You have asked me, Mr Rutledge, what motive I had for seeking my father yesterday. I may seem to you to be a long time in coming to that, and what I have told you may seem rather to supply reasons why I should have avoided him. But there is just this thing more: when Captain Mandeville disclosed to me the bitterness of my father's rancour, the depths of his scheming hatred, the extent to which a word from him could destroy me, he made me realize that if my father knew him under arrest, that word, supported by Heaven knows what lies, my father might speak at once. To prevent this I went to my father at the earliest moment. I assured him that, as I believed, Captain Mandeville was detained only as a precautionary measure, but that his identity was not suspected, and that presently he would be released. My father's conduct confirmed all that Captain Mandeville had told me. He no longer made any pretence to me. He showed himself compounded of vindictiveness and hatred. He warned me that if harm befell Mandeville he would denounce me and my husband with me. He had information of the American troops and of their movements which he would swear were obtained from me, to whom my husband had confided them. And if I failed to bring him word every day of Captain Mandeville's position, he would assume the worst, and act at once. And now you know why I visited him again yesterday. It was to reassure him, so that I might keep him quiet." She ceased. "That is all I have to tell you. It is all that I know, and I swear to you that every word of it is true. Deeply, bitterly do I regret the folly into which cowardice has led me. But I repeat that, however the British may have been warned, they were not warned through me."

Her words had that quality of sincerity that compels belief, and there was a spell of silence after she had finished. Gadsden was the first to speak, and his words were an expression of amazement rather than unbelief.

"It is incredible that a father should carry vindictiveness the length of destroying his own child."

Rutledge made philosophy: "Nothing that is evil is incredible in man."

And then Middleton came in bringing the letter Rutledge had requested. The Governor took it, and spread it on the table, face downwards, studying some pencilled notes with which its back was covered.

As the lieutenant went out again, Moultrie shifted uncomfortably in his chair, his broad tanned face creased in lines of ill-humour.

"All this does not dispose of the fact that Prevost had warning. That the warning can have proceeded only from your husband or myself, and we have now your word for it that your husband did convey that secret to you yesterday afternoon."

Nothing here perhaps terrified her more than this hostility in one whom she had come to regard with almost filial affection, one who had never shown anything but love for herself and Harry.

Rutledge looked up from the sheet of paper on which he was beginning to scribble.

"How exactly, did your husband convey the information to you?" he asked, remembering that question of time which Latimer had raised.

"How?" She knit her brows, puzzled by the question. "He told me."

"He told you? By word of mouth?" She nodded, wondering why Rutledge should lay such stress upon those questions. "When did he tell you?"

"Yesterday morning, before he went to the lines."

"No, no, madam! You are mistaken. Bethink you."

"I am not mistaken, it was, as nearly as I can remember, at about ten o'clock yesterday morning."

With the exception of Latimer, who was sitting forward, anxiety and eagerness blending in his face, there was on every countenance a reflection of scornful amazement.

"Madam," said Moultrie. "This is not the truth. He could not have told you then, because he did not know it. He did not learn of it from his excellency until close on twelve."

She looked at them in bewilderment. But his sphinx-like excellency met her gaze in silence. "Nevertheless, he told me then," she insisted.

"But don't you see that it is false, ma'am," cried Gadsden. "That what you say is impossible."

"It sounds impossible," said Rutledge slowly, "and yet… It is necessary to remember that Carey was arrested an hour before Major Latimer returned from the lines. That Major Latimer could not possibly have sent a message is, I think, within our knowledge; certainly within General Moultrie's and my own. For from the moment that I told him this secret until he went with Colonel Smith to meet the British commissioners, he was never out of our sight for a second."

"Egad! That's true!" Moultrie agreed.

"And yet the damning fact remains. There is something here that baffles reasoning." He turned to the prisoner. "Major Latimer, I recall now that you were singularly reluctant to go upon this errand for me; that the communication of the secret excited you very oddly; you made excuses: at first you urged your exhausted condition as a reason why you should not be sent; then you put forward a foolish objection based upon your rank. Will you be frank with us now?"

It was the only thing to be, since his silence must condemn him; and so he chose, as his wife had chosen, a course of utter candour. He began by telling them how he had discovered for himself that his wife was deceiving him with those falsehoods to which she had now confessed.

Moultrie interrupted him at that stage. "Are you telling us that you knew the real identity of this man Neild?"

"I am. I discovered it when I examined him."

"And you kept it to yourself?"

"For the very reasons my wife has given you. Mandeville used the same arguments with me that he had already used with her. He showed me that he and Carey had so entangled and compromised my wife that I could not denounce him without endangering her. So I contented myself for the present with detaining him, thereby rendering him at least powerless to harm us by espionage."

Thence, after a pause, he resumed the tale of his suspicions, his torment of doubt on the score of the extent of his wife's faithlessness, and his resolve, so terrible in its consequences, to put her to the test.

"In that evil hour, sir," he told Rutledge, "I remembered something you first said years ago and repeated lately, in connection with the traitor Featherstone: that when a person is suspected of spying, it is possible by means of false information to establish his guilt and mislead the enemy at one and the same time."

"But this test, sir...the nature of this test!" cried Moultrie. "Would you have us believe possible so extraordinary a fatality, so extraordinary a coincidence?"

"It is hardly a coincidence at all. If General Moultrie will recall words said to me a little while before – words similar to those which he used to your excellency a few hours later at the meeting of the Council."

"Ay! I remember!" Moultrie interrupted him.

"You deplored, sir, civilian intervention in military affairs but for which Lincoln's army would have been where it was required instead of idling at Savannah. When you said that you suggested the obvious test, and I applied it. Now, sirs, you know all, and I hope that you believe as firmly as I believe that my wife is innocent."

"You overlook, sir," said Rutledge gravely, "that if we believe you now – and I scarcely see, all the facts considered, what other explanation fits – the case against Mrs Latimer is stronger than it ever was. The extraordinary test you tell us you applied makes possible what seemed impossible before: that she should have communicated to her father, before he was arrested, this false information, which yet was true."

Latimer's eyes dilated in sudden fear. Only now did he perceive how his trust in truth had been misplaced. In his candour he had overshot the mark.

"Oh, my God!" he groaned, and sank down again into his seat.

"But it clears him," cried Myrtle. "You cannot doubt the truth of what he has told you. Your excellency has said that it fits."

"Do you admit, madam," Rutledge asked her, "that you conveyed this information to your father?"

She looked at them a little piteously, obviously hesitating. And Latimer instinctively apprehending the reasons for her hesitation, and in terror lest out of her desperate anxiety to save him she might have recourse to a lie that should incriminate herself more deeply than ever, cried out commandingly:

"The truth, Myrtle! The truth, without regard to anything!"

That clear command afforded her the guidance that she needed "I did not," she answered firmly. "I swear that I did not."

Rutledge bowed his head. "If there are no further questions for the witness – " He paused his hand upon the bell, and after a moment, none of associates making shift to speak, he rang.

Shubrick was prompt to answer the summons.

"Is the man who calls himself Neild here yet?"

The ensign replied that he was waiting.

"Bring him in," said Rutledge, and to fill in the pause that followed, he returned to the notes he was making in pencil.

Chapter 17

Judgment

Major Mandeville came in between two troopers, erect, firm of step, confident and composed of countenance.

Myrtle, at the end of her examination, had been led aside by Tom Izard to another chair. And now, in obedience to a sign from Rutledge, Shubrick and the guards fell back a little, leaving the prisoner face to face with the Governor.

The Englishman's dark piercing eyes took in the situation at a glance. Whilst much of it still remained mysterious, he perceived his own danger in the intent scrutiny to which he was subjected, and he suspected at once that his identity was known. He was not left in any doubt.

"We understand," said Rutledge, "that you are Captain Mandeville, a British officer."

The abruptness of the challenge startled him a little: so much his face betrayed. But only for a moment was he thrown off his balance. In the next he was bowing, cool and urbane, to Rutledge, and correcting him precisely as in similar case he had corrected Latimer.

"Major Mandeville, if you please." And he added, not without irony: "Your humble obedient."

"You confess yourself of course, a British spy?"

"Considering the garb in which you behold me, the confession is surely unnecessary."

Far from evincing any sign of fear, he spoke almost with a trace of humour. To the end he would be the correct representative of the artificial age and the artificial society to which he belonged. As he had lived, so he would die, true to his code, and whatever else he might forget, he would never forget the deportment that he owed to himself, to his birth and his race.

"You know, Major Mandeville, what awaits you?" Rutledge asked him.

"Naturally. It by no means exhausts my perspicacity."

Rutledge considered him a moment before putting his next question.

"Have you, yourself, any notion why Major Latimer should not immediately have denounced you upon discovering your true identity?"

Mandeville looked round at Latimer, and a faint smile curled his lip. Then his eyes shifted to Myrtle, and meeting the condemnation in her glance, his smile perished. He drew himself stiffly to attention, a tall figure, of great dignity, despite his abominable disguise.

"I gave Major Latimer excellent reasons why he could not denounce me without grave danger to his wife and even to himself."

"Will you repeat these reasons?"

"That is my intention. The game, I see, is lost, like most games I ever played. I was always an unlucky gambler; but at least always a good loser." And the story he told them now was one that confirmed in every particular what they had already heard.

When he had done, Rutledge asked a question, musingly.

"You say that you disclosed to Mrs Latimer the monstrous part her father has played towards her in the past six months?"

"That is what I said."

"Yet in this, upon your own confession, you assisted Carey. Why, then, do you betray him now?"

"Set it down to a common human weakness to speak the truth in the face of death. If that does not satisfy you, assume that whilst I stood to make an ultimate gain from it I was willing enough to forward the matter. But the inducement ends with the hope. I was never one to practise villainy for its own sake."

It was, I suspect, less than the truth, and yet the truth was contained in it.

Rutledge's next question was a little startling to them all.

"If you were told that after having learnt these facts from you, Mrs Latimer had conveyed to her father secret information obtained from her husband, which could be of use to the British what should you say?"

"Say?" Mandeville's astonishment was unfeigned. "What does your excellency say? What does any man who reasons say?"

"Ah!" said Rutledge. "And yet, conveyed such information certainly was."

"By Mrs Latimer?" cried Mandeville. He spoke contemptuously. "Sirs, your wits need furbishing."

Rutledge invited his associates to question the witness if they so desired. They did not, and Shubrick was ordered to remove him, and to bring in Sir Andrew Carey.

Mandeville's glance sought Myrtle in a pleading farewell. He had done his best for her at the last, and gratitude now invested her eyes with a look of compassion.

After that he took his place between his guards, and went out, his step as firm, his head as high as that of any man who ever faced the fate of a detected spy. His proud bearing dignified his end. It made those who watched him go remember that execrable as is the spy accounted by the side against which he works, the cause he serves may well regard him as a heroic martyr.

When he had gone, Rutledge repeated to them in a slightly different form the question he had put to Mandeville himself.

"If you believe what that man has told us of his interview with Mrs Latimer – and it closely confirms her own and Major Latimer's stories – ask yourselves whether upon learning such abominable facts concerning her father it is credible that she would have conveyed information to him."

"But the fact," cried Moultrie in distress, "the damnable fact that the information was conveyed?"

"Ay," said Gadsden. "That's something that remains unshaken and unexplained."

And Colonel Laurens silently nodded his agreement.

"Carey's evidence may shake it," said Rutledge. "I do not know. But whilst we examine him, keep present in your minds what I have said."

That was the first word in his favour that Latimer had heard from his judges, and to him the amazing fact was that it should proceed from one whom he had come to regard almost as his personal enemy, one whom three days ago he had threatened with a challenge to follow when the settlement of the present troubles of Charles Town should make it possible.

Rutledge was speaking again. "It will be best, I think, if Mrs Latimer is not present at the examination of her father, in case we should afterwards wish to re-examine her." He made the statement interrogatively and upon receiving the acquiescence of the others, he begged Captain Izard to conduct her from the room.

"We leave her in your charge, Captain Izard. Take her into the dining-room until we need her again."

As she was passing out she looked very wistfully at her husband, almost as if in fear. Harry Latimer returned the glance with one which at first was no more than its reflected expression, but which ended in a smile of confidence and encouragement.

Rutledge was bending over his sheet of paper, referring now to one, now to the other of the documents before him, his pencil travelling faster than ever.

At length Sir Andrew Carey, under guard, was ushered in by Shubrick. It was the first time that Latimer had seen him since that night of their duel at Brewton's, four years ago, and he was amazed at the change in the man. His bulk had shrunk, so that his clothes hung loose and empty about him, and he seemed to have lost height.

His face, so full, ruddy and hearty in the old days, was now grey and hollow-cheeked. He carried himself aggressively, but his feebleness was not to be dissembled, and he leaned heavily upon a cane. In his eyes alone was there vigour and life. They smouldered balefully as they fell upon Latimer; then glowed with a sardonic smile as they raked the faces of the others present.

Rutledge wrote on, without raising his head, so engrossed now in his task that he did not even look up when, in fierce expression of his hatred, Carey mockingly addressed the little gathering.

"But where is the hero of the hour? Your great General Lincoln?"

"What do you know of Lincoln?" Moultrie sharply questioned him.

"Faith, I know him for a damned rebel, and that's all I want to know of him."

Shubrick ventured to interpose an explanation. "The orderlies in the ante-room, sir, have been talking too freely before him."

Carey laughed at them. "What discipline can you look for in a pack of seditious curs?"

Rutledge laid down his pencil, at last, and looked up. There was the ghost of a smile on his thin lips, but his voice was as cold as ever.

"If General Lincoln has not yet arrived, at least General Prevost has departed. The reflection may serve to cool your insolence, when I add to it that I have documentary evidence before me that you have been acting as an enemy agent in Charles Town."

"An enemy agent? Why you pitiful traitor – "

"A British agent, if you prefer it. You know enough of the world, I am sure, to have some notion of what may happen to you."

"Bah!" said Carey, attempting bravado. But he was none too successful. His lips quivered, and his glance fell away before Rutledge's.

Moultrie asked a question: "Have you any notion, sir, how the British came to be informed of the approach of General Lincoln?"

A shade of annoyance crossed Rutledge's face, as if this were not a question that he desired.

Carey's eyes gleamed. He paused a moment before answering. "I have. They were informed by me upon information obtained from Major Latimer."

If any doubt could still have lingered in Latimer's mind of the truth of what he had heard from his wife and Mandeville this deliberate cold-blooded lie must finally have dispelled it.

"You are very eager, sir," cried Laurens, "to swear away your life."

"My life?" He shrugged his still heavy shoulders. "Haven't you just told me, you murderers, that my life is forfeit?"

"But not the life of Major Latimer," said Rutledge. "Nor would you swear it away so glibly if what you say is true. By doing so, you testify in his favour."

Carey's smouldering eyes considered the Governor in repressed fury. He realized his false step, and he set about retrieving it.

"You are right, Mr Rutledge," he said quietly. "It serves no purpose to deceive you." Then in a voice vibrating with passion he went on: "You all know the wrong, the unpardonable wrong this man did me. Like a coward he bound my hands so that I could not take satisfaction from him in an honourable way. Was that to be borne? Was I to lie for ever under that intolerable debt? Since I might not pay it one way, I have paid it another. Pretending to yield to my daughter's intercessions, I secretly made my peace with him, and I converted him back to the cause from which he had traitorously seceded."

"When? When did you do this?" Moultrie asked. "Be more precise."

"Six months ago," he answered impatiently, as if the interruption were frivolous; and he swept on with his tale of infamy. "Why, do you think, did I do it? That I might entangle and break him in the end. For months now he has been supplying me with information which I have been forwarding to the British, and which has brought about the frustration of your rebel aims. Thus he has doubly served my ends."

Again Rutledge was surprising. "Of that we were already more or less persuaded. It but required your own testimony to confirm us."

"Ha, ha!" The baronet almost gloated. "And now you have it. There he stands; as false to you as he was false to me; false and rotten to the core of him."

Latimer was on his feet, his face inflamed.

"Mr Rutledge, in God's name, if I am to be shot on the word of this vindictive madman – "

Rutledge quelled him sternly. "Major Latimer, you shall be given opportunity to answer, never fear." And he resumed his questioning of Sir Andrew. "You have said that it was yourself conveyed to the British the information that Lincoln was approaching to surprise them. Was this information received from Mrs Latimer?"

"She was the bearer of a note from her husband, which contained it."

"You have this note?"

Carey smiled. "It is not a document a prudent man would keep."

"But you are not a prudent man in this matter, Sir Andrew. And for your purposes of vengeance what evidence could have been more conclusive now? But we will pass on. You were arrested within a few minutes of your daughter's visit, and your papers were seized at the same time. They include this letter which you were just finishing. It is in cipher, which of itself sufficiently proclaims its object. It was intended for the British, was it not?"

"For General Prevost."

"Yet it was never dispatched. How do you reconcile that with your assertion that the information you received was actually conveyed to the British?"

It was a question that startled them all, with the possible exception of Latimer, who, from his own reasoning of yesterday, knew already what the answer must be. Yet it was not as obvious to Carey. For a moment or two he floundered in the trap before he perceived the clear way out, and took it.

"I was arrested a quarter of an hour after my daughter left me; but three quarters of an hour after she arrived. The letter informing General Prevost of Lincoln's approach was dispatched a half-hour before my arrest. Otherwise how did the news reach Prevost? And you know that it did reach him."

"Ay," growled Moultrie, "that's the damning fact to which all roads must lead in the end, however they may seem to be taking different directions."

"A moment, please," Rutledge repressed him. "What, then, Sir Andrew, was the object of this further letter, which also, as you have told us, was intended for General Prevost?"

Carey's answer was prompt. "It duplicated the information. The news was too important to be left to a single messenger. I was sending a second one against the danger of the first being arrested."

Rutledge sank back in his chair with bowed head, and half-closed eyes, thoughtfully tapping his teeth with the pencil he had taken up again. Then suddenly he looked round at the others.

"Have you any questions for the witness?" There was something odd and very unusual in his manner, a certain slyness in his glance, than which nothing could normally be more alien to John Rutledge.

"What more can he tell us?" said Gadsden between irritation and regret. "He has cast a new light on what we have already heard."

Rutledge looked at Moultrie, as if inviting him to speak. The sternness that had hitherto supported the general suddenly deserted him. He sank forward leaning his elbows on his knees, resting his chin in his cupped palms, his troubled eyes on Sir Andrew, standing there almost exultant, recking nothing of what might befall himself now that at last he had pulled his enemy down.

"You unnatural, kite-hearted monster!" Moultrie growled at him.

Carey eyed him with contempt. "Your insults cannot touch me, you rebel dog."

"God keep us all from such loyalty as yours," Gadsden answered him. "Stab me, sir, you're a worthy servant of your besotted King George."

The baronet looked at him in speechless fury, whilst Rutledge rapped the table sharply with his pencil.

"Gentlemen, gentlemen! Let us keep to the matter before us. If you have no questions for the witness, we will get on."

And now, at last, seeing that no one had anything further to say, Latimer judged that his time was come.

"Your excellency!" he appealed to the Governor.

But he was not destined to be heard in his own defence. At that moment there was uproar in the hall outside. A voice excitedly raised was demanding instant audience of the Governor. Others were presumably representing the impossibility of this, for the voice grew ever more clamant and was accompanied now by the sounds of a scuffle, ending in a heavy blow upon the door.

"See what is happening," Rutledge ordered Shubrick.

The ensign went to open. Instantly a tall, loose-limbed man, without coat or hat or wig, his white waistcoat and buckskin breeches bedaubed with mud, his Hessian boots, from one of which the spur had been wrenched, squelching water as he stepped, precipitated himself almost headlong into the room. He recovered his balance, and presented a furious, excited countenance, ghastly white under the filth and blood that masked it.

"Governor Rutledge!" he cried, stridently, and his bloodshot eyes raked the room. "Which of you is Governor Rutledge?"

"Stab me!" cried Gadsden, getting to his feet. "What new madman's this!"

The fellow stiffened to attention at that question from a general officer. He presented himself.

"Lieutenant Eaton of Captain Fall's Light Horse, attached to General Rutherford's Brigade."

"What?" It was an ejaculation from Rutledge, sharp as the crack of a whip. Rutherford's Brigade was part of Lincoln's force.

He waved away the guards who had charge of Carey, and obediently they withdrew their reluctant prisoner into the background, so that they no longer intervened between the Governor and the newcomer.

"Approach, sir. I am John Rutledge."

The man staggered forward. It was now seen that he was in the last stage of exhaustion and that only his excitement had made possible his last outburst.

"I am an express rider from General Lincoln," he further announced himself.

"Where is General Lincoln?" Moultrie interrupted him.

"When I left him at noon yesterday he was approaching the Edisto. He should be at Willtown or thereabouts by now."

"At Willtown?" echoed Moultrie in amazement, for Willtown was thirty miles away. "What has delayed him?"

"He explained it in his letter to your excellency," Eaton informed the Governor.

"Letter? Do you say you had a letter? That General Lincoln was so imprudent as to send a letter?" His cheeks were scarlet. Probably no man had ever seen him in so royal a rage. But no one was observing him at the moment. All eyes were upon the messenger, and none more eager than Latimer's, who already foresaw the real explanation of how the news had reached the British.

Lieutenant Eaton explained himself. "I had orders to destroy it if in danger of capture. Unfortunately I was taken unawares. I stumbled into the British lines on the Ashley just after midnight, and I was knocked over, searched and the letter taken from me before I knew what had happened. I escaped just before dawn, in the confusion of the British retreat, and I swam the Ashley in the dark."

"My God!" groaned Moultrie, and with eyes that were now almost afraid he looked across at Latimer, who smiled back at him, though not without a touch of bitterness.

"Yes," said Rutledge voicing the thought in every mind. "That affords another explanation of how General Prevost was warned." He looked at Eaton. "What was in your letter? Do you know?"

"Yes, sir. It was to inform your excellency that the general was making and would continue to make every exertion for the relief of Charles Town; that he would abandon his baggage so as to hasten progress; to assure you that the men are full of spirit; and to exhort you to stimulate your people into every effort for the defence of the Town until he could bring up his troops."

The scarlet tide of anger had ebbed from Rutledge's cheeks. He was white now to the lips. His utterance came thick and tremulous with passion.

"He deemed it necessary to write me that! And it was only yesterday beyond the Edisto that it occurred to him to leave his baggage! His baggage! What did he think himself? A pedlar, taking wares to market? And then to write to me! That he should not be here at the time appointed was bad enough. But to write to me that he was coming! God of Heaven! That I should have to work with such clumsy blunted tools!"

He sank back in his chair, everything else forgotten for the moment in the bitterness of his realization that through sluggishness aggravated by an act of crass stupidity, his elaborate plan should have been wrecked, with the result that the war might continue for years to afflict his distracted country.

But if he had no thought at the moment save for the effect of this blunder upon his plans, Moultrie had no thought save for the effect of the news upon the charge against Latimer, and it was he who now took up the questioning of the express rider.

"When you were seized in the British lines, what was the condition of the camp?"

"The British were asleep, sir. I was dragged off to General Prevost's quarters, and kept waiting whilst they roused the general. He came in a bedgown to examine me."

"So that until he read the letter you carried, General Prevost had no knowledge, no suspicion even, that General Lincoln was creeping upon him?"

" 'Creeping' is the word, Moultrie," sneered the livid Rutledge.

"That, he certainly had not, sir," Eaton answered. "He went almost mad in his surprise. Within ten minutes the bugles were blowing and the drums were beating to rouse the men. Within a half-hour the British had begun to break camp."

Moultrie swung to the Governor. He was shaking with excitement.

"You hear that, John? You perceive how that bears upon the case against Latimer? How it proves Carey's evidence a wicked lie?"

In the background Carey uttered a sneering, confident laugh. Rutledge glanced at him in silence.

"So much," the Governor surprised them all by saying, "was no longer necessary to prove that." Then he waved the express rider away. "You may go, sir, and get the rest of which you appear to stand in need. No blame attaches to you for what has happened."

Eaton thanked him, and staggered out.

Rutledge sat forward again, to return to the considerations that had been so startlingly interrupted.

"Now, Major Latimer, I do not think we need detain you long."

"Don't you?" quoth Carey with a malicious chuckle.

"Have you more lies for us?" demanded Moultrie.

Unbidden Sir Andrew advanced, his guards keeping close. He leaned heavily upon his cane.

"You think this evidence acquits him, do you? You purblind fools! All that it proves is that Lincoln's messenger reached Prevost before mine. It is even possible that mine miscarried. It was the danger of that made me prepare a second message."

"Ah, yes," said Rutledge. "This cipher message." He took up the letter. "Will you read it to us now?"

"Gladly. Then perhaps you will be convinced."

In silence Rutledge handed him the letter, and Carey read:

"Dear General – These to inform you again in case my letter of this morning should not have reached you, that Lincoln is rapidly advancing upon your rear, so that should you remain in your present situation, you may find it become one of extreme hazard. I have this from a sure source, namely my son-in-law, Major Latimer, who is aide to General Moultrie, commanding here."

Moultrie, Gadsden and Laurens frowned at one another in fresh perplexity. Their minds rebelled now against believing. And yet the letter was in cipher, and out of that alone it followed that some secret intelligence must be contained in it. It was written immediately after Myrtle's visit to her father, and that Latimer had told her this thing, she had admitted. So, too, was Latimer himself in danger now of reasoning, although earlier he had cast all doubt of his wife from his mind.

"Sir," he exclaimed passionately to Rutledge, "he is lying! Lying to destroy me, which he has avowed to be his aim. Whatever the letter contains, it cannot contain what he has said. Compel him, sir, to produce the cipher. In justice to me you must do that – now that we have had the express-rider's story."

"Produce the cipher!" Carey laughed. "Give you so precious a key as that! Not I, indeed!"

"It is not necessary," said Rutledge quietly. And his pencil tapped the papers on the table. "I have it here."

Carey's mouth loosened. His face which had been flushed turned now a sickly grey. "You have it there?" he echoed thickly. "It...it isn't possible!"

But Rutledge showed him that it was. "A messenger of yours, a spy named Quinn, was taken yesterday with a cipher message upon him. It was deciphered at leisure by my secretary, who is an able and patient fellow. Thus I was supplied with the key. With that key I have been deciphering your letter for myself whilst sitting here. Shall I read it to you?"

Sir Andrew swayed a little, his face convulsed. His mouth opened and closed; but no words came forth.

Rutledge lowered his eyes to the sheet he had taken up, that sheet upon which his pencil had been busy.

"Here is what you really wrote: ' Dear General – I regret to inform you that Mandeville has been arrested; but I am glad to add that his true identity is not yet discovered, and that he is being detained merely as a measure of precaution by order of the rebel Governor, who is afflicted with the cowardice of his kind. His observations before his arrest led him to estimate at not more than three thousand the forces defending the town, and many of these are raw militia who will never stand after the first British fire. So forward with confidence, and deliver us from these traitors.' "

He looked up. "That sir, is what you wrote. If anything had still been wanting to establish completely the innocence of Major Latimer and his wife – "

He broke off to look at Carey, who was no longer listening to him.

The baronet had let fall his cane from a hand which had suddenly grown nerveless. Purple now of face, he was clawing the air wildly with his hands, like a man fighting for breath. Suddenly he crashed back at full length upon the ground, rolled half over, and lay still.

There was a general forward movement of awe and horror. Rutledge, who had sprung up, went round to the side of the fallen man. A moment he stood looking at him. Then he went down on one knee, and held a hand for a moment over the region of Sir Andrew's heart.

He rose, and looked at the staring eyes and startled faces about him. Without any trace of emotion he announced to them:

"Judgment has overtaken him."

Chapter 18

Reconciliation

When presently they came out into the hall they found the members of the Privy Council assembled there in penitent and chastened mood, to wait upon the Governor.

It was Ferguson, who yesterday had sworn to see Rutledge hanged, who now acted as their spokesman.

"Your excellency," he said, "on my own behalf and on that of my fellow-councillors, I humbly offer you an apology for having lacked towards you the faith which your every past action should abundantly have inspired. I am also to express our profound admiration of the sagacious plan by which you had looked to destroy the enemy forces, of your fortitude in keeping the matter secret in the face of our reprehensibly untrusting opposition – "

Rutledge cut him short. "Is more of this necessary, sirs? The plan has failed, through – shall we say? – the malignancy of fortune. As for what happened yesterday, I am as ready to believe that you performed your duty according to your lights, as I know that I was performing mine. If you will oblige me by waiting upon me at my house presently, I shall be glad of your counsel in matters now to be determined."

Thus coldly dismissed, they made shift to depart, uncomfortably conscious of having merited his displeasure.

Without paying further attention to them, Rutledge turned to Latimer who lingered at his side.

"Don't stay now," he said. "Your wife is waiting."

And Moultrie, at his elbow, curiously moved for such a man of war, a suspicion of moisture about his kindly eyes, urged him in the same manner.

"Ay, ay, lad, go to her. Go to her. And ask her to forgive me. Maybe she'll understand when you tell her that it was love for you made me hate so when – God forgive me for an old fool! – I thought you'd turned against us."

Latimer smiled into the kindly stricken eyes of his father's friend, and turned again to Rutledge.

"I can't go without thanking you, sir."

"For sitting in judgment upon you?"

"No, sir. For acting as counsel for my defence."

"That," said Rutledge, "is the true function of any upright judge. Besides there were two other reasons why I must exert myself to save you. In the first place I was reminded by the Council's condemnation of myself only yesterday, that appearances may conspire to establish the guilt of an innocent man; and I could not forget that at that meeting you were the only one who did not condemn me on those appearances. In the second place," he continued, with now a gleam of sardonic humour, "there is between us a certain matter which, unless I exerted myself to acquit you, might have left upon me a slur of doing cowardly service to my own interests. There was something said the other day of a challenge to follow when the affairs of the State should leave more leisure. That leisure I am now likely to be afforded – "

"Sir, can you forgive me?" exclaimed Latimer, in penitence.

Rutledge laughed outright, and held out his hand.

"Perhaps we have never quite understood each other," he said. "But all things considered, it is a remarkable fact, Latimer, that yesterday in Beekman's tent you were the only one who did not call me a scoundrel."

"I have always understood you too well for that!" said Latimer as he gripped the proffered hand.

Then he plunged away down the hall to find his wife. Rutledge's voice followed him:

"It is possible that we may yet be friends."

But to that Latimer did not trouble to reply. He went on and opened the door of the dining-room.

She was sitting on the window-seat, and Tom Izard, large, benign and protecting was standing over her. Her face, white and tear-stained, but eager and half afraid was turned towards the door when he opened it.

She sprang up half-choked by fear, to be instantly reassured, both by his expression and by Tom Izard's cry:

"He is free! They have acquitted him." And he pointed to the sword that swung at Harry's side.

Two faltering uncertain steps towards him she took, then swayed into his arms, and lay half swooning in relief against his breast.

"You know now, Harry, my dear. You know now..." she said.

Tom Izard, whose letters to his sister, Lady William Campbell, then in Jamaica, relate this last episode, went out of the room at that point, closing the door upon a husband and wife who in reality had only just found each other. It was discreet of him, both as a man of feeling and a chronicler.

Rafael Sabatini

Captain Blood

Captain Blood is the much-loved story of a physician and gentleman turned pirate.

Peter Blood, wrongfully accused and sentenced to death, narrowly escapes his fate and finds himself in the company of buccaneers. Embarking on his new life with remarkable skill and bravery, Blood becomes the 'Robin Hood' of the Spanish seas. This is swashbuckling adventure at its best.

The Gates of Doom

'Depend above all on Pauncefort', announced King James; 'his loyalty is dependable as steel. He is with us body and soul and to the last penny of his fortune.' So when Pauncefort does indeed face bankruptcy after the collapse of the South Sea Company, the king's supreme confidence now seems rather foolish. And as Pauncefort's thoughts turn to gambling, moneylenders and even marriage to recover his debts, will he be able to remain true to the end? And what part will his friend and confidante, Captain Gaynor, play in his destiny?

'A clever story, well and amusingly told' – *The Times*

Rafael Sabatini

The Lost King

The Lost King tells the story of Louis XVII – the French royal who officially died at the age of ten but, as legend has it, escaped to foreign lands where he lived to an old age. Sabatini breathes life into these age-old myths, creating a story of passion, revenge and betrayal. He tells of how the young child escaped to Switzerland from where he plotted his triumphant return to claim the throne of France.

'…the hypnotic spell of a novel which for sheer suspense, deserves to be ranked with Sabatini's best' – *New York Times*

Scaramouche

When a young cleric is wrongfully killed, his friend, André-Louis, vows to avenge his death. André's mission takes him to the very heart of the French Revolution where he finds the only way to survive is to assume a new identity. And so is born Scaramouche – a brave and remarkable hero of the finest order and a classic and much-loved tale in the greatest swashbuckling tradition.

'Mr Sabatini's novel of the French Revolution has all the colour and lively incident which we expect in his work' – *Observer*

Rafael Sabatini

The Sea Hawk

Sir Oliver, a typical English gentleman, is accused of murder, kidnapped off the Cornish coast, and dragged into life as a Barbary corsair. However Sir Oliver rises to the challenge and proves a worthy hero for this much-admired novel. Religious conflict, melodrama, romance and intrigue combine to create a masterly and highly successful story, perhaps best-known for its many film adaptations.

The Shame of Motley

The Court of Pesaro has a certain fool – one Lazzaro Biancomonte of Biancomonte. *The Shame of Motley* is Lazzaro's story, presented with all the vivid colour and dramatic characterisation that has become Sabatini's hallmark.

'Mr Sabatini could not be conventional or commonplace if he tried'
– *Standard*

9773452R0

Made in the USA
Lexington, KY
27 May 2011